Praise for Ryan Steck

"Ryan Steck's *Fields of Fire* busts out of the chute with nonstop action and it never lets up until the final page. A magnificent debut with a terrific sense of place in Big Sky Country and a hero to root for in Matthew Redd."

C. J. BOX, #1 *New York Times* bestselling author of *Shadows Reel*

"Ryan Steck hits it out of the park with his debut, *Fields of Fire*. Part military thriller, part spy novel, part good old-fashioned Western—Matthew Redd has cemented himself as the go-to man in a bad situation. It starts off with a literal bang and never lets up, with an ending that will leave readers scrambling for more."

BRAD TAYLOR, *New York Times* bestselling author of *End of Days*

"The stakes—and tension—don't stop building until they explode into a denouement readers will never forget. The debut thriller of the year."

KYLE MILLS, #1 *New York Times* bestselling author of *Enemy at the Gates*

"You know Ryan Steck as the Real Book Spy. Now get to know him as the author of *Fields of Fire*, his debut thriller featuring Marine Raider Matthew Redd in a battle that will leave you speechless and begging for more. Lock and load!"

JACK CARR, Navy SEAL sniper and #1 *New York Times* bestselling author of *The Devil's Hand*

"The Real Book Spy becomes the real spy. Action! Suspense! And the introduction of former Marine Raider Matthew Redd, a formidable new hero who doesn't like being told no. Ryan Steck's *Fields of Fire* kicks off an exciting new series. Check it out."

BRAD MELTZER, #1 *New York Times* bestselling author of *The Escape Artist*

"Ryan Steck's *Fields of Fire* breathes fresh life into the thriller genre with his hero Matty Redd, a hard man forced to fight for those he loves in the harsh wilderness of Montana. A compelling premise strongly executed. Fans of C. J. Box and Vince Flynn will anxiously await the follow-up to *Fields of Fire*."

MARK GREANEY, #1 *New York Times* bestselling author of *Sierra Six*

"Ryan Steck has gone from writing about thrillers to writing a first-rate thriller himself. All you have to do is start reading about his new hero named Matthew Redd to understand. This is a book that does exactly what books like it are supposed to do: keeps you turning the pages to find out what happens next. And spoiler alert? Every time you think you know, you don't."

MIKE LUPICA, *New York Times* bestselling author of *Robert B. Parker's Payback* and *Robert B. Parker's Stone's Throw*

"A flawless story with a stellar cast of memorable characters—Ryan Steck's stunning debut, *Fields of Fire*, is a twisty, electrifying thriller reminiscent of the very best of Brad Thor that will keep readers flipping pages well into the night."

SIMON GERVAIS, former RCMP counterterrorism officer and bestselling author of *The Last Protector*

"Thriller fans, debuts don't get better than this. Explosive from page one and rarely letting up, *Fields of Fire* heralds the arrival of hard-charging, even harder-hitting Marine Raider Matthew Redd to the genre's pantheon of mesmerizing franchise heroes. First-time author Ryan Steck writes with the expertise of a seasoned pro and delivers 1,000 percent. Get your hands on this book!"

CHRIS HAUTY, nationally bestselling author

"*Fields of Fire*, Ryan Steck's long-awaited debut novel, is loaded with action, emotion, and plenty of authentic details. I could not put it down!"

NICK PETRIE, author of *The Runaway*

FIELDS OF FIRE

RYAN STECK

FIELDS OF FIRE

A **MATTHEW REDD** THRILLER

Tyndale House Publishers
Carol Stream, Illinois

Visit Tyndale online at tyndale.com.

Visit Ryan Steck online at therealbookspy.com.

Tyndale and Tyndale's quill logo are registered trademarks of Tyndale House Ministries.

Fields of Fire

Designed by Dean H. Renninger

Edited by Sarah Mason Rische

Published in association with The John Talbot Agency, Inc., a member of The Talbot Fortune Agency, LLC, 180 E. Prospect Ave. #188, Mamaroneck, NY 10543.

Scripture quotations are taken from the *Holy Bible*, King James Version.

Fields of Fire is a work of fiction. Where real people, events, establishments, organizations, or locales appear, they are used fictitiously. All other elements of the novel are drawn from the author's imagination.

For information about special discounts for bulk purchases, please contact Tyndale House Publishers at csresponse@tyndale.com, or call 1-855-277-9400.

Library of Congress Cataloging-in-Publication Data

A catalog record for this book is available from the Library of Congress.

ISBN 978-1-4964-6286-2 (HC)

Printed in the United States of America

28	27	26	25	24	23	22
7	6	5	4	3	2	1

To my best friend, father, and hero, James Steck, who always believed this book would be written . . . even when I didn't.

"I am in love with Montana. For other states I have admiration, respect, recognition, even some affection, but with Montana it is love, and it's difficult to analyze love when you're in it."

JOHN STEINBECK, *TRAVELS WITH CHARLEY*

"Home is the place where, when you have to go there, they have to take you in."

ROBERT FROST, "THE DEATH OF THE HIRED MAN"

Prologue

Matthew Redd wasn't afraid to die, but first he had some killing to do.

Listening to the rhythm of the incoming fire, he read the shooter's intentions with each passing round.

Pop, pop . . . Pause . . . Two, three, four . . . Pop, pop . . . Pause . . .

The rounds split the air above him with an audible crack, then smacked into the back wall of the log cabin. Each impact raised a puff of woodsmoke.

He's shooting high, Redd told himself. *Suppressive fire. Keeping us pinned down so that his buddies can move in close.*

In his mind's eye he could visualize their approach—at least a ten-man element, with a sniper providing overwatch and suppressive fire. They would sweep wide in a flanking maneuver . . . No, a better approach would be to use the trucks for cover.

That was how he would have done it.

Not gonna let that happen, Redd thought, gripping the Winchester.

The cycle repeated again. *Pop, pop . . . Pause.*

Redd made his move, combat rolling through the door and out into the night, where he immediately pivoted to the right so that he wouldn't be silhouetted in the doorway. He knew the sniper would be counting off the seconds and that it would take the man a moment to realize what Redd was attempting.

Not varying the shot interval had been the sniper's first mistake. And even if the shooter spotted him, it would take a fraction of a second for him to lower his aim and find Redd in his crosshairs.

Putting his shots in the same exact place had been the sniper's second mistake.

It would also be his last.

Redd came out of the roll and duckwalked across open ground to take cover behind the old pickup. Despite his size, he moved quickly, reaching his destination before the sniper could let loose with another shot.

As he moved, he passed the headless corpse of the sniper's first victim. That man's blood was on Redd's hands, literally if not figuratively, but Redd didn't allow his thoughts to go there yet. He had other priorities.

He scuttled along the passenger side of the truck, halting at the front end to slowly peek around the corner. As he edged out, he saw the protruding muzzle of a carbine—an M4, if he wasn't mistaken—barely visible in the moonlight. Redd immediately drew back.

The Winchester was good for long-distance engagements but unwieldy for close-quarter battle. Redd enumerated his options, which didn't take long, and made a decision that flew in the face of conventional wisdom.

He was going to literally bring a knife to a gunfight.

Gripping the old Case folder in his right fist, he edged forward again. The carbine muzzle was much closer now. The shooter had advanced several steps and was about to turn the corner . . .

Redd launched himself from a crouch, rising up inside the assaulter's reach, close enough that the man's weapon would be of no use to him. He rammed the blade up into the soft flesh under the man's jaw and slashed sideways. The razor-sharp edge sliced through muscle, tendon, arteries, and anything else in its way.

Redd punched his free hand into the mortally wounded assaulter's sternum, feeling the solid SAPI plate inside the man's tactical rig against his knuckles. The blow sent the man staggering backward, both hands futilely trying to stanch the flow of blood pulsing from his neck.

Redd ducked back behind the truck as incoming rounds began to pepper the opposite side of the vehicle. He stayed behind the wheel, knowing that it would provide the best protection, and took up the Winchester once more.

Off to his left, he spied two more assaulters moving out of the tree line and approaching the cabin from the opposite side. They appeared to be singly focused on reaching their objective, unaware of his position.

Tunnel vision when they ought to have three-sixty awareness, Redd noted. *Big mistake.*

He sighted the rifle on the point man, center mass, then remembered that the men were wearing body armor. Elevating his sight picture for the head shot, Redd squeezed the trigger.

Crack! The rifle bucked hard in his hands and the man went down.

Redd worked the lever quickly and snapped off another shot, but the second man had already dropped to a prone position to return fire.

Redd dropped flat as well, then squirmed back around the front end of the truck. Rounds continued to smack into the front fender of the vehicle, but he was able to pinpoint the location of another hostile from the bright-yellow muzzle flashes that accompanied each shot. The shot groupings were coming from the same location, indicating that the assaulter was holding his position when he ought to have been shooting and moving, hopping and popping.

Amateur.

Redd drew a bead on the shooter and let lead fly. He didn't wait around to verify the kill, instead rolling immediately back behind the truck's wheel.

Bullets were now sizzling through the air mere inches above him. This time, the rounds were coming in from the woods at the side of the cabin, where the surviving member of the flanking pair was trying to pin him down. A few shots fell short, kicking up dirt that sprayed over Redd.

Whoever was firing clearly had an idea of where he was but was having trouble dialing in the shot.

Spraying and praying. No discipline.

Staying calm, Redd put the Winchester's iron sights on the muzzle flash, inhaled, and then slowly let his breath out as he began taking the slack out of the trigger.

The weapon barked once, and the incoming fire ceased.

Another one down, Redd told himself. *One to go.*

For a few seconds, the only thing Redd could hear was the ringing in his own ears. The shooting had stopped, but he was certain that the last hostile was lurking nearby—the sniper who had been providing covering fire for the assault team. The man had evidently learned from the mistakes of his fallen comrades and was now content to play a waiting game.

One-on-one.

Under any other circumstances, Redd would have liked his odds. He was a trained killer himself and had spent most of the last decade honing his skills on the battlefield. But the old Winchester only had one round left, and he didn't think the sniper would let him get close enough for blade work.

Only one way to tilt the balance back in his favor.

Redd squirmed under the front end of the pickup and began low crawling toward the motionless body of the assaulter he had knifed. One booted foot rested about eighteen inches from the front right corner of the vehicle. To reach the man, Redd would have to risk exposure, but he reasoned that if the sniper knew where he was, he would have already taken the shot.

Moving slowly to avoid attracting notice, he slid out just far enough to get a firm grip on the boot and then, with equal patience, wriggled back under cover, dragging the smaller dead man along with him. The expected shot never came.

Redd reeled in the body like a prize trout, then groped his way up the dead man's torso until he felt the nylon web sling attached to the assaulter's M4. He ran his hands over the weapon, inspecting it. Even in the near-total darkness, he could have fieldstripped it and reassembled it in a minute flat, but there was no need. The barrel was cold and smelled of Break Free. The man hadn't gotten off a single shot.

Just to be sure, Redd buttoned out the thirty-round magazine and weighed it in his hands. It was heavy.

Fully loaded.

He reseated the magazine, then probed the dead man's plate carrier until he found a pouch with two more magazines. He took one and jammed it into the back pocket of his jeans. If he couldn't end this fight with sixty rounds, he might as well give up now.

He wriggled back to his original position behind the right front tire and took a moment to mentally review the battle space. He recalled approximately where he'd seen the sniper's muzzle flash earlier, but until the man took another shot, Redd could only guess at his exact position.

Not a problem.

He rose to his haunches, then rolled forward out into the open, where he sprang to his feet and sprinted for the tree line.

I'm up, he sees me, I'm down.

The words, drilled into his head back in boot camp, were a way of measuring the three to five seconds that it would theoretically take for an enemy to spot, aim, and fire. On the last beat, he threw himself flat, rolled twice in the direction of the cabin, and then bounded up to do it all over again. He was exposed, but because he was constantly moving, and never in a straight line, he would be a hard target to hit.

The sniper held his fire. Redd continued zigzagging, varying the length of time he spent up or down, daring his opponent to take a shot and betray his location, but the man did not oblige.

Then, just as he was about to make a final dash for the wood line, there was a bright flash behind him, like a distant bolt of lightning, followed by a tremendous concussion. It was not just a sound but a palpable force that passed through every cell of his body like the deep thrum of a bass subwoofer.

He knew that sound, and his heart sank.

Grenade.

Redd spun around to face the cabin entrance. All was dark within, but smoke and dust billowed out from the open doorway.

"No!" he gasped and then was running toward it, heedless of the fact that he was now fully exposed to the sniper.

He had not gone a step when a shadowy figure darted out from behind the truck and headed straight for the cabin door. As the last man in the kill team, the sniper had left his place of concealment and chosen to assault the objective himself, using a frag grenade to kill those Redd had left inside and then moving to capture the sturdy old cabin in order to make his last stand there.

Redd tried to bring the M4 to bear, but the man was moving too fast, plunging headlong into the gloomy interior.

The smoke flashed twice as the man fired his own weapon.

Redd reached the door a heartbeat later, carbine at the high ready, fire selector switch set to burst. He did not look around the destroyed interior of the cabin. His eyes were laser focused on the man standing just a few feet away, and as the shooter started to turn, somehow sensing Redd's presence, Redd dropped his aim a few degrees and pulled the trigger.

The weapon bucked as three rounds in rapid succession tore into the man's unprotected groin. Redd let the weapon rise, triggering another burst that stitched the man's abdomen and then a third that drilled the SAPI plate covering his heart. The man jerked backward with each burst but somehow stayed on his feet until the last one caught him in the face. He went down like a marionette whose strings had just been slashed.

Redd kept the smoking weapon trained on the man a moment longer, just in case, then finally lowered it and began to survey the devastation inside the cabin.

He was just about to breathe a sigh of relief when he heard a voice behind him.

"You're a hard man to kill, Matty Redd."

Despite the ringing in his ears, the voice was clear as day. Redd immediately recognized the speaker—the last person in the world he expected to hear—and felt adrenaline dump into his bloodstream.

How? he wondered, knowing that he had just made a fatal mistake of his own. His mind raced. He had only one play left.

"Any last words?"

"I wish I would have killed you when I had the chance," he said, looking down at the carbine in his hands. Redd knew he didn't have time to turn and level his weapon, but trying to get a shot off beat the alternative. Giving up wasn't in his DNA, and he'd been through too much in the last two weeks to get shot in the back.

He refused to go out that way.

Without warning, Redd spun on his heel, bringing the carbine up. He saw the indistinct figure in the doorway, limned in moonlight, the dull black pistol aimed at his chest.

A second later, a single shot filled the night's air.

ONE

Matthew Redd swung the eight-pound Fiskars maul like a Viking berserker, splintering the heavy wooden door at the hinges and blasting it open.

"Go! Go! Go!" Redd shouted. As the first member of the fire team passed through the opening, Redd slung the maul over one shoulder and filled his massive hands with an M4 carbine, equipped with an Aimpoint M68 close-combat optic sight and a PAQ 4 infrared targeting laser. A second shooter went through, and then it was Redd's turn.

But as he charged through the doorway, the blaring of alarms drowned out the staccato pop of rifle fire. Overhead lights flashed on. On both sides of the door, the fourteen members of the Marine special operations team stopped in their tracks and immediately lowered their weapons.

The alarm went silent a moment later, replaced by an electronically amplified voice. "Cease fire, cease fire, cease fire. Safe and secure your weapons." There was the briefest pause, and then, "Redd! You broke my shoot house!"

Redd glanced up at the catwalk above. The range safety officer, Sergeant Baker, a grizzled-looking staff sergeant, face partially eclipsed by the bullhorn clenched in his right hand, glared down at him. The team commander, Captain Perez, stood next to the RSO, along with the team chief, Master Sergeant Miller.

When all the weapons were cleared, Miller's voice boomed out. "Sergeant Redd, why do you have a ten-pound sledgehammer in your kit? Don't you have enough weight to carry?"

Redd gripped the thirty-six-inch-long fiberglass shaft in his oversize fists and held the tool up as if for inspection. He was six foot three, two hundred forty pounds of muscle, and it looked like a child's twirling baton in his hands. "It's not a sledge, Top. It's a splitting maul." He rotated the tool, showing the heavy steel head, one side of which tapered into a wedge-shaped blade. "And it only weighs eight pounds."

Perez coughed to cover a chuckle, then leaned out over the rail of the catwalk. "All right, Sergeant Redd. Why do you have an *eight*-pound splitting maul in your kit? And why use it to breach that door instead of a shaped charge? We put those in your loadout for a reason."

"Our orders are to take Willow alive, sir. You just put him in that room. Enough demo to blast the door might be enough to kill him. That's why I carry a maul in my kit, sir."

"Sergeant Redd?"

"Sir?"

"You nailed it. Outstanding."

"Thank you, sir."

Perez liked Redd. Though he'd only been with the team a little over a year, the kid had shown exceptional initiative. While his impressive physique led people to think of him as a typical hard-charging jarhead—all brawn, no brains—the truth of the matter was that he had brains aplenty. The stunt with the sledgehammer—*splitting maul,* he corrected himself—was proof of that. At first glance, it had seemed like a demonstration of macho excess, but the reasoning behind it had been solid.

Redd would go places in the corps. He was a natural leader—the kind who inspired men to follow him and would lead from the front. If he had a failing, it was his tendency to come across as aloof. He got along well with his teammates but rarely socialized with them when off duty, which probably kept him out of a lot of trouble. Where most Marines lived for raising hell, pounding suds, and chasing tail, Redd preferred to spend his free time working out or learning some obscure martial art, looking for a new challenge. None of that would keep him from putting rockers under his chevrons. In fact, Redd was already eligible to advance to E-6, but doing so would mean finding an open slot somewhere, probably in another unit, and Redd had expressed a distinct aversion to the idea of giving up his slot on the team.

"Do you want to run the exercise again, sir?" Miller asked.

Perez gazed down at his Marines, all of whom were still breathing hard and streaked with perspiration. He shook his head. "We've been pushing them pretty hard. Maybe we should save something for game day."

Pretty hard was an understatement. Although they didn't look it, the men were bone-tired. Even the indomitable Redd. They'd been running training scenarios fourteen hours a day for the last three weeks prepping for the mission, running contingency scenarios ranging from HALO jumping onto the objective to making a covert approach over land. For the last nine days, they had run endless drills in the 41 Area shoot house, which had been hastily remodeled to approximate the building they would soon be assaulting.

"Game day keeps getting pushed back," the team chief countered. "This is the only way to keep our edge."

"You can only sharpen a blade so much before there's no steel left." Perez leaned on the railing and projected his voice down into the pit. "Listen up, Marines. You've done good work. Now I know you're all sick of being in a holding pattern. Believe me, I'm right there with you. But until we get the green light, that's where we're going to stay. We're only going to get one shot at this."

There were a few nods of acknowledgment from the men, but no cheers of "Oorah!" or anything else. These men had advanced beyond the need for the kind of cheerleading and chest-thumping that the grunts used to stay fired up. They were Marine Raiders. The Army had the Green Berets, the Navy had the SEALs, and the Chair Force . . . well, who knows what they had . . . but the corps had outdone them all with the Raiders.

But even Raiders needed a break once in a while.

"Get your stuff stowed," he went on. "Once you're squared away, I'm authorizing a thirty-six-hour liberty. Go home. Get some rack time. Hug your kids and kiss their mamas . . . if they'll let you. Just keep your phones with you and on at all times. If you get the call, I want you back here and ready to rock in thirty minutes."

This was a departure from SOP. Tier one units were, as a matter of operational security, kept on lockdown for a minimum of forty-eight hours before a mission, and since the go order might come at any time, letting the team wander off the reservation, even if it was only for a few hours and electronically tethered, was not without risk.

This time, the men did give a raucous cheer, which was abruptly truncated by a barked order from Miller. "As you were, Marines."

Instant silence.

Miller leaned over the rail and singled out one of the Raiders with his gaze. "No liberty for you, Redd. I've got a special assignment for you."

Redd looked back at him, uncomprehending. "Top?"

"Once you're squared away, you need to get in that fancy truck of yours and head out to the nearest Home Depot. You owe Sergeant Baker here a new door."

TWO

Running the lake circuit this late in the morning was nice, Gavin Kline thought. Despite the humidity that accompanied the sun's creep toward midday, he had McMillan Reservoir mostly to himself. Everyone else in the capital was slaving away in their air-conditioned cubicles. It was just one perk of working at the annex and having flexible hours.

Not that he was ever truly off duty. Intelligence Branch was a 24-7-365 job, at least as far as Kline was concerned. The bad guys didn't work bankers' hours, so why should the good guys?

It wasn't like he had any kind of life outside the job. He'd sacrificed everyone and everything he ever cared for—*love* wasn't a word in his vocabulary—to serve his country, first as a Marine and then as a special agent in the Federal Bureau of Investigation. He'd fought America's enemies at home and abroad for three decades.

And what have I got to show for it? he thought, overcome by a rare moment of self-recrimination.

He was fifty-three and getting nowhere fast. Things had started off on the right foot. After leaving the corps, he'd transitioned to the bureau, joining and eventually supervising a special operations "fly team"—the bureau's equivalent of SEAL Team Six. From there, he'd been promoted up to counterterrorism and had been on the fast track to senior management in CTD or maybe even higher. At least, that was what he'd been promised.

Then his fortunes changed. He had transferred from CTD to the Intelligence Branch on the promise that there would be a desk on the seventh floor for him just as soon as his mentor moved up to the number two spot in the bureau. The plane crash that killed his "rabbi" and four other senior executives, however, had resulted in a massive change in FBI leadership. That promise, and Kline's career, had corkscrewed into the ground along with that plane.

His career trajectory flattened by office politics, he had been relegated to a make-work unit buried in a remote location on the far side of the District, punching the clock, counting the days until he had his thirty and could start pulling that fat pension check.

He shook his head, dropping the curtain on his personal pity party. It wasn't over, not by a long shot. *He* wasn't over.

Fifty-three wasn't really that old. He was still in good shape, partly because he ran religiously, but mostly because nature had blessed him with an athletic physique and a metabolism to match. He was six foot two, lean, but with the kind of build that would have easily allowed him to pack on the muscle if he so desired.

Of course, rugged good looks and cardio wouldn't help him climb the next rung of the bureau ladder. To do that, he would need a big win, and Willow was going to be it.

Willow—a code name, but the only one they had for a notorious bio-weapons expert—had ties to at least six different terrorist organizations on five continents, which was why it was so important to take him . . . or possibly her . . . alive.

Kline would have preferred to run the snatch and grab he'd designed with his old fly team, but his new boss, Rachel Culp, had put the kibosh on that. The FBI would not send a fly team into Mexico.

"Too political," she'd said. She couldn't deny the value of Willow as a target, but pushing it off onto the Marine Raiders was a chicken move meant to cover herself if things went sideways. As a former Marine, Kline resented that decision, though he didn't doubt that the Raiders were more than up for the challenge.

The Raiders . . .

His Apple Watch buzzed with an incoming call. The number was a reroute, shielding the identity and location of the caller, both of which he knew well. An old friend in Mexico, his most trusted contact, Hernán Vasquez.

Without breaking stride, Kline tapped his watch face to accept the call, which was transmitted wirelessly to the AirPods in his ears. "Talk to me."

"Twelve hours."

Kline didn't need an explanation. He knew exactly what the terse message implied.

In developing the Willow operation, based in no small part on intel provided by Vasquez himself, Kline had determined that Willow made frequent visits to a remote facility in the Yucatán Peninsula. It would be the perfect place to grab Willow, provided they had advance notice of the scientist's next visit.

And Vasquez had just given him that.

But there was something else that Vasquez wasn't saying. His tone was grim where it ought to have been ecstatic.

Kline stopped in his tracks, his gut dropping like a free-falling freight elevator. "What's wrong, Hernán?"

There was a long silence. "It's probably nothing, *jefe.*"

"Which means it could be something. Spill it."

"Can't say, exactly. I just got a bad feeling about this one."

Kline glanced around the tree-lined lake. No one in sight. At least, not in earshot. He dropped onto a bench shaded underneath a weeping willow. His feet hurt anyway.

"Is it your intel?" Kline prompted. "We're only going to get one shot at this, so if there's a chance he's not going to be there, then we don't go."

"It's not that," Vasquez said. "This is a solid lead. It's just . . . I don't know—it feels too easy. Like someone wanted to make sure I heard about it."

Kline weighed the statement. Easy was always cause for suspicion. Easy was the cheese in the mousetrap.

On the other hand, sometimes you got lucky and it only felt easy.

I'm gonna be knocking down TUMS like PEZ candies until this is over, Kline thought. "So what is your gut telling you?" he asked. "Do we take a pass?"

"No," Vasquez finally said, after another torturous pause. "Who knows when we'll get a chance like this again."

"So do we pull the trigger?" Kline pressed.

"*Sí.* Let's do this, *jefe.* But listen. The problem might not be on my end."

"What are you saying?"

"I'm saying you better watch your six."

"You too, *hermano*. The hammer's gonna fall soon."

Vasquez rang off.

"Crap," Kline muttered. He wiped away the sweat on his forehead. Vasquez was an old pro. The best. He could be counted on to strike a perfect balance between caution and audacity. It wasn't like him to drop a bomb like this at zero minus twelve hours.

And he had dodged Kline's question. *"What is your gut telling you?"*

Well, I've got a gut, too, Kline thought. *And right now it's in knots.*

He pulled a burner phone out of his running belt. He'd never bring it into the annex. Couldn't risk the random frisk or security desk check by the counterintelligence team that swept through on a regular basis. He also knew CI monitored all phone signals inside the building. A burner phone would pop up on their screens like a Roman candle on a moonless night.

But out of the office on his own time, he was probably okay. Certainly here, with no one in earshot. He flipped the phone open and punched in the number.

A voice picked up on the other end after just two rings.

"I need you to drop everything and take care of something for me."

"Name it."

"There's not enough time, and it's a long shot, but you've got to try," Kline said. "If anyone can pull this off, it's you." He laid out his plan.

"No promises," came the reply. "I'll do what I can, but in the end, it's not up to me."

"I know," Kline said, ending the call.

Then he stood and pulled out the burner phone's SIM card and battery and tossed them into the lake.

All he could do now was wait.

THREE

CALIFORNIA

No wife, no kids, not even a dog.

It sounded like a bad country song, but to Matthew Redd, it was heaven. Who needed any of that clutter in their lives?

Besides, unlike that sad sack in the song, the one thing he *did* have was a truck.

An agate-black 2020 Ford F-150 Raptor. He loved his Raptor like the brother he never had. It was a beast of a machine and a mirror image of himself: massive power, breakneck speed, unstoppable.

Truth be told, he loved it more than he loved most people.

It had cost him more than a year's wages—he'd been raised to pay for everything in cash—but it was more than worth it. His needs were simple, and his wants—aside from the Raptor—were virtually nonexistent. He was a thirty-year man, and the corps would take care of him when he got out. Who needed a retirement account? He had watched the markets over the years and would rather HALO jump without a chute than put his hard-earned money in the Wall Street casino.

And now he was rolling down a remote two-lane county road on a classic California morning, the blue Pacific white-capped in the far distance. Not going anywhere in particular, just cruising. There were still six hours of liberty left. He had the windows down and Jimmie Allen's "Good Times Roll" blasting on the radio.

But even as he bobbed his head to the rhythm, his mind was still on the shoot house drills. They had all gone well, no matter how many curveballs Captain Perez threw at them. The commander, like Redd, hewed to the old axiom *The more you sweat in training, the less you bleed in battle.* They were ready for anything.

Despite the very real risk, Redd was amped about the mission. HALO down—with a chute—in and out with no resistance, grab Willow, rendezvous with a pair of Ospreys sent to pick them up, and get back over the border before the Mexicans knew they'd been there.

Man, he loved his job. He'd never felt more a part of something than in the corps. And he was good at it. No, if he were honest, he was great at it.

He had joined up almost before the ink on his GED was dry, left the pine-studded granite mountains of Montana behind, and never looked back. Despite an impressive score on his ASVAB, he had known from the start that he wanted to be infantry, because the infantry took the fight to the enemy. For three and a half years, that was exactly what he'd done. He'd had his eye on the Raiders, and as soon as he made E-4, he signed up to attend the MARSOC Prep Course / Selection Screener at Camp Lejeune.

He breezed through the three-week course, which was designed to make candidates question their choices, and not long thereafter proceeded to phase two of the prep course, which featured more of the same.

Embrace the suck became his mantra.

He had loved every minute of it.

After passing selection, the fun really began with the seven-month-long individual training course. It had been like drinking from a fire hose. He had become an expert in almost every facet of special operations, received advanced training in sniper skills, communications, intelligence, diving, and language training. He became proficient with foreign weapons and attended SERE—survival, evasion, resistance, escape—school. Learned small unit tactics, received fire support and medical training. He'd even learned intelligence collection.

Because of his size, the instructors made it their mission in life to break him off, but in true Marine fashion, he had improvised, adapted, and overcome all obstacles put before him.

When it was done, he stood proud with seventy-two of his fellow Marines—down from 121 at the start. From there, he'd been assigned to Captain Perez's team, which was heading to the Philippines for a ten-month deployment.

No time to slow down, and certainly not for relationships. He wasn't exactly wired for them anyway.

The only two people who had ever really mattered were both out of the picture now. Mostly anyway. He still talked to his adoptive dad, J. B., once in a while, though he hadn't seen the old man face-to-face since his graduation from boot camp.

Emily, on the other hand . . .

He pushed thoughts of her out of his mind, cranked the music up louder, and hit the gas.

He rounded the next curve and saw a late-model Toyota Tacoma pickup parked in a wide turnout on the side of the road. Well, not exactly parked. It was jacked up and the rear left wheel missing. The bright-yellow surfboard in the bed caught his eye, but it was the stunning redhead in shorts and a bikini top that made him do a double take. The woman was clearly frustrated, staring at the spare tire at her feet, hands on her hips.

His first thought was that he should stop and help. Not because she was smoking hot . . . He was always a little wary of attractive women, mostly because in his experience, they felt their good looks entitled them to special treatment, especially from men. No, his impulse to help her arose from the same place as his decision to enlist. It was the cowboy way.

The way J. B. had raised him. He would have done it for any little old lady in a similar situation.

His second thought, however, was for the mission. What if he pulled over and somehow another car came by and struck him? Someone else could come along and help her, but nobody could replace him on the team.

He passed her.

But that was crap. He was far more likely to get killed in a head-on collision back on the I-5 than get hurt changing her tire.

"Get over yourself," he muttered in J. B.'s gruff voice.

He turned around.

✖ ✖ ✖

Fifteen minutes later, Redd had the full-size spare tire bolted in place and the flat tossed in the Tacoma's bed along with the surfboard.

"I can't thank you enough," the woman said. She'd introduced herself as Sammy. She opened the truck cab and pulled out her purse, grabbing for money. "Let me pay you something for this."

Redd shook his head. "It was no big deal. Really."

She smiled at him, then set her purse down. "I just can't believe I left my phone back at my place. Kinda stupid. And then the flat. You'd think I'd know how to fix something like that."

"That's what AAA is for," he replied. "Of course, I guess if you don't have your phone, that's not much help."

"I can't let you just leave. It's almost lunchtime. How about I buy you lunch?"

"No, really. It's fine. I should get going."

"Look, my Airbnb is just up the road, five minutes from here. Let me at least offer you a beer. You do drink beer, don't you?"

A beer sounded great, but he wasn't so sure that was a good idea. One beer had a way of turning into more than one beer.

But Sammy had surprised him. She seemed genuinely nice, and that was enough to get him to lower his guard. There was a fierce intelligence dancing behind her dark-green eyes.

"I don't want to impose," he said, half-heartedly.

She cocked her head to the side. "Are you military?"

The question surprised him. Like most tier one special operations units, the Raiders were permitted relaxed grooming standards. While not exactly shaggy, he had a full, albeit well-groomed beard and wore his dark-brown hair considerably longer than a jarhead buzz cut. And unlike most leathernecks, he did not advertise his affiliation with T-shirts and bumper stickers. "Uh, yeah. I mean, yes, ma'am. I'm in the corps."

"I knew it. I can always tell. My grandfather was a Marine. He fought in Vietnam. Wounded at Khe Sahn in '68."

"God bless him. He doing okay?"

"He passed a few years ago. Agent Orange." She shrugged. "I miss him like crazy."

"I'm sorry."

"If he were still alive, he'd chew me out if I didn't buy a thirsty Marine a beer. Whaddya say?" She smiled again, her teeth almost blindingly white. "I'm not asking you to marry me. Just have a beer with me. I don't like owing anybody anything."

J. B. had taught Redd that a cowboy doesn't take advantage of women . . . or anybody else. But she obviously wanted to buy him that beer. Maybe saying yes would be doing her a favor. In fact, saying no would be kind of rude.

Redd checked his watch. He wasn't supposed to report back to base for another five-plus hours. How long could it take to have just one beer?

He shrugged. "Well, I'd hate to disappoint your grandpa."

She brightened. "Thank you. It means a lot to me." She pulled open the door of her truck. "Just follow me."

As he watched her firm body slide into the cab, he felt a sudden pang. This wasn't what he wanted. He wasn't looking for a relationship, and he had no interest in a one-night stand.

But then again, all she was offering was a beer.

Right?

FOUR

Master Sergeant Scott Miller gazed down the aisle of the C-130 Hercules, unconsciously counting heads.

Unlucky thirteen, he thought. He was not a superstitious man, but he could not shake an uncharacteristic feeling of apprehension as he surveyed the uneven parallel columns.

Where are you, Redd?

The call had gone out only two hours before the originally scheduled return time, and more than half of the team had already been either in the team house or en route. The rest showed up within thirty minutes, except for Redd. He hadn't answered that call nor any of the subsequent calls and texts.

In a regular line unit, Miller would have immediately sent out the shore patrol to reel him in, but the Raiders didn't operate that way. They were adults, professionals, not wayward children in need of a babysitter. If Redd was unavoidably detained, it was because stuff happened. Murphy's Law was as much a factor on the home front as the battlefront. Redd would show up eventually, Miller had assured Captain Perez. He wouldn't let them down.

But Redd had not shown up, and as the cutoff time expired, they had been forced to make two very difficult decisions: drive on with the mission, and report Redd as UA—unauthorized absence.

If Redd wasn't dead in a ditch somewhere, a UA would probably kill his career in special operations. It wouldn't do Perez or Miller any favors either. But they would deal with the fallout later, after they had Willow in hand.

Miller mentally ran through the mission brief again. Compared to the training scenarios they'd run through, the execution promised to be easy— or at least, as easy as a night HALO jump could be. Any jump was risky, but a high-altitude, low-opening insertion added a whole new level of possible applications of Murphy's Law. Altitude sickness and decompression sickness could strike even a seasoned jumper without warning. The long free fall had a way of dulling the reflexes, which could cause an operator to hesitate just a fraction of a second too long when the time came to deploy his chute. The low-opening part of the equation left only a razor-thin margin for error. If the main chute failed, there might not be time to deploy the reserve.

Accidents happened. *Stuff happens* might as well have been a secondary Marine Corps motto, scribbled beneath *Semper fi* with a jittery, adrenaline-fueled hand.

By that calculus, Redd's absence would not significantly impact the mission. Nevertheless, it felt like a bad omen.

What if Redd really was dead in a ditch?

A chirp issued from his headset, and then a voice. "Two minutes."

Miller nodded unnecessarily, then relayed the news to the team. "Showtime, ladies!"

✖   ✖   ✖

Hernán Vasquez stood on the side of the road next to his Jeep Cherokee, the night-vision binoculars glued to his eyes. This was mostly flat country and where he stood was only ten meters higher than the compound a half mile away, but it was the best view he could get.

Three hours earlier, he had observed a small convoy of trucks and SUVs pulling into the compound. Since then, all had been quiet within.

And without.

That was about to change.

His naked eye couldn't make out the small, dark shadows he knew were plummeting toward the earth, but then the Marine Raiders' chutes blossomed into gray-green flowers drifting lazily above the field. One by one, they touched down and then seemed to disappear as quickly as they had come.

He tracked them as best he could as they dashed forward in cover-and-move formation. They moved like ghosts, advancing to the edge of the dark compound and then vanishing inside. Vasquez held his breath, waiting for the night to erupt into violence, but nothing happened. No gunfire, no explosions. Not even a flicker of artificial light.

Too quiet, he thought.

Several minutes passed. Vasquez's eyes were starting to burn with the strain of peering into the monochrome display of the binos, but he didn't dare look away. Finally something moved in the otherwise-static display. The ghosts were leaving the compound, moving back toward the field.

Fourteen ghosts, all of them separated by a good five meters.

Fourteen in, fourteen out.

Where was the captive? Where was Willow?

Vasquez's heart dropped into his stomach.

As if to underscore his rising dread, the stillness was broken by the dull roar of aircraft engines in the distance. He scanned the horizon with the binos until he at last found the infrared marker lights of two V-22 Ospreys coming in low, flying nap of the earth to avoid showing up on Mexican radar. The Osprey was neither plane nor helicopter but could function like both. With its enormous twin rotors tilted up, it could take off and land like a heavy-duty helicopter, but once in the air, with the rotors tilted forward, it could travel at 275 knots—even faster at higher altitude.

As the two birds made their approach, the pilots tilted the rotors up so smoothly that Vasquez didn't notice it happening until it was done. One of the aircraft continued hovering a hundred feet off the ground, providing overwatch, while the second touched down, its cargo ramp opening to allow the Raiders to board. Though the camouflaged figures were almost indistinguishable against the background, Vasquez thought he could read disappointment in the way they moved. The mission had been a bust.

Vasquez knew that he should depart, slink away into the shadows, just as the Marines were doing, but he kept watching through the binos, desperate to find some cause for hope. Maybe the Raiders were rallying at the aircraft just long enough to hand off some crucial piece of physical intelligence before returning to the compound to bring Willow out . . .

But as soon as the last man was aboard, the pulse of the engines deepened, and the Osprey began to loft skyward again. They were leaving. No doubt about it.

Suddenly a blinding light raked Vasquez's eyes like jagged fingernails. He winced reflexively, tearing the binos away from his eyes. Too late. The damage was already done. Long green streaks crossed his vision, but everything else was pitch-black. An instant later, however, the night lit up as the hovering Osprey was transformed into a fireball.

The boom of the rocket-propelled grenade's ignition reached his ears almost simultaneously, but it was nothing to the thunderclap that followed the destruction of the aircraft. Even as flaming debris rained down, two more rockets streaked up from a distant corner of the field, lancing into the second Osprey before it could clear the ground.

Vasquez staggered backward, one hand groping for the Jeep's hood.

"No," he whispered. "No. No. No!"

"Too easy," he had told Kline. *"Like someone wanted to make sure I heard about it."*

Why hadn't he trusted his gut? Willow had set a trap, and they had all fallen into it. Fourteen Marines dead. His own cover almost certainly blown.

That revelation sizzled through him like a bolt of lightning. *I have to go.*

But as he reached for the door handle, he sensed movement around him. He reached for his holstered pistol, but before he could break leather, something crashed into the back of his head, and then there was nothing.

FIVE

WELLINGTON, MONTANA

Anastasia Petryk despised Montana. It was, she thought, America's Siberia.

She had never been to Siberia—had never even left Odessa until she and her husband, Viktor, took jobs at the bioresearch facility—but her old *babusya* had told stories of her own childhood, growing up under Soviet rule and the constant threat of exile to a frozen gulag in the Siberian wilderness. It sure sounded a lot like Montana.

She wasn't an exile, of course. She and Viktor were here of their own free will and were in fact being handsomely compensated by their employer. *It's just not what I thought America would be like,* she thought as she leaned her elbows against the bar and contemplated the shot glass in front of her. Where was the nightlife? The restaurants and retail stores? Even in Bozeman, which was a good hour's drive away, the pickings were pretty slim. Wellington, the Stillwater County seat, was just a bump in the road in the middle of a beautiful nowhere. It was the kind of place you only found by accident or word of mouth. What few businesses survived here were more than content to keep things as local as they could for as long as possible. All the town had to offer was a couple of outfitter shops and Spady's Saloon.

Spady's, she had been told, was a local favorite, which meant the whiskey was good, the steaks fresh, and the tourists scarce. Ana wasn't quite sure why the last criterion was counted as a positive, but the first two were at least accurate.

Spady's was . . . She supposed the only word for it was *quaint*. Dusty trophy heads of grizzly bear, elk, moose, and deer stared down at them from their high perches on the log walls, a jury of slaughtered witnesses judging the crimes and misdemeanors of the drunken humans below, including the two Ukrainians. An old jukebox wired into a surround sound system played classic country-western tunes, mostly Hank Williams and Johnny Cash, with a little Gene Autry thrown in.

She and Viktor had decided to sit at the tall bar rather than waiting for a table. Despite its remote location, the place was hopping on a Friday night, probably because of the three-dollar well drinks, of which Ana and Viktor had already polished off quite a few.

Like Viktor had said, they deserved a treat.

Their work had consumed them for eleven months straight, and when the schedule finally allowed for a week's getaway—a too-long-delayed honeymoon—they'd grabbed it. Tonight was their last night to let loose. Tomorrow they would be back at the grindstone.

As much as they had enjoyed the time off, though, work was never far from their minds. For all of their complaining to themselves, they were in fact utterly consumed by the project. The work was exciting—cutting-edge stuff that promised to make a real difference in the world—and the fact that there yet remained a few obstacles to success felt almost like a personal affront. Viktor was the first to raise a problem that they'd both been struggling with at the lab.

Ana glanced around nervously. "Careful what you say," she cautioned. "Someone might overhear."

Viktor waved a dismissive hand. "I cannot even hear myself," he practically shouted, but he had, she noted, switched to their native Ukrainian language. And then, his tongue loosened by all the alcohol he had imbibed, he began opining on the one subject about which they had been sworn to absolute secrecy.

Anastasia felt the hairs stand up on the back of her neck. It might have been the chill wind blowing through the door. It was the middle of May, but it was snowing lightly outside. "Viktor, I really don't think you should be talking about this in public."

Her husband's bloodshot eyes narrowed. "Why? No one can understand us," he slurred, his words oozing out of his mouth like syrup.

"It's against the security protocol. We don't want to get in trouble." She had always been the more circumspect one in their partnership, both in and out of the lab. Also the smartest. She glanced around the room, so quickly that it made her head spin, and caught the eye of an old cowboy with a drooping white mustache.

He looked away quickly as if embarrassed.

Or guilty.

Her face flushed.

"Viktor—"

"You want another round?"

"I think we should go."

"I'm not sure I can drive. How about some coffee first?"

She frowned and jerked her chin in the direction of the old man, who had risen from his booth seat and was leaning on a cane, counting out bills onto his table.

Viktor turned around on his stool to see what had so alarmed her. "So?"

"That man. I think he heard us."

"So he heard us. You think some dumb cowboy speaks Ukrainian?"

Anastasia's eyes narrowed. "I don't know."

"It's not possible! He talks to cows all day, and there are no Ukrainian cows in Montana. Stop being paranoid."

Anastasia watched the old man shuffle out the door. "Pay the bill."

"Why? I want some coffee."

She switched to English. *"Pay the bill."* She stood up.

"Where are you going?"

She ignored him and crossed over to the jukebox, pretending to study the playlist. But she was stealing glances through the window. She saw the old man climb with great difficulty into a battered old Ford F-250. A moment later, he stuck a cell phone to his ear. Her pulse began to race.

She nearly jumped out of her skin when Viktor laid a hand on her shoulder. "You don't actually like this music, do you?" he asked in Ukrainian. Even drunk, he knew not to let the locals hear him insult their music.

"Look," she said, pointing to the window. The truck was pulling out of the parking lot, but the old man inside was still visible, a mobile phone pressed up under the brim of his Stetson.

"What? That old man again?"

"I'm telling you he heard us. And he understood."

"I don't believe it."

She gripped his arm. "But what if I'm right?"

Viktor weighed the question for a moment, his expression sobering rapidly. "We need to call it in."

"You call while I drive." She held her liquor better than her husband, so it made sense for her to take the wheel, but the real reason she wanted to drive was that she was scared to make that call. This breach of security would have consequences.

They pushed open the glass door and stepped into a chill wind. What had been just a dusting of light snow now felt like splinters of ice, stinging their faces. As Ana slipped into the driver's seat, Viktor began dialing the company's emergency hotline. As he waited for the call to connect, she wondered if it might have been better for her to make the call after all. Driving drunk was dangerous, to be sure, but if Viktor screwed it up, said just one wrong word . . . they were both dead.

SIX

Matthew Redd was dead to the world.

Or he was until he felt the first rays of sunshine warming his face, a sensation that made him realize he was only just now becoming conscious. Sort of.

His mind began to open, but try as he might, he couldn't will his eyelids to do the same. He was so tired . . .

"No such thing as too tired," J. B. had told him, waking him before dawn every day, even Sunday, to work the ranch.

It had seemed like a harsh lesson for an eleven-year-old, but that discipline had served him well.

So why are your eyes still closed, Marine?

He felt himself slipping back into a dark well, his mind narrowing to a single point of oblivion. So tired . . .

"Screw that," he murmured.

Still lying flat, he palmed his face, rubbing his eyes until he could coax them open. He blinked, momentarily unable to focus. His vision was blurred, and the sunlight didn't do any favors for the headache thundering inside his skull.

Through the fuzz, he glimpsed a slow-turning ceiling fan.

Where am I?

A familiar smell, salty and feminine, struck him.

A woman. *That* woman. He saw her face, her copper hair and green eyes.

What was her name? Sandra? No, Sammy.

His memory returned in snippets. A small beach house . . . Sammy's Airbnb.

He had followed her here, accepted her invitation to come in, but refused the beer. *"A glass of water will be fine,"* he had insisted. *"I have to report for duty soon."*

He probably should not have told her that—OPSEC—but it was the politest way he could think of to refuse the beer.

"How 'bout a Coke?"

"A Coke would be great," he'd allowed. *"As long as you don't splash some Jack in it."*

She had fetched a can from the refrigerator and poured it into a glass over ice. He would have been fine with sipping it from the can, but whatever.

And then . . . what?

He couldn't pull it up.

"Wait. What time is it?"

He barely had enough energy to turn his head on the pillow and bring his wrist close to his face. Through the blur, he could just make out the display of his G-Shock.

8:37 a.m.

Panic dumped adrenaline into his bloodstream, clearing his mind though the headache remained.

"Oh, crap."

He fell out of bed but rose up on one elbow, only now aware that he was still fully dressed.

"Phone? Where's my—?"

The bedroom door burst open.

Three beefy figures in cammies and bump helmets charged into the room, brandishing what Redd's bleary eyes took to be semiautomatic pistols.

A second jolt of adrenaline almost brought him to full wakefulness, and a single thought went through his head.

Hit squad.

He launched on wobbly legs straight at the first man who'd come through the door. If they were going to kill him, he'd take at least one of them out. It wasn't a decision. It was instinct. A killing instinct.

Shocked by Redd's headlong charge, the lead operator hesitated before pulling the trigger.

Big mistake.

Redd's fist crashed into his face like an anvil, tossing him backward into the other two men, jamming them up before they could get all the way through the door.

Redd swung his other fist, smashing the first man again just beneath the chin, slamming his jaw shut. The man uttered a bloody howl through broken teeth.

But the two other men pushed forward as if joining a rugby scrum. One man wrapped his big arms around Redd's waist; the other swiped the butt of his sidearm toward the top of Redd's bare skull. Although immobilized, Redd had the wherewithal to duck his head, and so the blow, while painful, did not render him unconscious. In fact, it had the opposite effect. Fueled by rage, Redd reached down, seized hold of the arms pinioning him, and ripped them loose as easily as stripping off a belt. Then, still gripping the man's wrists, he snapped his body around, swinging the man like a whip and slamming him into the other man. There was an audible thud as their skulls made contact, and both men went flying across the room.

Then a fourth man poured into the room and immediately discharged his weapon.

Twin barbs struck Redd's broad chest and stuck there like fishhooks. He knew what was coming next, but before he could sweep the wires away, fifty thousand volts of electricity coursed into him.

His entire body convulsed in a single spasm of pain. He fell dead away and crashed onto the hardwood floor, a faux sheepskin the only thing that kept his skull from cracking wide-open.

Even before his muscles could unclench, a second pulse ripped through him. With only 8 percent body fat, there was almost nothing to insulate him from the jolt. Still convulsing, Redd felt powerful hands roll him over. Another man none-too-gently flex-cuffed his arms behind his back, putting his knee in Redd's spine for leverage.

"Why are you doing this to me?" Redd tried to say, though with his muscles still quivering and a mouth full of fake wool, his words were incomprehensible.

"You're under arrest," the man said and then leaned in so close that Redd could smell the stink of stale tobacco on the man's breath. "I hope they hang you for the traitor you are."

SEVEN

Redd hadn't slept so much as passed out and woken up over and over all through the night. The brig's hard cot didn't help. Neither did his bruised ribs or the quasi-beating he'd received in the form of rough handling from the shore patrol. His muscles still ached from the hard contraction caused by the Taser . . . which he supposed was preferable to what a bullet might have done, but in the moment, it didn't feel like it.

Yeah, he hurt pretty good, but he'd been beaten a lot worse by some of the assorted jerks and druggy boyfriends his mother had dragged into their various trailer homes over the years.

He pushed away that thought. Thankfully, those memories of childhood, of the time before J. B. took him in, rarely rose into the light.

Exhausted, starving, and sore, his body demanded sleep. But his mind would not comply. *Treason* was a big word, an accusation that could get you life in prison—or worse. As far as Redd was concerned, *traitor* was just about the worst word in the English language. There was nothing lower, not even *coward*. Sometimes a man just lost it in battle—brain chemistry, shot nerves, who the heck knew?—and even the bravest man could find cowardice washing over him under the wrong circumstances. He'd seen it happen.

But treason was a choice. It was a decision to betray all that you and your friends fought for, bled for, and sometimes even died for. It was the unforgivable sin.

A sin he'd been accused of.

No one would tell him what had happened. They wouldn't even give him the time of day in his windowless room. But he had an inkling of what lay behind the charge.

Something bad had happened.

The team had gotten the green light, gone after Willow . . . and somehow the crap had hit the fan.

Why else accuse him of betrayal?

Lying on his cot, he imagined a thousand scenarios where things went sideways and his teammates got killed. It made him want to puke. When fatigue overcame him, self-loathing guilt would seize him by the throat and throttle him awake again.

Sammy.

The chick had drugged him. He was certain of it.

And then? Had he spilled his guts? Told her about the mission? Revealed operational details?

If he'd learned anything in SERE school, it was that everybody talked eventually, especially under the influence of exotic pharmaceuticals.

Something bad had happened on the mission. Someone had probably died.

I should have been there. I could have saved them . . .

He tried to shout down the voice of his guilt. *Quit running to your worst fears. "Fear is the mind killer."*

He'd loved that quote ever since he'd read it in the novel *Dune.*

Fear was what separated animals from human beings. An animal would chew its leg off to escape from a trap, but a human being—at least as defined by the mystics in the novel—knew that fear only made the situation worse.

Detach. Don't get emotional.

Observe, orient, decide, act—OODA.

But if something did go wrong? And it all went to hell because I wasn't there?

Guilt seized him again. He should have been there no matter what.

He fell back onto his hard cot and closed his eyes, trying to will it all away. But he failed.

The nightmare rolled on like a riptide, sucking him under again.

✖ ✖ ✖

The cinder block interrogation room was as spartan as the rest of the brig, and even more humorless, if that was possible. The freshly mopped floor, still wet, gave off the sharp, pungent odor of old Pine-Sol. Redd was seated at the table in the center of the room, his handcuffs now in front of him and chained to an eyebolt in the center of the table.

Out of habit, he tried to stand while his battalion's commanding officer, Colonel Olson, entered the room along with another short, middle-aged officer with distinctively Asian features and wearing Navy whites. One of the SPs flanking him shoved the chair into the back of his legs. "Sit back down, traitor," the man growled.

Olson and the other man approached and sat across the table from him. The Naval officer spoke first. "Sergeant, I'm Commander Kim from the JAG Corps. I'll be overseeing the case against you. Before we get started, I need to advise you of your rights under Article 31 of the UCMJ—"

"I know my rights," Redd said in a deliberate manner.

Kim's lips twitched with something that might have been a smile; then he reached out and turned on the small recording device in front of him. He read in the particulars of name, place, and date, then turned his eyes on Redd. "Do you wish to have legal counsel?"

"I don't need an attorney. I didn't do anything that needs defending, except for maybe being stupid."

"'He who represents himself has a fool for a client,'" Kim said. "Abraham Lincoln."

"Actually, there's no evidence that Lincoln ever said that," Redd countered. "However, he most definitely did say, 'Resolve to be honest at all events; and if in your own judgment you cannot be an honest lawyer, resolve to be honest without being a lawyer.'"

Colonel Olson leaned forward. "You sure about this, son? You're in deep trouble."

Redd nodded. "I didn't do anything wrong, sir. I swear."

Olson acknowledged this with raised eyebrows but said nothing.

Kim filled the silence. "Sergeant Redd, you were UA while the rest of your team was engaged in a critical operation. Can you explain your actions?"

"I didn't go UA, sir. At least, I didn't choose to. Like I said in my first statement, I was driving home to my place when I saw this girl on the side of the road with a flat tire. She looked like she needed help, so I stopped."

"You said her name was Sammy? No last name?"

"None that I recall, sir."

"And you had never met her before?"

Redd glanced at the colonel. Olson was one of the most squared-away Marines he'd ever met. He had more parachute jumps under his belt than any other officer on base, and in six combat tours, he'd earned a number of awards including a Navy Cross and two Purple Hearts. Somewhere along the way he also found the time to earn a PhD in history from Cambridge University. If Colonel Olson led a charge into the mouth of hell, the entire First Division would fall in behind him, Redd in the lead. It was Redd's admiration that made him wither beneath the cold, searching glare in Olson's clear-green eyes. It seemed a mixture of contempt and pity, neither of which Redd could abide.

"No, sir," Redd continued. "Never laid eyes on her before."

"And yet you put your entire team at risk by pulling over to change a stranger's tire? That's the story you expect us to believe?"

"I can't make you believe anything. I can only tell you what's true. She had a flat; she needed help; it was a deserted road. It was the right thing to do."

Kim shrugged. "Too bad we can't find any trace of this 'Sammy.'"

This did not come as a surprise to Redd. "The Airbnb—"

"Was rented in your name, using your debit card for payment. I guess you thought it would be a good place to lie low while the rest of your team fell into the trap you helped set for them."

So there it was. Confirmation of Redd's worst fear. He squirmed in his chair, rattling his chains. "What happened to them?"

"You don't ask the questions here, Sergeant. I do," Kim said, his hard eyes narrowing. "Your job is to answer them."

Redd cast a glance at Colonel Olson. Unlike the JAG lawyer, Olson was a combat officer. He understood what Redd was feeling. Redd silently pleaded with his battalion commander to tell him about the mission and the team, but all he got in return was an icy stare.

"So you claim you stopped for this woman we can't locate, to help her change her flat tire," Kim went on.

"Yes, sir."

"But you didn't go home afterward?"

"No, sir."

"Why not?"

"She wanted to buy me a beer."

"At her place?"

"Yes, sir."

"This was . . . what, about noon? You drink a lot of beer that time of day, Sergeant?"

"I turned down the beer, sir. Drank a Coke instead. Honestly, sir, it's hard to say no to a girl like that." He managed a half-hearted grin.

"So you were just hoping to get laid, is that it?"

"I don't know. Maybe? She was nice. Said her granddaddy was a Marine in the Vietnam War. She was real insistent."

"And then?"

"She poured me a Coke. We sat and talked—"

"Talked? About what?"

Redd pursed his lips together. He knew he and Sammy had talked, but everything they had exchanged was like something from a dream. "I don't remember. We were drinking Cokes, and the next thing I knew, I was waking up in her bed."

"Nothing else?"

"No. Nothing. I don't even remember passing out."

"What are you suggesting? That this mystery woman drugged you?"

"It's the only explanation. It's like someone edited out a big chunk of the movie."

"If your timeline is correct, about twenty hours of your 'movie,'" Kim said. "Funny thing, though. You submitted to a urinalysis after we brought you in. Tox screen indicates nothing in your system. No drugs, no alcohol."

"But I *could* have been drugged."

"You also could have been kidnapped by aliens, but I doubt it. I'll say it again. The tox report shows no indication of drugs in your system."

For the first time since the interrogation began, Redd was truly bewildered. "Then why don't I remember anything?"

"You tell me."

"How can I tell you why I don't remember anything when I don't remember anything?"

Kim shook his head with a pitying smile. "Are you listening to yourself, Sergeant?"

Redd's hopes fell. What had happened to him?

Kim sighed through his nose, loosening up. He grinned a little as he leaned on the metal table. "I think I know what happened, Sergeant. Maybe there was a Sammy. But I don't think you found her on the roadside. I think you met her in a bar somewhere. You wanted to impress her, so you started bragging on yourself. Told her about the glorious Raiders, that you're a badass operator, and that you're about to go on this top secret mission. And then you realize that you've sold your team out. You know they're heading into a trap, so when you get the recall order, you panic. You hide out in a rental, trying to figure out your next move, and the best you can come up with is this weak story about some surfer chick slipping you a mickey."

"No. I didn't do that. I didn't do anything wrong."

"Do you know how many times guys like you sitting in that very chair have said those exact same words?"

"I got suckered. I freely admit that." Redd knew he wasn't going to get any traction with Kim, so he shifted to Colonel Olson. "Sir, I have to know. What happened to the team? You wouldn't be throwing the word *traitor* around unless something really bad happened . . ."

Kim's face darkened. "Oh, something happened, all right."

Panic rose in Redd's throat like bile. He twisted in his chair toward Olson, the chains scraping on the table. "What happened to them, sir?"

Olson was as hard as steel. "You want to know what happened to the team, Sergeant? To the men you abandoned? Betrayed?"

"I swear I didn't!" Redd pounded his big fists onto the tabletop. The ringing steel echoed like a shotgun blast. Kim jumped, completely startled.

The shore patrol guards moved to restrain Redd, but Colonel Olson held up a hand, stopping them cold in their tracks. He folded his hands on the table, leaned forward. His eyes locked with Redd's, angry and searching. "I'll tell you what happened, Sergeant Redd. You opened your smart mouth and got your entire team killed. Blown out of the sky in an ambush."

Redd began to tremble, his eyes watering. "I should have been there . . ."

"They're all dead. Every last one of them."

Redd lowered his head to the table, resting it on hands clenched into white-knuckled fists. Somehow he had known all along.

I should have been there.

Olson let the news sink in for a moment. When he broke his silence, it was only to say, "Haul this sack of crap back to his cell before I put a bullet in his brain."

EIGHT

Kline had about thirty seconds to prepare for the meeting with Culp. That she should deign to visit him at the annex was unusual to say the least. Normally, the head of the FBI's directorate of intelligence would have called him into her office on the seventh floor of the Hoover Building to deliver a thorough chewing out, if not an outright termination. That she should pay him this visit without calling ahead to schedule the meeting was ominous.

Kline hated being blindsided.

She was waiting for him in the conference room, seated at the end farthest from the door like an empress holding court. Attired in a tailored pin-striped suit, tall and lean with short, bobbed hair—blonde but streaked with silver—Culp looked like the CrossFit trainer she still was in her off-hours. The woman was as tough as she was smart.

For a woman—any woman—to rise so high in the old boys' club that was the bureau was remarkable, even in the supposedly enlightened twenty-first century, but Culp's rise had been almost meteoric. Kline knew her from his time in the Counterterrorism Division. While he had advanced steadily through the ranks after years of faithful service, she had appeared seemingly from out of nowhere. A reputed superstar at Quantico, she had gone straight to CTD in Los Angeles, then rocketed past Kline and a dozen other more qualified field agents to begin climbing the ladder of upper management. It was clear her career was being guided by an unnamed mentor who was no doubt anxious to see a woman in charge, no matter how many necks she stepped on to get there.

She waited until Kline closed the door to speak, and when she did, her tone was severe. "What happened?"

He did not need to ask for clarification. Before answering, however, and without waiting for an invitation, he pulled out a chair midway down the table from her and sank wearily into it. "Short answer: it was a trap."

"I don't want a short answer, Gavin," she snapped. "We've got over a dozen dead Marines, two destroyed aircraft, blowback from the Mexican government for an unauthorized military operation on foreign soil, and Willow in the wind. So please, take some time with this."

Kline winced at the mention of the dead Marines. Sending them in, instead of a fly team as he had advised, had been her call. But because the operation had been his from its very inception, he would be held responsible for this failure.

"My contact—"

"Vasquez?" she cut in.

He nodded. "He was worried that the intel we received on Willow might be bait for a trap."

"But you still gave the green light?"

"It was his call."

"Have you heard from him?"

Kline shook his head. "No. It doesn't look good."

"How well do you know him?" Culp asked.

Kline recognized the unasked question. *Could Vasquez have sold us out?*

"I met him a few years ago on an operation against the Sinaloa cartel. They were attempting to smuggle Quds Force operators across the border into the US. Hernán was a Federale but working for Interpol. A real stand-up guy. He had his own sources down there, but he was too smart to expose himself to anybody. It's how he survived his undercover work in the cartel."

"So how was he compromised?"

Kline shook his head. "I don't know, *yet*."

Culp pondered this in silence for a moment. "What about this AWOL Marine?"

"UA."

Culp stared at him as if he had just sprouted a second head. "Excuse me?"

"AWOL is what they call it in the Army. For Marines, it's UA—unauthorized absence. But to answer your question, it doesn't appear to have any relation to what happened."

"The JAG prosecutor doesn't share that opinion. He thinks the Marine sold his team out."

"I really doubt that," Kline said. "*Semper fi* isn't just a motto. It's a core belief for every Marine."

"I know Commander Kim from my time in LA. He's a fine prosecutor and doesn't make mistakes."

"'Guilty until proven innocent' is how those JAG guys roll. I don't buy it. The kid's what, twenty-six? He's full of piss and vinegar. I think he just wanted to get laid and wound up getting drunk or stoned and missed his flight. Now he's too ashamed because of what happened and he's playing stupid."

"Stupid for sure, if you're right."

"Stupidity isn't treason. If it was, half of Congress would be hanging from lampposts all over this town, and the other half would be waiting in line for their turn."

Culp smiled. "It's hard to believe you aren't FBI director with that kind of wit."

"My day job is stand-up comedy."

"Then take my advice and *do* quit your day job if you want to get out of this place."

Kline ignored the barb. "Bottom line, the kid is a Marine *Raider*. A Marine's Marine. Young or old, he's loyal to the corps—and to the core."

"Loyalties can be bought and sold pretty cheaply these days."

"Not a Marine."

"Oh, that's right. You were a Marine yourself. Hope I didn't hit a nerve."

Kline decided to keep his thoughts on that to himself. "Look, the kid says he was drugged. Now I know he tested negative, but we both know there are substances that won't show up on a tox screen."

"What are you suggesting?"

"Maybe he's just the fall guy." Kline spoke slowly so that his mouth wouldn't run out ahead of his brain. "Maybe he was targeted *because* he was on the team that was supposed to execute the Willow op."

Culp's eyes narrowed. "Targeted by whom?"

Kline didn't have an answer ready. *"The problem might not be on my end,"* Vasquez had said. *"Better watch your six."* "Someone who knew what we were planning. Someone on the inside."

"A mole."

Kline nodded. He chose his next words carefully. "I need your authorization to do a top-down review of everyone who was read in on this operation. If there's a leak, we need to find it. It could be that we've got another Robert Hanssen on our hands."

Kline had once met the FBI's most notorious traitor. A counterintelligence officer with a wife and six kids, who went to Mass daily, Hanssen had sold out his country to the Soviets for the bargain price of $1.4 million in cash and diamonds. It was hard to believe that there was another traitor in their ranks now, but how else could he explain the Willow debacle?

Unfortunately, mole hunts had a way of uncovering a lot more than just the identity of a traitor.

Culp studied him for several long seconds. "Finding Willow is your priority. I'll handle the mole hunt."

NINE

Two hours later found Kline sitting in a second-story booth in his favorite DC burger joint, Good Stuff Eatery on Pennsylvania Avenue, just a stone's throw from Capitol Hill. He was digging into a Greek goddess salad when a good-looking young woman fell onto the bench opposite him. Matthew Redd would probably have recognized the woman right away, even though her hair was now jet-black and the green lizard tattoo on her shoulder had been washed off.

Her dark-green eyes narrowed. "A salad? Seriously? I can't eat that crap."

"As if I didn't know," Kline retorted.

Right on cue, a giant Colletti's smokehouse burger arrived, stuffed with bacon, onion rings, Vermont cheddar cheese, and dripping with barbecue sauce. A mess of hand-cut fries seasoned with thyme, rosemary, and sea salt landed next to her as well, along with a soda.

"Double onions, double barbecue," he said. "Just the way you like it."

The woman, whose name was not Sammy but Stephanie Treadway, flashed an ear-to-ear grin. "Thanks, boss. You spoil me."

"You earned it." He stabbed a forkful of olives and cucumbers.

She crammed the burger into her mouth and took a giant bite, then wiped away the barbecue drool on her chin with the back of her hand.

Kline loved watching her eat. She always attacked her food like a shark on a feeding frenzy. She claimed it was because she was the youngest child in a family of ten, all boys except her. Treadway ate like a barnyard hog but was built like a purebred rottweiler. She must have had a small nuclear reactor for a stomach and the metabolism of a hummingbird to eat like that and stay in her kind of shape.

"You did a good job out there without much notice," he said as she took another bite.

She said something through a mouthful that might have been *thanks*.

"Unfortunately, there's a complication."

Her green eyes flashed at him, but she did not stop chewing. He quickly summarized the meeting with Culp. By the time he was done, so was she.

"So is there a leak? One of us?"

"I don't know. Maybe. What concerns me is that she'll be looking into us as well. If she finds anything to connect either one of us to Redd . . ."

She shook her head. "Not a chance. My bases are covered."

Based on what he'd read in the report, Kline couldn't help but think that Treadway had covered her bases a little too well. But there were other threads Culp might be able to tug on that would unravel everything.

"Then that just leaves us with one big problem," Kline went on. "We still don't know who the leak is."

"I thought Culp was going to handle that?"

"You really want to trust that to her?"

Treadway pondered this while taking a long sip from her drink. "Careful how you poke that bear, boss."

"I haven't survived in this world as long as I have by being careful." He jabbed his fork into the salad in a futile attempt to find something palatable, then dropped the fork onto the plate with a loud clatter. "I hate salad."

"So what do you want me to do?"

"Who else knew our plan to grab Willow?"

Treadway's eyes went up to the ceiling for a moment. "Well, only a few of us had the whole picture. You. Me. Dudek. O'Brien. Jackson . . . Culp, of course."

Kline nodded thoughtfully. "Start with Dudek."

"Boss, are you serious? Have you seen his service jacket? He was a rock star with CTD in Dallas. Three commendations. He's third-generation FBI. Has a wife and two small kids."

Kline thought again about Robert Hanssen. He shook his head. "Then you probably won't find anything. But he still gets a turn under the microscope."

"Then I better get moving. I'll be in touch." Treadway shoved a couple of fries into her mouth as she stood. "There's one thing I still don't get."

"What's that?"

"Redd."

"What about him?"

"We—I—just torpedoed his career. He'll probably do time for this."

"Was there a question?"

She stared at him, then shrugged. "Why?"

Kline leaned back in his seat and placed both hands on the table. "You better get going. Let me know what you find out on Dudek."

Without saying another word, Treadway turned and headed for the door.

TEN

The few days spent in the brig were the longest of Redd's life. He'd humped through backbreaking training cycles and ops that had put him nose-deep in putrid swamps, running all out in sandy deserts, and climbing high-altitude mountain slopes at night, but always for a purpose and always with fellow Marines beside him. Pain, exhaustion, even sleep deprivation could be endured and overcome when there was a mission at stake and brothers beside you to keep you going.

But a week alone in his cell was hell because all he had was himself. He tried doing body-weight exercises to keep his mind occupied but to no avail. No matter what he did, his brain ran back to what had happened on the side of the road and at the beach house. He'd been escorted three times a day by two armed guards to the brig cafeteria, where he ate in silence and alone for fifteen minutes at a stretch, wearing jailhouse BDUs. Twice a day he was given latrine privileges. Through it all, he refused three more offers of legal representation. He sensed Kim was glad that he'd done so.

The only respites from his self-imposed mental torture were the repeated interrogations by Commander Kim, or on occasion, the military police assisting Kim with the investigation. They kept throwing the same questions at him, trying to trip up his recollection of words, moments, thoughts. But Redd stuck to his story because it was the only one he knew, and it was true.

True or not, it wouldn't bring his teammates back from the dead. Nor would it give him absolution.

Redd didn't care what happened to him now. He expected the worst, and in his heart, he felt like he'd deserved it. A week of solitary reflection only fueled his raging guilt as the faces of his friends—his brothers—burned in the wreckage of their Ospreys.

Kim was right in one sense only: there was no way to prove with metaphysical certainty that he hadn't betrayed the operation or his team. Maybe, under the influence of some kind of exotic truth serum, he had. Maybe he was a traitor by accident.

✖   ✖   ✖.

On day five, he was escorted back to the interrogation room, where Colonel Olson and Commander Kim were already waiting.

"Have a seat," the colonel said.

Redd sat. His hands were still cuffed, but the hovering shore patrol guards made no move to secure them to the shackle on the table.

"I've gone over everything that Commander Kim and his team have uncovered," Olson said. "Frankly, it doesn't look good for you, but I went back over your service records. I had forgotten that you and I had actually been in the field together three years ago on the operation in Mali with the French Second Para against the local jihadi gang. Do you remember it?"

Redd nodded. It was an unforgettable firefight. The Frenchies lost two men KIA and eleven wounded. The Marines took two casualties from an IED but both survived. Redd's captain had written him up for "exceptional and meritorious service in the execution of his assigned duties" and recommended him for a commendation, which Olson himself had approved.

"You were a special Marine, Sergeant Redd. One of the best we had."

Redd's grief-numbed soul barely heard what the colonel was saying, but he did not fail to notice the use of the past tense.

Olson continued. "In light of your exemplary service record, I'm offering you a onetime deal, right here, right now. You take it or leave it—it's up to you."

A glimmer of hope fluttered in Redd's chest. "Sir?"

Olson held out the file folder. "If you agree to an other than honorable discharge immediately and leave the base today, all charges against you will be dismissed. Of course, an OTH means you'll never be able to rejoin the corps or any other DoD organization. You'll also forfeit all veteran's benefits."

"And if I don't take this deal?"

Kim's dark eyes bored into Redd's. "Under the Uniform Code of Military Justice, subchapter 10, and relevant US Code, you will be charged under Article 86, absent without leave; Article 85, desertion; Article 81, conspiracy; Article 87a, resistance to arrest; Article 92—"

Olson raised his hand. "I think he gets the idea. Commander Kim assures me you would receive a minimum five years in the DB. Possibly longer. After which you would receive a dishonorable discharge."

An OTH was a black mark, particularly with respect to future service in the military or other government jobs. A dishonorable discharge, on the other hand, was tantamount to exile from polite society.

"For the record, Sergeant Redd," Kim intoned, "I am opposed to Colonel Olson's offer. It amounts to a pardon. In my juridical opinion, you should be in jail for your crimes."

Olson held out the file folder for Redd. He took it and flipped through the pages listing the charges, along with the discharge papers awaiting his signature.

The idea of leaving his beloved corps physically sickened Redd. He hadn't even thought about the possibility. He just assumed he could beat the charges and get his life back. But it was clear from the demeanor of these two men and the stack of papers in front of him that he had miscalculated badly. Even if he were to retain a lawyer now, the most he could hope for was a ruined career and eventual discharge anyway—but only if he could beat the rap. Right now he wasn't so sure.

Redd knew enough law to know that prosecutors didn't bring cases they didn't think they could win to trial, and a military court would be comprised of combat officers who would view the brutal deaths of a whole team of Marines with extreme prejudice. Kim's case would be backed by Olson's approval, and Redd had absolutely nothing to prove his case.

J. B. had taught him that in the end, truth wins out. Redd's insistence that he didn't remember doing anything wrong that night was the absolute truth. But no matter how he squared it, Redd couldn't see that as an exonerating defense strategy. Men had died after he had been in the presence of a woman with a false identity, and he had failed to take part in the mission in which they were killed.

There was really only one choice to make.

Redd signed the papers.

ELEVEN

As soon as the big 4x4 Raptor cleared the base, Redd felt a sudden chill, as if he'd passed through an invisible membrane and into a cold, airless vacuum. For the first time in nearly a decade, he was no longer a Marine. It had been the greatest source of pride in his life. Now his discharge from it was his wrenching shame.

What was he going to do? He'd trained to lead men into combat, to break things, to kill. Not exactly the skill sets the corporate world was clamoring for these days. At least, not the kinds of companies he wanted to work for. He had no qualms about killing bad guys to protect his country. But killing men for money, even bad men, didn't sit right with him. There were some security outfits he might work for—guarding nuclear facilities or even corporate executives. But the legit outfits were all ex-military. One look at his OTH and they'd blow him off.

Could he be a cop? Again, not with his OTH discharge. No government agency would touch him with a ten-foot pole. And there was no way he was going to be a security guard or an armored car driver.

Who was he kidding? They might not want him either.

The fact that his dream life had been ripped from him was agonizing enough, but now the hard, undeniable reality hit him. There wasn't going to be anything worthwhile to replace it. The thought sent a terrifying shudder through him.

He punched the gas and pointed his truck north to his apartment. He knew there were a couple of frozen pizzas in the freezer and a pound of organic chicken he could grill down by the pool. What he needed more than food, though, was to get stone-cold drunk, and that meant a stop at the store.

Drunk probably didn't make any sense, but nothing did anymore.

✖ ✖ ✖

A bottle of Tito's vodka and two six-packs of ice-cold Modelo Negra on the seat next to him carried the promise of the altered consciousness to come.

Then again, why wait? It was five o'clock somewhere.

He grabbed one of the Modelos and started to pry the cap off to take a swig right there in the parking lot, but J. B.'s steady voice echoed in his mind.

"Crap happens to everybody, Son, but stupid is a choice you make on your own."

Redd chuckled despite himself. Jim Bob Thompson was no church-going teetotaler. His tolerance for alcohol was legendary, and Redd never once saw him drunk despite the copious amounts he could consume. His adoptive father wasn't against drinking, but he firmly opposed bad choices. Getting drunk never made anyone smarter.

He put the bottle back in its slot, cranked the engine, and pulled out of the parking lot with J. B. still on his mind.

His love of country and the corps had come from J. B., the first adult male he could ever call father and, yes, even loved—though that was a hard word for Redd to come by. He and J. B. just didn't talk like that. In fact, they didn't talk much at all. Didn't have to. Actions always spoke louder than words. Actions cost you something. Words were cheap, especially when they were used too often and too lightly.

Now he had to tell J. B. that he'd been discharged from his beloved corps for his actions—*discharged without honor,* he reminded himself—and there were no words he could say to make up for that disgrace.

Losing everything was bad enough. Losing J. B.'s respect was the last, blood-chilling straw.

As he raced down the highway, Redd's despair grew, boiling up from his chest like lava and oozing through his arms and into his fingers clutching the steering wheel. Just a quick flick of his wrists and he could fling his speeding Raptor over the edge, plunging the vehicle onto the rocks below. There'd be an explosion and fire, and then he'd pay for his sins . . .

"Man up, Son," J. B. said. *"You never run from the fight 'cuz there's worse things than losing one."*

Redd snapped out of his trance. Running from trouble no matter how bad it was just wasn't in the cards. It was part of the code that J. B. raised him with.

He wasn't J. B.'s biological offspring, but he could be his son in every other way, following in his footsteps with the same honor, pride, and dignity with which J. B. had served. Now, all he had left was integrity.

Redd pulled out his phone to make the call he dreaded but quickly discovered that a week of sitting in a locker had completely drained the battery.

Maybe that was for the best. He'd call after a shower to wash away the stench of failure.

Or maybe he could just wait until tomorrow.

✖   ✖   ✖

His skin red from the scalding hot water, Redd toweled off, free at least of the crud he'd felt crawling all over him after nearly a week in the brig. Being clean brought only a small measure of relief. Hot water couldn't wash away emotional crap.

And he still needed to tell J. B.

He'd plugged the phone in before hitting the shower and knew that it would be sufficiently charged for use, so even though he wasn't yet ready to talk to J. B., he unplugged the phone, intending to take it with him to the living room. As he did, the screen lit up, displaying the words *Missed call* along with the name of the caller.

J. B.

J. B. hated talking on the phone and had staunchly refused to purchase a mobile phone. He had relented somewhat after Redd bought him an iPhone so they could keep in touch, but aside from Redd's birthday and Christmas, J. B. never initiated a call.

Had someone told him what happened?

Redd unlocked the phone and saw that there was a message waiting. He frowned. J. B. was a man of few words and what few he spoke he didn't waste on something as superfluous as a voice mail.

What had changed?

He pulled up the voice mail and hit the Speaker button. It was J. B.'s voice for sure, but the recording was broken up and filled with static.

"Matty . . . I heard . . . Trouble's come knocking . . . Might need your help."

Redd's blood suddenly ran cold. He had never heard J. B.'s voice sound like that before. It might have been a weak cell signal or maybe he had a cold, but the man had a parade ground voice that could make a cast-iron statue jump off its pedestal.

He played the message again.

"Might need your help."

J. B. was the most self-reliant man Redd had ever known. For him to call and ask for help meant that something was terribly wrong.

Ten years earlier, J. B. had been thrown off his horse and broken his back. He had not asked for help—not from Redd, who was a junior in high school, and not from any of his local acquaintances. It just wasn't "the cowboy way."

They'd always lived hand to mouth on J. B.'s small and mostly unprofit-able cattle ranch, which had been in his family for four generations. It was a one-man operation—two when Redd wasn't in school—and J. B. made ends meet as a part-time hunting guide, shoeing horses and sometimes providing informal farrier service.

With his injury putting him out of commission, it had seemed inevitable that the ranch would be lost, breaking a 170-year chain of sacred trust handed down to him through the generations.

J. B. couldn't afford to hire anyone to take over, and Redd was in school, excelling in academics and also starting as the tight end for the county high school football team, which was suddenly a contender for the state championship because of Redd's undeniable talent. J. B. refused to even consider asking Redd to sacrifice his future to work the ranch.

Redd had made that decision on his own, because that was how J. B. had raised him. That decision had cost Redd his high school diploma, to say nothing of college and professional prospects, as well as ending his relationship with the only girl he'd ever loved. But he'd saved the ranch.

J. B. had called him an idiot for throwing his life away, but Redd knew the old man had secretly been proud of him. For his own part, he'd never regretted his decision. Once J. B. was back on his feet, Redd had gotten his GED, enlisted in the Marines, and . . .

Redd shook his head, refusing to follow that thought to its logical conclusion. He punched the Call Back button and waited for J. B. to pick up. As it rang, another wave of guilt pounded into him. He hadn't spoken to J. B. since last Christmas. Between deployments, workups, and training, Redd's days were maxed out. Whenever they did speak on the phone, J. B. always said the same thing. "All good. Don't worry about me. You just keep your head on a swivel." He'd add, "Happy birthday, Son," and "Merry Christmas, Son," as the occasion required.

J. B. didn't want to be a bother. He just wanted to hear his son's voice every now and then.

The last ring turned to the automated message telling Redd to leave a voice mail after the tone. A voice mail that J. B. would never pick up anyway.

"J. B., it's me. I got your message. Call me back."

He dressed quickly, pulling on a pair of jeans and a Bravo Company T-shirt, and then tried calling again.

No answer. And no point in leaving another voice mail.

He realized only then that he had forgotten to check the date and time of J. B.'s call.

"Oh no."

J. B. had called at 6:31 p.m.

Last Friday.

The day before Redd had been arrested.

Struggling to hold in the toxic mix of emotions that had been coursing through him over the last week, Redd couldn't shake the feeling that as bad as things were at the moment, they were about to get much worse.

TWELVE

According to his GPS navigational map on the dash, it was going to take just over seventeen and a half hours to get to Wellington. The fastest route ran through the Mojave Desert up to Vegas. Then it was a long haul all the way up to Salt Lake City before the final dash through Idaho and into Montana.

A real beatdown.

He planned for at least three stops for gas, bladder release, and caffeinated beverages to keep him moving. This would add at least another half hour but would let him drive straight through to J. B.'s ranch in Stillwater County just north of Wellington. Whatever had happened to his dad—*"Trouble's come knocking"*—might still be happening, and there was no way he'd let fatigue slow him down.

He thought about trying to call the local authorities to do a welfare check on J. B. but knew that J. B. would have called them if he thought they could solve his problem. Obviously they couldn't. That's why Redd knew he had to get to Wellington immediately.

He'd already let the old man down enough.

❌   ❌   ❌

Over the next several hours, Redd flipped through country-western sta-
tions, classic rock, and even an old *Dragnet* radio episode—anything to
keep him from crawling back into his own skull and hearing the shouts of
condemnation and guilt. But hours of head-banging guitar and twangy
country vocals finally took their toll. Redd punched off the music and
listened instead to the rhythm of his pounding headache.

The pale-red sunset against the thin, high clouds above the Arizona
desert wasn't particularly striking. But it signaled the end of a truly terrible
day that began inside a solitary confinement cell.

When dusk finally faded into the fathomless dark beyond the reach
of his headlights, Redd's world changed again. The blue glowing light
of his dashboard controls couldn't keep the black from closing off the
world from him, reducing it to the interior space of the Raptor's high-
tech cabin area. He suddenly felt like an astronaut in a capsule hurtling
through space. The hiss of his big, meaty tires on the asphalt and the
steady thrumming of the 450 horsepower 3.5L EcoBoost engine only
added to the spaceship effect. The black isolation and hypnotic road
noise fell on him like a warm blanket on a cold night, hitting his eyelids
like fishing weights.

Assorted energy drinks and triple-shot espressos wired him up but
made him antsy too. For all of the chemical stimulation, he found himself yawning more than he wanted to and rubbing his blurring eyes with
his big hand. He rolled down the window for the noise and rush of air.

He tried finding a talk radio station that wouldn't drive him crazy
but soon gave up. He settled for an AM sports station yapping about ice
hockey, booming off the ionosphere all the way from Minneapolis to his
Raptor flying through southern Utah on the I-15.

In the moments he managed to push away the horrors of the last week,
Redd found new avenues of self-recrimination. After a quick count in his
head, he suddenly realized he hadn't been back to Montana or J. B.'s ranch
since he joined the Marines eight years ago. Where did the time go? He

knew J. B. didn't like to travel and was always busy keeping his place up. Redd's hectic deployment and training schedules weren't exactly amenable to extended vacations either.

In truth, lately everything Redd wanted and needed he'd found with his Raider unit. What he'd needed most as a wounded, orphaned child he'd already received from the old cowboy years ago, absorbed by osmosis more than anything else as the two of them did the backbreaking work of running the small cattle ranch. He loved the Montana wilderness and its dangerous beauty, but that love had not been enough to keep him rooted in Big Sky Country.

Redd made his ninth call to J. B.'s phone just outside of Provo, Utah, but it was another futile gesture and the final confirmation that something was horribly wrong.

Redd kept his boot steady on the throttle, fighting the urge to floor it. No point in getting pulled over or, worse, tossed into jail.

Again.

✖   ✖   ✖

The long night spent in the solitary confinement of his own pickup truck finally yielded to a dim glow in the east. The subtle change was less the coming of the light and more the fleeing of the dark. He sensed more than saw gloom boil away in the gray shimmering light of a bashful sunrise.

His spirits rose as the black veil lifted. The world beyond his windshield was flat and still nearly featureless. But his eyes caught the looming shadows in the east, the jagged teeth of the great Teton Range clawing at the purpling sky.

He could have shouted for joy.

He knew that when the sun finally hit those snowcapped granite peaks, they would blaze white and blue in the light, even this far away in Idaho. This wasn't home but it was the West, the place where he'd grown up, the land as much a part of him as the blood coursing through his veins. He'd be too far up the road when those magnificent mountains did finally stand up in their fiery glory, but for now their monstrous shadows were enough to satisfy him with the promise of what was to come.

Home.

✼ ✼ ✼

Skirting Yellowstone National Park in Wyoming just east of the Idaho border, Redd crossed from Idaho into Montana on the winding, ascending two-lane Route 20. The scenery felt as familiar as the old hiking boots he wore. So did the weather. The sun was little more than a silver disk veiled by slate-gray clouds that spat rain. His wipers slapped away the small drops that turned to tiny shards of ice as the temperature dropped, which it always did at first light. Patches of snow hugged the base of the Douglas fir trees on either side of the road. Winter was gone and spring was nearly over, but the weather was the weather, and in Montana it was always unpredictable. The outside temperature gauge read thirty-seven degrees and the forecast had promised midfifties by noon, so no chance of snow falling here in the lower elevations. Farther up, snow was always possible.

He made the turn north onto the 191 in the small town of West Yellowstone and punched the gas, the mountains of the Gallatin Range far up ahead, though still out of sight, drawing him like a mama bear to her lost cub. He passed a roadside café billboard that read, "Fresh Mountain Oysters: The Original Sack Lunch."

Montana, he thought. *No place like it.*

Highway 191, also known as the Gallatin Road, curved and climbed steadily through the steepening foothills. Redd was still hours away from J. B.'s place, but this part of the state was his home, a feeling that only quickened the higher the road climbed and the sharper the pine-studded hills rose above.

The two-lane followed the valley cut eons ago by whatever volcanic or glacial activity had carved it out. Running alongside Redd was the green-gray white-capping Gallatin River, boiling and surging from snowmelt. The river was running too high for white-water rafters and kayakers and even for the fishermen who flocked from all over the world to fly-fish here. This was the part of the state where *A River Runs Through It* had been filmed decades ago and single-handedly revitalized the fly-fishing industry in the area. That was good news for local guides and their well-heeled customers but bad news for the locals who wanted their peace and quiet. People didn't move to Montana to socialize. Most folks who had settled here had come for the beauty and solitude. Those that landed in Big Sky Country just a few steps ahead of the law weren't exactly looking for more neighbors either.

When at last the snow-laden peaks of the Madison Range rose high in his windshield, Redd's heart began to race. With his window down and the rush of the chilled air to keep him awake, the cabin was filled with the familiar smells of rain-washed mountain air carrying the scent of pine.

Ironically, now that he was closer to home than he'd been in eight years, Redd was feeling homesick. Even when he left the ranch for Marine boot camp eight years prior, he'd never felt the longing for home or the pang of loneliness as so many in his barracks did. He was self-sufficient even then, in part because of the way he'd been raised, but also because he'd learned to trust no one, especially adults.

His mother had never been a loving figure during his early childhood days growing up in Detroit, Michigan. Though he'd heard rumors about how smart and beautiful she had been as a young woman, an honor student in high school and a gifted track athlete, in his memories of her—which were thankfully few—she was drunk or high and groveling before a series of stoner boyfriends who would beat both her and Redd for no discernible reason. When she had finally died of an overdose, his biological father—Redd had not even known the man existed until then—had appeared as if from nowhere, but rather than accepting responsibility and stepping into the role of father, he had abdicated a second time. He was some kind of petroleum executive who was always traveling and so had no time for family. His one concession had been to entrust young Matthew Redd to the care of his old friend Jim Bob Thompson.

That had probably been the first thing to go right in Redd's life.

J. B. had not been a conventional father. He was not affectionate in the slightest, and he did not pepper Redd with platitudes. Life on the ranch was hard—tough, grinding, relentless work. Redd had grown tall and strong on that kind of work, fed by thick-cut steaks from cattle he himself had branded, fed, raised, and even butchered. Those seven years with J. B. had made him the person he was. But man, it was a beatdown. Between the ranch and the tiny town of Wellington, Redd had felt small and cramped. He needed to get out. Spread his wings. See the world.

Now that he was here again, the best memories of this place returned. For once, he longed for those things he'd left behind. Life on the ranch was hard but simple, the rewards deferred but earned, like muscle. But it didn't take a psychologist to tell Redd why he was feeling homesick.

It was the rising fear that J. B. was beyond his reach. Ageless J. B. was like the mountains he loved, strong and eternal, as much a part of the wilderness as any grizzly roaming the woods. The idea that J. B. might be gone was like saying the mountains had been felled. It simply wasn't possible.

Was it?

✕　✕　✕

Redd turned off the two-lane highway and onto a paved service road that eventually ran out of asphalt. He found the sharp turn he was looking for between stands of maple and pine, then steered the truck down the long, winding dirt track rutted by years of abuse from J. B.'s old Ford dually.

A one-lane wooden bridge—little more than old railroad ties set up on cement pylons—crossed the river bordering J. B.'s property at its narrowest point. On the other side, a rusted cattle guard fronted the entry gate, which was composed of two ancient but giant tree trunks stripped of their bark and surmounted with a hand-painted sign that read simply *Thompson Ranch*. The paint was peeling, the words barely legible. The fence posts bordering the property were rotting and crooked, and the rusting barbed wire had seen better days. It wasn't like J. B. to let things go. More to the point, there wasn't a cow or steer to be seen on the property.

Even with the four-wheel drive, the Raptor's big tires spun in the rutted, muddy track. He fishtailed over a rough patch, making his way through the wide pasture that led up to the old rambling log ranch house nestled at the foot of the mountain.

The first place he'd ever called home.

Redd pulled up next to J. B.'s battered old Ford F-250 and climbed out. He stretched his long legs and torso, cramped and sore after so many hours on his butt. He glanced around. No horses. No cattle. No chickens. Nothing. It was as if the place had been abandoned.

But it hadn't. J. B.'s truck was here. He loved that thing even more than Redd loved his Raptor. It suddenly occurred to Redd that maybe he was even more like J. B. than he realized, even with trucks.

Redd laid a hand on the hood of the F-250. It was as cold as the rainwater puddled on the sheet metal. It hadn't been driven in hours if not days. The mud caked on the sidewalls was bone-dry.

From where he stood, the barn and the outbuildings looked worn down, neglected. He glanced over at the house, expecting to hear the familiar crash of the screen slamming open and shut and J. B. striding out onto the porch.

No such luck.

But there was something on the door—an official notice of some kind, though the words were obscured by the screen mesh. He jogged up the steps, the boards creaking underfoot.

Not like J. B. to leave loose nails in the treads like that.

He flung the screen door open and read the notice:

DO NOT ENTER
UNDER PENALTY OF LAW
BY ORDER OF
SHERIFF S. W. BLACKWOOD
STILLWATER COUNTY, MT

Redd's legs felt like rubber. He staggered back, catching himself on the porch rail.

He needed to get inside.

He ripped the sign off the door and shoved it into his back pocket, then tried the doorknob.

Locked. Probably the sheriff's doing. Like many rural Montanans, J. B. rarely locked his front door. He lived too far out in the boonies for such foolishness. Fortunately, Redd still carried the brass key J. B. had given him the day he arrived at the ranch all those years ago.

"This is your home," the man had said when he slapped it into Redd's small palm. *"Hang on to it."*

At the time, Redd assumed J. B. was talking about the key. Now he wasn't so sure.

He turned the key in the old lock and pushed his way into the house. Mixed with the familiar smells of pipe tobacco and burnt firewood was an obtrusive mustiness. No one had occupied the house for several days.

Redd went from room to room, but all he found were the familiar sights he'd grown up with and taken for granted. He saw the same worn overstuffed leather chairs, the deer antler chandeliers, even the dusty trophy head of Redd's first white-tailed deer, a four-point bruiser. Unlike on the East Coast, hunters in Big Sky Country only counted the points on one side of the rack. The mounted head still hung on the wall over the fireplace mantel, though the majestic antlers were crisscrossed with cobwebs.

In one corner stood the Old Glory gun safe, which J. B. had grudgingly purchased not long after Redd came to live with him. What good was a gun if it was locked up in a bombproof vault when you needed it quick? But Redd's biological father had convinced J. B. that gun security was going to become increasingly important as the world grew more connected and unsavory types retreated into the backcountry. Redd was relieved when the combination he remembered still worked. Inside, he found J. B.'s lever action Henry .45-70, along with an old double-barreled Purdey shotgun. The Ruger .44 Magnum was in its holster, resting on the shelf underneath.

Everything looked normal and in its place, even if somewhat neglected. A former Marine, J. B. liked his corners squared, edges lined up, things generally straight and proportional. The kitchen and bathroom were clean but not sparkling. Everything seemed just slightly off, and that didn't sit right with Redd.

He headed to his old bedroom and stopped dead in his tracks as he stepped through the door. His room hadn't changed one iota since the day he'd left for boot camp. His Led Zeppelin, Nirvana, and Creed posters were still pinned to the walls. They had often quarreled over his music selection. Redd had never told J. B. how he used to listen to his Waylon Jennings and Johnny Cash albums when he wasn't around. He loved that music but was never gonna tell the old man that.

Now he wished he would have.

He headed into J. B.'s room. Everything looked like he remembered it. If anything seemed out of place, it was the old Thompson family Bible resting on the nightstand. Growing up, Redd only ever saw it stacked on a hallway bookshelf, unopened and unused by J. B. except to point out to Redd the Thompson family history in the front. The family lineage began with a marriage in 1842 and ended with "James Robert Thompson, b. 1956." J. B. was the end of the family line.

J. B.'s small desk was neat and cleared away except for a thin film of dust and a framed picture of J. B. and Redd grinning ear to ear the day Redd graduated from boot camp.

Redd wasn't sure if he was being memorialized or if J. B. just kept everything exactly as Redd had left it hoping it would draw him back home. Either way, it was a gut punch.

Redd headed back out the front door and took another look around the place. He had not found any clues about where J. B. might be, but deep down inside he knew.

He's gone.

THIRTEEN

Wellington was almost exactly as Redd remembered it. Eight years wasn't really that long, and this far from the center of the known world, time moved differently. The colors seemed a little duller than in his memories—washed-out, sun-faded—but that might have been just in his head. As he neared the northern city limits, he began to see familiar establishments—the tire store, the self-storage place, the Diamond T Motel, Spady's. Everything right where it had been the last time he passed through.

It was almost as if he'd never left.

He drove to the center of town and took the left onto Broadway. He could see the municipal water tower, half a mile away, rising above the town like a waypoint marker on a map. He recalled that the tower was in a park right across the street from the courthouse.

Despite its ambitious name, Broadway was a two-lane street with room to park on either side. It was lined with storefronts that dated back at least to the 1970s—specialty shops, professional offices, a tavern that advertised poker and keno, an American Legion post.

It occurred to Redd that, in all his years growing up in Stillwater County, he'd never had occasion to visit any of the businesses on this stretch of road. That entire chapter of his life had unfolded in a handful of locations—J. B.'s ranch, the feedstore, school. On rare occasions, usually after a game, they'd go to the pizza parlor, but there had never been much reason to deviate from the routine in order to wander down the town's main street.

Redd drove past the two-story brick building that contained the courthouse, sheriff's department, and other county offices, and took the next left onto Oak Street. He parked and made his way back to the front of the building without passing a single living soul. As he reached the glass double doors, emblazoned with a six-point star in a circle and the legend *Stillwater County Sheriff's Office*, he felt as if the weight of the world had landed squarely on his shoulders.

The loss of his team . . . The end of his career . . . And now J. B.

I've lost everything.

He didn't know for a fact that something had happened to J. B., but he refused to indulge in hope. He couldn't survive one more disappointment.

Inside, he found a reception counter but nobody occupied the chair behind it. Farther back, he spied a half-open door. Beside it, a black placard announced, *Stuart W. Blackwood, Sheriff.*

Redd dinged the bell on the counter. He heard the springs of a swivel chair creaking from behind the open door and a metal desk drawer slamming shut.

"Back here," a voice boomed.

Redd stepped around the desk and headed to the open door. He rapped his knuckles on the wall below the placard, then pushed the door all the way open and stepped through.

It was, he realized, the first time in eight years that he had stepped into an office of any kind as a civilian. He had to fight the impulse to approach the desk, snap to attention, and announce himself with a salute.

The office was dark, unwelcoming. The overhead fluorescents were off, the only light in the bland room, aside from what crept in through the closed window blinds, coming from the illuminated screen of the sheriff's computer. The air was stale, and the stink of institutional deodorizers was almost strong enough to make Redd gag.

The man behind the desk wore a rumpled brown uniform shirt, open at the collar and decorated with a gold badge. He had thick silver hair and a bushy, untrimmed handlebar mustache that drooped over his upper lip and cascaded down the sides of his mouth. Silver stubble sparkled on his face and neck. The harsh light exaggerated the dark circles under his eyes. He looked like he hadn't slept in days. A Stetson hung from a peg on a coatrack mounted to the back wall, along with a black leather duty belt, holstering a stainless .357 Smith & Wesson.

"Can I help you, son?"

"You're Sheriff Blackwood?" Redd asked.

"I am. And you are?"

"Name's Redd." He had to stop himself from saying *Sergeant Redd*. "Matthew James Redd."

Blackwood's expression did not change. "What can I do for you, Mr. Redd?"

Redd opened his mouth, but suddenly the words weren't there. He frowned, then tried again. "I grew up near here, sir. My father is J. B. Thompson."

Blackwood looked him up and down. "You got any identification to prove what you're saying?"

Redd's heart began hammering in his chest. He struggled to draw breath in the stifling room.

"I don't have a card that says I'm J. B. Thompson's son," he said, striving for a patient tone. "But you can ask anyone who knows him. They'll tell you." He wanted to say, *Just ask J. B.,* but some part of him already knew that wasn't an option. "Sheriff, has something happened to him?"

The old sheriff's eyes narrowed, wrinkling in the corners. He leaned forward in his chair and tapped some keys on his computer. Redd couldn't see what was displayed on the screen, but he could tell from the change in light level that the sheriff was browsing through several different screens.

Finally he looked up again. "You said your name is Redd? I'm still gonna need to have a look at your ID."

Redd ground his teeth together but fished out his wallet and extracted his driver's license.

Blackwood took it, squinting to read the small print in the dim light. "California?"

"Yes, sir."

"What were you doing there?"

"I was in the Marines. I just got discharged." Redd saw no point in telling him why or under what conditions.

"I was in the Army. Desert Storm," Blackwood said, handing Redd back his license. "Well, Mr. Redd, I guess some wires got crossed. You should have been notified. You were listed as next of kin. I'm sorry for your loss, son. It's a hard thing to lose someone."

Redd sank into one of the chairs positioned to either side of the door. "When?"

"My deputy found him dead on his property last Monday. Our best guess is that he'd been dead for at least twenty-four hours. Hard to tell exactly since he was found outside. Affects the body temperature."

"How did—?" He faltered.

"Looks as if he was thrown from his horse. Landed wrong and broke his neck. Heck of a thing."

Through his black despair, Redd felt a surge of crimson rage. "No. That's not possible."

But wasn't it? J. B. had been thrown before and seriously injured. Sometimes accidents just happened.

But J. B. had called him.

"Trouble's come knocking . . . Might need your help."

"Horses spook, son," Blackwood was saying. "Even Superman would have a tough time hanging on to a horse that's spooked. It happens to the best of us."

Redd's jaw clenched. He considered telling Blackwood about the voice mail message from J. B. but then thought better of it. He didn't know anything about this man. When he'd left Stillwater County, the sheriff had been a man named Robert Littleton. He and J. B. had been casual acquaintances, exchanging nods whenever their paths crossed. "Where's his body?"

"He's at the Pitt-Bateman Funeral Home. You know it?"

Redd recalled that Pitt-Bateman had made generous contributions to the high school football boosters back when he'd played. He had no idea where the funeral home was located but figured he could find out. He nodded. "What about his personal effects?"

Blackwood sighed deeply, then stood, using the arms of the old banker's chair to heave himself up. He was nearly as tall as Redd but badly out of shape, his belly straining the buttons of his uniform shirt.

He strode past Redd and poked his head out into the reception area. "Maggie?" When there was no reply, he returned to his desk. "I swear, sometimes I wonder about that woman." He dug into his pocket, pulled out a smartphone, and tapped off a quick message. "I'll have them brought over from the evidence locker."

"Evidence?"

"Don't read anything into that, Mr. Redd. It's just where we put things for safekeeping. Won't take a minute." He gazed at Redd with just a hint of curiosity in his dull eyes. "What are your plans?"

Redd had no immediate answer. He had come here with a single purpose—to help J. B.—and like everything else in his life, it had been an act of futility. He had failed his team, the corps, and now he had failed J. B. too. J. B. had asked for his help, and he hadn't been there.

"Trouble's come knocking."

He was in trouble, and now he's dead . . .

He knew what he had to do. Straightening in the chair, he said, "I'm going to stay at my dad's place for a few days, get things sorted out." He pulled the crumpled sheriff's notice out of his back pocket and tossed it on the desk. "You can have that back."

Blackwood's eyebrows arched at this violation. Redd silently dared him to say something about it, but Blackwood met his gaze again. "You'll need to submit an application to the state Department of Public Health and

Human Services to get a copy of Mr. Thompson's death certificate. You'll need that in order to take care of his business. They can help you with that over at the courthouse."

As he finished this discourse, a plump woman in civilian clothes stepped into the office and handed the sheriff a manila envelope. Blackwood slid the envelope across his desktop, indicating that it was now Redd's to do with as he pleased.

Redd summoned up the energy to rise from the chair and seize the envelope. He opened the flap and tipped the contents out onto the sheriff's desk.

J. B.'s wallet, keys, pocket change, and a bone-handled Case pocketknife he'd carried for decades. Redd opened it. The blade was ground down after years of hand-sharpening on a whetstone but it still cut just fine and got the job done. Redd closed it up and stuffed it into his own pocket. "He had an iPhone. Where is it? Wasn't it on him?"

Blackwood glanced at the desk. "Everything that was found on his person was put into that envelope." His tone softened. "Take another look around the place, son. Did you check his truck?"

Redd frowned but shook his head.

"If it doesn't turn up, give us a call. Ask for Deputy Hepworth."

"Shane Hepworth?"

"You know him?"

"Yeah." Redd scooped J. B.'s possessions back into the envelope and made his way toward the door without another word.

It was obvious that the sheriff had failed to properly investigate things before ruling J. B.'s death an accident. Redd wasn't sure if the man was lazy or had another reason for the shoddy work.

Could he be trying to cover something up? he wondered as he pushed the door open and stepped into the cold air.

Two things were for sure. Redd didn't trust Blackwood. And if the sheriff wouldn't investigate, Redd would do it himself.

FOURTEEN

The Pitt-Bateman Funeral Home turned out to be right across the street from the American Legion post Redd had passed earlier. The building was plain-looking—gray stucco, with a sign so unobtrusive as to be invisible. It was only when he pulled into the parking lot behind the building that he saw the white Cadillac hearse parked beneath the portico.

Redd cut the engine on his Raptor and leaned back in his seat.

Sitting in front of the funeral home made it all seem real, yet Redd was becoming numb. There would be time to grieve later, he promised himself. But first there was a job to do.

He needed answers.

A bell tinkled as Redd pulled the front door open. He stepped into a showroom with several polished ebony and metal caskets on display. Decorative funeral urns in stone, polished steel, copper, brass, pewter, and even hardwoods stood on shelves on the far side of the room. To his right was a glassed-in office with an executive desk and chairs. In the showroom itself, an indoor water fountain gurgled next to a plaster cast reproduction of Michelangelo's *Pietà*, the crucified body of Christ draped in Mary's grieving lap. Soft music played in overhead speakers.

A middle-aged man in a business suit rose from behind a desk in the office and hastened to greet him. "Are you Mr. Redd?"

He spoke in a low, sympathetic tone, eschewing the ordinary pleasantries, which Redd supposed was a way of avoiding awkward answers to commonplace questions.

Redd just nodded.

"Sheriff Blackwood told me you would be stopping by. I'm Malcom Pitt. I'm so sorry for your loss."

"Thank you."

"It's a difficult time. If there's anything I can do to help you to make any kind of arrangements, please let me know."

"I appreciate it but I won't be making any."

"Not even a church service?"

"He wasn't religious."

"A small memorial is quite fitting. We can make the showroom available if—"

"I'd like to see him," Redd said in a flat tone that cut off further inquiry.

Pitt's eyebrows drew together. "Sheriff Blackwood didn't tell you?"

"Tell me what?" Redd asked.

"He, uh . . . Well, there's no good way to say this, but he was cremated."

"What?" The news was yet another gut punch.

Pitt must have sensed the spike in Redd's ire, because he hurriedly added, "The disposition of the remains was stipulated in Mr. Thompson's will."

"J. B. had a will?" *Why didn't he tell me about it?*

"Mr. Blanton took care of the arrangements. I'm surprised he didn't try to reach you."

"I was . . ." Redd trailed off, not wanting to finish the sentence.

Pitt stepped into his glassed-in office and retrieved a business card, then came back and handed it to Redd.

Farley "Duke" Blanton, Esq.
Attorney-at-Law
Wills, Trusts, Real Estate

The address was also on Broadway, just a couple blocks west. Redd shoved it into his shirt pocket.

"Was there an autopsy?" he managed to say.

"I don't believe so, but you'd have to ask the sheriff."

"Yeah, I guess so."

"I can transfer the ashes to an urn of your choice," Pitt went on. "If you'd like to step into my office, I can show you some inexpensive options."

Redd shook his head. He needed to talk to this lawyer. "I don't need one," he said. "Just give them to me. I'll take care of the rest."

Pitt pursed his lips together in a mild show of irritation but then bobbed his head in an obsequious nod. "Just a moment."

As Pitt moved back into his office and then disappeared through another door behind his desk, Redd leaned against a wall. He was still reeling from the news of the cremation. He had come here because without seeing J. B. with his own eyes, there would always be doubt. Doubt about how he died. Doubt about what killed him.

Doubt about whether he was really dead at all.

But no, in his heart he knew that it was true. Trouble hadn't just come knocking. It had walked in through the front door and subtracted J. B. from the world.

And now I can't even say goodbye to the old man.

Pitt returned bearing a black plastic container a little bigger than a shoebox. Without being asked, he lifted the molded lid to reveal a plastic bag stuffed with chalky white powder.

"That's . . . him?" Redd asked, barely able to get the words out.

Pitt nodded and then, as if he felt Redd needed an explanation, added, "Seventy percent of the human body is water. The ashen remains of the average adult male is approximately six pounds." He reseated the lid and extended the container to him.

Redd took it carefully, like he was picking up a ticking time bomb. He felt the weight of it in his hands.

He remembered the man who sat tall in the saddle, who swung a blacksmith's hammer like a Nerf bat and carried lost calves home on his broad shoulders when they strayed.

Cowboy, warrior, father.

Was this all that was left?

Six pounds of ashes?

No. This isn't how it ends, Redd promised himself. *I'm going to find out what really happened.*

FIFTEEN

Duke Blanton was a big man, but not necessarily in a healthy way. He had a bright-red face—sunburn or rosacea, it was hard to say which—and the rough, dry hands of an avid outdoorsman, which he clearly was. Trophy heads, fly rods, and rifles hung on the walls along with framed photos of him on elk and pheasant hunts with local politicians and celebrities. Despite his considerable girth, he bounded up and moved out from behind his oversize mahogany desk, a huge smile plastered across his face with his big meaty paw extended to shake.

"Matthew Redd! So glad you came by." Blanton jacked his arm like a pump handle, then waved at one of the two leather chairs facing his desk. "Goodness, but you sure grew."

Sensing that Blanton might try to talk his ear off if given the chance, Redd got right to the point. "I spoke with Mr. Pitt at the funeral home. He said that J. B. left a will. Is that right?"

Blanton studied Redd across the desktop the way an angler might study a river, looking for the best place to cast. Then he placed his palm flat on a brown file folder resting on the desktop and slid it across. Redd opened the folder and glanced down at the first page. At the top in big bold letters were the words *Montana Revocable Living Trust of James Robert Thompson*.

Below was the date. Fifteen years ago. Just a few weeks after Redd's arrival at the ranch.

Redd's eyes began to blur with tears.

"That man sure was proud of you," Blanton was saying. "When you graduated from boot camp, I swear I thought he'd bust every button on his shirt. He thought you hung the moon, son."

He paused a beat and then in a more formal tone said, "You'll see on page four that you are named as the sole beneficiary. Because he put everything into a revocable living trust, there won't be any probate. It all just goes to you directly—titles, property, bank accounts, everything."

The idea of inheriting everything J. B. owned was utterly foreign to Redd. Never in his wildest dreams had he envisioned a world without J. B. He shook his head. "Mr. Blanton—"

"Please, call me Duke."

"Duke. The reason I actually came here is that Mr. Pitt told me J. B. left instructions to be cremated. Is that true?"

Blanton did not spend even a second thinking about it. "It is." He pointed to the folder. "It's in the attachment at the end of the document. He didn't want a lot of fuss . . . as I'm sure you can imagine. Honestly, too many of my clients forget to formalize little details like that, and then you end up with the heirs squabbling about what to do at the worst possible time for it."

Redd frowned. "The thing is, I would have liked a chance to see him . . . you know, before . . ."

Blanton spread his hands apologetically. "I'm sorry, Matty. We tried. Every effort was made to track you down."

"Was there an autopsy?" Redd pressed.

Blanton shook his head. "Again, in accordance with Jim Bob's wishes, and because the circumstances of death were not suspicious, it was determined that no postmortem examination was necessary."

Redd studied Blanton's fleshy visage. He had an instinctive distrust of lawyers, and his recent experiences with the JAG prosecutor back at Camp Pendleton had only reinforced it. *Not suspicious?* "I was told that he was thrown from his horse," Redd said in a measured tone. "But I didn't see a horse, or any other animals, at J. B.'s."

"I believe Deputy Hepworth recovered the horse and made arrangements for its care."

It felt like half an answer. *Just what I'd expect from a lawyer.* He chose his next words carefully. "Was J. B. having any trouble?"

Blanton cocked his head to the side. "I take it you weren't in regular contact with him?"

"We didn't talk a lot. The corps keeps me pretty busy." He used the present tense out of habit and winced a little as soon as he said it. "He called me last week. Left a message that made me think he might be having some difficulty. I was out of contact at the time, but when I got the message and couldn't get through to him, I dropped everything and came running up here only to find out he was dead."

Blanton's eyes drilled into Redd. "What did he say in the message he left?"

Redd didn't like that. It was none of Blanton's business. "It wasn't so much what he said as how he said it."

Blanton leaned back in his chair, picking up a heavy ballpoint pen absentmindedly. "I have nothing but the greatest respect for Jim Bob. He was a hard worker, honest as the day is long, and a man of his word. I probably don't have to tell you how tough it's gotten for the independent operator, but he was worse at the business side of it than most."

"He was never into ranching for the money. It was the land he loved, not the idea of getting rich."

Blanton uttered a noncommittal grunt. "Truth is, he was drowning in red ink. There are several small liens against the property for money J. B. owed around town. I know he intended to pay everyone off, but he was struggling toward the end. There's a considerable tax lien against the property for unpaid taxes. A real whopper of around twenty-seven thousand dollars."

Redd didn't know what to say.

"I think he knew he was going to have to sell," Blanton went on. "I expect that's what he wanted to tell you. If there's a ray of sunshine in this mess, it's that the property is worth a heck of a lot more than he owed."

Redd did not immediately grasp the significance of this. "Excuse me?"

"I'll speak plainly, son. Another client I represent has expressed an interest in purchasing the property. Now, I can't talk specifics, as that would be a conflict of interest, but my advice to you is to find a real estate broker and let them negotiate on your behalf. I can confidently say that you would walk away with a tidy sum, even after all the accounts are settled."

"Someone wants J. B.'s ranch?"

"Well, technically, it's yours now."

"Who wants it?" Redd asked, confused as to why anybody would be interested in purchasing a run-down cattle ranch that had failed to turn a profit.

Blanton looked uncomfortable. "I really shouldn't say. Client confidentiality, you know."

Redd sat up straight in his chair and laid his meaty forearms on the wood armrests. "Yeah, well, J. B. was your client too, but that didn't stop you from telling this other client of yours that the land might be available."

Blanton frowned, evidently dismayed at having fallen into a trap of his own creation, but then he shrugged. "Well, I suppose there's no harm in telling you. It's not like it's any kind of secret. The man is actually one of your neighbors. Wyatt Gage."

The name was vaguely familiar to Redd, but not one he recalled from his childhood. "I don't remember any neighbors named Gage."

"No, he's new to the area, but he's brought a lot of money into the community. He's already bought up the adjacent properties and would like a continuous spread. He made a generous offer to Jim Bob a few weeks back, but you know how stubborn that old cowboy was."

So this Gage has had his eye on J. B.'s land for a while, Redd thought. *And now J. B. is dead in an "accident." I need to know more about this Wyatt Gage.*

"Gage," he mused aloud. "The name rings a bell."

"You might be thinking of his father, Anton Gage."

Redd raised an eyebrow. "The tech billionaire?"

"The very same." Blanton shifted in his chair again. "Look, it's probably not my place, but if you like, I'd be happy to act as an informal go-between with Wyatt. I know he'll offer you a fair price. It's the way he does business, which is why most folks around here like him, even if he is from California. It's the least I can do for Jim Bob. We can get those debts paid off and leave you with a nice little nest egg. What do you say?"

Redd managed a smile. "I appreciate the offer, Mr. Blanton. This is a lot to take in all at once."

Blanton inclined his head. "I do surely understand that, my boy. I'm only trying to make this as painless for you as I can. Give yourself a couple of days to get settled and put your thoughts together; then you come back in and we'll talk it all over and figure out what's the best thing for you to do. Sound like a plan?"

Redd stood. They shook hands. Redd held up the file folder. "Thanks for everything, Mr. Blanton."

"My pleasure, Matthew. Anything I can do to help. No point in you getting stuck in a one-horse town like this."

SIXTEEN

Redd sat behind the wheel of the Raptor, still parked in front of Blanton's office, and stared at the box with J. B.'s ashes. "What kind of trouble were you in, old man?" he asked. He did not believe in ghosts or psychics or any of that nonsense and had not made up his mind about the afterlife, but at that moment, he would have done almost anything if it meant he could have one last chat with J. B.

He dug out his iPhone and was pleasantly surprised to see full bars on LTE. When he'd left eight years ago, not many folks in Wellington bothered with smartphones. Most places outside town didn't even have regular cell coverage, to say nothing of 4G.

Maybe some things did change.

His search for Wyatt Gage yielded only a few tangential references, mostly archived news items and usually in the context of being Anton Gage's son.

There was plenty of information about Anton Gage. He was like some kind of Frankenstein's monster, cobbled together from the cloned tissue of several different high-profile tech billionaires. He had Bezos's money, Musk's penchant for elaborate schemes, and Branson's breezy good looks. Like the first two, he had made his initial stake in e-commerce—his particular contribution had been an encryption protocol that had revolutionized secure online transactions—and had subsequently reinvested in more audacious enterprises. Unlike them, he had turned his attention not to colonizing space but to "saving" Mother Earth. His primary focus was on reimagining the world food supply, using genetically engineered cereal crops to feed the world's hungry while advocating a plant-based diet for all. Anton's press was mostly positive. The worst thing his critics could say about his vision for the future was that it was unrealistic.

In contrast, Wyatt had mostly flown below the radar. One of the hits, however, directed Redd to the webpage for the Bozeman-based Gage Land Development company, of which Wyatt was the president. There was very little biographical material, but Redd nevertheless spent several minutes browsing the website, which looked and read like a slick brochure designed to entice wealthy investors. Wyatt intended to develop the area outside Wellington into a kind of wilderness playground for the uberwealthy—the next Jackson Hole, perched on the northern edge of Yellowstone. One picture, which showed a field of bison roaming free, was tagged with the caption "Give yourself a home where the buffalo roam." It might have added, *But where the local yokels are kept at a safe distance.* Most of the folks who called Stillwater County home would eventually find themselves working minimum-wage service industry jobs and priced out of the housing market.

The only thing J. B. would have hated more than having Wyatt Gage for a neighbor would have been letting the ancestral ranch get assimilated into Wyatt's scheme.

Unfortunately, Wyatt Gage was not the only person who would have stood to gain from the acquisition of J. B.'s ranch. Wyatt's development would mean big money for local politicians, bankers, and chamber of commerce types—connected people—who might have seen J. B. as an impediment to their success. And because Sheriff Blackwood and Duke

Blanton were both on that list, Redd would have to proceed carefully in his investigation.

He wasn't a cop, but he had been trained to gather intelligence and conduct interrogations. More importantly, because he wasn't a cop, he would not be constrained by the rule of law, nor would he have to meet some arbitrary burden of proof.

When he eventually found J. B.'s murderer, he would know. And then he'd settle accounts the cowboy way.

✖ ✖ ✖

After a stop at Roy's Thriftway for provisions—during which, thankfully, he didn't encounter any familiar faces—he was back on the highway, headed north.

He was about a mile from the turnoff to the ranch when he saw brake lights up ahead. The mere fact of stopped traffic on the highway shook him from the trancelike state into which he'd slipped. The stoppage made no sense. There hadn't been any road construction going on when he'd passed this way earlier, and Montana drivers weren't likely to be stopped in their tracks by an accident—they would just go around. Fully alert, he tapped the brakes and then, when it became evident that traffic ahead was at a complete standstill, brought the Raptor to a full stop half a car length behind a Subaru Outback with Minnesota license plates and a back window festooned with hiking stickers and pro–social justice messages. Such a display would not have even registered in his conscious mind in California, but here, it seemed wildly out of place. The folks in Montana, at least the ones he'd known during his childhood, had tended toward more traditional conservative values albeit with a strong independent streak. He supposed if men like Wyatt Gage got their way, that would change.

After waiting a few seconds, Redd stuck his head out of his window to see what was going on. He was surprised and a little dismayed to see that the line of unmoving cars stretched ahead almost a quarter mile. In the distance he saw some people in tie-dyed shirts and jeans standing in the middle of the road blocking traffic in each direction as a couple of big bison and their calves ambled across the asphalt. Several more bison and their rust-colored calves—called "red dogs" locally—had already gathered in the open field on the right side of the road. Redd surmised that the bison were probably grazing their way down to the banks of the Missouri River, a few hundred yards east of the highway. This far north the river was relatively narrow and running blue with spring snowmelt.

Redd was a little surprised to see the herd. While bison roamed free in the state, their normal migration patterns did not bring them through Stillwater County, which was still largely given over to domestic cattle operations. The exception was places like Ted Turner's sprawling Flying D Ranch. The cable television mogul was one of the biggest private land-owners in Montana and had devoted much of his land to the restoration of native species, including the American bison. Redd recalled mention of buffalo on the Gage Land Development website—evidently that plan was already moving forward.

From his vantage point, Redd could see that the road was now clear of the shaggy creatures, but the flow of traffic was still reduced to a dribble. A moment later, he saw why.

One of the tie-dye–wearing figures—a bearded guy with long, shaggy hair and tattooed forearms, carrying an orange bucket—shuffled up to the Subaru's driver's window. After a brief exchange, the driver of the Subaru reached out and dropped a fistful of greenbacks into the bucket.

Shaggy lifted a skinny arm in a gesture of gratitude, then turned and ambled toward Redd. The Subaru remained where it was, as if intention-ally blocking Redd's path of escape. Normally, Redd had little patience for panhandlers and would have just driven around the motionless car, but this was such an unusual sight for rural Montana that he found himself overcome by curiosity.

The young man looked like some of the people Redd had seen on LA's skid row when he did some charity work for homeless veterans. Most of those people were seriously damaged by drugs or mental illness or both, but some of them were flat-out lazy panhandlers too shiftless to find a real job.

Redd guessed Shaggy was in the latter category.

The man smiled through his rat's nest beard as he approached Redd's window. A bison graphic stood in profile in the middle of his psychedelic shirt surrounded by the words *Buffalo Warriors, Giving Nature a Fighting Chance.*

"Nice truck, man!" Shaggy said, his face close to the window.

Redd could smell the stale marijuana on the man's breath.

"Hey, sorry to stop you but we're watching out for the red dogs, ya know? Hate for you to hit one of them little guys—it'd really mess up your truck, too." He held the bucket up. *SAVE MONTANA'S WILDLIFE* was clumsily inked with a Sharpie across the front. "Thanks for helping out, man."

Redd fought back a smile and stared into the bucket. It was loaded with small bills and loose change. "What's it for?"

"Money makes the world go round, man. Every little bit helps out the buffaloes over there." He pointed helpfully toward the big animals standing in the field. "You like buffaloes, don't ya?"

The brake lights in front of Redd released and the Outback moved off.

"They're actually called *bison*," Redd pointed out.

Shaggy gave him a blank stare. "Oh, sure, man."

"I surely do love bison," Redd went on genially.

"Yeah. They're great." He shook the bucket, rattling the coins, trying to coax a donation.

"But you gotta cook 'em just right," Redd said and then put the Raptor in gear.

As he pulled away, he heard the guy shout, "Not cool, man! Not cool!"

There were four more Buffalo Warriors on the roadside—two men and two women, all in their twenties or thirties, all cut from the same cloth. They didn't look much like warriors, eco or otherwise. In his rearview mirror, Redd saw Shaggy flipping him the bird and laughed.

He hadn't done that in a while.

But as he got back up to speed, his smile faded. Something about the encounter with the Buffalo Warriors rubbed him the wrong way, and it wasn't merely because of his reflexive distaste for them.

Quite simply, they didn't belong. Maybe in downtown Bozeman or Billings, but not here, out in the middle of nowhere, fifteen miles from the nearest town. He didn't believe for a second that they were earning enough from panhandling to sustain themselves. No, they had to be getting support from someone. He was curious to know who was helping them, but what he really wanted to know was why.

What if they were the trouble J. B. was worried about?

He was going to have to take another look at the Buffalo Warriors.

After some much-needed shut-eye.

SEVENTEEN

Redd left his groceries on the kitchen counter and J. B.'s ashes on the big fireplace mantel beneath his trophy deer head. He'd figure out what to do with them later. Thus unburdened, he set his phone timer for two hours, flopped down on the sofa, covered his eyes with a forearm, and surrendered to oblivion.

Sleep, however, was as elusive as a unicorn. Every time he started to drift off, he would suddenly jolt back to wakefulness, panicked at the thought of waking up in the brig or, even worse, waking up in a stranger's rental with a quartet of shore patrol busting through the door.

Kim's voice mocked him. *"I'll tell you what happened, Sergeant Redd. You opened your smart mouth and got your entire team killed. Blown out of the sky in an ambush."*

He was almost grateful when the alarm sounded. He heaved himself to a sitting position. He had a splitting headache and needed another six to eight hours of uninterrupted rack time but knew that if he went back to sleep now, his body rhythms would be completely out of whack. Besides, he had plans for the night. He decided instead to make some coffee and get his head together.

First, a couple of aspirin.

He went back to the main bathroom, where J. B. kept his medicine cabinet. He pulled open the mirrored door and was surprised by what he saw.

Two dozen pill bottles, at least.

Redd checked a couple of the labels. He recognized some of the generic names as pain meds. Some serious stuff. The other stuff he didn't recognize. He'd google it later.

Why all the meds?

Redd swallowed a couple of aspirin and washed them down by cupping his hands under the faucet and lapping up the water. He thought about grabbing a shower but decided he was hungrier than he was dirty. As a grunt he'd spent enough time in the dirt that a little stink and sweat didn't bother him as much as it should have. Now that he was a civilian, he probably needed to get civilized again.

Just not today.

He stumbled into the kitchen and went straight to the cabinet where J. B., a man of habit, kept his coffee and filters. Redd stuffed a paper filter into the coffee maker and scooped ground coffee into it from a half-empty Folgers can, then poured in a full pot of water and hit the On button.

While the coffee maker gurgled and wheezed, Redd decided to make something to eat. He yanked open the old Frigidaire and did an inventory. There wasn't much in there. He found a couple of rubbery carrots in the vegetable drawer and a half-empty jar of dill pickles. There was sliced turkey in the meat drawer, but it had a slight green tinge to it. He sniffed it and tossed it straight into the garbage. There wasn't any milk or juice, but there were a couple cans of Dr Pepper, J. B.'s longtime favorite. He was, indeed, a man of habit.

The top shelf was full of Ensure meal replacement drinks stacked in neat rows, the labels all facing the same direction.

Ensure? What was that about?

Some part of him already knew the answer, but he didn't want to accept it.

He moved from the nearly empty refrigerator to the cupboards, which were surprisingly bare. Neither he nor J. B. had a knack for the kitchen, though his dad was a wizard with smokers, grills, and open fires. Half the meals Redd had eaten in the last eight years had been MREs, so he wasn't exactly a foodie anyway. Still, J. B. had always kept the cupboards stocked with canned goods—lots of heat-and-eat items like soup and chili. The empty shelves sent another ominous message that he wasn't ready to process just yet.

He stowed his purchases in the cupboard, leaving out a can of Dinty Moore beef stew. He had just popped the lid on it when he heard the sound of tires crunching in the dirt outside.

Who's that?

He glanced out the big front window and saw an official-looking black SUV parked alongside his Raptor. Redd opened the door just as a pair of boots hit the porch.

Though it had been almost ten years since he'd last seen the man who now wore the brown uniform of a Stillwater County Sheriff's deputy, Redd recognized him immediately.

"Matt Redd, you old dog. How the heck are you?" Shane Hepworth flashed a million-watt smile and stuck his big hand out.

Redd took it and nodded. "Doing all right."

Hepworth was just a few years older than he and nearly as tall. He had California surfer good looks with thick blond hair and blue eyes that made the cheerleaders swoon back in the day. Hepworth had been the starting senior quarterback when Redd first started working out with the varsity squad. They got along pretty well on the field, but Shane ran in social circles Redd didn't have access to. The handsome quarterback lived in the better part of the county and came from money—his father was a cattle broker and his mother had her own dental practice down in Bozeman. Nevertheless, the two of them had been magic on the gridiron. Hepworth saw a path to his own future glory in Redd's ability to catch his hard-thrown passes, break tackles, and score touchdowns. But when Redd suddenly disappeared from the squad to take care of the ranch, Shane Hepworth hadn't even bothered to check in on him. That's when he learned who his real friends were. One of his buddies, Mikey Derhammer, would show up to lend a hand when he could and still hung out with Redd until he left, but Shane was nowhere to be found.

"I'm really sorry about Jim Bob," Hepworth said. "Sheriff Blackwood told me you stopped by. I just got off shift and thought maybe you could use some of this." He held up a plastic bag emblazoned with the Thriftway logo.

Redd took it and saw that it contained a six-pack of beer.

What's that old saying about Greeks bearing gifts?

"Appreciate it," he said. "Come on in and let's crack one open."

Hepworth grinned. "Don't mind if I do."

EIGHTEEN

Redd pulled out two bottles from the bag—Deschutes Black Butte porter from Oregon—and shoved the rest in the fridge. He popped the tops off with a bottle opener and handed one to Shane, who had, without waiting for an invitation, taken a seat at the big table in the dining room.

"Hope you don't mind the dark stuff," Hepworth said. "I can't stand those IPAs. They taste like old gym socks to me."

"I only like beer that's wet and cold," Redd said. "Mostly wet."

"To Jim Bob Thompson," Hepworth said, raising his bottle. "The last of the real cowboys."

Redd tapped the neck of his bottle against Hepworth's but found his voice deserting him when he tried to say, "To J. B."

Redd savored the dark beer, which had a lot more heft than the Modelo Negra he usually drank. "Not bad," he remarked. He studied his house-guest as the other man took another pull on his bottle. "So . . . you're the law around here now. Last I heard you went to Idaho on a full-ride football scholarship. I thought you'd be throwing in the NFL by now."

Hepworth flashed a rueful grin. "Yeah, I made starting QB in Idaho. Then I busted up my knee in the first season."

"That's too bad."

"Stuff happens. At least I got a college education out of it. Criminal justice is always gonna be a growth industry, and it sure beats sitting at a desk all day." Hepworth threw back his beer, finishing it in a long gulp. "What about you? Marine Corps, right?"

Redd nodded but did not elaborate.

"I'll bet you've seen some real things."

Redd nodded again, then, to avoid having to tell war stories, went back to the refrigerator. "Have another?"

"Thought you'd never ask."

Redd brought two bottles over to the table. Hepworth took his and immediately took another long sip.

"I'm a little surprised you came back here," Redd went on. "Why not do policing in one of the big cities like Bozeman?"

"Me? In Boze-Angeles? No thanks. I mean, I don't mind chasing tail down there—plenty of pretty sweet honeys running around in that part of the world. But I'm not big on kombucha or quinoa salad and avocado toast. And all things considered, I'd rather be a big fish in a small pond. A couple more years of putting in my time here, and I'll be ready to run for sheriff myself."

Hepworth then leaned in, lowering his voice to a conspiratorial whisper. "Between you and me, brother? Blackwood's a mess. He's mad at the world or something. Doesn't do anything. Half the time he's back at his place liquored up and I'm the one running around doing all the policing."

"I kind of picked up on that," Redd admitted. "Is he local?"

Hepworth shook his head. "Nah. Showed up a few years back. Some of our new *locals* invited him here and staked his run against Sheriff Littleton. When old Bob saw how much money they were throwing at Blackwood, he decided it was time to retire and spend the rest of his days fishing."

Redd raised his bottle. "To Sheriff Hepworth."

"I'll definitely drink to that," Hepworth said and then promptly did.

He brought the half-empty bottle down hard on the table, like a judge calling a trial to order. "We tried everything to reach you when we found Jim Bob. Where were you?"

Redd wondered if the abrupt change in subject was some kind of questioning tactic that Hepworth had learned in the pursuit of his criminal justice degree. If so, he needed to work on his technique.

"I was off-grid," Redd replied.

Hepworth gave a knowing nod. "Secret Marine Corps stuff, right? You could tell me, but then you'd have to kill me."

"Something like that."

"Still, we called the Navy's bureau of personnel. They refused to give us a contact number for you. Even when we told them it was a family emergency."

"Your tax dollars at work," Redd muttered, hoping that Hepworth would let it drop. "I was offline for a while, but when I finally got around to checking my phone, I saw that I'd missed a call from J. B. When I couldn't get in touch, I hopped in the truck and hauled as fast as I could to get here." He paused a beat, then added, "The sheriff told me you're the one who found him?"

The deputy picked at the label on the bottle. "Yeah. Heck of a thing." He drained the rest of the beer in one long chug.

"You want another?"

"Man, I guess I should have brought a case." He grinned. "Set me up."

Redd went to the kitchen, then came back with a bottle for each of them. "So tell me what happened."

"Well," Hepworth said, letting out a heavy sigh, "there's not much to tell. I was driving by after a call up the road about a mountain lion in someone's yard and thought I'd swing by. I used to check in on him every now and then. You know, just to keep an eye on him."

Redd frowned. He did not *know*. "You got that much time on your hands?"

Hepworth shrugged. "Well, I bumped into Jim Bob at Spady's a while back. He didn't look so good. I could tell he wasn't feeling all that great either. So I just took it upon myself to check in on him. I mean, he didn't have anyone around, did he?" Hepworth took a swig of his beer, letting the none-too-subtle rebuke hang in the air.

It was a fair point, but Redd still felt like shoving Hepworth's Black Butte porter down his throat.

You should have been there, he told himself for the umpteenth time since he first heard J. B.'s message.

"Where'd you find him?"

Hepworth chinned toward the rear of the house. "About a quarter mile up the road to the old hunting cabin."

"No sign of foul play?"

The deputy gave him an odd look. He shook his head. "Nothing like that. His horse got spooked and threw him. Probably startled a rattler. Or maybe caught a whiff of a cat. Who knows? Just one of those things. When I found him, there was blood on a rock where he hit his head, but the coroner said it was a broken neck that did him in." Hepworth sat forward in his chair and looked Redd in the eyes. "On this job I've found that what you see at first is most likely what happened. Poor old Jim Bob lay on the ground all night next to his horse, who just waited there like a watchdog standing guard over him."

Redd took a sip of beer as he thought things through. "There's no horse in the barn."

"Your neighbors have him. They'll take good care of him, trust me. I can fetch him for you tomorrow if you want, or whenever."

"I can take care of it."

Hepworth shrugged. "Suit yourself. Just trying to help."

"Was it the Jacobys that took him?"

"The Jacobys? They've been gone for four years. Bought out by Gage."

"Wyatt Gage?"

"You heard about him?"

"Duke Blanton mentioned he was buying up land around here. Told me he might even want to buy this place." He watched Hepworth for any reaction, saw none. "So Gage has J. B.'s horse?"

"Not him personally, but his wrangler promised he'd take care of the horse until we could figure out what to do." The deputy paused a beat. "So you gonna sell to him?"

Redd shook his head. "I'm still trying to process everything. This land was in J. B.'s family for generations. That's a lot to think about."

"You've moved on, brother. I can tell. Trust me, there's nothing here for you. Wellington hasn't changed much since you left, except maybe for the worse. These little ranches around here can't make it, so the Richie Riches from out of state like Wyatt come swooping in and buy them up. All the old hands are getting laid off and then hired back at minimum wage. And there's more people than jobs, so everyone's hurting. You can't imagine what that does to a community like this."

Redd was pretty sure he could but decided to let Hepworth keep talking. "What do you mean?"

"Drugs have hit this area hard. Opiates. Meth, especially. And where you have drugs, you've got everything that goes with it. Theft. Prostitution." He shook his head. "Stillwater County is a great place to be *from*. If you've got a chance to cash out, do yourself a favor and take it."

Redd gave a noncommittal grunt. "Speaking of things going to hell, I got ambushed by a bunch of tie-dyed tree huggers on my way back from town."

Hepworth laughed. "The Buffalo Warriors? They're mostly harmless."

"Not really something I expect to see out here in the boonies."

"The Gage family is very involved in the environmental movement. I don't have to tell you what kind of people are drawn to that." He gave a derisive snort. "Freaking environmentalists. A bunch of California liberals flying all over the world in their personal jets, then try to convince us that we're the ones killing the planet."

"You mean Anton Gage?"

"Don't get me wrong. I appreciate what he and his family are trying to do. But you know how it is with these rich guys. They think they're all smarter than us. But it's people like us—people who grew up here on the land—who are the real conservationists. We know the value of this land because our families have worked it and lived on it for generations." Shane stabbed the table with his index finger. "The land and the water and the blue sky above ain't no theory for us. We've hunted it. We've fished it. It's our way of life. We don't need outsiders like Anton Gage telling us about it. We live it."

This dude either forgot we grew up together or he's starting to believe his own BS.

Redd barely managed to hide a look of incredulity. Hepworth sounded like he was already stumping for public office, but his "man of the people, defender of the land" schtick would ring hollow for anyone who had grown up with him. Hepworth came from money. Hunting and fishing had been leisure activities for his family, not a lifestyle, and certainly not something he did to put food on the table. He wondered if Hepworth would have been so forthright without three bottles of Deschutes ale providing some lubricant.

"Now Wyatt on the other hand . . . ," Hepworth went on. "I get along with him real good. He's a little more practical being a real estate guy. A real sharp operator. Makes sense he'd want to buy your place since it borders his. You oughta consider it. He'll make you a fair offer. More than fair."

The abrupt shift left Redd momentarily speechless. One minute, Anton Gage and all the other "Richie Rich" elites were a plague, grinding everyday folks under their bootheel, and the next, Wyatt Gage was a "sharp operator"?

Maybe he's looking to get some of that Gage money to bankroll his run for sheriff, Redd thought.

Hepworth made a show of checking his watch. "Well, it's getting to be dinnertime, and you're out of beer, so I'll head on down the road." He lowered his voice and added, "I know you've got a lot to take care of. If you need anything, give me a call."

Redd inclined his head but then said, "Hey, before you go, I was wondering something."

"Shoot."

"I can't find J. B.'s phone. Any idea where it is?"

Hepworth shrugged. "There wasn't one on him when I found him or anywhere near him. His front door was unlocked, so I checked inside because I wanted to call you, but I didn't find one. Not in his truck either. At that point I just assumed he didn't have one."

"I know he had one because I bought him one and we talked on it every now and again. I found his phone charger in one of his drawers."

The deputy shook his head, twisting his mouth into a curl. "Hmm. Sorry I missed that. But then again, I didn't go rifling through his drawers or anything. I saw his address book on his desk, though, and checked it for your phone number to call you. It wasn't in there."

"He had it programmed into his phone."

Hepworth sighed again, and Redd sensed he was becoming irritated with the matter. "Well, if you say he had a phone, then he must have dropped it out there somewhere by accident. If you want, I can go out and take a look around for it."

"I'll check it out tomorrow."

"Try calling it when you go searching. There's a chance the battery isn't dead yet."

"Good idea," Redd said, but he already knew there was no way the battery would last that long. Besides, something told him that no matter where he looked, that phone would never turn up. *The question is, who would have wanted to make it disappear?*

"Like I said, I'm sorry we couldn't get through to you." He paused a beat and then, as if struck by inspiration, went on. "You want to give your number to me now in case I hear anything?"

Redd shook his head. "Nah, you know where to find me."

If Hepworth found the dodge suspicious, he gave no indication. "Your call. Let's catch up soon."

Redd followed him out to his SUV. "You sure you're okay to drive, Deputy? I'd hate for you to get a DUI."

Shane snorted and climbed inside. "You're buying next time."

"You know it."

"If you want, I'll call Wyatt, let him know you're interested in selling."

"Don't know that I am."

"Whatever, dude. Let me know if you change your mind."

Redd just shrugged. As he watched the SUV drive away into the waning afternoon, he allowed himself a smile of satisfaction. He didn't have all the answers yet, but he'd learned a lot. His headache was better too, which was good because he had a long night ahead of him. He was glad that he'd limited his intake of beer to a single sip—the toast to J. B.

Deputy Hepworth hadn't even noticed.

NINETEEN

After Hepworth's departure, Redd returned to his postponed dinner, eating the Dinty Moore right out of the can and washing it down with a cup of coffee. The combination of food and caffeine helped beat back the last vestiges of the headache he'd woken up with. He poured the rest of the pot into an old Thermos and took it outside to J. B.'s F-250. He had been a little worried that the battery might have gone dead after sitting idle for more than a week, but it started right up. The radio came alive, blasting out a Merle Haggard song, which brought a smile to Redd's face. He let it play.

J. B.'s truck was strictly a working rig, no frills. Redd could only imagine what the old man would have thought about the Raptor—how much Redd had spent on it and how much time he spent maintaining it inside and out. He couldn't remember J. B. ever washing his Ford though he kept it in top mechanical condition. The old man saw vehicles as tools, not fashion statements.

Despite the lack of creature comforts, J. B.'s old truck possessed a couple features that the Raptor just couldn't provide—Montana license plates and a virtually anonymous appearance. He supposed some of the old hands might recognize it and wonder why J. B.'s rig was rolling into town a week after his death, but that was a small price to pay for avoiding the kind of attention the Raptor would be sure to draw.

He drove back in the direction of town but didn't go far. As soon as he spotted the bison herd grazing in the field, he pulled off to the side of the road and watched the animals through a pair of binoculars while he drank the rest of the coffee. He wasn't the least bit surprised to see brightly colored shapes lurking at the edge of the herd. But the five tie-dyed Buffalo Warriors were doing more than just acting as crossing guards. Two of them sat astride quad bikes and were zipping back and forth behind the animals. With each close encounter, the herd turned away, bolting fifty or so yards to get clear of the noisy little ATVs.

The reason for the harassment soon became apparent. The Buffalo Warriors were nudging the herd in the direction of the highway, no doubt hoping to provoke the animals to cross, at which point they would be able to stop traffic and solicit more donations. Redd shook his head in disbelief.

So much for defending wild animals. Where's a game warden when you actually need one?

The traffic snarl lasted nearly an hour, with the Buffalo Warriors somehow managing to move the herd across in small groups of a dozen or so animals at a time, and short intervals in between where they were able to hit up stopped cars for donations. From what Redd could tell, their appeals were rebuffed more often than not, but this did not seem to trouble the scruffy-looking bunch much.

The sun was brushing the mountains to the west when the herd finally made it safely across. Four of the Buffalo Warriors departed, riding buddy-style on the quad bikes and heading east, toward the river. Redd figured they must have a camp down there. Shaggy, who had pocketed a considerable amount of the take, remained behind, standing on the shoulder of the southbound lane with this thumb extended. Redd was frankly surprised when, after only about five minutes, a blue pickup stopped to give him a ride.

He wasn't quite sure what it was about Shaggy that bothered him, but something felt off. He decided to follow.

The blue pickup traveled south as far as Spady's Saloon on the northern outskirts of town. Spady's was a veritable institution in Wellington. In Redd's lifetime, it had transformed from a watering hole for weary ranch hands at the end of the workday to a slightly more family-friendly establishment, at least until happy hour.

When the pickup pulled into Spady's parking lot, Redd pulled to the shoulder about two hundred yards back from the turnout to observe. He couldn't imagine that things in Wellington had changed to the point where a ragamuffin like Shaggy would be allowed past the front door, and sure enough, as soon as the pickup was off the highway, the driver stopped long enough to let Shaggy out, after which the Buffalo Warrior made his way back to the roadside where he continued walking south.

When he was nothing but a smudge of color in the distance, Redd pulled out and drove forward a few hundred yards before pulling off again to continue watching Shaggy's progress. Following on foot would have been easier, but Redd didn't want to get separated from the truck, so instead he jumped forward in small increments, keeping the man just within his view. Shaggy plodded forward, blissfully unaware and evidently untroubled by the walk.

Upon reaching Broadway, some twenty minutes later, Shaggy crossed the highway and headed east but then turned south again after only one block. Redd was obliged to get closer than he would have liked, turning onto the cross street—Apple Street—just twenty-five yards from the striding figure. The darkening sky necessitated turning on the Ford's headlights, but Shaggy never even glanced back.

Apple Street was a mixture of residential and commercial spaces—a tax preparer, a chiropractor, an irrigation specialist—with a lot more of the former. The farther they got from Broadway, the more dilapidated the houses began to look. Ranch-style houses with immaculate lawns gave way to mobile homes with tangled weeds and derelict vehicles. Shaggy walked through the neighborhood as if it were his own, which Redd supposed it might actually be.

Shaggy's eventual destination was a neglected-looking house nestled behind some trees in a lot sandwiched between a pair of similarly decrepit mobile homes. Redd pulled over and quickly shut off his lights, then got out the binoculars to follow his subject's subsequent movements. Through the glasses, Redd spotted a late 2000s model Chevy Silverado, parked near the trees, and closer to the house, a pair of customized hogs—Harley-Davidson motorcycles. Shaggy stepped around the truck and disappeared through the trees. Redd cursed under his breath, then set the binoculars aside, preparing to go extravehicular.

He switched the interior light to the off position so that it would not illuminate when the door opened. Before he could work the door lever, however, he spied movement in the trees behind the Silverado. He grabbed the binos again and trained them on the spot just as a figure stepped into view.

It was not Shaggy but a middle-aged man wearing the customary local uniform of jeans, western shirt, and a Stetson. Though Redd could not see the man's face, his not inconsiderable beer gut gave the impression of middle age. The man seemed to be in a hurry, looking around nervously as he circled to the left side of the Chevy and climbed in. The truck started up with a puff of smoke, but its lights remained off until it hit the pavement.

Redd waited until the Silverado rounded the corner before exiting the truck and heading toward the house. He chose a casual gait, as if he knew exactly where he was going and had every right to be there. He was halfway across the empty lot when he saw two things that almost caused him to stop in his tracks. The first was a homemade sign—black Sharpie on poster board—attached to one of the trees, which showed a smiley face next to the words *Smile. Your on camera.* The second was a glimpse of a porch light through the tree branches.

A *red* porch light.

No way, he thought. *They can't possibly be that obvious.*

But the more he thought about how the old rancher with the beer gut had slunk away from the house, the more certain he was that the red porch light was not signaling the householder's support of heart health awareness.

Evidently Shaggy was planning to use the donations he'd solicited to support a different kind of wildlife.

Redd continued walking, aware that breaking off now would look suspicious to anyone watching the feed from the camera, and he did not doubt that there really was a camera. He closed the distance, his mind working furiously to come up with an exit strategy that would not complicate the situation.

As he stepped between the trees, the front door of the little house opened and a man almost the same size and build as Redd stepped out. The guy had dark unruly hair and a bushy beard and wore black jeans and a black silk-screened T-shirt, mostly hidden by a black leather vest. The man crossed his arms over his chest, revealing not only full-sleeve tattoos on both arms but bulging biceps and pecs that strained the fabric of his shirt. The red light gave his skin a pallid, bloodless hue. Redd guessed the man had ridden here on one of the hogs out front. The fact that there were two motorcycles meant a second biker dude was probably lurking nearby.

After sizing Redd up, the man squared his shoulders and said, "Get lost."

Redd knew that if he complied, it would only reinforce the idea that he had no business there, so he mounted a half-hearted protest. "Dale told me that I could find someone to party—"

"I don't care whatever Dale told you," the man said. He advanced a step, uncrossing his arms and letting them come to rest on his hips. "Get. Lost."

Redd raised his hands in a show of surrender and then backed away slowly. When it became apparent that the biker dude wasn't going to pursue, he turned on his heel and headed back to the truck.

No sooner had he settled back into surveillance mode than Shaggy strolled out from between the trees.

"Wow, buddy," Redd muttered. "That was quick."

For a moment, he felt sorry for whomever had been required to provide "entertainment" for the unwashed and fragrant Buffalo Warrior, but something about the way Shaggy was moving caused Redd to reevaluate the situation.

If Shaggy hadn't come here to buy sex, then what?

Drugs?

That seemed a lot more likely.

Shaggy retraced his steps, heading back the same way he'd come. Redd didn't think he would be visible inside the darkened interior of the truck, but ultimately it didn't matter. Shaggy walked past without even a glance in his direction.

Redd watched the other man's retreating form in the side mirror for a few seconds, then reached a decision. Stepping out onto the running board, he lifted himself high enough to look over the top of the cab and called out, "Hey, you need a lift?"

Shaggy wheeled around, clearly startled by the shout, but after a moment, his bearded face split with a grin. "Dude, thanks!"

As he started moving toward the truck, Redd got out and circled around to intercept him. Shaggy's forehead creased in sudden recognition, and the grin became a frown. "Hey, I remember you."

He started to take a step back, but Redd was faster, clamping a hand down on the young man's shoulder, pinning him in place. "Hold up a minute, Mr. Buffalo Warrior. I just want to have a little talk."

Shaggy tried to pull away, then grimaced as Redd's grip tightened. "Ow. Let go, man. This ain't legal!"

Redd laughed. "That's funny. You know what else isn't legal? Buying drugs."

"I didn't buy any drugs," Shaggy shot back, but even as he said it, his eyes flicked to the right, in the direction of the house with the red porch light.

"Look, I don't care what you do on your own time," Redd told him. "But I think it's pretty low to take money that's supposed to be used to save wildlife and instead use it to buy . . . what, crystal?"

Shaggy didn't deny it.

"Tell you what, though," Redd went on. "I'd be willing to forget about this if you just answer a couple questions."

Shaggy made another futile attempt to squirm out of Redd's grip. "I don't know anything, man."

"Oh, I bet you know more than you realize," Redd assured in a soothing tone. "You spend a lot of time out there with the bison, right? You got a camp out there? That's private property, isn't it?"

"Yeah. So what? We got permission."

"Permission from who?"

Shaggy tried to shrug but was only partly successful. "The owner."

"The owner," Redd echoed. "Would that be Wyatt Gage?"

Another half shrug. Redd took it as an affirmative. "You must hear things," he went on. "Rumors. Did you hear anything about that rancher who died about a week ago?"

When Shaggy tried to shrug again, Redd gave his shoulder a squeeze that elicited a painful yelp. "I need you to use your words," he said, moving his face in close. "Did you hear anything about the rancher—?"

"Yes, okay? I heard he fell off his horse."

"Is that all you heard?"

"Yes—ow!" Shaggy writhed in Redd's grip for a moment, then rasped, "He was sticking his nose where it didn't belong. Okay? Just let me go, dude."

Redd struggled to maintain his blank mask. Here at last was confirmation that there was more to J. B.'s death than he had been led to believe. "What do you mean he stuck his nose where it didn't belong?"

"I don't know. I swear. I just heard someone say it."

"Who?" Redd pressed. "Who said it?"

Before he could squeeze the answer out of Shaggy, Redd heard the sound of gravel crunching and was instantly on guard. He snapped his head around and saw the biker dude striding toward him.

As soon as eye contact was established, the man's hands clenched into sledgehammer-like fists. "Gonna have to mess you up," he growled.

From the corner of his eye, Redd detected movement behind him, and a sidelong glance revealed a second figure trying to sneak up from the street side, using the truck for concealment.

Redd didn't waste time or breath with challenge words or posturing. Reluctantly he released his hold on Shaggy, then spun on his heel to meet the man who was trying to blindside him.

Biker Dude Number Two was smaller than his counterpart—both in height and build. To make up for this apparent disadvantage, he had armed himself with a thirty-six-inch bolt cutter, which he held in a two-handed grip, the cutting head resting on his shoulder like a baseball bat. Perhaps because he was counting on being able to catch Redd by surprise, he was completely unprepared for Redd's preemptive attack. As Redd closed toward him, Number Two stopped short, eyes widening in alarm, but seemed rooted in place. The bolt cutter never left his shoulder.

Redd didn't hesitate but advanced in two quick strides, driving his right fist forward into Number Two's solar plexus. The impact lifted the man off the ground and sent him flying backward into the street. He landed with a thud, followed immediately by the clank and hiss of the bolt cutter hitting the pavement and sliding away.

Redd pivoted back to Biker Dude Number One, who looked almost as shocked by the suddenness of Redd's attack as his fallen buddy. Despite the fact that he might have looked like a match for Redd mano a mano, he nevertheless retreated a step and unclenched his right fist, reaching behind his back.

Gun.

With no time to close the fifteen-foot gap between them, Redd quickly reached for the bolt cutters, grabbed them, and threw them one-handed toward Number One's chest. The large tool made a sickening thud as it crashed into the man's left rib cage. The biker grunted in pain and staggered back another step.

"You're dead," he hissed. "You're—"

Redd struck like Thor's hammer, driving forward so fast that Number One didn't even get to finish the threat. He led with a right uppercut that slammed the biker's mouth shut so hard that the crunch of broken teeth sounded like gravel in a cement mixer. But the punch was only the beginning. A millisecond later, Redd's right elbow—with every ounce of his full mass and momentum behind it—drove into the biker's sternum. Unlike the punch that had laid out Number Two, Redd did not simply knock the man flying but instead drove through, bearing the biker to the ground and landing on him so hard that his breath blew out in a spray of blood and tooth fragments. Redd's left hand shot out, grasping the stunned man's throat, pinning him in place while his right came up, poised to deliver one final blow.

In Redd's book, the threat the man had just made against him was all the provocation needed for him to execute a permanent solution. If he let these men live, they would make good on that threat, no matter how long it took, and so killing them, right now, whether incapacitated or not, was simply a matter of self-defense. It would probably even hold up in court . . . in a perfect world.

The problem was, it wasn't a perfect world. For one thing, there was a very real possibility that the county sheriff and others in the local law enforcement community were corrupt. The simple fact that the biker dudes were operating a whorehouse and dealing crystal within the city limits was proof enough of that. And he wasn't Sergeant Redd, hero of the USMC anymore. Getting kicked out of the military would weigh heavily against him, even if the circumstances of his separation were not revealed. So if it came down to a legal case, there was no guarantee that the verdict would go his way . . . or that he would even survive long enough to get his day in court.

Simply making the men disappear wasn't an option either, not now that he'd shown his face to a surveillance camera, never mind that Shaggy could also put him at the scene.

No, like it or not, he was going to have to tolerate the looming threat, at least until his business in Stillwater County was complete.

He lowered his fist, then pushed away from Number One. The man wasn't moving, but Redd could tell by the bubbles of blood popping around his nose and mouth that he was still breathing. He rolled the biker onto his side so he wouldn't aspirate, and as he did, he got a look at the image embroidered onto the man's leather vest. It was a variation on the skull and crossbones theme, but instead of bones, there were crossed pistons. Above the image, in Gothic letters, was the word *Infidels* accompanied by the letters *MC*. Below it was written *Bozeman*.

He considered cutting the patch off, then thought better of it. Instead, he lifted the bottom of the vest to reveal the butt of a holstered pistol. Redd tugged out the weapon, which appeared to be a 1911 variant. In the darkness, he couldn't distinguish a manufacturer. He dropped the magazine into his palm, then racked out the chambered round and slotted it back into the magazine. After picking up the bolt cutters, he deposited both weapons in the bed of the truck, then walked over to where Number Two was just beginning to stir. After a moment's contemplation, he reached down and scooped the man up as easily as he might a sack of potatoes, heaving him up onto one shoulder and carrying him around the truck to where Number One still lay unmoving.

He dropped Number Two alongside his buddy, knelt down, and began slapping his face to rouse him. The man came awake with a start, then grew still as he realized that Redd was looming over him.

"Infidels, huh?" Redd said. "That's kind of on the nose, don't you think?"

The man just glowered at him.

"I want you to listen very carefully," Redd went on. "I didn't pick this fight with you. I don't give two craps about you, your motorcycle club, or any of the messed-up stuff that you guys are into."

This was a lie, of course, but there was nothing to be served by revealing his real feelings about motorcycle gangs.

"Now, I'm sure you're going to want payback . . . save face or whatever. You should know that's a really bad idea. Before you even think about coming after me, just know that next time I won't be throwing bolt cutters at you. I'll put a bullet right between your eyes and bury your body someplace nobody will ever find you. You feel me?"

The man's head bobbed with a slow nod.

"Good. Now, in the Old West, I would give you until sundown to get out of my town, but since it's already after dark, I'm going to be generous and give you until sunrise. I'm gonna swing by here tomorrow. That little love shack of yours better have a For Rent sign on it. Got it?"

Another nod.

"Good. I'm going to leave now. You should probably stay down until I'm gone." With that, Redd rose to his feet, headed back to the pickup, and started it up. When he drove away, the two bikers hadn't moved.

He kept an eye out for Shaggy on the way back, but the scruffy Buffalo Warrior was nowhere to be seen. Redd figured he'd probably gotten all the useful information out of the man already.

"He was sticking his nose where it didn't belong."

That didn't track. It wasn't in J. B.'s nature to go looking for trouble. The old man had been a firm proponent of MYOB.

"Trouble's come knocking . . ."

Translation: Trouble had caught up with J. B. even though he had been minding his own business.

That sounded like more than just a negotiation for property, but Redd's gut still told him that the land was involved. Somehow.

I think it's time to have a chat with Wyatt Gage.

TWENTY

Gavin Kline sat in his private car, a late-model Cadillac Escalade, his eyes glued to the tablet in his hands and his mind focused on the voice in his earpiece.

Two blocks away, Kevin Dudek paced the floor of his two-story townhome, obviously still unaware of the cameras and recording devices Kline had planted in light fixtures throughout the residence.

It's his own fault, Kline told himself. He'd warned all the agents under his command to check for bugs at home on a regular basis because "you just never know."

Dudek had dismissed the warning and now Kline was exploiting his willful negligence.

Kline would have preferred to wait for Dudek to leave for work tomorrow morning so he could retrieve the devices and download them for later review. But the young agent's wife and two small children were due home from a visit to relatives out of state first thing in the morning, which made that impossible. Most important of all, time was critical. He needed to get the Willow situation figured out fast.

So here he sat at the maximum limit of broadcast range, which was too close for comfort, getting the intel via a live feed. Like nearly every stakeout he'd ever been on, Kline was bored out of his mind.

Dudek had come home, made himself some dinner, and watched the final episode of the final season of *Homeland*. Judging by Dudek's reaction, he shared Kline's opinion that it was a pretty good show. Then Dudek got himself ready for bed. Thirty minutes after taking care of business, Dudek's head hit the pillow and he was out like a light.

Kline hung around for another hour before deciding to call it a night. Just as he was about to punch the Escalade's Start button, Dudek's cell phone rang—a private phone not registered with the bureau, Kline noted.

Naughty boy.

He wished he had the number to Dudek's private cell—then he could have patched his way in to the call. For now, he had to guess the identity of the caller and the questions they posed by Dudek's responses. The young agent was clearly surprised and agitated by the call, which had awakened him out of a deep sleep. The man had ripped the covers off the bed, jumped up, flipped on the lights, and snatched the phone out of a drawer. As he talked, he paced the room in pajama shorts and a faded FBI Academy T-shirt.

Obviously not his wife, Kline thought. *She'd have called on the registered cell.*

"Yeah, I know it's you. No one else has this number," Dudek began.

Was it a man? A woman? Kline turned up the volume but Dudek's receiver wasn't broadcasting the caller's voice loud enough to pick up anything. He willed Dudek to put the caller on speakerphone but apparently his telepathic powers were worthless.

Worse, Dudek headed for the hallway stairs, where Kline hadn't put any bugs.

By the time Dudek emerged in the kitchen and yanked open the fridge, he was already deep into a conversation.

". . . I don't know what she knows. She's suspicious by nature."

Dudek grabbed a half-gallon jug of milk and bumped the fridge door closed with his hip. "I can't do that right now." He unscrewed the milk jug cap with one hand, still talking. "I don't think that's a good idea. Better to stay where you are."

He took a swig of milk one-handed, still listening to the voice on the other end. Before he could swallow, he nearly spat it out of his nose. "Then you'd be putting us both at risk. We just need to be patient. A little more time and things will all work out. Trust me, okay?"

Dudek pulled the fridge door back open, shoved the milk inside, and hip-closed it again, his face making clear that he was intently listening to the voice on the other end. He bounded upstairs—out of range again.

Kline swore in frustration.

When Dudek reached the bedroom, he'd already ended the call. He paced the floor for a few moments, running his fingers through his hair. He was a caged animal with no way out.

He powered off the phone, pulled the battery, and stuffed the phone into his shorts pocket.

Kline watched Dudek jog back downstairs, open a cabinet, and pour himself a tall bourbon. An hour later, Dudek was drunk and back in bed, sound asleep.

Kline called it a night. As he drove away, he began working on a plan to get his hands on Dudek's phone.

TWENTY-ONE

MONTANA

Twelve hours after he threw the two bikers a beating, Redd awoke feeling better than he had in weeks. He still didn't have all the answers, but he felt like he was making some progress. Or at the very least doing something, and that was better than wallowing in self-pity. After a cup of black coffee and a Clif Bar—breakfast of champions—he headed out to the barn and hooked the horse trailer to the hitch of J. B.'s truck, then drove up the road to what had formerly been the entrance to the Jacoby Ranch.

A hundred yards up the recently graveled road, he passed through a ranch gate hung with a massive timber sign that read, *Dancing Elk Ranch*, so named, he presumed, for the little river that passed through J. B.'s property and into the Gage spread.

Redd rumbled up the dirt road to the entrance and hit the brakes, the rusted bumper of the F-250 nearly touching the wrought iron. A guard shack stood to the right with a neatly carved Private Property sign attached to it. Redd did not fail to notice several high-end security cameras covering the approach from all angles.

Two men ambled out of the shack. They wore clean Wranglers, flannel shirts, straw cowboy hats, and ropers—just like every other ranch hand working the high-end estates in the area—but it was the pistols strapped to their hips that Redd noticed first. Glock 19s by the looks of them.

Not exactly the type of gun you normally see on a cowboy.

Both men were in their early thirties, bearded but well-groomed, and clearly in great physical shape. Their confident, easy gait gave them away at a distance. But as one of them approached the window with searching eyes scanning for possible threats, Redd knew for sure these two boys were former military, almost certainly from a special operations background.

"Good morning, sir. How can I help you?" the man asked, draping his left arm over Redd's door and leaning close, blocking Redd's view of his gun hand with his body.

"I'm here to get my horse."

His eyes locked with Redd's. "I don't know anything about a horse pickup today. Maybe you have the wrong address."

An apex predator, no doubt, with an instinct for violence that combat training only enhanced. Redd recognized the breed. Saw one just like him every morning in the bathroom mirror.

He knew he could have cleared things up simply by telling the truth, but after what he'd learned the previous night, he was curious to see just how far Gage's security forces were willing to go to keep uninvited guests out, so he simply returned the steely gaze and said, "Nope."

They stared at each other for another moment, neither willing to blink. The guard's eyes scanned the truck cab and bed one more time just to be sure it was clear of weapons. There was nothing to see. Redd had left the pistol he'd taken off the biker the night before in the gun safe back at the house and had stashed the bolt cutters behind his seat in the cab.

The guard stepped back from the old Ford and called over to the other guard, "You got any horse pickups on the schedule for today?"

The other guard stepped into the shack and came back out with a tablet. He approached the truck reading from it.

"What's the name?" the second guard asked.

"Redd."

He scrolled through the tablet again.

"Sorry, sir. No Redd here. You must be mistaken. You're going to have to turn around and head back."

"No mistake. I know who I am and I know where my horse is. It's you boys who are confused."

"I'm sorry, sir, but we can't let you in."

"If I get out of this truck, believe me, you won't have to. I'll do it myself."

As if on cue, a Jeep Wrangler scrambled out from behind a stand of trees. The driver slammed the brakes just short of the gate, kicking up a cloud of dust. Then a man who looked to be in his forties, dressed the same as the two guards—including the Kydex-holstered Glock on one hip—jumped out of the Jeep, marched through the guard shack, and approached the vehicle.

Nice response time, Redd thought. *I guess those cameras aren't just for show.*

"Is there a problem here?" the older man asked the first guard.

"This gentleman says he's here to pick up a horse. But there's no horse pickup on the schedule and his name isn't on today's roster."

The supervisor shot a hard glance at Redd, sizing him up quickly. "That true, sir? You're here for a horse?"

"Yes, sir."

"Then why aren't you on the roster?"

"Didn't know there was a roster. Didn't know I was supposed to call ahead. Deputy Hepworth said I could just run up here and fetch him."

"Your name, sir?"

"Redd. With two *d*'s."

The supervisor pulled a cell phone out of his phone holster and placed a call. "Sorry to bother you. There's a gentleman here, last name Redd.

Says he's here to pick up a horse? He's not on the roster—yes, of course. Right away."

Interesting, Redd thought. *Wyatt Gage knows my name.*

The supervisor snapped his phone back into its holster and pointed at the second guard. "Open the gate and let him in." He turned to Redd. "Sorry for the confusion. Mr. Gage likes his privacy."

Redd returned a terse nod, then turned his eyes forward, watching as the supervisor moved his Jeep while the guards opened the gate. Redd pulled through the gate and pointed the old Ford at the hill looming in the distance. The trailer behind him bounced on the cattle guard, its ancient leaf springs screeching with the effort. In the rearview mirror, he saw the three security men watching his every move.

✖ ✖ ✖

Redd crested the hill, his window down, taking in the smell of pine that filled the air. From the top, he could see the Crazy Mountains off in the distance, tipped with snow and stark against the azure blue of the Big Sky. What he'd taken for granted as a boy now stunned him as if he'd never been here before. He loved SoCal beaches, but these mountains called to the depths of his soul.

Redd didn't need to be told to follow the track left to the horse barn because the two-story structure stood tall and broad in the middle of acres of emerald grass ringed by fresh-cut split rail fencing. A dozen thorough-bred horses grazed beneath the postcard mountain sky.

You could fit two of J. B.'s ranch houses inside that thing, Redd thought, as he neared the barn. *Maybe three.*

It was obviously new construction, but it was well-done and fit right in with the log cabin aesthetic common to the area. On the hill rising far behind the horse barn, he saw a massive, modern-looking log cabin, though *cabin* didn't seem like the right word for the three-story, glass-fronted residence. Not far from it stood a matching but smaller residence. Another Jeep Wrangler was parked in front of the big house and another security guard was posted on the porch, a long gun in his hand.

Interesting.

Redd swung his rig around and backed the trailer up to the only open barn door. He put the truck in park, hopped out, and headed for the interior. He noted the security cameras over the doorways and on the lampposts.

Stepping into the cool, dark barn brought the familiar smells of sweet hay, old leather, and horse crap. His eyes took a moment to adjust, but when they did, he spotted Remington, J. B.'s dappled gray quarter horse.

Recognition brought with it a flood of memories. He remembered the day J. B. had brought the horse home, purchased at auction from a rancher who had been forced to downsize during the recession of the late 2000s. J. B. had owned three other horses back then, but Remington had always been Redd's favorite, maybe because they were both relative newcomers.

He had ridden Remington over nearly every square foot of J. B.'s spread, running down strays and checking the fence line for breaks. Remington had always been an even-tempered creature. Redd could not remember a single instance where the horse had been jittery, much less spooked by anything, but that had been many years ago. Remington had been eleven back when J. B. had acquired him, still relatively young as horse life spans were reckoned. Now, at twenty-four, the horse was entering into his twilight years.

But as Redd approached, he saw a horse standing tall and proud in the center aisle between a long row of stalls occupied by a dozen magnificent thoroughbreds, their heads peering out over their gates like a jealous audience to the grooming the visiting gelding was receiving.

Redd's attention was drawn to the groomer.

She was five-foot-ten, with long blonde hair quilted in a thick French braid that reached between her shoulders. She wore no makeup, at least not that he could tell, and was attired in old jeans, dirty ropers, and a T-shirt, which fit quite nicely. The finely toned muscles of her bare arms flashed as she brushed Remington's dappled steel-gray-and-brown coat with loving care. She was, Redd thought, achingly beautiful, and for a few seconds, all he could do was stare.

Then he recalled what had happened the last time he'd allowed himself to be distracted by a beautiful woman, and with an effort, he tore his gaze away from her and focused on Remington.

He made a nickering sound. Remington's head bolted up, awakening from his trance. He sniffed the air, nickering in return, and when he spotted Redd, he began moving toward him. The woman turned as Remington moved, and when she beheld him, her smile lit up like a mountain sunrise.

Remington trotted over to Redd and leaned his head down. Redd wrapped his hands around the velvet soft ears. "So you remember me, do ya?"

"You must be Matty, Jim Bob's son?" She extended a strong right hand, her brush still in the left.

Redd winced but accepted the hand, noting the strong grip. "My friends call me Matt."

That wasn't actually true. What few men he had counted as true friends always called him Redd, following military custom. Of course, he wasn't in the military anymore, and every one of those friends was dead.

"Oh, I'm sorry. Jim Bob always called you Matty." She held his grip a little longer than he expected before letting go. "Okay. Matt it is."

Redd tried to relax his face, but he couldn't bring himself to smile. He'd gone through too much in the last few days. "I didn't catch your name."

Her dark-blue eyes sparkled with amusement. "It's Hannah."

He nodded to her as if tipping an invisible hat. "Hannah. Pleased to meet you. Thanks for tending to Remington."

As if responding to the sound of his name, the horse nuzzled Redd's chest with his massive head, snorting. Redd pulled a rubbery carrot out of his pocket and offered it. "Hey, sport. What are you up to? Huh?"

The horse's teeth immediately latched on.

"Remi's a magnificent animal," Hannah said. "One of the smartest horses I've ever known."

"I appreciate you watching out for him."

"Of course. It was the least I could do. Jim Bob and I rode together a few times. We shared a love of animals, especially horses. I know how much he loved Remi."

Redd had difficulty imagining J. B. letting someone else into his life, even a beautiful young woman.

Especially a beautiful young woman.

"Nice spread you got up here," he said, trying to change the subject. "Used to be the Jacoby place."

She smiled and shrugged. "I'm afraid I don't know anything about that. My brother, Wyatt, handled all those details. I just take care of the animals."

Brother?

"Speaking of that," Redd said, trying not to think about the fact that he was conversing with one of the richest women on earth. "How did you end up with Remington?"

Hannah waved dismissively. "Deputy Hepworth called as soon as he found Jim Bob. It was so sad. Remi was just standing there, like a loyal watchdog."

Redd recalled Hepworth saying almost exactly the same thing. "So you came and got him?"

She nodded. "He—the deputy, I mean—couldn't leave the scene until the medical examiner arrived. He knew that Jim Bob and I were friends, and I was happy to help. I came right over."

"Where's his tack?"

Hannah's forehead creased in consternation for just a moment but then was smooth porcelain again. "Oh, I left everything in Jim Bob's barn. It didn't make sense to drag it all the way over here." She smiled. "When they weren't able to get in touch with you, I figured maybe we'd have to give Remi a new home with us."

Redd felt the old familiar guilt flush in his cheeks. "Well, I'm here now. And I really should get going. I've got things to attend to." He patted his thigh, coaxing Remington to follow. "You ready to go home, boy?"

The horse complied without any additional goading. Hannah walked alongside them as if reluctant to let the encounter end. To fill the silence, Redd asked, "What do I owe you for boarding him?"

Hannah laughed. "Don't be silly, Matt. It was my pleasure. In fact, I'd be happy to keep him a few more days. Or . . ." She hesitated a moment. "I don't want to speak out of turn, but what are your plans for him? If you're going to put him up for sale, I'll make you an offer right now."

"Sale?"

"Or I'd be happy to board him here for you, as long as you'd like."

"I'm not selling him."

Her perfect eyebrows came up. "I'm so sorry. I just assumed . . . Jim Bob told me that you've got a career with the Marines. I just assumed that you'd have to get back to that. I mean, you can't very well take care of a horse if you're off in Afghanistan or wherever." She stroked Remington's neck as if to soften the impact of the statement, but Redd felt it slam into him nevertheless.

You left. You weren't here when he needed you. I was.

"He thought the world of you," she was saying. "He was so proud. He knew how important your service was to you."

"To tell you the truth, things are kind of up in the air right now."

She laid a hand on his forearm. "Matt, I'm so terribly sorry for your loss."

"Thanks."

"If you ever need to talk about it, I'm a pretty good listener." She reached into her pocket and pulled out her business card.

Gage Wildlife Conservancy
Hannah Gage, President

"Do you have a pen?"

Redd dug the stub of a pencil from one pocket. Carrying writing materials at all times had been drilled into his head in boot camp. Memory was not to be trusted, not when your life might depend on the accuracy of a set of coordinates or knowing the digits of a secure radio frequency.

Hannah scribbled a phone number on the back of the card and then handed both pencil and card to Redd. "That's my private cell number. Call me if you need anything, okay?"

Redd pocketed the card into his dirty jeans. He had no interest in pouring his feelings out to Hannah Gage or anyone else, and while he felt an almost-primal attraction to the woman standing before him, he knew better than to let himself indulge in those feelings. She was part of a world he could never comprehend, one he wanted nothing to do with. The real world wasn't some fairy tale where the princess and the huntsman lived happily ever after.

And there was a very real possibility that Hannah Gage's brother was somehow involved in J. B.'s death.

"That's neighborly of you," he said equivocally. "I'll keep it in mind."

"I don't know what I'd do if I lost my father," she went on, either not picking up on his attempt to disengage or simply refusing to accept it. "I just can't imagine."

"I've read about your father," Redd said as he continued coaxing Remington into the trailer. "I mean, who hasn't? Everything they say about him true?"

Hannah smiled. "I'm the luckiest girl in the world to be the daughter of a man who cares so deeply for the environment. Everybody knows my dad made his billions in the tech industry, but not as many people know his work on behalf of the planet. He spends his fortune on humanitarian issues and food security. That's why he wanted a place here in Montana."

"Food security?" Redd asked, curious despite himself. He wasn't sure why she was still talking to him, much less why she felt the need to defend her father's reputation from some unspecific accusation.

"There will be nearly 10 billion people on this planet by 2050, and most of them will be hungry. My father founded the Gage Food Trust to end world hunger. And you know what? He's going to do it."

"I can see why you're so proud of him." Redd stepped up into the trailer and Remington followed. Redd patted him on the neck. "Good boy."

He stepped out, then closed and secured the gate. "Well, I best be on my way. Thanks again."

Hannah just gazed back at him with a *Mona Lisa* smile, then brightened as if struck by a revelation and darted back into the barn. Redd shook his head and turned away, but as he reached for the door handle, something heavy thumped into the bed of the truck. The noise startled him. He whirled around and saw a bale of hay resting in the truck's bed and Hannah Gage brushing flakes of grass off her jeans with her gloved hands.

"When I was stowing Remi's tack, I noticed that your hayloft is empty as a banker's heart. That should hold you over until you restock."

Redd was genuinely grateful. "Thank you, Ms. Gage."

"It's Hannah, remember?" She flashed a smile that made him question his resolve.

He nodded. "Hannah."

"You know, now that I think about it, maybe you do owe me for boarding Remi. How about you buy me a coffee sometime and we'll call it square."

"Something tells me you're not the kind of person who takes no for an answer."

She grinned. "See, you're already getting to know me."

✖   ✖   ✖

Redd tapped the old Ford's brakes as he approached the main gate. One of the security guards he'd met earlier was leaning next to the driver's side of a black Range Rover, speaking with the driver, his face hidden by the windshield's glare. The other guard entered the shack to open the gate.

The first guard glanced up from the Range Rover and pointed at the Ford as Redd pulled to a stop. The driver's door opened just as Redd pulled through the gate and stopped.

The driver was six feet tall, narrow-hipped, and wide-shouldered. He affected what he must have thought was a cowboy look, but his designer jeans were creased and his boots polished to a high gloss. He was clean-shaven, dark-haired, and was, Redd supposed, handsome in the way movie stars and male models were. His eyes were the same sapphire hue as Hannah's, and Redd realized that he was looking at none other than Wyatt Gage himself.

But it was the monster that emerged from the Range Rover's passenger door that really caught Redd's eye. The man was so big he looked like Andre the Giant climbing out of a Mini Cooper. His face was hard, round, and flat as a cast-iron skillet, and his massive chest filled out a Montana State University T-shirt with the Bobcat logo on the front, and a matching ball cap sat on his big, balloon-shaped head. The doughy features looked Slavic to Redd, putting him in mind of a Russian mob enforcer, but his black eyes focused on Redd like targeting lasers.

Redd recalled Sheriff Blackwood's account of J. B.'s death. *"Landed wrong and broke his neck."*

A guy like that could break someone's neck like he was swatting a fly, he thought.

"Are you Matthew Redd?" called out the man Redd assumed to be Hannah's brother. He approached, his hand extended. "I'm Wyatt Gage."

Redd fought to maintain a neutral expression as he accepted the handclasp.

Wyatt's grip was solid but not insistent, and after a couple of quick pumps, he let go and nodded at the horse trailer. "Is that old Remington in there? Good horse, according to my sister. And she knows horses."

Redd nodded. "Taking him back home. I appreciate you folks watching after him."

"Anything for Jim Bob. He was a proud man, stood his ground. I admired him for that."

Wyatt paused as if waiting for Redd to acknowledge what must have seemed like a compliment, then went on. "I know you've got a lot on your mind right now, but we should have a drink. My treat. Drop by Spady's for happy hour and let me talk to you about a big opportunity." He spoke with the confidence of someone used to getting his way.

Just like Hannah, Redd thought.

"I'll think about it," Redd replied. "Like you said, I've got a lot going on. Thanks again for taking care of my dad's horse."

Wyatt smiled. "Anything for old Jim Bob. But seriously. Call me." He dipped a hand into his pocket and brought out a business card embossed with the logo of Gage Land Development.

Redd took the card and dropped it in a shirt pocket, then put the truck in gear and hit the gas. In the mirror, he saw the big Slav's eyes tracking him as he pulled away.

TWENTY-TWO

Hannah Gage had not been wrong about J. B.'s hayloft. There was maybe a week's worth of loose grass and alfalfa scattered around. Redd wondered how J. B. could have let things get to that point. He would have to make a trip to the feedstore soon, but that could wait until he had a better idea of what he was going to do with the rest of his life. He could not think much past finding J. B.'s killer.

During his teen years, it had only ever been him and J. B. at the ranch, yet it had never felt like a lonely existence. Now that the old man was gone, however, it was too quiet.

After putting Remington in the stall and scattering some of the hay Hannah had provided, Redd stuck his head into the tack stall. Remington's saddle rested astride an old wooden sawhorse, and his bridle hung from a peg on the wall. Redd ran his hands over the saddle, noting the empty scabbard that usually held J. B.'s Henry rifle. Hannah had not mentioned putting the rifle away in the house, nor had Shane Hepworth mentioned J. B.'s guns when talking about entering the house to find Redd's contact information. These omissions were conspicuous to Redd because he knew that J. B. would not have ridden out on the trail without the Henry in the saddle scabbard and his Ruger on his hip.

One more thing that just doesn't add up.

Switching gears, Redd turned his thoughts to the Gage family. He knew he had not heard the last of Wyatt Gage. The man's first impulse would be to use his wealth to get what he wanted. If Redd refused his offer, then he would turn to strong-arm tactics.

Like siccing his big brute bodyguard on me.

If he was right about Wyatt ordering J. B.'s death, then a showdown was inevitable. And while J. B. had raised him to never back down, the Marine Corps had taught him the importance of decisive action.

Happy hour at Spady's. That would be something new.

But first, he had some work to do.

✖ ✖ ✖

After a quick bite to eat—a can of Bush's baked beans, which he ate without heating—he returned to the barn and saddled Remington. Despite the passage of time, he still recalled all the lessons J. B. had taught him—how to set the bridle, how tight to cinch the saddle. Remington stood by patiently, knowing what was expected of him, and when the process was finished, Redd rewarded him with a couple sugar cubes.

After a final check of the saddle strap, Redd stuck the toe of his boot into the left stirrup, rested a steadying hand on the saddle horn, and stepped up, throwing his right leg up and over. It was a move he had done hundreds of times as a teenager, but he wasn't that person anymore. He had experienced a final growth spurt in his early twenties, and his muscle memory for mounting a horse was calibrated to someone smaller. His right foot dragged across the saddle and he almost didn't make it over. Any other horse might have reacted by trying to throw him, but Remington endured the discomfort until Redd was finally able to get his leg over and balance his weight. He let out a sigh of relief when he was finally astride. Riding a horse wasn't like riding a bike; it was a perishable skill, and he was rusty.

He had trouble keeping the toes of his Danners—the only footwear he'd brought up from California—in the stirrups. There was a reason cowboy boots had pointed toes, but his old ropers were about two sizes too small now.

Even something as simple as coaxing Remington forward by squeezing his thighs together felt completely alien—a skill he had to relearn. Still, after a little trial and error, it came back to him, and soon he was sitting easy in the saddle and letting Remington do most of the work.

He had J. B.'s Magnum holstered to his hip and the Henry in the scabbard. Both were loaded with HSM Bear Load bullets. J. B. only ever loaded Hunting Shack ammo because HSM was a reliable, veteran-owned Montana company.

Back when he taught Redd how to shoot, J. B. had warned him that Bear Load *"kicked like a mule,"* especially the Magnum round for revolver, and that it would *"put the hurt on him"* if he didn't handle it the way he'd been taught. But young Matty Redd had his own way of learning—from his mistakes.

Redd could still remember raising the Henry up to shoot and wrapping his finger around the hair-set trigger before the stock was snugged into the pocket of his shoulder. The Henry had bucked. The blue-steel barrel had cracked Redd in the face, and the recoil knocked him off-balance, dropping his skinny, twelve-year-old butt into the dirt.

"Always the kid who had to touch the burner for himself just to see how hot it was," J. B. used to say.

Redd absentmindedly rubbed the thin scar cutting through his left eyebrow. It had hurt like no other when it split open, and he'd bled like a stuck pig. J. B. cleaned him up and taped it shut as Redd fought back tears.

A good lesson for a young boy, he thought, smiling at the memory. He never made that mistake again.

Redd led Remington across the pasture behind the house and found the overgrown two-track that cut across the ranch and eventually snaked up the mountain that bordered it to the east. He could see where the grass had been flattened by recent traffic—Deputy Hepworth's patrol vehicle.

The trail plunged into the woods, and Redd found himself surrounded by lodgepole pines and memories. The upturned petals of bright-yellow avalanche lilies waved in the whispering breeze.

Remington stopped to drink from the fingerling creek that ran a crooked track down the mountain, a sluice of cold water now brimming with snowmelt that ran most of the year. After a few minutes, and without any coaxing from his rider, the horse resumed his unhurried trek up the gentle incline.

A little ways farther along, the track opened up to a clearing on the right—one of several pastures where J. B. used to graze his cattle as he rotated them around the property.

Remington stopped in his tracks. Knowing better than to question his mount's instincts, Redd glanced around, looking for the cause of Remington's unease, but neither saw nor heard anything, save for the cool wind rustling the trees.

Remington lowered his big head and nibbled the pasture grass on the side of the trail.

Redd laughed. "Snack time? Seriously?"

But then his eye was drawn to the trail, just up ahead. About twenty yards in, the grooves left by Hepworth's four-wheel-drive vehicle abruptly ended, leaving four deep depressions where the rig had probably sat idle for a while.

Redd dismounted and moved ahead on foot. There wasn't any crime scene tape or anything else to mark the area—just a lot of boot and hoofprints stamped into the ground. Then Redd's gaze fell upon a large, sharp stone half-buried in the dirt like an iceberg, the tip pointing upward. There was a black stain on the gray rock. Redd knelt down, brushing his fingertips against the rock. The black substance flaked away. Dried blood.

J. B.'s blood.

Remington raised his head suddenly, still chewing. Redd looked up at him, tracking Remington's eyes. The horse was shifting nervously, his attention rooted on something off to the side of the trail. Redd did not immediately see what it was, but a moment later, he heard the distinctive crackle of a rattlesnake's tail.

Redd felt adrenaline dump into his bloodstream. He was no stranger to rattlers, but that didn't make him take them any less seriously. The noise helped him fix the snake's location—about ten feet away—which gave him time to stand, back away, and draw the Ruger. Now he could see the serpent, a five-foot-long prairie rattler, coiled and thrashing its warning.

Redd put the front blade of the Ruger's sight on the viper's triangular head but then hesitated. The snake wasn't a threat. It just wanted to be left alone. Redd could sympathize.

Back when he and J. B. had been running the ranch together, he wouldn't have thought twice about killing the rattler. Snakes were a danger to both humans and livestock. Let one live, and tomorrow you might lose a steer or get bit or have your horse spooked out from under you . . .

Had it been as simple as that? Was he being paranoid, looking for crazy conspiracies to explain why J. B. had been taken and refusing to accept the simplest explanation for his death?

Redd shook his head. He didn't want that to be true, but *why* didn't he? Was it because he really believed someone had murdered J. B., or was it his guilt over not being there for the old man?

But J. B. had called him.

"Trouble's come knocking . . ."

Redd lowered the Ruger a few degrees, aiming at the ground in front of the snake, and pulled the trigger. The heavy Magnum bullet punched the ground, and the snake wriggled away as if it had been scalded.

Redd wasn't wearing ear protection, and the report felt like a hammer blow to his eardrums. A high-pitched whine filled his ears.

A few steps away, Remington shook his head violently. The gun blast hurt his ears, too.

But he hadn't bolted. Not at the gunshots. Not at the rattler.

Redd took a step toward Remington. The horse shuffled sideways a step, uncertainly. Redd holstered the revolver. "There, there, boy. Sorry about the noise." He patted Remington on the neck. "That was stupid of me, wasn't it? Now we're both deaf as stones."

He cooed and rubbed Remington behind his ears until he felt the animal's tense muscles relax.

"You didn't throw him, did you?"

Remington nickered and shook his head. Redd knew the horse wasn't really answering him, but it felt like confirmation.

He spent the next hour tramping around the area on foot but did not find J. B.'s iPhone. He hadn't expected to, but that wasn't the point. The more he thought about it, the more convinced he was that someone killed J. B. and dumped the phone. He still didn't know why, but as he mounted Remington and headed back to the barn, he promised himself and the old horse that he would find out.

TWENTY-THREE

Spady's was hopping when Redd pulled his Raptor into the lot and cruised the length of it, looking for a place to park. Two dozen battered pickups stood door-to-door with each other along the row except near the front entrance, where a familiar black Range Rover sat with about fifteen feet of unused space to either side. As Redd rolled by, he saw the two Reserved signs, with the Range Rover parked on the line separating them. There was a third reserved spot, empty.

"Reserved." Redd spat the word like a curse. Even if Wyatt Gage had nothing to do with J. B.'s death, he deserved to have his bell rung at least once.

Rich idiot.

Redd backed the Raptor in next to the Range Rover, getting as close as he could to the passenger side without hitting it, then hopped out and headed for the door.

✖ ✖ ✖

Redd hadn't been to Spady's since J. B. brought him here the night before he left for boot camp. Old man Spady had fought with the 101st Airborne at Hamburger Hill in '69, and even though Redd had only been eighteen, Spady had closed the place early so that the three of them could hoist a few shots of Wild Turkey. They drank to friends lost and, in Redd's case, to the good things to come.

The place had changed since then. It was bigger than he remembered, and refurbished. The hundred-year-old dark mahogany bar was still in place but refinished. The barstools were brand-new, replacing the old ones that had been duct-taped where they had split over the years.

The main dining room was packed, mostly locals judging by the trucks outside and the flannel shirts inside, but a few wore the wide-eyed look of tourists wanting to experience local color. Over the din of hungry, chatty diners, classic country music blared on the jukebox and billiard balls clacked in the lounge out back. Wyatt Gage and his guard dog were not in evidence.

Redd spotted an empty slot at the end of the bar and hurried to claim it.

One of the two bartenders ambled over. He was dressed like Redd in a clean work shirt and jeans, mid- to late thirties, judging by the dusting of silver in his beard. His smile seemed genuine enough. "What'll ya have?"

"What's local on tap?"

"Bozone Amber Ale's pretty good."

"One of those."

The man's smile turned to a curious frown.

"Is there a problem?" Redd asked.

"You seem familiar. You wouldn't be Jim Bob Thompson's boy, would you?"

Redd nodded. "I am. Have we met?"

"No, we haven't. But Jim Bob showed me your picture a couple of times. He was right proud of you. My name's Jarrod." He stuck out his hand. Redd took it. "Sorry for your loss."

"Thanks."

"Heck of a thing. I just saw him last week not too long before, well, you know." Jarrod got embarrassed. "Let me grab you that brew."

As Jarrod moved down to the tap handles, Redd scanned the room again. A lot of older guys with their wives. Some of them he recognized. He hoped they didn't see him. He wasn't here for condolences.

His head swiveled in the other direction, and he at last caught sight of Wyatt Gage. The land developer looked like a prince holding court at a large, round table in the back lounge—no doubt reserved just for him. His arms were stretched out wide along the tops of the chairs next to him like he owned the place, along with the two beautiful blondes who occupied the chairs. A third young woman, a brunette, sat on the other side of one of the blondes. All wore tight-fitting cocktail dresses that looked to be painted on their firm bodies. They were laughing at something he'd said.

Jarrod showed up with a pint glass full of dark ale and a rocks glass half-full of whiskey. "Here ya go, Mr. Redd. On the house, in honor of your dad. He was a good man."

Redd raised the bourbon. "To J. B." He took a sip, savoring it, then asked, "How's old man Spady doing?"

Jarrod shook his head. "Drunk driver took him last year."

"That's too bad. Who's running the place now?"

"Corporate outfit from Bozeman."

Redd's frown was automatic. "Corporate?"

Jarrod grinned. "I know, but they ain't so bad. Spent a ton a money on the place. Making repairs and improvements."

Redd thought about the Reserved signs out front. He had a pretty good idea who was behind the corporate takeover. He glanced back over at Wyatt's table. "Say, is that Wyatt Gage back there? The billionaire's son?"

Jarrod chuckled. "Sure is. He's tight with the new owner. A nice enough fella once you get to know him. A good tipper, too."

"He looks like a privileged, pampered idiot." Redd took a long sip of beer.

"The smart play is to stay on his good side. He can make things happen."

"Smart is overrated, Jarrod." Redd chugged the rest of his beer down and pushed away from the bar. He tossed a crumpled five-dollar bill on top. "Thanks for the drink," he said and started toward the lounge.

Jarrod hurried around the end of the bar to head him off. "I wouldn't mess with him if I were you. He's not alone." Jarrod nodded toward the back of the dining room, where Gage's skillet-faced pet monster was hovering near the men's room doorway, black eyes scanning the room, searching for threats. The big man wore the same MSU Bobcat T-shirt as this morning but without the ball cap, revealing a shaved head. Even from where he sat, Redd could see the deep scars cut into his scalp.

"That's one big, ugly gorilla," Redd said.

"I saw him mop the floor with a half-dozen ranch hands one night trying to get frisky with one of Wyatt's ladies. It was like a John Wayne movie in here. Wyatt was good enough to pay for the medical bills of the boys his goon beat up."

"What's the goon's name?"

"Shev-something. Shevchenko, I think. Russian, I guess."

"Ukrainian," Redd corrected. It was something he'd picked up during his time in the military. He wasn't fluent in anything but English, but he'd been trained to recognize a number of different languages and was well versed in surnames as well.

Jarrod shrugged as if he didn't really understand the difference. "Best to just steer clear of him."

One of Wyatt's long-legged female friends got up and crossed the length of the room, heading for the jukebox. Her tight dress hugged her ample curves, inching up her thigh with each step. Every man's head turned as she passed by, and half the women too. By the look on her face, she not only knew she was the center of attention, she relished it.

She bent over the jukebox, giving even more display of her ample wares as she studied the play selection. Satisfied, she stood, slid the credit card in her long-nailed hand into the pay slot. She punched out several selections and marched back like a runway model to Wyatt's table.

Redd's eyes tracked the woman as she resumed her place beneath Wyatt's outstretched arm. Wyatt caught his eye and shot Redd a wink and a smile, then waved him over.

Redd had stormed enemy positions, cleared houses filled with hostile insurgents, moved under fire, but as he strode across the floor of Spady's lounge toward Wyatt Gage and his bunnies, he felt as if he was going into battle unarmed and naked. He could handle combat, but this was an infinitely more dangerous fight.

"You made it," Wyatt called out. He did not rise or offer another handshake. "I was hoping you would. As you can see, I found some friends to make it a party." He rattled off the girls' names. Redd made no effort to remember them.

"You mentioned an opportunity," Redd replied. He pulled out a chair on the opposite side of the table and settled into it. "I figured you wanted to talk business."

"I mix business with pleasure whenever I can." Wyatt waved to a waitress who had been hovering near the end of the table. "A drink for my friend Matty here. Whatever he wants."

Redd locked eyes with Wyatt. "It's just Matt." The declaration was simple enough, but it burned in the air like dry ice. He glanced at the server. "I'll have a Coke, please."

She cast a quick, nervous glance at Wyatt, as if she feared she had done something wrong, but then nodded. "Coming right up."

Wyatt's grin had slipped, but only a little. "Bring him a shot with that," he called out. "Jack, I think." He eyed Redd across the table. "You look like a Jack Daniel's man."

As the server hurried off, Wyatt said, "My sister told me about the name thing. Sorry. No offense."

"If none was intended," Redd said easily, "then none taken."

Wyatt laughed as if Redd's comment was just about the funniest thing he'd ever heard. The girls chorused in. "How long will you be in town?" he said as the mirth finally trailed off.

"Long as it takes."

Just then the waitress reappeared with a tray full of drinks. She passed Wyatt a pint and a shot glass, then set a tall red plastic tumbler full of ice and soda in front of Redd, along with another shot glass containing the whiskey Redd had not ordered. Lastly, she passed out three cocktail glasses, each with some kind of syrupy fruit concoction for the girls.

Wyatt picked up his shot glass. "It's bad luck to drink a toast without booze." He raised the glass. "To Jim Bob Thompson, last of the true cowboys."

Almost exactly the same words Shane Hepworth used, Redd noted.

Wyatt tossed back his shot in a gulp. Redd tossed his as well.

"I bet you hunt," Wyatt said, picking up his beer.

"I have."

"I've got a gun range up at the house. You're welcome to come over anytime. I've got ARs and AKs. And one of the best sporting clays setups you've ever seen."

"No disrespect, but I'm not exactly in a sporting mood these days." Redd took a sip from the Coke. He had a feeling he was going to need a clear head to get through this evening. "Besides, the last moving targets I shot at had two legs and skinny beards."

Wyatt gave another uproarious laugh. "Oorah! Marines!" He hoisted his beer glass for Redd to toast. Redd left him hanging. Wyatt just shook his head and took another swallow.

"Well, to business then," Wyatt went on. "I wanted to talk to you about your place."

"What's to talk about?"

"I thought someone might have told you." Wyatt flashed his winning smile. "I'd like to buy it."

"I'm not sure I'd like to sell it."

"You might want to hear my offer before you turn it down."

Redd shrugged. "Okay. What's the offer?"

"I'll pay you double the market value. Let's shake hands on it right now, and you'll be a multimillionaire and then some by this time tomorrow."

Redd kept his eyes on Wyatt. "Double, huh? Did you make that offer to J. B.?"

Wyatt's mouth twitched, but the smile came back. "Matt, I think we both know what a stubborn cuss your father was. I could have offered him five times what it was worth, and he'd still have spit in my eye."

Redd raised an eyebrow as if giving this serious consideration. "Five times. Now that might get my attention."

"Double fair market value," Wyatt said, and this time he wasn't even pretending to smile. "All cash, no inspection, quick close. In fact, I'll cut you a check right now if you're ready to do the deal. And I'll give you thirty days to gather up whatever you want—or hey, take as long as you need. Rent free, of course. I'll even cover the utilities. You won't get an offer this good. Ever."

Redd took another sip of Coke. He glanced over at the big bodyguard, Shevchenko, who despite his dull affect seemed to be intensely interested in the discussion. When he noticed Redd's scrutiny, the big man uncrossed his tree trunk arms, as if moving into an alert posture.

Redd turned back to Wyatt. "I haven't been in town forty-eight hours and I've been told at least three times that you want to buy my place."

"People know I'm in the market for good properties."

"Good property? The place is a wreck, and there are liens against it."

Wyatt's smile came back, albeit noticeably dimmer. "Yeah, you're right. It's kind of a dump. Jim Bob owed money all over town. He really let the place go. Frankly, I'm doing you a favor."

"Seriously, why do you want the place?"

"We want what we want, right? And when you've got as much money as I have, you usually get what you want. So last chance . . . Double, take it or leave it."

Redd sat up straight and leaned forward, both hands flat on the table as if he was about to hurl himself at Wyatt. "Listen, Wyatt. At a time like this, I have to think, what would J. B. do? I think he'd tell you to take your money and shove it up your—"

In his peripheral vision he saw Shevchenko lurch into motion, marching in his direction.

Wyatt raised a hand, freezing Shevchenko in his tracks.

Redd smiled. "Nice trick."

"Roman tends to overreact when it comes to my security," Wyatt said. "But it's what I pay him for."

"Can you make him roll over too?"

"You're a funny guy, Matty. Take my advice. Don't piss him off. His bite really is far worse than his bark."

Redd glanced back at Shevchenko. Hate radiated off the bodyguard like heat waves. "He doesn't look that tough—or that bright."

"Roman's English is better than yours. So is his German, Spanish, and Mandarin."

"If I ever need a grammar lesson, maybe I'll give him a call."

Wyatt leaned back in his chair. Without looking, he made a dismissive gesture, and the three girls promptly vanished, leaving their half-finished drinks behind. Wyatt stared across the table for a few seconds, then said, "Look, I've obviously offended you. My timing is terrible. Let's talk about this later next week. You have my card."

"No need to talk. I'm not selling you his place."

Wyatt snorted. "You've got no more sense than your old man, do you?"

"I wish I was half the man he was. If you made him the same offer you just made me, then I know he *really* didn't want to sell it to you." Redd stood up. From the corner of his eye, he saw Shevchenko bunched up like the Incredible Hulk about to bust out of his shirt.

Wyatt held his stare. "You're going to regret this, Redd."

"I promise you I won't," Redd said as he got up to leave. He glanced at Shevchenko. "And make sure you keep your animals off my land."

TWENTY-FOUR

Outside, the night air felt good on Redd's face. Not cold enough to freeze but cool enough to remind him it wasn't summer yet. As he walked through the parking lot, enjoying the soft breeze, he took a moment to assess the results of his confrontation with Wyatt Gage.

There wasn't a doubt in his mind that Wyatt was responsible for J. B.'s death, but Wyatt's parting threat fell just short of an admission of guilt. The real proof would come in the form of direct action, which meant the next move would be Wyatt's. Would he, as he suggested, wait a few days before restating his offer in hopes that Redd would come to his senses? Or would he use the interval to begin planning for Redd's eventual "accident"?

Redd hated playing defense, waiting for the enemy to initiate contact, but for the time being, it was the only play he had.

The attack came a lot sooner than expected.

Redd was just reaching for the Raptor's door handle when something that felt like a falling tree trunk slammed into his back. The force of the impact crushed him against the door and sent his keys flying from suddenly nerveless fingers. His chin hit the window first, then turned so that his right cheek was jammed against the glass. The rest of his body was driven into the door so hard that the panel buckled inward with an audible *pop*. Redd could taste blood in his mouth, but in that instant, he felt no pain—just the pressure of whatever had hit him holding him pinned against the side of the truck.

A voice hissed in his ear, "You stupid cowboy. How dare you speak to Mr. Gage like that!"

There was no mistaking the Slavic accent.

Shevchenko.

Redd was a little dismayed by the fact that Wyatt's bodyguard had been able to sneak up on him. It seemed impossible that the big man could have moved so quickly, so quietly.

Was I that distracted?

He didn't think so.

It took only a second for the initial shock of the surprise attack to wear off. Shevchenko had essentially bodychecked him into the truck, and while the experience was by no means pain-free, it was far from the worst thing the Ukrainian could have done to him.

"Big mistake," Redd grated, the words distorted by the pressure of the glass against his cheek and the blood filling his mouth.

"Is that right?" Shevchenko retorted, spitting out a laugh. He leaned forward as if to squeeze Redd between the anvil that was the Raptor and the hammer that was his own body.

"Yep," Redd said, then planted his hands against the door of the truck and drove himself backward into the other man.

The Ukrainian might have outweighed him by fifty pounds . . . maybe even a hundred . . . but Redd could bench-press four hundred pounds, and unlike his opponent, he had something stable from which to push off.

He did not hold back one iota but put everything he had into the push. The Raptor rocked on its springs, but most of Redd's energy went straight into Shevchenko. The big man's first instinct was to plant his feet and resist, but the forcefulness of Redd's push, combined with the fact that he did *not* have a stable position, gave Redd the edge. Shevchenko started to topple backward. As soon as Redd's body peeled away from the truck, he brought his legs up quickly, flexing his knees and planting his boot soles against the stove-in door panel. Then he pushed off again, adding even more momentum to the maneuver. The combined mass of Shevchenko's upper body and Redd's thrust took the already-unbalanced bodyguard the rest of the way over.

At the last second, Shevchenko tried to throw his arms around Redd, but the latter was already two steps ahead of him. As his opponent fell back, Redd whipped his legs up and curled into a backward somersault, and in the instant that Shevchenko crashed down, Redd rolled over his face and came up on his feet in a fighting stance.

He spat a mouthful of blood on the gravel.

Astonishingly, Shevchenko was up almost as quickly, bounding back to his feet and spinning around for another charge. Redd saw what was coming and pivoted at the last second, grasped Shevchenko's outstretched left arm with both hands, and pulled him along, adding his own energy to the big man's considerable momentum. As the Ukrainian came even with him, Redd pulled the meaty arm across and down and then threw his hip into Shevchenko's side.

The other man should have gone pinwheeling into a judo throw, but instead it was Redd who suddenly found himself flying through the air.

What the—?

Redd slammed into the door of the Raptor again. His head bounced off the glass, and he saw stars. Before he could even begin to make sense of what had just happened, something that felt like a sledgehammer rammed into his kidney.

Redd grunted, trying not to cry out with the pain.

This just got real.

Shevchenko grabbed Redd's shoulders and spun him around like a top. Then his massive hands slammed into Redd's chest, pinning him against the truck.

Shevchenko leaned in close. "If you ever disrespect Mr. Gage like that again—even in your dreams—I will break you in half."

Redd used the only weapon he had left. He launched his forehead at Shevchenko's face, striking the big Ukrainian just above the bridge of his nose. Redd saw another flash of stars as he made contact and knew the hit had been solid. The headbutt should have dropped any man, even a monster as big as Shevchenko, but the pressure against Redd's chest barely eased.

Shevchenko shook off the stinger, then pulled back his massive right arm and drove it like a two-hundred-pound crossbow bolt into Redd's gut.

The door panel popped again as the energy of the blow traveled through Redd. Shevchenko stepped back to let him fall, and Redd doubled over, writhing on the ground. He had been in plenty of fights before and taken plenty of hard hits, but never anything like this. Shevchenko wasn't human.

As the boot started to swing forward, Redd twisted out of the strike path. His timing was perfect. Shevchenko had neither the time to check his kick nor to redirect his energy. Redd felt a whoosh as the boot streaked past his head, connecting with nothing but air.

And as Shevchenko's foot reached the end of its forward arc, with all his weight resting on his left leg, Redd rolled to the side, drew his knees up together, and then drove them out into the side of Shevchenko's left knee.

There was a satisfying pop—like the sound of a drumstick being torn from a roast chicken—and Shevchenko's leg folded under him. He went down hard, his big, round head the last thing to make contact with the ground. It bounced off the gravel surface of the parking lot like a basketball.

The sudden reversal, not to mention the fact that his breath had returned, gave Redd a much-needed boost. He rolled over onto all fours and threw himself at the Ukrainian, pummeling his exposed face with his fists. Shevchenko's head rocked back and forth under the assault, blood flying from mouth and nose. The withering assault stole away whatever animal fury Shevchenko had possessed. He was clearly beaten, dazed, possibly unconscious, and yet Redd did not relent.

But as Redd raised his fist for one more blow, a thunderclap detonated above him.

TWENTY-FIVE

Redd flinched at the sound of gunfire and looked up to find Jarrod the bartender standing over him, shotgun in hand, smoke curling from the barrel, which was pointed skyward. In the frozen moment that followed, Redd realized that a crowd had gathered in the parking lot and was watching the titanic struggle with rapt fascination.

"That's enough, Mr. Redd!" Jarrod said. He was shouting, probably because the shotgun blast had left him a little deafened, but there was a noticeable quaver in his voice. "You should clear on out now!"

Redd stared at him, then looked down at the unmoving form of Shevchenko. He wondered what it would take to kill the man. Could he do it with one more strike? That didn't seem likely—the Ukrainian was like a bull. And yet if he didn't finish this fight now, decisively, Shevchenko would be back with a vengeance.

Before he could reach a decision however, the matter was taken out of his hands. Jarrod swung the barrel of the shotgun down and pointed it directly at Redd.

"Jarrod." Redd's voice was low, unnaturally calm. "I think you know better than to point a gun at a man unless you intend to shoot him. Do you intend to shoot me?"

The bartender's face registered genuine shame as he moved the weapon away from Redd. "It's only rock salt load," he confessed. "But you need to move off. I can't have no trouble here."

Redd knew the window of opportunity had closed. He rocked back on his haunches, then rose to his feet. Darkness swelled at the edge of his vision—he'd stood up too fast—and he had to lean against the side of the truck to keep from blacking out. The pain arrived a moment later, pulsing through his body in waves.

On the ground, Shevchenko had begun to stir. His piggish black eyes fluttered open, darting to look first at Redd, then at the shotgun. Then, like some kind of fairy-tale gargoyle turning from stone to flesh, he slowly roused himself and shuffled toward the main entrance.

Redd stared at Jarrod, incredulous. "So I'm eighty-sixed, but he gets a free pass?"

"Please, Mr. Redd. Just go home."

Redd threw his hands up to signal that he was done listening. He retrieved his keys, moving slower than before so as not to aggravate his injuries, and got into the truck without another word.

As the Raptor roared to life, the crowd outside broke up and dispersed. A few moved deeper into the parking lot, searching for their own vehicles, but most headed back inside Spady's.

Redd curled his fingers around the steering wheel, squeezing as if it were Shevchenko's throat. Of course, there was no way he'd ever be able to get even his massive hands around the Ukrainian's thick neck.

No, the next time they faced off, Redd would be loaded for bear. *Literally.*

As he put the truck in gear and started forward, he thought about racing back up to the ranch, grabbing J. B.'s trusty Ruger, and then coming right back to take care of business.

What did it matter if he got arrested, sent away for life? His life was effectively over anyway. He'd let everyone down—his team, the corps, J. B. . . .

Emily.

So why hold back? What did he have to lose? If he could at least bring J. B.'s killer to justice—not the kind dispensed in the circus that was the American legal system, but real, rough justice . . . the cowboy way—then at least some part of his life would have meaning.

But even as his foot drove down on the accelerator, with all the amassed weight of his rage and guilt, Redd heard J. B.'s calm, deliberate voice whispering words of wisdom in his ear.

Three words to be exact.

Words that had guided him over the years in those moments when he was about to charge into a dangerous situation.

Words that had saved his life on missions while he was in the Raiders.

Words he trusted.

"Don't. Be. Stupid."

Not exactly Marcus Aurelius. But wisdom nonetheless.

Despite his righteous rage, self-justification, and wounded ego, J. B.'s three words had drilled down to the core issue.

He was being stupid.

Again.

Redd knew that he'd have to deal with the big Ukrainian sooner or later, but the truth of the matter was that he couldn't control the outcome. He could lose the fight or even get killed, and how would that serve the cause of justice?

When that showdown eventually came, and Redd knew it would, rage would not serve him well. He would need a cool head.

He eased off the accelerator and then pulled over onto the side of the road. He took a few deep breaths, then noticed a Rorschach-like smear on the window. The print he'd left when Shevchenko had slammed him into the door.

"Perfect," he muttered, recalling how the door panel had buckled with the impact. The thought of it almost reignited his rage afresh.

He got out to inspect the carnage. Dented, but at least the paint wasn't ruined.

He got out his phone and googled *body shop near me*. Back in California, he would have found half a dozen within a ten-mile radius, but out here, there was only one choice, unless he was prepared to drive to Bozeman or Helena.

Lawrence Auto & Body Repair.

"Perfect," he muttered again. He'd rather face down a dozen Ukrainians than approach old man Lawrence.

He was still pondering his options when he saw flashing blue police lights coming down the highway, heading away from town. He quickly got back inside the Raptor and closed the door to give the cop plenty of room to pass, but to his dismay, the patrol SUV slowed as it approached and then swooped in behind him, braking in a cloud of dust.

"What fresh hell is this?" Redd muttered as he watched the SUV's door pop open. He could now see the Stillwater County Sheriff's logo, reversed in his side mirror, but still easy to read. Then Sheriff Blackwood stepped out.

The sheriff pulled on his stained Stetson, shut his door, and ambled toward Redd's truck, the big .357 Smith & Wesson that had been hanging on his coatrack now pinned to his hip. Redd lowered the side window, then put his hands on the steering wheel at two and ten o'clock. Nothing made a rural LEO more nervous than to walk up to a window with a driver hiding his hands. Blackwood approached, his right hand flicking open the holster's thumb break as he passed the Raptor's rear bumper.

"Problem, Sheriff?" Redd asked as Blackwood peered into the cab.

The sheriff smoothed the ends of his bushy mustache with his left hand while the other remained on the butt of his sidearm. "You tell me, son."

"Was I speeding?"

Blackwood ignored the question. "Heard you had a couple drinks at Spady's."

Redd kept his expression neutral. "That's what people do there."

He braced himself for what he knew would follow. First, Blackwood would administer some kind of field sobriety test. Redd wasn't worried about that. He wasn't feeling even a slight buzz. A Breathalyzer, on the other hand, might tell a different story. Two shots and a pint of craft ale might just be enough to put him over the legal limit.

Blackwood, however, had something else in mind. "I heard you and Mr. Gage had words."

If Blackwood knew that, then he surely knew about the altercation with Shevchenko. He was a little surprised that someone had brought the law into it. That wasn't normally how things were handled in Wellington. At least, not in the Wellington he remembered.

"We had a few words," Redd admitted. "Sure hope words ain't been outlawed in Stillwater County."

"I don't need any new trouble around here," Blackwood said. "I got plenty enough as it is."

"I'm not looking for trouble."

Blackwood sighed as he pushed the brim of his Stetson further up on his head. "I got a feeling trouble comes looking for you."

Redd measured his words. "Sheriff, I came back here to bury my dad and settle his affairs."

"That a fact? And do you reckon on selling his place?"

Redd held the other man's gaze and spoke slowly. "I haven't made up my mind."

Blackwood leaned in closer as if worried they might be overheard. He looked tired but sober. Even concerned. "Gage and his posse are nobody to mess around with. You hear me, son?"

Ten minutes earlier, Redd would have countered with *I'm nobody to mess around with either.* But that would have been a stupid thing to say.

"Don't. Be. Stupid."

"Heard, understood, and acknowledged, Sheriff."

"Good." He patted Redd's door with a couple of quick taps. "You get right home now, Mr. Redd."

Redd sat tight as he watched the lawman climb back into his SUV. Blackwood killed the blue lights, put his vehicle in gear, and gunned it, whipping across the two-lane in a 180-degree turn and speeding away.

Redd put the Raptor in gear and eased back onto the empty road, careful to keep the speed limit on the drive home.

If he was going to be arrested, it wasn't going to be for a speeding ticket.

TWENTY-SIX

WASHINGTON, DC

It was a warm spring night. Not quite like the swampy kind of heat they'd get in summer, but warm enough that Stephanie Treadway felt a trickle of sweat slither down her muscular spine.

She had a pair of infrared binoculars glued to her eyes. The binos had a photo option, which was handy. She'd already shot several of Culp earlier that evening but only out of boredom. Right now she sat in a parked car far away from any light source on a sleepy Alexandria street. The two of them had been there for forty minutes.

"She's one very cautious lady," Treadway whispered into her comms. "Not reading her phone, no radio, no smoking. If she's that afraid of the light, maybe she's a vampire."

"She didn't get to be where she is by being careless." Kline's voice spoke in her comms. He was on the other side of town keeping Dudek under surveillance.

"So she's a cautious vampire?"

"Stay focused, will you?"

"What's going on with Dudek?"

"On the couch with the little wifey, bouncing a kid on his knee."

Treadway smirked in the darkness. "Sounds wholesome."

"How would you know?"

"I read about it in a book."

They sat in silence for a few more moments.

"You scanned your car?" Kline said.

Following the disastrous outcome of the Willow operation, they would all be under intense scrutiny, and Kline had become increasingly paranoid about the possibility that Culp had *them* under surveillance. Culp might have been a suit now, but she remained a skilled field operative.

"Not my first rodeo, chief," Treadway assured him.

"No bugs?"

"I found three."

"And?"

"And I left them there, just the way you trained me. I can feed her all of the bull crap that I want, when I want."

"Please tell me you're in a rental right now."

"Stolen, actually. But same idea."

Treadway adjusted the light intensity on her glass to get a better picture. Culp just sat there, staring out of her windshield.

"Our lady is either one very cool customer or she's not meeting anybody after all," Treadway said.

"What's the street address?"

Treadway checked her GPS and read it off to Kline.

"Give me a second," he said.

A small light popped on in Culp's lap. In Treadway's IR it looked like a bonfire. A text message on her phone? Culp looked like she was typing something out.

Kline came back on. "You're not going to believe this."

"Hold on. She's on the move."

Just then Culp got out of her car. She glanced around to be sure she wasn't being watched, then scampered up the long walkway to a stately, two-story brick colonial. As she reached the door, it opened.

"Holy crap," Treadway said. "It's the DAG."

She did not have to elaborate. Kline knew Deputy Attorney General Hunter Baldwin from years past, working together on a couple of task forces. Baldwin was a fast-tracker like he had been back in the day and a real stand-up guy, or so it was generally believed. Kline had visited Baldwin after he was confirmed as DAG following the death of his old boss in the plane crash. He'd told Baldwin about the job his boss had promised him. Baldwin said he'd look into it and, days later, gave it to Culp.

Baldwin kissed Culp briefly before ushering her in and shutting the door.

Treadway laughed. "Culp is doing the DAG! No wonder she got the promotion over you, boss."

"Please tell me you got a photo."

"Do you know who you're talking to? Of course. If you want, I can sneak in and get some really steamy—"

"I've got a better idea. Let's call it a night."

"You know, maybe if you did the DAG, you'd get the next bump. Or wait, maybe I can, and then you can work for me. Or—hey, are you listening to me?"

He wasn't.

She was talking to dead air.

She packed her binos and comms up, hit the Start button, and pulled away, keeping the lights off for a block past Culp's parked vehicle.

Kline was an angry man these days. She should have known better than to try and cheer him up with a stupid joke. With so much on the line, she couldn't blame him for being scared. Both of their lives were hanging by a thread, and he felt responsible for the two of them. When he got scared, he got mad.

She was more into gallows humor.

Treadway smiled in the dark.

If things didn't break their way, she'd be laughing her head off soon enough.

TWENTY-SEVEN

MONTANA

Wyatt Gage sat behind his desk in his spacious second-story office at his palatial residence. His gaze rested on the sparkling, snowcapped peaks of the Crazy Mountains, but his focus was on the matter presently being discussed on an open phone line.

"You're the county tax assessor," he said. "You can do what you want."

His tone was forceful, but as he said it, he shot a wink at the buxom brunette lounging sideways with one leg draped over the arm of an over-stuffed chair-and-a-half, positioned in front of the window. She was wearing Wyatt's dress shirt and nothing underneath. She giggled when he winked, and blew a kiss back at him before exiting the room.

"It has to go before the judge first," the man said, his voice cracking. "We'll have to issue a levy—"

"Then do it."

The brunette came back in, silent as a cat on stocking feet, carrying a tray of fluted glasses and a pitcher of bright-orange mimosa.

"There's a process," said the weary, disembodied voice. "The landowner must be notified of the county's intention in writing, and then there has to be a hearing. It all takes time."

"You let me handle that. Just get the process started. I want Redd's place up for auction by the end of the month."

"But, sir. It's not—"

"I don't care about your buts."

The brunette, high on crank, burst out laughing at his joke. Wyatt shushed her with an index finger to his mouth. She covered her mouth and quieted.

"Yes, sir. I'll get it started."

"Good. Call me when it's on the calendar." He killed the call before the tax assessor could finish groveling.

Wyatt stood, beaming. He loved nothing more than winning.

The brunette resumed her giggling as he poured two glasses of sparkling mimosas.

Over the trill of her giggles, he heard his phone buzzing with an incoming call. He scowled, readying a harangue for the hapless civil servant who just didn't understand how to get things done, then saw the name on the caller ID.

His scowl deepened, but when he accepted the call, his tone was obsequious. "Well, good morning, Sister dear. How are things in the Mile High City?"

Hannah had been summoned to Denver to conduct business on behalf of their father. Wyatt was more than a little put out by that. Why hadn't he been looped in on that business meeting? Hadn't he demonstrated his abilities by making a success of the Stillwater County project? But no . . . his *sister*, the bleeding heart, was their father's favorite, the one being groomed to take on greater responsibility.

The worst part was, he couldn't let it show. He had to bow and scrape and pretend like they were all one big, happy family . . . . that he was delighted to follow Hannah's orders like a good little trouper.

Her brisk voice filled his ear. "I'm not in Denver. We're en route to Bozeman. Father wants you to come pick us up in the Rivian."

Anton Gage always rode in his Rivian R1T pickup whenever he visited his holdings in Montana. The fully electric, extended range truck was his concession to the region's love of big pickups, while remaining faithful to his genuine commitment to avoid driving an internal combustion engine if at all possible.

Rivian was only just beginning to fill preorders for their production line of trucks and SUVs, but Anton Gage had been an early venture capital investor in the company and so had received one of the first preproduction prototypes. *"Risk hath its privileges,"* his father always said.

Wyatt rolled his eyes. Now he was reduced to playing chauffer. Bozeman Yellowstone International Airport was nearly an hour's drive away. "This is kind of last minute. Can't you just fly him up in the Lilium?"

The Lilium was a German-engineered, all-electric airplane with both flight and hovering capabilities—essentially, a VTOL aircraft. Built with lightweight carbon composite materials and powered by thirty-six single-stage high-thrust electric motors, the six-passenger vehicle required no tail, ailerons, or rudders, its direction controlled by the articulation of its ducted fans. With a short front wing forward of the bulbous cabin and wide rear wing behind it, the Lilium looked like a small, flying hammerhead shark. The current prototype had a limited range of less than two hundred miles.

As with the Rivian, Anton Gage had been one of the Lilium project's first investors. Besides the obvious contribution to the aircraft's development, there was a purely practical side to the Lilium. The ostentatiously rich Hollywood entertainers, Silicon Valley executives, and wealthy socialites who lived in gated communities like the uber exclusive Yellowstone Club flew helicopters to and from the Bozeman airport to avoid the long drive. But their convenience came at the expense of climate-killing carbon pollution that fouled the pristine mountain air they all claimed to love. With the Lilium, Gage could have the best of both worlds.

Thanks to his connections with the FAA, he had received special permissions and certifications to operate the still highly experimental aircraft in short flights of less than two hundred miles. Both Anton and Hannah were fully qualified to fly the Lilium. Wyatt had no interest in learning that particular skill set. Not that anyone had asked him.

"The Lilium is temporarily out of commission," Hannah said, sounding irritable. She was tired, having been summoned by their father late the previous day, and had likely been going nonstop ever since. "Software update."

Wyatt laughed.

"Look," Hannah said with a sharp edge. "We're going to be landing in about forty-five minutes. Father doesn't have time to waste standing around the airport, so you need to get moving."

Wyatt scowled again. "Fine. I'll be there as soon as I can."

He thumbed the screen to end the call, then raised his eyes to his houseguest. "Sorry, party's over. Get lost."

✳   ✳   ✳

"I'm hungry," Milo complained. His dirty tie-dyed Buffalo Warrior T-shirt hung loosely from his slight frame, and a multicolored, Inca-styled chullo hat covered his mop of matted red hair.

"You're always hungry," countered his companion (who Matthew Redd had dubbed "Shaggy" but actually went by the name Pan).

"It's 'cuz I have a fast metabolism like my mother. How much further we gonna have to walk? My feet are killing me." His paper-thin leather moccasins had holes where the uncut nails of his big toes had broken through. They were on their way into Wellington to panhandle for grocery money.

"As long as it takes unless—hey, wait. Someone's coming." Pan turned around in the direction of the oncoming vehicle. He tugged at his shirt to smooth out the wrinkles. Nothing much he could do about the sweat stains.

"Finally," Milo said. He held up one stubby thumb.

"Make sure you're smiling. Look real friendly-like."

"No kidding, Sherlock." The redhead flashed his tobacco-stained teeth.

The dark vehicle on the horizon suddenly loomed larger, blowing along at a high rate of speed.

"Oh, crap," Pan said. "It's him."

"Maybe he won't see us."

"Are you for real? How can he miss us?"

The sheriff's SUV braked hard without skidding, slowing fast, the rear end rising up on its haunches. It came to a complete stop next to the two Buffalo Warriors. The passenger window lowered with the push of a button.

"Gentlemen! Out for a little stroll, I see."

"Hey, Sheriff," Milo said.

"Deputy," the man corrected. He turned to Pan. "What are you two hooligans up to now?"

Pan scanned the wide blue sky. "Oh, you know. Just communing with the earth spirit, soaking it all in."

"In other words, not a thing."

"It's a free country."

"Who told you that? Ain't nothing free in this life. You gotta earn your way if you want to make something of yourself. You do want to make something of yourself, don't ya?"

"We're fighting to save the planet," Milo said, scratching himself.

"Is that why you're humping along on the hot asphalt in those house slippers you call shoes? A commitment to clean air?"

"Actually, we were just—"

The popping door locks cut Milo off midsentence.

"Get in," the deputy ordered. "Both of you."

Pan frowned. "Why?"

"We need to have us a little powwow."

"About what?" Pan asked.

"Climb in and you'll find out."

"And if we don't?" Milo's face soured with anxiety.

The deputy smiled. "Trust me, it'll be a whole lot better for you if you do."

The Buffalo Warriors exchanged a worried glance. Their shoulders slumped in resignation as they climbed into the back seat of the big SUV.

Deputy Shane Hepworth was nobody to screw around with.

TWENTY-EIGHT

It had been a long night for Redd. He'd slept fitfully, sitting in J. B.'s easy chair, with the shotgun across his lap and the unholstered Ruger on the coffee table in front of him. He didn't think Wyatt would launch another attack against him so soon after the altercation in the parking lot of Spady's, but he was going to remain on high alert nonetheless.

He sat up with a groan as his stomach reminded him of the beating he'd taken the night before. At least he'd given better than he'd got. He stood uneasily, working out the kinks while trying to protect his abdominal wall, where he'd taken a hard hit to the gut when he wasn't expecting it. *The same sort of thing killed Houdini, didn't it?* If it didn't feel better in a day, he'd get it checked out.

Just one more reason to want to take down Wyatt's goon.

He headed for the kitchen and turned on the faucet, splashed cold water on his face, then went about brewing a pot of coffee.

Forget Shevchenko. He'd deal with him later.

While the coffee maker burbled, Redd cut up and fried a can of Spam he'd picked up from Roy's. He would need to reprovision soon, especially if he planned on staying here a while.

That was really the question, of course. He knew with absolute certainty that J. B.'s murder had to be avenged, but he hadn't thought much past that. He wasn't going to sell to Wyatt—another certainty—but he would have to make a decision about the future of the ranch, not to mention his own future.

Two weeks ago, he would not have believed it possible that he would be back in Stillwater County, much less facing a career choice.

He had never thought about coming back here, being a rancher for the rest of his days, but the idea was not without some appeal. He had run the place almost single-handedly when J. B. had been laid up, and while it was hard work to be sure, it beat the heck out of any number of other jobs he could think of, especially now that so many doors were closed to him.

And yet running a ranch was more than just doing hard work. He would have to turn a profit, and quickly, if what Duke Blanton had told him was correct, and to do that, he would need money. He would have to buy stock and make repairs. He had some savings thanks to eight years of frugality—the Raptor had been his only indulgence—but that would evaporate quickly without regular income.

Was it even possible to save the ranch?

He might have no alternative but to sell.

Can't think about that now, he thought, forking another bite of Spam into his mouth.

✖   ✖   ✖

After breakfast, Redd stripped down and put his clothes in the washing machine. The jeans were filthy and spotted with blood, some of it his, some Shevchenko's. He'd pretreated and scrubbed as best he could but had a feeling the stains might be permanent.

He'd left California without even taking the duffel bag stuffed full of his personal belongings out of the truck bed. It contained a couple sets of cammies—one standard green MARPAT digicam, and one desert beige—along with some clean T-shirts and socks. Redd's plan had been to strip off his name tapes and donate the battle dress uniforms to a homeless veterans' charity—the old vets loved wearing cammies. He didn't feel right wearing the uniform out in public, but aside from what he'd been wearing, they were the only clothes he'd brought along, so after a hot shower, he pulled on the green cammie trousers and an olive-drab T-shirt. He would have to swing by the outfitters store and grab a couple pairs of Wranglers and maybe a new pair of ropers.

He headed out to the barn to check on Remington. The horse nickered happily when he opened the stall. Redd slid open the barn's side entrance, which let out into the pasture, so that the horse could get some fresh air and exercise if he wanted, then headed back inside to get ready for a face-to-face encounter that he'd put off too long.

Before leaving the house, he grabbed the Ruger in its holster, along with the pistol he'd taken from the Infidels biker. Having a weapon that couldn't be traced to him might come in handy, though carrying it was not without risk. He stuffed it into a thigh cargo pocket. The Ruger, which would be his first choice if things got western, he placed on the passenger seat of the Raptor.

He did not need GPS to find Lawrence Auto & Body Repair. He had been there too many times to count during his high school years. The garage, along with the Lawrence family residence, was located on Elkhorn Road, about a mile north of Wellington. The razor wire–topped front gate was open but not exactly inviting. Redd threaded his way past a red Mahindra tractor and a faded-yellow Stillwater County school bus converted to a Methodist church bus. The hood was up and old man Lawrence stood on the front bumper, bent over at the waist, working on the engine.

As the Raptor's big 3.5L EcoBoost rumbled to a stop, Lawrence poked his head up. Redd saw the normally cheerful, welcoming face darken like a storm cloud when Lawrence saw who'd pulled into his place. The old man's steel-gray eyes narrowed, and the grease-stained wrinkles on his face deepened.

Apparently eight years away hadn't changed much between them.

Redd took a deep breath and then got out. By the time he'd made his way around the front of his Raptor, old man Lawrence, still spry as a cat, had jumped off the front bumper of the bus. He slipped a heavy crescent wrench into his rear pocket before wiping the oil and engine crud off his ironhard hands with a rag that was even oilier and cruddier than the bus engine.

"Hello, Mr. Lawrence. Remember me?"

Lawrence shot Redd a look like he was out of his mind.

Hard to forget a man you hate.

Redd had no idea why that idiot question rolled out of his mouth. But Lawrence made him nervous. Always had. The Reverend Lawrence—as he liked to be called owing to his "true calling" leading a small congregation—had to be pushing eighty, Redd thought. He stood nearly a foot shorter than Redd even with the shock of thick, white hair piled on the top of his head. When the old man wasn't bent over an engine block or lying beneath a dripping oil pan of a car on jacks, he stood ramrod straight, his shoulders squared, just as he was doing at the moment. His blue work coveralls, greased and oiled, read Eli on the name tag.

Lawrence ignored Redd's question. "I'm sorry to hear about your daddy, Matthew. I always liked him, but he and I became especially close this last year. He was a fine Christian man."

Redd had to fight to keep a look of incredulity off his face. J. B. believed in God and tried to live a Christian life but wasn't one for organized religion. The only time Redd could remember J. B. darkening the doorway of a church was to attend a wedding or a funeral. Church attendance was, Redd knew, a big part of Lawrence's idea of what constituted "a fine Christian man."

"Thank you, sir."

Lawrence squinted at him. "What are you here for?"

Redd could tell the old man was struggling to maintain his Christian bearing. He desperately wanted to tell Redd to go to hell.

When Redd had first met him, Lawrence had been a warm and welcoming spirit. It came with the territory, him being a preacher and all.

But that was before Redd got together with Emily.

Emily Lawrence was the apple of her father's eye. She was his only child, born to him and Mrs. Lawrence very late in life. Emily was his "Isaac," the child he'd prayed to God for over many long and barren years of marriage.

It wasn't lost on Lawrence that his little girl, who once sang in the church choir and talked openly from a young age about being the wife of a pastor herself one day, had suddenly begun skipping Sunday evening services to be with Matthew Redd.

They were just high school kids, but they were in love—first love—and they did what so many young kids in love did when their parents weren't around. After that, Emily's outlook changed, albeit gradually. At least at first.

She started asking more questions, wondering what she wanted to do with her life, as opposed to living the life she thought her parents wanted for her.

The Reverend and Mrs. Lawrence tried to break the young couple up, but that only drew them closer together—until they eventually broke up all by themselves.

As far as Lawrence was concerned, the split, and his daughter's ensuing broken heart, was mostly Redd's fault. In the reverend's eyes, Redd hadn't tried hard enough to be the young man that his daughter deserved. He'd liked Matthew at first and had tried to encourage the then teenager to straighten up and get his priorities in order. But first came trouble at school, which spilled over into his personal life. And no matter how many times Lawrence had told Redd that the Bible was full of men who'd lived troubled lives before cleaning up their acts, the young man carried a chip on his shoulder and refused to listen.

At least, that's what Lawrence thought. He'd never been interested in hearing Redd's version of it. Never figured out that it was two years of backbreaking work on J. B.'s ranch that had caused Redd to drop out of high school, which had kept him away from Emily until they just stopped seeing each other. And he didn't realize until too late that Emily was, in many ways, the only thing Redd really had.

After Redd, Emily never married an evangelist or a missionary. She didn't even go into the ministry. Last Redd heard she was living in Texas. Lawrence probably blamed Redd for that too. He had never understood it was a full-ride scholarship to a Texas nursing school that took Emily away from them both.

"I asked you a question. What are you here for?" Lawrence repeated, snapping Redd out of his trance.

Redd rubbed his face, thinking. Lawrence's question was a claymore mine, primed to shred him to pieces if Redd dared cross into the kill zone.

"My truck picked up a dent." Redd walked back to the driver's side of his truck and Lawrence followed. Redd pointed at the damage.

Lawrence ran his calloused fingers over the dents. "How'd it happen?" His unblinking gray eyes were lie detectors.

"Parking lot. I got too close to somebody."

It wasn't a lie.

Lawrence looked Redd up and down, deciding. "Be right back."

The old man marched back into his shop, disappearing in the shadows.

Redd heard the sound of tools banging around. Then Lawrence reappeared with a device in his hand. It looked like a giant suction cup with a handle.

Lawrence wedged the suction cup against the door panel and turned the handle, then pulled on it. The sheet metal popped beneath the rubber. Lawrence loosened the suction device, inspected the damage again with his hand, moved the cup over a few inches, and repeated the process. He pulled the device away and inspected it one last time before stepping aside.

"That do ya?"

Redd ran his hand over the smooth door. *If Lawrence preaches as good as he repairs stuff, he might even convert me. Not that God would waste His time on a man like me.*

"Yes, sir. What do you I owe you?"

Lawrence waved a hand. "No need."

"I insist." Redd reached for his wallet.

"Put that away."

Redd felt a chill in his gut. The old man would have made a great drill sergeant with a command voice like that. "Yes, sir."

"Consider it my gift to your father. He deserved better than what he got."

Redd caught the double meaning like a shot to the mouth. The problem was, the reverend was right.

"Well, I best be going."

"How long are you in town for?"

"Not sure just yet."

"Then you have time for us to hold a proper funeral service for your father."

Redd shook his head. "I don't think so. He said in his will he didn't want a fuss made, and he never was much for religion."

"I'm sure he made those arrangements a long time ago. He was a changed man these last few months. In fact, I baptized him myself just a few weeks ago."

Redd would never have called Lawrence a liar, but he found the notion of a born-again J. B. utterly ludicrous. He shook his head again. "He's already been cremated. I'm gonna scatter him on the ranch, just like he wanted."

"Then at least let me hold a memorial service. Jim Bob was a well-known man in this community. Folks will want to pay their respects. You owe him at least that much."

Redd frowned. This was a complication he didn't need. But Lawrence wasn't wrong. He nodded. "Okay."

"Good. We'll hold it at my church on Tuesday at 5 p.m."

Redd squared up. "No disrespect intended, sir, but I prefer the ranch."

The reverend started to say something but caught himself. "If you insist."

"I do."

"Who you gonna invite?"

Redd shrugged. "I don't know anybody around here anymore."

"Would you allow me to take care of it?"

Redd thought the old man was being unusually deferential. "No more than ten people."

Lawrence's left eye twitched. "The whole county'll want to pay their respects."

"I don't care."

"Give me at least fifty."

"Twenty, max. Or we can forget the whole thing."

Lawrence made a noise in his throat. "You gonna say a few words?"

Redd was not looking forward to expressing his feelings for J. B. publicly but figured this too was something he owed the man who had raised him . . . who had saved him. He nodded. "A few."

"You want me to preach it?"

Redd saw the determination in the man's eyes. "Keep it short."

Lawrence gave a terse nod. "It's settled then. Tuesday. Now, as I don't think there's anything else we need to discuss, I've got work to do." He turned and marched back to the church bus.

Redd wanted to call after him, *How's Em doing these days?* But instead, he climbed back into his Raptor, threw the truck in gear, and pulled away. He saw the reverend peek out from beneath the bus hood, watching him leave and shaking his head in disgust.

Redd couldn't blame him.

He had thought about trying to make contact with Emily a thousand times over the years. But what was the point? She had her career, and he had his. They both made their choices. And they were both stubborn as mules.

But at moments like this, he wondered what he'd lost when he let her go.

Redd swore.

Coming home sucked.

He decided right then and there that once his account with J. B.'s killer was settled, he would sell the ranch and leave Montana for good.

TWENTY-NINE

"Over here!"

Hannah looked up to see her brother standing in front of their father's silver Rivian pickup, which was parked outside their private fixed-base operator terminal at the Bozeman Yellowstone International Airport. Wyatt was flashing a hopeful smile and waving.

Beside her, Anton Gage nodded slightly as he began moving toward his son. Anton's gestures, like everything else about him, were simultaneously engaging, cool, and energy efficient. Taller than Wyatt, with broader shoulders, Anton moved like a much younger man. His thick straw-white hair was tucked behind his ears, revealing the strong, handsome features of a clean-shaven, old-world Nordic face. Fierce blue eyes betrayed his incredible intelligence, but his winsome smile charmed even his most implacable enemies when face-to-face—and lured more beautiful women into his bed than even he could remember.

Hannah kept pace with his long stride. Their gaits, like their features, were a mirrored reflection of the other. Her mother, unlike Wyatt's, was a fashion model, but it was her father she favored in form and grace.

They each carried a canvas luggage satchel; leather was inappropriate for either of them given their status in the environmentalist community. Anton wore an off-the-rack light linen suit, white T-shirt, and a pair of Toms canvas slip-ons. Behind his back, his detractors said he was the most poorly dressed billionaire on the planet. What they never understood was that Anton Gage knew his cool came from somewhere else.

Hannah was surprised her brother had left Shevchenko back at the ranch or in the fighting pit or wherever else he kept the big Ukrainian thug when he wasn't around. Though utterly loyal to the family, Shevchenko was a stone-cold killer. When she was around him, she had the sense she was standing next to an unexploded artillery shell that could erupt at any moment and slaughter everyone within his reach. She knew the trick to managing him was to keep him pointed in the right direction, like a loaded rifle.

Most of the time her father saw Shevchenko as an unnecessary accoutrement, like vanity plates on a Lamborghini. Not that Shevchenko's protective services weren't occasionally needed. But Wyatt's large security entourage was more often than not merely a vulgar display of his power and wealth and, hence, his insecurity.

Hannah, unlike her brother, viewed Shevchenko as a tool to be used only as needed.

So did her father. Anton Gage was no fool. There were bad people in the world who meant to do him and his family harm. But Anton also fervently believed in his destiny, which, at least in the short run, made him invulnerable. He also liked to think that his selfless efforts on behalf of the planet and its hungriest inhabitants were an added buffer against evil. Good karma—which he believed was a primitive though accurate description of quantum principles—went a long way against overcoming human malevolence.

Wyatt didn't open his father's door because it wasn't expected by a man who hated class distinctions, nor his sister's because it would offend her feminist sensibilities. They tossed their luggage into the back.

"Good flight?" Wyatt asked as he buckled in.

"Of course," Hannah said from the back seat. "Why wouldn't it have been?"

Wyatt shot her a glare in the rearview mirror. "Just asking."

"It was an excellent flight." Anton glanced at the nearby Bridger Mountains, topped with snow. He often remarked on how he loved this little regional airport with its global ambitions. Convenient, easy, and quaint. "Beautiful here, isn't it?"

It wasn't really a question.

"Another day in paradise." Wyatt punched the Start button. The nearly silent engine engaged. "Your meeting go okay?" He glanced at his father, clearly hoping for a response.

But the world-renowned tech genius was completely captivated by a young student pilot receiving instructions from his teacher, the two of them seated in the open cockpit of a tiny trainer parked on the service tarmac.

"Just drive," Hannah said. "I'll fill you in later."

"The ranch, Father?" Wyatt asked, ignoring his sister.

"Yes, please," Anton finally said. There was iron in his voice.

Wyatt pointed at the onboard GPS map display. "Looks like an hour and ten minutes."

"I don't mind the drive, really."

But she knew he did. Anton Gage's time was, in fact, far more valuable than that of the vulgar, self-absorbed celebrities he often socialized with. He tolerated their hypocrisy in order to gain their support for his environmental initiatives, but it was a character fault that Anton Gage simply couldn't abide within himself.

Hannah could also tell that Wyatt was seething behind a well-practiced smile. He must have caught her mocking gaze in the rearview because his eyes turned back to the road ahead. Wyatt probably had a thousand questions for their father, but he knew to keep them to himself. If his father wanted to speak, he would.

Anton pulled out his encrypted tablet and began scrolling through his email.

The three of them rode home in total silence, as relentlessly quiet as the Rivian.

THIRTY

Gavin Kline sat in his FBI annex office thinking about Dudek's mystery burner phone. He had not yet been able to get into Dudek's home to recover the surveillance devices, but he had been able to search the agent's office a couple of times, even patting down his sport coat hanging on a rack. He had checked out Dudek's work car but found nothing.

Kline needed to find that phone, had to know if Dudek was the leak.

His intercom buzzed. "Gavin, there's a call for you on line two, says it's urgent," Amy, his executive assistant, said. He could see the pretty young woman at her station through his office window, her mouth moving silently while her voice boomed over the intercom.

"Who is it?"

Amy turned to look at him through her window. "He didn't say. But it's a 406 area code. Where's that?"

Kline knew it well. Montana only had one area code to remember.

"Fly-over country," he said with a dismissive laugh. "Probably some farmer reporting an alien cow killing or a squadron of UN black helicopters on patrol."

"You want me to take a message? Tell him you're busy?"

Kline sighed. "No, that's okay. He's a taxpayer. I might as well earn my paycheck." He checked his watch. "Say, why don't you take an early lunch?"

"It's only eleven. I'm not hungry yet."

"Then take a long lunch. Go see that new boyfriend of yours over at the DOE."

"Are you for real?" Amy sounded cautiously optimistic.

"See you at one."

Amy giggled. "Thanks, boss."

"Now."

"Gotcha." Amy hung up, grabbed her purse, and shot out the door.

Kline waited for her to clear her space before he picked up. He had been expecting a call like this after what had happened in Mexico. "Kline here."

But the voice was not the one he expected. "We need to talk."

THIRTY-ONE

MONTANA

After leaving the Lawrence place, Redd drove toward Wellington and headed straight for Hohman's Ranch Feed & Supply. His future plans notwithstanding, he would need more hay for Remington.

His visit to Lawrence's had brought back too many memories—some of them good, but all of them painful because of what had subsequently happened. Emily had been Redd's first and only love. And he had let her go.

He had tried to shut those feelings away, bury them in his military service. And it had worked, right up until everything blew apart.

Now, with J. B. gone, it felt like everything in his life had gone down in flames.

Hohman's feedstore was another familiar place he hadn't thought about in ages. It was more than just a place to buy stuff for the ranch. He had a lot of good memories of this place. Unfortunately, J. B. was a part of all of them, and that only underscored his sense of loss.

J. B. had brought him here to buy his first rifle, a Savage .22 bolt action that he'd worked all summer to pay for, along with his first box of ammo. J. B. decided that Redd would learn how to shoot better with the smaller rifle after fighting the big Henry and getting whacked in the face for the effort.

Over the years, just about anything and everything they needed for the ranch—tools, building supplies, insecticide, paint, and of course, feed for cattle and horses—they bought from Mr. Hohman.

It was also Mr. Hohman who had caught Redd trying to shove a thirty-two-ounce bottle of Coors into his pants when he was fourteen. He was kind enough to call J. B. instead of the sheriff, though Redd would have preferred jail time to the icy-cold silence he endured for the next week. His dad never raised his voice, never hit him, never denied him food or shelter. But the bitter disappointment in his face was more unbearable than any physical abuse he'd endured from his mom's junkie boyfriends. It took Redd days to find the words to apologize—really apologize, not just mouth the words. J. B. had nodded his forgiveness. But it was a good, long while before Redd earned back his dad's respect, and once re-earned, he fought even harder to keep it.

"Matthew Redd, is that you hiding behind that beard?" Mr. Hohman said with a broad grin and open hand as he stepped out from behind the counter.

"Sure is, Mr. Hohman. Good to see you." They shook hands.

Hohman wagged his head in mock amazement. "Boy, you're even bigger than I remember. I guess military life suits you."

Redd had to fight the urge to look at his feet. "Three squares a day and a little sunshine never hurt anyone."

"Yeah. 'Sunshine.' I bet you can do a hundred push-ups straight, can't you?" Hohman seemed to sense that Redd wasn't in the mood to talk, so he quickly added, "Sorry for your loss, son. Jim Bob will be missed."

Redd nodded. "I hear J. B. got behind on some of his bills. Do I owe you anything?"

Hohman gave him a sidelong glance. "I'll print up an invoice. I guess you're planning to sell the place, then?"

Although that particular issue had just become clear to him, Redd hesitated to confirm it openly. "Don't see as there's much choice."

Hohman nodded. "See, the thing is, if there's a chance you might want to keep the place . . . in the family, so to speak . . . then I might be able to see my way clear to work out some kind of payment plan. Maybe even extend your credit so you can get some new stock. If you were so inclined."

The offer caught Redd flat-footed. With so many people in Wellington telling him he ought to sell, ought to cash in and check out, the last thing he expected was for someone to extend a helping hand.

"Might even be able to recommend someone to manage things for you," Hohman continued.

Of course. He thinks I'm still a Marine.

"That's something I'd have to think about," Redd said slowly.

"Tell you what. Why don't you do that and then come back and see me before you leave town."

Redd nodded. "I need to pick up a few things today. Couple bales of grass, one of alfalfa."

"Sure thing. I'll add those to the account."

Redd shook his head. "I'll pay you for it now. J. B. always told me, when you're in a hole, the first thing to do is stop digging."

Hohman smiled. "Sound advice. He taught you well."

✳ ✳ ✳

The visit to Hohman's lifted Redd out of his black mood, if only a little. Even with an extended line of credit from the feedstore—and he wasn't keen on the idea of buying things on credit—it would still take a lot of time and money to get the ranch back in the black.

Still, it seemed like a worthy challenge and a better way to occupy his mind and body than simply wallowing in self-pity. Maybe he *would* stick around a while, give it a try . . .

If he wasn't dead or in jail.

He made another quick stop at Roy's, this time buying enough food to fill both the cupboard and the refrigerator, then headed back out to the ranch. His slightly improved mood lasted only until he parked the truck in front of the house. That was when he saw that the front door was open.

He immediately went into tactical mode, shutting off the truck and exiting from it by dropping into a crouch behind the front wheel, the Ruger in his right hand. He scanned the surrounding woods, checking all angles of approach for any sign that someone was lurking nearby, then cautiously made his way around the truck and crept up to the front door.

A quick glance revealed gouges in the doorjamb around the strike plate. The door had been jimmied open.

Redd eased inside, leading with the Ruger, listening after each step forward. Despite his best efforts at stealth, the old boards creaked under his weight.

He cursed under his breath.

Though there did not appear to be anyone in the house, there was abundant evidence of the intrusion. The place had been trashed. The furniture had been kicked over, pictures pulled down from the walls and tossed aside. There were scuff marks on the gun safe, indicating that someone had made a futile attempt to smash it open. Even so, Redd punched in the combination and checked to make sure everything was still as he'd left it.

He breathed a sigh of relief when he saw that it was. Then he glanced up at the mantel, and his heart sank.

J. B.'s box was gone.

Then he saw the black plastic box tossed onto the sofa, the lid popped open but the ashes still contained within the bag. He gently retrieved it and returned it to the place of honor.

A glance into the kitchen revealed the refrigerator door wide-open and completely empty. Redd went in and found the cupboards likewise pillaged.

He moved through the house, his alert posture relaxing as each cleared room confirmed the fact that the miscreants had moved off. There hadn't been much for them to steal, though they'd given it one heck of a good try. In every room Redd found drawers pulled out, beds torn apart, cabinets opened. Their biggest haul appeared to be the stash of pain meds in J. B.'s medicine cabinet. Redd recalled Shane Hepworth's warning about drug-related crime in the area.

Was that what this was? Or was it just supposed to look that way?

Was this Wyatt Gage's latest effort to harass him into walking away from the ranch?

If so, then he's a terrible judge of people.

And then he thought about the barn.

Would they steal a horse? Or even . . .

Redd hurried outside and made a beeline for the barn door, which, he was a little relieved to see, remained closed, just as he had left it. Once inside, he was immersed in darkness. It would take a moment for his eyes to adjust, but he nevertheless hurried to Remington's stall.

It was empty.

Then he remembered that he'd left the side door open so Remington could graze. With a mixture of hope and concern, he jogged over to the side entrance and stared out into the pasture, where Remington was lazily browsing.

Redd let out a breath he hadn't even realized he'd been holding.

Then something cracked into the back of his skull, and Remington, the pasture, and everything else in his world swirled down into darkness.

THIRTY-TWO

"Matt! Matt!"

Redd's eyes fluttered open, his head aching. He'd felt this way before when a grenade went off inside a cinder block apartment outside Manila. The medics told him he had suffered a slight concussion then.

This was worse.

He felt like Remington had stomped his skull.

Hannah Gage hovered over him, her beautiful face lined with worry.

"What are—?" he tried to say, but the words were so slurred and garbled that even he couldn't tell what he was attempting to ask.

She gripped his bicep. "I thought you were dead. We need to get you to a hospital."

"No." That at least came out clear. He raised himself up on one elbow and felt the back of his head. His hand came away covered in blood.

"I'm calling an ambulance." She pulled her cell phone out of her pocket, but Redd wrapped his bloody hand around it.

"No. I'll be okay. Just get me inside." He tried to stand. His legs felt wobbly as if partially disconnected from his brain, but he steadied himself against the wall and managed to get to his feet.

"You need stitches," she insisted. "Not to mention a head CT. If you won't let me call an ambulance, at least let me drive you to the clinic."

Redd almost laughed at the suggestion that the Wellington clinic might be able to do a CAT scan. They'd probably give him a bag of ice and tell him to walk it off, which was exactly what he planned on doing.

Then he saw the puddle of bloody mud where he'd lain until Hannah found him. A fresh wave of pain shot through his head like a sniper's bullet.

"I think you better drive."

✖ ✖ ✖

Hannah Gage stomped on the gas pedal when she pulled out of the ranch and never let off. The trip down the old service road had been pretty brutal, but once her white Mercedes G-Wagon reached the highway, she'd made the jump to warp speed.

Redd had a towel pressed against the back of his skull but he still managed to bleed onto the bone-white quilted Nappa leather.

"I'm sorry about this," he said, his eyes shut against the headache.

"Good thing I found you when I did. You might have bled out."

"Yeah, lucky me. What were you doing there, anyway?"

"Just wanted to pay Remi a visit," she replied. "Make sure you're taking good care of him. And I thought maybe I could talk you into having that cup of coffee you promised me."

He grunted. It was a plausible enough explanation, except for the fact that she was Wyatt Gage's sister.

But if she was in on Wyatt's scheme, why hadn't she just let him bleed out?

Doesn't make sense.

"What happened?" she asked, keeping her eyes on the road.

"Somebody whacked me pretty good."

"Who?"

"Never saw 'em."

She cast a suspicious eye his way. "Someone just tried to kill you, Matt. You must have some idea who."

Oh, I've got an idea, Redd thought. What he said was "Tweakers, I think. Deputy told me that's a problem around here."

As he said it, he wondered if maybe he'd discounted that possibility too quickly. The Buffalo Warriors' camp wasn't really all that far away. He could easily imagine them breaking in to steal stuff to pay for a bump. Maybe they had even brought along their Infidels biker buddies looking for payback.

My third day here, and I've already made more enemies than I can keep track of.

✖   ✖   ✖

The Stillwater County Health Center was a bland, institutional complex occupying half a city block, just north of the courthouse. It was not a full-service hospital but provided basic medical service and was mostly contained in a horseshoe-shaped utilitarian structure, built around a small central parking area. It was just one story, except for a recent addition—built sometime after Redd had moved away—which had added a second story to the east wing, where the long-term care facility had been located. The urgent care clinic, which served as a de facto emergency room, was located on the inside of the top of the horseshoe. It mostly served as a triage facility for walk-ins, where minor injuries and illnesses could be attended to, and where more serious cases could be stabilized for ground or air transport to Bozeman.

Hannah had offered to drive Redd all the way to Bozeman for treatment at a proper hospital, but Redd refused. While his stated reason was that he didn't think the injury warranted that level of attention, the real reason was that he didn't want to be even farther away from the ranch, especially as it had already been targeted.

The sight of blood moved Redd to the front of a very short line of people waiting to be seen, though all that meant was that he was moved out of the reception lobby and into a small examination room.

Despite her fierce protests, Hannah had not been permitted to accompany him. As he was wheeled into the secure examination area, she gripped his arm. "I'll be waiting for you out here, okay?"

Redd managed a smile. "Thanks. For everything."

As the triage nurse conducted his assessment, Redd gradually began to realize that the reason for this separation had very little to do with medical privacy.

"So what happened?" the young man asked as he gently irrigated the wound. Since the injury was located at the back of his head, he sat on the low-slung examination table while the nurse worked.

"My horse got spooked," Redd said, deciding it was a useful fiction. Since he wasn't sure he could trust local law enforcement, he was loath to admit being the victim of an attack. "I was backing away from him and tripped over a rock. Must have whacked my head when I hit the ground."

"Is that right?" the nurse replied. "Was your girlfriend out there with you at the time?"

Redd suppressed a smile. "She's not my girlfriend. Just an acquaintance. But no, I was alone at the time."

The nurse nodded. "She seemed pretty insistent on coming back here with you. I'll bet she's got quite a temper."

That was when Redd figured out what the man was driving at. "I wouldn't know. She didn't do this." He almost laughed at the thought of Hannah breaking a board across his skull but then remembered that she was only one or two degrees removed from the person most likely responsible for the attack.

"I understand. We have to ask these questions. Domestic violence can go both ways. If you ever need anyone to talk to about it, this is a safe space."

"I'll keep that in mind."

The nurse gently laid a gauze bandage over the wound, then activated an instant cold compress, which he placed atop that. When he was done, an older woman carrying a tablet computer came in and began asking Redd questions.

"Name?"

"Redd, Matthew."

She raised an eyebrow from behind her glasses as if unamused by the order in which he'd answered the question. "Address?"

He gave the address of the ranch. She entered the information without the slightest indication of recognition. "Who can I list for emergency contact?"

That stumped him. He had always listed J. B. There was no one else. "I don't really have anyone."

Another arched eyebrow. "What about the woman who brought you in?"

He shook his head, then regretted it as a spike of pain went through his skull. He supposed it didn't really matter who he put down. He would be walking out of here soon. Still . . . he supplied his biological father's name. *At least he's good for that.*

She asked about his primary care physician—he didn't have one—and his insurance. He wasn't sure if his Tricare coverage would remain in effect for the rest of the month or if it had ceased along with all his other military benefits when he'd accepted his other than honorable separation.

"I don't have any," he said.

She accepted this without comment and moved on to medical history. Lots of minor injuries, but no illnesses, chronic conditions, or known allergies. The woman tapped her iPad one final time and then left him alone.

He closed his eyes and leaned forward, elbows on his knees and cradling his head in his hands, taking shallow breaths to keep the pain at bay. He felt his heartbeat pounding at the pinpoint of his wound on the back of his skull. It was starting to itch. He did not open his eyes when the door opened and he heard the sound of soft footsteps approaching.

A voice—female and hauntingly familiar—broke the stillness. "Matty Redd. Never thought I'd see the day that you came back here."

Redd's eyes popped open.

Before him stood Emily Lawrence.

THIRTY-THREE

Redd met Emily's stare. Her unblinking eyes were cold and clinical. If anything, he saw a tiny spark of anger flickering in them. He felt a tingling running through him like a low-level electric shock. Not enough to kill, just paralyze. He couldn't say a word, couldn't smile, couldn't sit up.

She had changed, and yet so much about her was familiar. Same blue-hazel eyes, thick reddish-chestnut hair, and cute, upturned nose. At five-foot-six she had the lean, athletic build of someone used to working hard, and yet there was a softness that he remembered too well.

She had always been a knockout, but somehow she was even more beautiful than he remembered.

He wanted to tell her he was sorry he stopped being around her, but he had to do it for J. B. and to save the ranch. That having a girlfriend seemed too selfish at that time.

He also wanted to tell her how sorry he was for not reaching out to her over the last few years. Tell her about the Marines. Explain what happened. Tell her how sorry he was about everything.

And he wasn't sure why.

What did he have to be sorry for? She was one of the only people he'd ever trusted. He loved her, and at a time when he wasn't sure he'd ever know how to love someone again. He never wanted to split; that part wasn't on him.

Did she ever come around to the ranch to check on him? Or was she just too busy getting her straight As while he was busting his hump?

And it wasn't as if she ever called him or wrote to him when he was serving his country. Last he heard, they had phones and email in Texas too.

Yeah. She had a lot of explaining to do herself.

He'd gone from smitten to smoldering in about half a nanosecond.

But she sure was beautiful.

And all he could do was stare.

Emily was the first to break off the staring contest. She glanced down at her own iPad. Only now did Redd see the long white lab coat over lavender scrubs. "So it says here you bumped your head. Let's have a look."

She set the tablet down on the small sink counter at the back of the room and snapped on a pair of nitrile gloves before he could think to check for a wedding ring, then approached and began gently removing the cold compress and gauze.

The nearness of her body sent another shock wave through him. A hundred sun-drenched, meadow-damp memories flooded back in. It took everything in him to not reach over and wrap his arms around her and pull her close. She smelled like antibacterial soap and iodine, but he'd never smelled anything better.

He felt her fingers parting his hair and gently probing the wound area. His scalp stung slightly when her gloved finger explored the edges of the cut.

"Honestly, it's not too bad. The bleeding has slowed quite a bit. The cut is long but not deep. You'll need a couple stitches, but I'll have to cut some hair away first. You okay with that?"

"Yep."

"You always did have a way with words."

He couldn't see her face. He wasn't sure if she was kidding or criticizing. His throbbing headache short-circuited any capacity for linguistic analysis.

She stepped back and faced him again. "Headache?"

"No," he lied. But her stern eyes saw right through him. "Maybe a little. No big deal."

She pulled out a penlight and checked his eyes. Her breath smelled like mint tea. "Blurred vision?"

"Nope."

"You're not dilated. That's good. What month is it?"

He actually had to think about that for a moment. "May. Last time I checked, anyway."

"Who's the president?"

"Are you serious?"

"Just checking for cognition. I could always order a CT scan to see if you have a concussion. How'd you do this? Fall?"

He couldn't lie to her. "Somebody hit me. I didn't see who."

She nodded slowly. "Anything to do with what happened at Spady's last night?"

"You heard about that?"

"You know how fast news travels in a small town."

He sighed. "It's possible."

"Judging by the wound, I'd say someone hit you with a flat surface. A two-by-four or a shovel. You're lucky it wasn't something sharp."

"Yeah. Lucky."

She pulled off the gloves and dropped them in a waste receptacle, then washed and dried her hands. Redd couldn't help but notice that her left ring finger was bare.

"Okay. I'll be back in a few minutes and we'll get to work sewing you up." She turned and headed for the door.

"Em, I—"

That was all he managed to get out before the door closed between them.

✖ ✖ ✖

She returned a few minutes later, pushing a small cart atop which sat a sealed plastic suture kit and a capped syringe. Redd made no attempt to engage her in conversation. He had received that signal loud and clear.

After numbing the wound area and shaving away just enough hair to work on it, Emily seized the curved FS-2 needle from its sanitary packaging with her needle holder in one hand and picked up the tissue forceps in the other.

When she finally spoke, her tone was flat and professional. "When was your last tetanus shot?"

"Uh, let me see. I think it was two years ago . . . when I was deployed to . . . Well, it doesn't matter where I went."

"I imagine you've seen some pretty rough stuff."

Redd thought her tone was softening just a little. "You mean, rougher than a tetanus shot?"

"Yeah."

"Flu shot was pretty bad." He waited for the laugh. It never came.

He'd forgotten about her iron will.

"Does that hurt?" she asked.

"Can't even feel it," he lied. It felt like she was peeling his scalp away with the forceps.

"Good answer."

Now he felt the tug of the suture needle piercing his skin.

"Still good?" she asked.

"*No hay problema.* That's Spanish."

"*¿De verdad? No sabía que podías hablar español. Tal vez—*"

"Point taken, Doctor."

"I'm actually an NP. A nurse practitioner, ER certified." Her voice was a low murmur in his ear. Her breath raised gooseflesh on his arms. He hoped she didn't notice.

"And I'm an idiot," he muttered.

"Also certified."

Redd felt the puff of breath from her silent laugh just beyond the wound area. He smiled. "Where'd you learn Spanish?"

Emily ran another stitch. "In college. It comes in handy when I volunteer with Samaritan's Purse in the summers down in Central America. You?"

"Part of my training for the Raiders."

"I'm guessing that's not a reference to the football team."

"Nope."

"Not that you asked, nor am I offering alternatives, but I'm using a nonabsorbable 4-0 nylon thread in a set-back dermal pattern. Since we both know you're not the type to lay around the house and watch *Gilligan's Island* reruns while this thing tries to heal up. That'll give you the best chance of not tearing the wound back open. Just don't be stupid and try to shoot head goals with it, okay?"

Was she trying to bridge the gulf between them, or was it just wishful thinking on his part? He wanted to believe it was the former. "Certified nurse practitioner? That's pretty impressive."

"Top of my class."

"Not surprised. You were never second-best at anything." Redd still couldn't see her face, but he hoped she smiled. For a moment her hand stopped. Redd swore he felt her rub the back of his head in a more tender way. Was there still something between them after all these years?

His thoughts were interrupted by the needle once more poking into his scalp.

"Quiet," she said, her hands moving again. "I'm trying to work."

THIRTY-FOUR

Hannah paced the waiting room, anxious for news about Redd. It had been more than half an hour since he'd been wheeled away, and nobody had told her anything.

She stalked back up to the reception desk. "Excuse me, can you tell me anything about Mr. Redd's condition? Is he okay?"

The woman on the other side of the desk gave her the same opaque nonanswer. "He's being treated now. I'm sure everything is fine."

Hannah placed her hands flat on the counter. She wanted to rail at the woman. *My family has contributed millions to your dingy little clinic. We're the reason you have a job.*

It was true. When her father and then Wyatt had begun purchasing property in Montana, one of the first things they'd done was invest in local services. As their respective ventures began to gain momentum, the number of people on the payroll would grow, both at their father's agricultural research facilities and at Wyatt's personal little ranch-resort. They would need thriving local businesses, well-provisioned schools, and adequate medical services. Gage money had funded extensive renovations at the health center and paid for cutting-edge diagnostic equipment. That should have bought Hannah a little respect, but evidently the stolid receptionist didn't understand how the world really worked.

Hannah wasn't sure why she even cared about what happened to Redd. He was nobody to her. She had her pick of men everywhere she went. It was like she had a superpower that turned the wealthiest and most desirable men in the world into utter and complete idiots.

Maybe that was why she was so fascinated by Matthew Redd.

Though not exactly movie star good-looking, he exuded masculinity. He had a rare sort of animal magnetism that was hard to resist.

And yet he hadn't fallen for her, at least not in any obvious way. Hadn't debased himself like a rutting pig, chuffing with impotent desire to seduce her. The fact that he didn't try to bed her made her want him all the more.

And the fact that he had been laid low, that he was vulnerable and wounded, only increased her attraction. The desire to hold him, care for him, and yes, dominate him in every way possible now consumed her.

She pulled out her black Amex credit card and slid it across to the receptionist. "I'd like to take care of Mr. Redd's bill now."

The woman remained unmoved. "We usually deal with that when the patient is discharged."

"Just take care of it," Hannah snapped.

"Of course, dear." The woman took the card, but before she could do anything with it, the desk phone rang. "Excuse me," she said and looked away from Hannah.

Hannah seized the opportunity. In a flash, she slipped past the reception desk and was through the door to the examination rooms before the woman could raise a protest.

Beyond was a small nurses' station and a short hallway with doors on either side—some closed, most open. A whiteboard on the wall listed the patients currently being seen according to room number. Hannah's eyes immediately found Redd's name on the list alongside the number three. She pivoted into the hallway and scanned the plastic signs beside each door until she found the right one and opened it without bothering to knock.

Redd sat on a low exam table in the center of the room, an odd smile on his face despite his present condition. Hannah's gaze immediately settled on the other person in the room, a strikingly attractive woman—presumably a nurse—who was sitting on a small stool right behind Redd, her head close enough to his to whisper in his ear.

Or kiss him.

Hannah flushed with anger but managed to force a smile. "Matt! There you are. I was so worried. Is everything going to be okay?" She brought her gaze back to the nurse. "Can I take him home soon?"

The nurse scowled at her. "You can't be in here."

Hannah affected a look of pure innocence. "The woman out front said it was okay—"

"No, she didn't. You need to leave. *Now.*" The woman's tone was firm, almost threatening.

Hannah definitely wasn't accustomed to anyone speaking to her that way. With an effort, she maintained her benign expression. "I won't get in the way." She dropped her eyes to Redd's. "Matt, it's okay if I stay, right?"

The nurse straightened, and Hannah saw the blood-tipped medical instruments in her hands. "It's not up to the patient. This is my examination room. Go."

Hannah's smile slipped. "Now you listen to me—"

"Hannah!" Redd's voice broke through her rising fury. "It's okay, Hannah. I'm okay. We're almost done here."

With an effort, Hannah brought the smile back to her lips. She fixed the other woman with her icy-blue stare. "I'm so sorry if I've upset you. I was just worried about Matt. I'm the one who found him and brought him here. I'd hate to think what might have happened to him if I'd shown up an hour later."

The nurse returned an equally humorless smile. "Well, I'm sure Matty will be very grateful. The sooner you leave this room, the sooner I'll be able to release him back to you."

The woman's tone spoke volumes, and it wasn't lost on Hannah that she'd called him Matty either. *She wants him,* Hannah thought. *But he's mine.*

"Well then," Hannah said, her smile turning into a smirk, "I'll just let you do your job."

✖ ✖ ✖

Emily had her suspicions from the moment the woman barged in, but Redd confirmed them when he named her.

Hannah Gage.

She had seen the woman before, at fundraising dinners for the clinic, as well as on the pages of magazines, but that person had been done up and dressed to kill, whereas this version of her was dressed like she'd just come off the ranch.

Even so, she looked stunning.

Hannah Gage. The billionaire's daughter.

Good for you, Matty.

Emily stared at the closing door as if her eyes might bore straight through it and into the departing woman. When she heard the click of the latch resetting, she shook it off and went back to work.

Redd's scalp was unusually tough, and she had to really push the needle hard to pierce the skin.

"Ouch." Redd winced. "You might want to sharpen up that wrench you're using."

Emily took a deep breath to calm herself down. "Sorry. Won't be much longer." She threaded another stitch. Against her better judgment, she said, "Congratulations."

"Excuse me?"

"You and Hannah. I'm glad you found someone that can make you happy." She expertly knotted the stitch and moved on. "One more should do it."

"We aren't together," Redd said.

"Could have fooled me."

"We're neighbors. She was just . . ." He trailed off, and when he spoke again, there was a hint of irritation in his voice. "No. You know what? I don't owe you an explanation."

"No, you don't," Emily agreed.

"Maybe you haven't heard, but J. B. died last week."

The declaration felt like a slap, and she placed the needle and forceps back in the tray until her hands stopped shaking. "I know."

"Yeah? Well, I came up here because he called and said he was in trouble and that he needed my help. You know J. B. He never asked anyone for help in his life. But I got here too late. He was already dead. So contrary to what you might think, I didn't come here looking for a girlfriend."

Emily bit back an angry retort.

"Hannah was taking care of Remington. That's how I met her. And that's it. There's nothing between us."

She stepped around so that he could see her better and raised her hands in a *whatever* gesture. "Like you said, you don't owe me an explanation."

"Em, would you just listen for once?"

"Really? You want *me* to listen?"

"I think somebody killed J. B." He glanced furtively at the door, then dropped his voice to a whisper. "And I think it might have been her brother. I don't know if she's involved."

She stared at him, incredulous, and shook her head. "You really don't know?"

"Know what?"

She opened her mouth to tell him but found herself unexpectedly choked up. She took a deep breath, then tried again. "He was terminal, Matty."

"What?"

"Pancreatic cancer. Stage III when they finally caught it. It metastasized and spread to his lymph nodes."

Redd's shoulders slumped. Emily thought he looked like a lost little boy. "He never told me."

"I think he was trying to when he told you he was in trouble."

Redd just stared at her, looking stunned.

"I think he held off as long as he did because he worried you might get some notion to quit the Marines and come home and take care of him."

"I would have."

She searched his face. "Yeah, I think you would have."

"How much time did he have left?"

"I wasn't his primary, but I consulted with his oncologist. With a full course of treatment, he had a fifty-fifty chance of making it another five years. There's a chemotherapy unit here at the clinic so locals don't have to go all the way to Bozeman or Helena for treatment. You know J. B. He was a fighter. He came in a couple of times to the ER because of shortness of breath. That's when he and I got reacquainted. That man was a rock. I hated to see the chemo waste him away like it did. Poor guy had to use a cane most of the time."

Redd looked like he was staring off into space, but then his eyes came back to her. "Could he have ridden a horse in that condition?"

"Are you kidding? I mean, don't get me wrong. He was stubborn, so I wouldn't put anything past him, but some days he could hardly get out of his chair. Watching him climb into his pickup was like watching a sloth climb a redwood. I don't think he could have climbed up into that saddle if his life depended on it."

"Shane Hepworth said he found J. B. dead by his horse, thrown off."

She blinked at him. "I hadn't heard that. When I heard that he passed, I just assumed . . ."

"He wasn't brought here?"

"No. We don't have a dedicated morgue facility. DOAs go straight to Pitt-Bateman." She winced as soon as she heard herself say, "DOAs."

Redd pursed his lips together, then seemed to relax. "You about done?"

The change in his demeanor both surprised and alarmed her. She had seen that look of determination before. He'd been the same way right before he'd dropped out of high school and disappeared from her life.

Fine. I didn't ask for him to come back. She returned to her work, threading the final suture. "There you go. I'll have Janice print up your discharge instructions. Basically, you need to keep the wound clean and dry. You don't want to get an infection. I'll write a prescription for a topical anti-biotic. Like I said, I know it's asking a lot to tell you to take it easy, but seriously . . . take it easy for a few days. Take Tylenol for pain. Avoid alcohol. How long will you be in town?"

"Long as I need to be."

Emily had no idea what he meant by that and was afraid to ask. She stared down at him, at his broad chest, his powerful arms. She still remembered what it had felt like to be held by those arms. She blinked away the memory. "That shirt is a mess. I'll have Janice find you something to wear home."

She started for the door, but his voice stopped her. "Em?"

"What?" She didn't turn to look at him.

"You'll come to J. B.'s memorial, won't you?"

That did get her to turn. "When is it?"

"This coming Tuesday. Five o'clock. Your daddy's preaching."

"You're kidding."

"I spoke with him this morning. It was actually his idea. I'm surprised he didn't tell you."

"I'm not," she murmured. She looked him up and down again. There was a lot of history between them, not all of it good.

But not all of it bad, either.

She nodded. "I wouldn't miss it for the world."

THIRTY-FIVE

Hannah drove the speed limit from the clinic back to the ranch, not because there wasn't an emergency, but because it gave her more time to talk to Redd.

Only he wasn't talking much. Mostly he just stared out the passenger window, clearly lost in thought.

She had a pretty good idea what he was thinking about.

"She called you Matty," Hannah said, breaking the silence.

He turned to face her. "Huh?"

Redd sat next to her in a red XL T-shirt, two sizes too small for his muscled frame. *MONTANA* and a stylized buffalo in silhouette were printed across the front, donated to the clinic by Montana Scene, an outdoor clothing store in Bozeman.

"That nurse who fixed you up. She called you Matty. I thought you hated being called that."

"She's a nurse practitioner."

There was something like pride in his voice.

"I take it you know her? That nurse . . . nurse practitioner."

He didn't meet her gaze. "Yeah. We went to high school together."

Hannah glanced at him sidelong. "That's all?"

"All that matters. We . . ." He hesitated a beat. "Dated. But we were just kids. That's all water under the bridge."

"You sure about that?" Hannah smiled. "Did you see the look in her eyes when I came into the room?"

"She was standing behind me."

"You could hear it in her voice."

"If you say so."

"Trust me, she still has a thing for you."

"I haven't seen or talked to her in years."

She liked that he was trying so hard to dismiss the obvious attraction the woman had exhibited.

He's keeping his options open.

She decided not to press the issue and instead changed the subject. "My brother said you and he had a somewhat-heated discussion at Spady's last night. Is that true?"

That evoked more of a reaction than anything she'd said about his love life. He gave her a sharp look as if staring straight into her soul. "What did he say?"

"Just that you're stubborn. I could have told him that already. You're Jim Bob's son, after all."

"He wants J. B.'s ranch . . . my ranch." Redd sounded defensive, like a grizzly bear protecting its den.

"Wyatt can be pigheaded when he wants something. He has a hard time with boundaries and especially with people who tell him no. I don't say that to excuse him. I'm genuinely sorry that you had to go through that."

Redd turned away, looking out the window once more. "A man's got to draw a line somewhere. Mine's around J. B.'s property. Maybe you should let your brother know that."

"Maybe I will," she said and meant it. Wyatt's recklessness had given her the perfect lever to bend Matthew Redd to her will.

A mile up, they passed three people walking along the side of the road—two women and a man—all wearing the tie-dyed attire that distinguished them as Buffalo Warriors. As the Mercedes drew close, they turned around, but instead of throwing up thumbs to hitch a ride, they flashed big, toothy smiles and peace symbols as the G-Rex raced past.

"What are those guys doing here?" Redd asked.

Hannah couldn't tell if the question was meant to be rhetorical. "They're the Buffalo Warriors. It's a group dedicated to protecting endangered wildlife."

"They look like dirty hippies."

She frowned. "That's kind of judgmental. They're really nice kids. It's all volunteer work. I convinced Wyatt to let them set up a low-impact campsite on the ranch, and my organization provides a small stipend for them, mostly for food and medical care at the clinic. In return, they collect data about the movement of the bison herds that roam our land."

"Gage Wildlife Conservancy. Right?"

She smiled. "That's sweet of you to remember."

"Those nice kids have quite a racket," Redd went on. "They're using that bison herd to extort donations, which they turn around and use to buy crystal meth."

Hannah had heard rumors of such behavior before and gave her patented response. "There are always a few bad apples."

Redd leaned forward and stole another glance at the Buffalo Warriors in the passenger mirror. "I think a tour in the corps would do them kids a world of good."

"Not everybody's tough like you."

"No, but everybody can learn how to stand up straight and take a freaking bath with soap." He leaned back in his seat.

"I think they're romantics."

"I'm glad you think so because you're the one paying for it."

Hannah let Redd's last comment slide. She liked the fact he didn't roll over for her like so many other men did, even if his viewpoints were a century out of date.

Just then her mobile phone rang through the car's media center. *Shane* popped up on the dashboard caller ID. She stabbed a finger out to accept the call, hoping that Redd hadn't noticed.

"Hello, Deputy Hepworth," she said. "You're on speakerphone with me and Matthew Redd."

There was a slight pause, and then Hepworth's voice filled the interior of the Mercedes. "Matt? You okay?"

"I'll live. Got a big mess to clean up though."

"Ms. Gage reported you'd been attacked. Any idea who?"

"Not really."

Hannah glanced over at Redd. She didn't think he was being completely truthful with the deputy.

"How soon until you two get back there?" Hepworth asked.

"We're about fifteen minutes out," Hannah answered.

"I'll meet you guys there and we'll see what's what." He hung up.

"I wonder what he really wants," Redd said, fixing her with his stare.

She did not fail to grasp the subtext but pretended otherwise. "Just doing his job, I imagine. Trying to find out who assaulted you."

"I remember Shane from high school. I hope he's better at solving crimes than he was at long division."

Hannah hid a smile. Was this jealousy she was hearing? "Can I ask you a serious question? About your financial situation?"

"Not like I can stop you."

"I'm sorry; I don't mean to pry. I'm a child of privilege—I get that—but I also know what money can do for you. The opportunities it provides, the doors it opens."

"Is this about your brother's offer?" Redd's voice was flat, but there was just a hint of ire in his tone.

"I'm not trying to push you or sell you—honestly, Wyatt drives me insane sometimes. But he's in charge of the family real estate program and he really wants your property. I'm not saying you should sell . . . But he's willing to pay you three times the market value."

"He offered me double."

"Counter with triple and see what he says. Think about what you could do with that kind of money. If it's land you want, there's plenty to be had out here."

Redd frowned. "Did your brother put you up to this?"

"Oh no. He'd kill me if he thought I was talking to you about this. He thinks he's the Jeff Bezos of real estate. He'd interpret what I'm saying as a personal attack on his ability to buy your property. I only raised the subject because I know you two went crossways last night, and I know a little something about stubborn men." She reached over and squeezed Redd's forearm. "I just don't want you to miss out on a big opportunity. I want good things for you, Matt. Money opens doors. And this would be your money. Not a handout."

Redd snorted a little, a laugh. "I'll have to think about it."

"Name your price. Sky's the limit."

"Don't know if I have one."

"Everybody has a price."

"Only whores and politicians have a price."

"Excuse me?"

"It's something J. B. used to say. Only whores and politicians know the price they'll sell themselves for."

She frowned. "This isn't the same thing."

"Maybe not." Redd folded his arms, closed his eyes, and leaned back. "Like I said, I'll think on it."

Hannah eased off the gas pedal to give them more time together in the Mercedes. She kept stealing glances at him, hardly able to contain herself. He was a force of nature. A headstrong stallion who refused to be saddled.

She was going to enjoy breaking him.

THIRTY-SIX

Hannah parked her Mercedes next to Deputy Hepworth's SUV. The deputy himself stepped out from the house and began walking toward them. Redd thought Hepworth looked a little guilty as he waved to the two of them.

Redd figured it was because he had been inside the house without permission, but then he noticed the deputy's eyes flitting back and forth between Hannah and him and realized there was something more going on. He recalled that when Hepworth had called Hannah, the ID had read *Shane*.

Redd wondered just how well the two knew each other.

"The door was open, so I poked my head inside," Hepworth said. "Looks like they trashed your place pretty good from what I could see."

Redd didn't need to see it again.

"Probably tweakers," Hepworth went on. "County's crawling with them." He clicked his tongue, disgusted. "They're running Stillwater County into the ground. We can't do anything about it unless we catch them with stolen goods."

"This time they did more than just steal," Hannah said. "They could have killed Matt."

Hepworth nodded. "They were probably raiding the barn when you showed up and figured the only way out was through you."

A memory hit Redd like a lightning bolt. He wheeled and ran toward the barn. Hannah and the deputy were right behind him. The exertion set his skull throbbing, but he ignored the pain until he reached the bloody spot where he'd fallen.

"What is it, Matt?" Hannah asked.

"The Ruger. J. B.'s Magnum. I had it on me when I got attacked. It's gone. They have it."

Hepworth put his hands on his hips. "Well, that's not good. You're lucky they didn't drill you with it. But I imagine they saw something like that as a big score." The deputy paused a beat. "I'll need a list of what's missing. That'll help if something turns up at a pawnshop, and it'll help you with insurance."

"I don't know if J. B. even had insurance. I'll have to check."

"Well, you let me know if there's anything else I can do for you."

Redd nodded dully.

"Do you need our help getting your place back together?" Hannah asked.

Redd saw a momentary flicker of anger in Hepworth's eyes. He really wasn't happy that Hannah was here with him.

"Thanks, but I'll manage."

Hepworth checked his watch. "Well, I gotta run. Get me that list as soon as you can." He turned to Hannah. "You leaving too? I can get the gate for you."

She smiled at him, but it wasn't a warm smile. "I'm going to say hi to Remington."

"Okay." Hepworth turned to Redd. "See you around, Matt."

As Hepworth left them, Redd turned to Hannah. "Are you two together?"

She leaned close. "Do you see anything in my eyes to suggest that?"

"No. But it was his eyes I was watching. He was a real lady-killer in high school. Starting quarterback."

"High school was a long time ago." She held his gaze. Her eyes were both playful and challenging. "For both of you. And we're all grown-up now."

Redd didn't miss the dig at his relationship with Emily.

"Well, if you don't need any help, I'll check on Remi, then head on out."

She stepped through the side door and out into the pasture. Even though he felt guilty for doing it, Redd enjoyed the view as she walked away.

❌ ❌ ❌

As he put the house back in order, Redd thought a lot about his conversation with Emily. The thought that J. B. had been dying of cancer and hadn't told him cut to the bone, and yet he knew that was classic J. B.

He could almost hear the old man's voice. *And if I'd told you? What would you have done then? You got a cure for cancer you ain't told no one about?*

Nevertheless, he was mad at J. B. for not giving him a chance to at least say goodbye.

But it wasn't cancer that killed him.

He recalled Shaggy's confession. *"He was sticking his nose where it didn't belong."*

And Emily saying, *"I don't think he could have climbed up into that saddle if his life depended on it."*

But Shane Hepworth had found J. B. on the ground next to Remington. So how did that work?

Was Hepworth in on it?

"Now Wyatt on the other hand . . . I get along with him real good."

Redd decided that he didn't trust Deputy Shane Hepworth any farther than he could throw him.

Maybe not even that far.

Making a list of what was missing was harder than he expected, partly because everything that he did find triggered a cascade of memories, but mostly because he hadn't lived there in years.

Redd never did see a tackle box—J. B. loved to fly-fish—and there were two empty slots in the fishing rod rack. But had the items been stolen, or had J. B., knowing that he would probably never be able to fish again, sold or donated them?

He finally got to J. B.'s bedroom. He started out by making the bed. The sheets and blanket had been torn off and the pillows tossed onto the floor. Even the desk lamps had been tossed. At least J. B.'s thick, black leather Bible was still on the nightstand.

"He was a changed man these last few months," Reverend Lawrence had said. *"I baptized him myself just a few weeks ago."*

He couldn't quite square with the idea of J. B. begging God to cure him of his ills, but he could absolutely see the old man trying to "get right with the Lord" before the end. Still, the more he heard about J. B.'s renewed faith, the more Redd found himself wishing he could have had just one more conversation with his dad.

Almost unconsciously, Redd picked up the Bible and flipped it open, something he hadn't done since his first year with J. B.

It read the same as he remembered it, beginning with the ornately inscribed names of Abraham Ulysses Thompson and Mary Francis Bonner, married in 1842.

On the last printed line, written in neat cursive handwriting, was still *James Robert Thompson, b. 1956.*

Redd knew it would be up to him to complete that entry.

Written just below that was a new inscription in his father's familiar, uneasy scrawl.

Matthew James Redd, b. 1994

Redd's eyes blurred with tears as he touched his name on the page.

He closed the holy book and set it back down.

He was about to call it quits for the night when his cell phone rang.

Only two people in the world had that number, and one of them was dead. The caller ID read Unknown.

He did not waste his breath with a cautious greeting. "Who is this?"

"Is this Matthew Redd?"

The voice was strangely familiar. "Answer the question."

"My name is Anton Gage. First, let me express how terribly sorry I am about your loss. I only met your father once, but Hannah simply loved the man."

Redd was momentarily struck dumb by the fact that he had one of the world's richest men on the line. But then again, he was on first-name terms with both of Anton Gage's children. "I appreciate the sentiment, but how did you get this number? It's private."

"Hannah gave it to me."

Redd was certain that he had not given Hannah—or anyone else—his number, but then he remembered that he had given it at the health center earlier in the day. No doubt, Hannah had found a way to exert just the right kind of pressure to get that confidential information.

"I'm afraid her concern for your situation outweighed her concern for your privacy," Gage went on. "My apologies. How are you feeling, by the way? I understand you were injured quite severely."

"A few stitches. No big deal." He almost added, *What do you mean by my "situation"?*

"That's wonderful to hear. Well, if you're up to it, I'd be more than honored if you'd come by the ranch house tomorrow for brunch. I'm only in town for a few days and there's something I'd love to discuss with you."

"If it's about buying my place—"

"Oh no. Quite the opposite. I'm afraid there's been a huge misunderstanding and I'd like to clear the air. Can I send a driver down to pick you up tomorrow? Say, 11 a.m.?"

The last thing Redd wanted to do was hang out with a billionaire, never mind one whose son had probably ordered J. B.'s death, but he was curious despite himself.

"I'll drive myself," he said. "I remember the way."

THIRTY-SEVEN

WASHINGTON, DC

Kevin Dudek found a parking spot on Belmont Street, a couple blocks east of Meridian Hill Park. He checked up and down the street, verifying that nobody was around, then headed toward the park entrance at Fifteenth Street.

This was quite a place for a rendezvous.

Despite its gentrified exterior and close proximity to the center of federal power—the White House was just a mile and a half to the south—Columbia Heights wasn't a great place to be after dark and certainly not after midnight. He was a federal officer, and he was armed, but that just meant that, if he ran into trouble, he would have a decent chance of surviving the encounter. He stopped at the concrete pillars that formed the park entrance, his hand resting on his hip, just a few inches from the butt of his holstered Glock, and peered down the dimly lit path, looking and listening for any signs of activity. Satisfied that he wasn't about to walk into an ambush, he started down the walk, rolling heel to toe to minimize the sound of his footsteps. Before long, he could hear the sound of running water—the centerpiece of the park was an elaborate water feature called *Cascading Waterfall*, which consisted of several tiered cisterns overflowing in a descending stairstep and augmented by numerous fountains.

Dudek only had a passing familiarity with the park's layout but was able to follow the trails up the hill to the designated rendezvous spot. In the muted darkness, he could just make out the shape of a statue—a warrior astride a horse.

He was starting toward it when he heard a familiar voice from the darkness whisper his name.

He froze but said nothing. Without being too obvious, he searched the nearby trees, looking for the other person.

"Were you followed?"

He shook his head once. Then his curiosity got the better of him. "What's going on?"

"You've been compromised."

Dudek shook his head again. "Impossible."

"You got sloppy."

He pursed his lips together, accepting the criticism.

"I need to show you something," the voice went on. "Come forward."

Dudek frowned, but then a human shape detached from the shadows and took a step toward him, one hand outstretched. Dudek could see the outline of something in the figure's hand. The object was too small to be a phone. A memory stick?

He closed the distance with the figure, reaching out to take the proffered item, but as his fingers were about to close on it, the hand moved, darting as quickly as a striking snake, and seized him by the wrist.

"Hey, what the—?"

The figure pulled hard on Dudek's trapped wrist, yanking him forward. Off-balance, he fell toward the shadowy figure.

He didn't see his assailant's other hand ram forward, into his chest, but he felt the blow—a hard punch that landed right below his sternum. The hand drew back, then pistoned out again and again, striking so quickly that Dudek didn't have time to even think about resisting.

When the seriousness of the situation finally hit home, he first tried to tear himself loose of the hand holding his wrist.

His arm didn't seem to work anymore.

He tried to cry out, but when he opened his mouth, nothing happened.

Then he felt the coldness spreading out from his diaphragm. He pressed his free hand to his abdomen and felt warmth and wetness against his fingertips.

Stabbed me.

The coldness continued to spread, and on its heels, the first hint of pain. His knees buckled, and then he was falling . . .

As he lay there, consumed by darkness, he shuffled through every emotion—denial, disbelief, despair.

How had he let this happen?

She suckered me.

With the last of his fading awareness, he felt the hands of his killer searching his clothes, his pockets. Then the voice hissed in his ear.

"Where's your other phone? Where's the burner?"

But Kevin Dudek couldn't have answered the question if he wanted to.

✖   ✖   ✖

Gavin Kline looked up as Rachel Culp marched into his office at the annex. It was seven thirty in the morning, way too early for him. An untouched cup of coffee sat at his elbow. "What's going on? I wasn't expecting to meet with you until tomorrow."

Culp shut the door behind her and took a seat opposite his desk.

She stared at him for a moment as if mesmerized by the dark circles under his eyes. It had been a late night.

"Agent Dudek was killed last night."

Kline sat up straight. "What? How?"

"His body was found by a jogger less than two hours ago at Meridian Hill Park. He bled out behind the Joan of Arc memorial."

"Yeah, I know it." Kline moved the coffee away so he wouldn't accidentally spill it. "What do we know so far?"

"According to the Metro PD, he was stabbed to death. Nothing was taken. Not his gun, not his wallet, not his watch or cell phone or wedding ring. And here's the part you're going to love. Metro PD says it was a robbery gone wrong."

"Let me guess," Kline said. "No cameras, no witnesses, no murder weapon, no DNA."

"You got it."

Kline leaned back in his chair. "That settles it, then. Dudek was our leak."

"Agreed. And someone decided to plug that leak."

"Someone connected to Willow obviously."

Culp's strong face turned flinty. "Or someone who wanted their own brand of justice."

Kline raised an eyebrow.

"It was your operation," she went on. "It went sideways badly, people died, all because of our leak. Maybe you found out Dudek was the leak and decided to take matters into your own hands."

"That would be rather brazen of me, don't you think? Kill the man I was assigned to investigate?"

"You don't strike me as a timid soul."

Kline waved a hand as if shooing away a fly. "Trust me, I'm not your killer."

She held his gaze a moment longer, then seemed to relent. "It's my job to ask these questions. But for the record, when was the last time you saw him?"

"Last night around 11 p.m. He went home from work, ate dinner, watched TV, pulled the curtains. I figured they were getting ready for bed, so I headed home. I can't pull twenty-four-hour shifts by myself."

"Did you ever put any bugs in his place? Tap his phone?"

"Still waiting on the warrant. The FISA court has been getting stingy about them lately. They act like they don't trust us anymore. We were supposed to get it sometime later today." He pointed at his computer. "I was just putting an email together to find out the status."

"I'm surprised you're such a stickler for details. I'd heard you cowboyed things up when you needed to."

Kline gestured toward his meager office and IKEA desk. "And maybe that's why I'm sitting here, and your office is on the seventh floor."

Culp stood. "I need you to get over to Dudek's place, see what you can find. You won't need a warrant to get in. Just make a house call on the grieving widow, then do your thing. If this was more than just a mugging gone bad, we need to find out who ordered the hit. More important, we need evidence proving he was the leak."

"Agreed." He took a sip of the coffee. "Oh, how's your surveillance of Treadway coming along? Are you dropping it now that Dudek is our most likely suspect?"

"Treadway lives the most boring life you can imagine. Unlike you, I pulled a few strings and put a few things in place. Apparently she watches a lot of reality television, and when she's really got her crazy on, she binges Hallmark Channel reruns. And by the way, *Love in the Sun* is her favorite."

Kline smiled. Good ol' Stevie. She had been his best student at the academy. "Makes sense. She's pretty boring at work too."

Treadway had done a good job covering her tracks, Kline thought. The Hallmark Channel stuff was priceless.

"Do you want me back on tracking Willow?" Kline asked.

"For now stay focused on finding out who killed Dudek. I have a feeling that will lead you straight to Willow."

"That would make my job a whole lot easier."

She stood, ending the meeting. "Keep me posted on what you find at Dudek's place. No telling how far down the rabbit hole you'll go."

Kline stood as well. "Only one way to find out."

"Just watch your six."

Just what Vasquez told me before he was butchered.

"Always do, boss. Always do."

THIRTY-EIGHT

MONTANA

Redd woke the next morning, his stitches itching like a volcano of fire ants erupting on the top of his head. He fought the urge to scratch as he unfolded himself from the couch and headed to the kitchen. It was only when he got there that he remembered he no longer had a coffee maker or coffee. The thieves had taken both.

He was contemplating making a run into town to address this deficiency when he heard a vehicle rolling up the drive. A look out the window showed it to be a sheriff's department SUV. Shane Hepworth was behind the wheel.

Redd stepped out onto the porch to meet the deputy, who got out with a paper coffee cup in each hand. Hepworth was out of uniform, wearing a sweatshirt and jeans.

Hepworth handed him one of the cups. "I've got cream and sugar in the truck if you need 'em. I would have called, but I don't have your cell number."

"Black's fine. Thanks. Don't you have J. B.'s landline?"

"It's disconnected."

Redd took a cautious sip. The coffee was lukewarm. "So what brings you out here on a Sunday morning?"

"Don't you want to go to church?"

"Seriously?"

Hepworth laughed. "Nah. Grab your stuff. I want to show you something."

✖ ✖ ✖

Hepworth drove him back out to the highway and then went off road, driving out across the meadow where the bison had previously grazed. There was no sign of the shaggy creatures today. The farther the SUV strayed from the highway, the more uneasy Redd felt. If Hepworth was secretly working for Wyatt Gage, then the deputy might well be leading him into an ambush.

As they rode, Redd watched Hepworth's expression and body language, looking for any hint of treachery or even agitation that might signal deception, but saw none. If Hepworth was up to something, he had a stone-cold poker face. They rode in silence for the most part, which was fine with Redd. He wasn't big on small talk. He had debated bringing along the pistol he'd taken from the biker but had ultimately decided that carrying an illegal weapon while accompanying a law enforcement official was probably a bad idea.

Besides, he didn't need a weapon to defend himself.

After about thirty minutes of cross-country driving, Hepworth stopped at the edge of a wooded area and got out. "It's just over here a little ways."

It was the first thing he'd said concerning their destination. Redd noted that the deputy left his sidearm on the center console. Hepworth led him into the forest a short way until they emerged into a primitive, and recently abandoned, campsite.

The area was littered with candy wrappers, empty beer cans, cigarette butts. A used syringe lay in the dirt next to a filthy, bargain-basement pup tent standing a few feet from a campfire that had been smothered with dirt.

"That look familiar?" Shane asked, nodding toward a tackle box. *J. B. T.* was written in permanent marker on the cover.

Redd nodded. "That's J. B.'s."

"Told you, man—tweakers. Two of them."

Redd scanned the ground. The area was thoroughly trampled. "Two? How do you figure?"

"There are two filthy sleeping bags inside that tent, that's how."

"And you said tweakers?"

"Druggies, meth heads, whatever."

"You know, I've seen these idiots running around dressed in rainbow-colored T-shirts. They call themselves Buffalo Warriors. Every time I turn around, they're on the side of the road, hustling money to 'save the buffalo.' I know for a fact that they're spending some of what they make on drugs."

Hepworth kicked the dirt and shook his head. "Folks around here call 'em buffalo hippies. I don't know that anyone's ever had trouble with them, but these days?" He shrugged. "Who knows?"

Redd surveyed the camp again. It was tucked back in the trees a good distance from the main road. "How'd you find this hellhole?"

"Smoke from the campfire. Someone called it in to the volunteer FD late last night—no fires allowed. I read the report this morning, thought of you."

Redd looked around. It would have been a solid hike from here to J. B.'s place, at least ten miles over wooded terrain. "You *really* think two meth heads hiked from here to the ranch just to steal stuff?"

"Nah. They *live* out here, man. Must have been running around the woods high on crank and found your place. Or maybe they had been in town and found out about J. B. dying, so they figured they'd have his place to themselves—until you showed up."

Redd put his hands on his hips, lifting his eyes to the treetops. He spun a three-sixty, trying to take it all in. "I don't know. It all seems pretty convenient."

Hepworth looked at him sidelong. "I don't follow."

"You found J. B. dead up on his property next to Remington, his neck broke. Right?"

"Exactly how I found him."

"And the coroner confirmed the cause of death—did he come out to see for himself?"

"Sure did."

"Funny thing is, J. B. was riddled with cancer. According to Em, he was too weak to climb a horse."

"Em?" Hepworth blinked uncomprehending for a moment, then broke into a grin. "You mean Emily Lawrence, your old flame? Man, she's a real looker. Always was. You were hitting that pretty hard back in the day, weren't you?"

Redd felt his fingers curling into fists.

"I tried to get me a taste of that," Hepworth went on. "I mean, you weren't around or anything, right? But man, she wouldn't give me the time of day."

"The point I was trying to make," Redd said, barely able to get the words out through clenched teeth, "is that she said it wasn't possible for him to be on that horse."

Hepworth scratched his chin. "Far be it from me to argue with a medical professional. But then again, you know old Jim Bob. He was tougher 'n nails. I wouldn't put anything past him."

"What was he doing out there?"

Hepworth folded his arms. "What do you mean?"

"He sold off all his stock and let the place go to seed. What possible reason could he have had for wanting to haul his cancer-riddled body up into the saddle?"

"Well, what's the alternative?"

Redd watched Hepworth carefully to see how he would react. "Could somebody have killed him and then staged the scene to made it look like an accident?"

Hepworth appeared to genuinely consider the question. "I suppose. But who would want to kill Jim Bob? You think the tweakers did it?"

"No, I was thinking of someone else."

Hepworth cocked his head to the side again. "Who?"

"Who stood to gain from his death?"

"I have no idea. He was in hock up to his neck. What could he possibly have that anyone would want?"

"His property. Wyatt Gage has been wearing me out over it—and so has half the county, including you."

"Just wait one minute, Matt. I never wore you out about it. I just said that there ain't a lot of good reasons to hang around this dumpster fire of a county if you don't have to. Do whatever you want. I don't care. All I was saying was that Wyatt would buy your property for more than it's worth if you want to sell it, that's all. And—" He flinched as realization dawned. "Whoa. Wait. You think Wyatt Gage killed J. B.? Are you kidding me?"

Redd didn't say a word.

"You must've been hit pretty hard in the head to think of something that stupid. Why would a billionaire's son kill an old man with one foot already in the grave? He could've just waited for him to die and get his property."

Redd's face hardened.

"No disrespect," Hepworth went on. "I'm just saying, why would Wyatt risk everything just to get title deed to a broke-down cattle ranch? It's no bigger than a postage stamp compared to his spread. It just don't make any sense."

"J. B. had a fifty-fifty chance of making it another five years," Redd said, his voice still ice-cold. "If Wyatt knew that, he might not have wanted to wait around that long. He probably figured I wouldn't want the place because I haven't been around. So he kills J. B.—or has that trained ape of his do it—and then offers me a deal I'd be a fool to refuse."

Hepworth shook his head. "If you're saying Wyatt wanted your property, what you're really saying is that Anton Gage wanted it, because Wyatt only buys property his father wants. Is that what you're alleging?"

Redd frowned. "I didn't know that. I thought Wyatt was just trying to build some kind of resort town."

"Anton Gage is a living saint," Hepworth went on, his voice rising with passion. "He's fed more than 10 million people over the last ten years and plans to feed a billion more over the next ten. He's not some Chicago gangster who orders hits on people."

Redd blinked. "I'm supposed to meet him later today."

"Really? Wow. How do you rate?"

"He invited me to brunch at his place."

"Wow, man. That's awesome. You'll see. Anton Gage is a good man."

Redd nodded dully. Had he read the signs wrong?

Hepworth pointed at the fishing equipment. "You want those, don't you?"

"Uh, sure."

"I'll have to come back later and take it in as evidence when I process the scene. I'll let you know when I can release them." He put his hands on his hips. "Look, Matt. We don't want to miss the obvious here. It's pretty clear a couple of dopers broke into your place, knocked you on the head, and left you for dead. As I think about it, they probably had J. B. under surveillance for a while. Maybe they even saw him fall off his horse. Or maybe they're the ones that spooked Remington. If J. B. was actually killed—and I'm not saying he was, I'm just following your line of reasoning—then maybe it was those tweakers that did it. If the evidence points in that direction, I promise you, we'll find out."

Redd didn't say a word. He'd learned during his time as an interrogator that it was best to let the other guy run his mouth. There were still some missing pieces to the puzzle. Maybe Hepworth would let something slip.

"What we need to do is find those tweakers; then we'll know for sure what's going on. When I get back to the office, I'll run this all by Blackwood, if he's sober."

"That doesn't exactly inspire confidence."

"He's got a bad drinking problem, but he hides it well. He ain't good for much, but Mr. Gage likes him well enough, and when he's sober, he's not a half-bad cop. The two of us will put our heads together and see if we can get a line on these guys. When I catch them—and I will, trust me—I'll give you a holler and we'll see what's what. Fair enough?"

Redd nodded. But his gut told him the tweakers angle was a false trail. He couldn't imagine someone like Shaggy getting the drop on J. B.

"Trouble's come knocking . . ."

No, J. B. wouldn't have called him because of a couple dirtbag tweakers. *"Sticking his nose where it didn't belong."*

Then he recalled what Hepworth had just told him. *"What you're really saying is that Anton Gage wanted it, because Wyatt only buys property his father wants."*

He managed a half-hearted smile. He could take Hepworth at his word, but then again, he could also ask the man himself.

"Thanks, Shane. I appreciate you looking into this. We should probably get a move on, though. Don't want to be late for brunch."

THIRTY-NINE

Redd slowed to a stop in his Raptor just in front of the entrance to Dancing Elk Ranch. It all looked the same as it did when he'd first visited and just as impenetrable.

The same surly supervisor was there, only this time he was wearing a grin on his face almost as big as the .45 he wore on his hip. He ambled up to Redd's window.

"Good morning, Mr. Redd. Good to see you again."

"I'm here to see Mr. Anton Gage."

"You're right on time, sir. I think you know the way, though I'm happy to show you if you prefer."

"I'm good."

"Of course." The supervisor leaned in close. "I hate to ask this, but you're not armed, are you?"

"And if I was?"

"Then I'd politely ask you to check your weapon with me. I'll secure it here at the shack and return it to you as you exit. It's SOP around here. Nothing personal. I'm sure you understand."

Redd shrugged. "No, I'm not strapped. Just curious."

Like I'd ever turn over a gun to these assclowns.

The supervisor's dark eyes scanned Redd once over, the smile never leaving his face. Redd could tell the man wanted to search the Raptor and pat him down. But obviously he was under orders to give him the VIP treatment.

"I understand." The supervisor stood and waved to someone in the guard shack. The gate began opening. "Enjoy your visit, Mr. Redd."

✖   ✖   ✖

Redd parked in front of the huge three-story, glass-fronted residence. It was made of rough-hewn timbers but its steep angles and stark lines were ultramodern. It perfectly fit the mountain setting but was completely original in form—a high-tech version of a mountain lodge if there ever was one.

Hannah's white Mercedes G-Rex was parked out front, and she appeared on the porch as if on cue as Redd climbed out of his Raptor.

"Matt! So glad you could make it," Hannah said, beaming. She wore a long black linen dress with ruffles from the waist down and a wide braided rope belt with a big silver buckle around her narrow waist. The high wedges on her feet had three-inch rope heels that added to her already-tall frame. The black dress really made the long blonde hair draped over her shoulders stand out, and the beaded turquoise necklace complimented her eyes.

She was, as always, stunning.

"How are your stitches?"

"They itch like a son of a . . . gun." Redd tried to watch his language on Sundays. That was about as religious as he got. "Other than that, I'm right as rain."

She radiated another smile. "I'm glad you're okay. Dad can't wait to meet you. Come on in."

She led him through the wide entrance and into a cavernous living area. The huge floor-to-ceiling windows of the three-story home brought the great outdoors straight inside—or maybe it was the other way around.

Large sectional sofas in thick, natural fabrics, custom wood tables and chairs, colorful hand-woven Native American rugs, and a dozen other features all spoke of extraordinary taste, style, and . . . money. Unlike every other Montana cabin he'd been in, there wasn't a single animal head on the wall—no bearskins, no stuffed fish or birds or cats. As he thought about it, there wasn't any leather in the place either except for the boots he was wearing and Hannah's belt.

As he followed her through the wide living area toward the deck, his eyes were irresistibly drawn to her graceful form. He had a feeling she knew he was looking, and liked it, so he tore his gaze away and looked up to find a tall, broad-shouldered man with thick, straw-white hair tucked behind his ears, dressed in gray linen slacks and a white T-shirt, standing near the glass rail of the panoramic deck, surveying the magnificent view.

Hannah swept up behind the man and laid a hand on his broad back. When he turned to her, his face lighting up with a loving smile, it was clear to Redd where Hannah got her good looks.

"Dad, this is Matt Redd. Matt, this is my father, Dr. Anton Gage."

Anton stepped forward, extending his long, wide hand. Redd took it. The man's skin was soft but his grip was firm.

"It's a genuine pleasure to meet Jim Bob Thompson's son. Thank you for taking the time to come visit us."

"Thanks for having me."

"I just want to say again how sorry I am for your loss. I only met your father once. He made quite an impression. He was one of the most self-possessed men I've ever met. They just don't make them like that anymore."

"Thanks. He was a good man and a hell of a Marine."

"That's a fine epitaph for any man. You must be very proud and rightly so." He gestured to a buffet table covered with a white linen tablecloth and loaded with covered serving trays on the other side of the deck. A pretty young woman dressed in a black chef's jacket was fussing over the prepared food. "Well, you must be hungry. Please, let's eat."

"I'll leave you two alone," Hannah said. "I've got a Zoom conference call I've got to take in ten minutes." She kissed her father on the cheek and smiled at Redd as she passed him by. "Enjoy your brunch."

Redd was a little surprised that she was leaving. He figured she'd be there for the brunch but quickly realized this meant that he would be alone with Anton Gage.

That might make it easier to feel him out.

"Thanks." Redd fought the urge to watch her walk away, especially with her father standing next to him. But he realized he wasn't thinking about Hannah Gage at all.

It was Emily who was on his mind.

✖   ✖   ✖

After days of eating straight from the can, Redd found the food offering impossible to resist. He loaded up on thick-cut bacon, fat link sausages, a cooked-to-order omelet, and a steak, fresh off the grill. Anton Gage just stood back and watched him shovel food onto his plate.

When they were both seated, the young chef brought over several plates of colorful grilled vegetables and freshly cut fruit, which she set in front of her employer. There wasn't one piece of animal protein anywhere near him. Not even a glass of milk or a pat of butter.

Redd took another look at the carnage on his plates. He had grudging admiration for people like Gage who had the ethical or moral conviction against the killing of animals. What he couldn't stand was hypocrisy. The absence of animal products on his person or his brunch plate suggested that Gage was a true believer.

"Please, don't be shy. Dig in," Gage said with a grin. "Erica is one of the best private chefs in the country and she specializes in proteins." He gestured at his plates. "I just happen to prefer these."

"I appreciate it."

Redd wasn't a hypocrite either. He was a carnivore from way back and there was nothing he liked more than steak. He cut into his blood-rare rib eye, releasing red juices onto the plate. He stole a glance at Gage, who seemed to enjoy his own food every bit as much.

"Everything to your satisfaction, sir?" Erica asked with a slight German accent.

Redd had never tasted better. The pepper-crusted, butter-soaked Angus beef practically melted in his mouth.

"Incredible. Thank you."

"Something to drink, Matthew? Coffee? Mimosa?" Anton asked.

"A Bloody Mary would be great, spicy if you've got it," Redd told the chef.

"Same for me," Gage said.

"Right away, sir."

"So, Matthew—do you prefer Matthew or Matt?"

"Matt's fine." Redd cut into his cheesy omelet, careful to snag a big piece of glistening ground sausage tucked inside.

"Well, Matt, I was at a fundraiser for homeless combat vets a few months ago and had the chance to meet with the commandant of the Marine Corps. A quite imposing gentleman. Have you met him?"

Redd finished chewing. "The commandant and I travel in different social circles."

"I imagine you've seen a lot."

"Yes, sir."

"I've seen a bit myself in my travels. So much suffering. So much of it needless. All of it caused by humans."

Erica arrived with their Bloody Marys, served in frosty cold mason jars rimmed with fresh crushed black pepper. Anton's was garnished with a dill pickle spear, Redd's with a slice of sriracha-smoked crunchy bacon. She stood nearby, her hands folded in front of her.

Anton lifted his glass toward Redd in an air toast. "To better things to come."

"Amen to that." Redd pulled the bacon out and set it on his plate and took a sip of his drink. He didn't have a sophisticated palate but he knew he wasn't slurping canned tomato juice.

"I forgot to mention that Erica is also an amazing mixologist." Gage gestured toward her. "I stole her from Elon Musk. Smartest move I ever made."

Erica blushed. "I'm glad they are to your satisfaction, gentlemen."

"Thank you, Erica," Anton said, dismissing her.

Redd bit into his bacon as she exited the patio. He waited for Gage to take a bite of his dill pickle before asking a question.

"Dr. Gage, I know that—"

Gage waved Redd into silence, fighting hard to swallow his food. "Please, please. It's Anton."

"Okay . . . Anton. I really appreciate you inviting me up here and the spread you've laid out. I'm not so white trashy that I don't understand the significance of you having me up here. I bet half of Congress and two-thirds of Hollywood wish they were sitting where I am sitting right now. But I just need to tell you up front: I'm not selling J. B.'s property to you—at any price."

Gage snatched up a linen napkin and wiped his face. "I'm so sorry you thought that's why I invited you here. That's the last thing on my mind. In fact, just the opposite. My son got way out over his skis on all of this and frankly, it's my fault."

Gage sat back in his chair and crossed his long legs as he lifted his Bloody Mary. "I haven't always been a presence in his life, and he's constantly trying to earn my approval. Fathers and sons . . . it's not always easy, is it? Trying to live up to expectations? Either the ones imposed upon us or, worse, the ones we put upon ourselves."

That hit Redd hard. Like Gage was seeing right through him.

"I'm sure Wyatt became aggressive with you. He likes to be the biggest rooster in the yard. So let me state here and now for the record, I don't want your property. Don't get me wrong; it's a beautiful piece of land. But it's *your* land, and it's been in your family for generations. I know how hard it is for small ranches to make it, and I'm as upset as anybody about what's been going on in this region for the last decade. It's rich guys like me who come swooping in to pick up smaller operations that can't compete in the marketplace. That's good old-fashioned capitalism but that doesn't make it right."

Redd tried to hide his surprise. "No, sir. It doesn't."

"The reality is, however, that a small cattle operation like the one your dad used to run doesn't make economic sense anymore. They can't compete with the big industrial farms and ranches."

"Yeah, it was tough a decade ago. We barely made ends meet. It must be harder now."

"So let me make you this proposal. If you decide to keep your ranch and work it yourself or even lease it out to someone else, I'll pledge to buy every pound of beef you raise on it. I'd prefer it to be raised organic . . . bison would be even better . . . but that's something we can figure out later. Of course, I'm a vegan, but I have friends in the restaurant business, and I'm sure I can persuade them to switch from their current suppliers. Is that something you might be interested in?"

Redd was stunned by the offer. He'd been looking for a way to keep the ranch alive, and now it was being dropped in his lap by the man he thought was trying to snatch the land out from under him. "Uh, yeah. Sure. That would be really helpful."

"Regarding the vandalizing of your place and the attack you suffered— it's just terrible. Unfortunately, it's not surprising. Rural communities are among the poorest, and they're disproportionately suffering from the drug pandemic. I'm talking to some friends of mine on Capitol Hill about getting a DEA unit assigned to Stillwater County. But until that happens, I want to make my security team available to you. Since our properties are contiguous, I would like your permission for them to include your property in their routine patrols."

Redd thought about the security team he'd encountered back at the gate. They looked competent enough, but he wasn't sure he wanted to give them the run of his ranch. "I'm taking up my own security measures, but I appreciate the offer."

"Of course, I understand completely. But just know the offer always stands."

Gage deftly switched the conversation to his love of Montana's stunning beauty, the wildlife he'd encountered, and his desire to curb the increasing demand for high-end residential development by rich out-of-state types.

"What do you love best about Montana?" Gage asked.

Redd didn't have to think too long about it. "It's a beautiful place. So are a lot of places. But the thing with Montana? It's still . . . *wild*."

Gage grinned. "Brilliant."

Redd relaxed under Anton's charming spell. He opened up about his best memories of J. B. and the joy of growing up in Big Sky Country.

A short time later, an urgent call came in from Belgium seeking Gage's help regarding a humanitarian crisis in South Sudan. Gage accompanied Redd to the front door and gave him a big hug—something Redd hadn't expected at all and, strangely, was glad to return.

By the time he cleared through the front gate and waved at the security guards, Redd couldn't shake the feeling that he'd just become best friends with the world's most famous billionaire environmentalist. The man was brilliant, humble, and utterly engaging.

And apparently he was just fine with having Redd as a neighbor.

So why was Wyatt Gage willing to pay triple market value for J. B.'s land?

That was the question Redd chewed on as he drove back to Jim Bob's ranch.

FORTY

Roman Shevchenko turned the big gun over in his hands and laughed. A cowboy gun for cowboy country.

He raised it to his lips, blew away the smoke that was still curling from the barrel, and had to resist the impulse to twirl it around his finger like some kind of gunslinger in a Wild West movie. Large-caliber handguns were interesting to own and fun to shoot. But as practical tools, they were far too heavy and loud.

Still, they got the job done.

He looked down into the shallow grave where the two bodies lay facedown . . . or rather they would have been facedown if there had been anything left of their faces. But those had been obliterated by the .44 Magnum rounds fired into the backs of their respective heads at point-blank range.

Shevchenko shoved the revolver back into its holster, then wiped the polished wooden grips and trigger clean using the Inca wool hat that had belonged to the shorter of the two. It felt damp in his hands, soaked with the tears and snot of its owner, who had bawled into it while pleading for his life. At least the one with the filthy dreadlocks had accepted his fate like a man. Or perhaps he had been so stoned, he didn't realize what was happening until it was too late.

Shevchenko tossed the hat into the grave, then laid the gun and belt on the ground nearby, exchanging the weapon for a shovel—the same shovel he had used to smack Matthew Redd across the back of his head.

That had been satisfying.

Not as satisfying as using the spade to take Redd's head off would have been, at least, not in the moment. But it was payback of a sort, and Wyatt was right. This was a much better plan.

Finding the Ruger had been an unexpected bonus. Killing these two had always been part of the plan, but he would have been content with bashing their heads in with the shovel or breaking their necks. Either one would have worked just fine, but a gun? Redd's own gun?

That was too perfect.

And if the plan didn't work? Well, then he might still get his chance for payback.

He smiled at the thought. Then he scooped a spadeful of dirt from the pile beside the grave and tossed it into the hole, where it partially covered a tie-dyed T-shirt.

FORTY-ONE

As he mucked out Remington's stall later that afternoon, Redd replayed his conversation with Anton Gage. He could not help but be impressed by the man's earnest humility, especially given his enormous achievements in science, business, and environmental activism. But now that he was beyond the gravitational pull of Anton Gage's charisma, with time to reflect, Redd began to wonder if the man's humility was actually a mask or, worse, a kind of patronizing condescension, the way a tall adult might kneel down to speak with a small child.

He was still mulling this over when he heard a vehicle pull up outside.

Starting to feel like Grand Central station out here, he thought as he stepped over to the door. He expected it to be either Hannah or Shane Hepworth, but the newly arrived vehicle was a graphite metallic Chevy four-wheel drive pickup. Redd did not recognize the truck, but he instantly recognized the face behind the wheel.

Em?

His heart began to race, and he unconsciously smoothed his untrimmed beard with his hand as he hurried out to meet her. He reached the truck just as she stepped off the running board. She was dressed in blue hospital scrubs and, as usual, wore no makeup. She didn't need to.

"Hey." He fought back a smile. Played it cool.

"Hey, yourself."

He smiled, and she did too. They stood there staring at each other.

He had so many things he wanted to tell her but just couldn't. Worse, he was afraid he'd say something stupid. He suddenly realized just standing there and staring at her was also stupid. "You want to come in?"

Emily shrugged. "Yeah, sure. I've got about an hour or so before I have to be at work."

She followed him inside. Redd shut the door behind her as she pulled up a chair at the kitchen table. "I'd make coffee," he said, "but I seem to have misplaced the machine."

"Ouch," she said. "I'd say getting a replacement should be the first thing on your list." She paused a beat, then went on in a more serious tone. "How are you feeling?"

"Fine. Why?"

"Why do you think?" Emily gestured at his head. "Blunt force trauma to your skull, stitches, that sort of thing. I just wanted to stop by and see how you're doing. I know for a fact you're too stubborn to see a doctor and too lazy to put on a hat. Has it been itching?"

"Nope," Redd lied.

"Because I can write you scrip for some anti-itch cream."

"I'm fine."

She rolled her eyes. "You find out who hit you?"

He looked away, afraid that she would see the deception in his eyes. "Deputy Hepworth thinks it was a couple of tweakers camped out in the woods."

"Yeah, sadly, we have a lot of those around here these days. I've had quite a few of them OD and come into the ER. Saved most of them." She shrugged. "I know they're responsible for a lot of theft and property crime, but this is the first time I've heard of them getting violent."

Redd uttered an indifferent grunt.

Emily looked away. "The place isn't the same without him here."

"I should've made more time for J. B. Should've been here." It was the first time he said as much out loud.

"Yeah, you should have. But don't beat yourself up. He was as stubborn as you are. He made choices; you made choices. What else can we do?" She reached out and squeezed Redd's hand, then just as quickly pulled away. "What are your plans? Put in your twenty and retire like J. B. did? That's what he figured you'd do. I think he was hoping you'd come back and take over the place and then he could retire for good."

"Actually, I'm done with the Marines."

"Really?" Her face drew into a concerned frown. "Why?"

"It's complicated." Redd stood up, his chair scraping the floor. "Anyway, I haven't really settled on my next move."

"Are you going to sell?"

"I haven't settled on that, either. Making a go of things here won't be easy. J. B. ran up a lot of debt . . . which I guess makes a little more sense knowing what he was going through. I don't know if there's a way to pay it all back without selling."

"I'm sure your girlfriend will be able to find you a buyer."

He shot her a hard look. "Really, Em?"

"Matty, she's into you. She's beautiful, smart, compassionate . . . oh, and she's loaded. You'd be a fool to pass up a chance like that." She refused to meet his gaze. "If you're playing coy because you're worried I'm carrying a torch for you, forget it. I mean, I still care about you, Matty, and I want to be friends, but let me make it easy for you. You have my blessing to pursue happiness."

Redd could see that he was standing in the middle of an emotional minefield. Was Emily truly trying to tell him she had no interest in rekindling their relationship? Or was this some kind of passive-aggressive ploy to force him to declare his undying love for her and no one else?

He took a deep breath. "No offense, Em, but I'm getting a little fed up with everyone around here treating me like I can't make up my own mind."

She flinched as if he'd just slapped her. "I wasn't—"

"I met Hannah two days ago. I know next to nothing about her. What I *do* know is that her family wanted to buy J. B.'s ranch so bad, they were willing to offer me three times what it's worth. I'm not convinced that Wyatt Gage wasn't willing to kill for it. So what I can't figure is why it's so important." Redd took another calming breath. His pulse had quickened along with his ardor. "I don't know anything about these people except that they have more money than God."

Emily swallowed. "Well, I can tell you that they're dedicated philanthropists. Anton Gage donated a lot of money to the clinic—we have a brand-new 3D mammography machine thanks to him. He's invested in half the businesses in the county and loaned money to the rest at low interest rates."

"When did all this happen?"

Emily's eyes went up to the ceiling as she did some mental arithmetic. "Four . . . maybe five years back. It was sort of happening in the background at first. A lot of ranches were going under. Gage Land Development started picking them off. Then pretty soon they were everywhere. The Gages must be one of the biggest property owners in Montana now."

"Why?"

She shrugged. "Isn't real estate always a good investment?"

"This isn't just real estate. These are ranches. The reason all those family operations went under is that ranching isn't profitable anymore. Never mind the fact that Anton Gage is a strict vegan. I really don't see him trying to turn a profit by bankrolling the cattle industry. So what's he doing with all that land?"

Emily shook her head. "Maybe he just wants his own private wilderness."

Redd considered this. Anton Gage *was* an environmentalist, so it was possible, but then he recalled something Gage had said during the brunch . . . something about "good old-fashioned capitalism." Gage was a businessman first. So what was he really after?

Emily squared her shoulders. "Well, it's been great catching up, Matty, but I should probably get going."

He brought his gaze back to her. Until that moment, he had not realized how much he wanted her to stay. "Em, can I ask you something?"

"Of course." She looked sincere, like she was genuinely intrigued by what he might ask.

That makes two of us.

Redd wasn't one to dance around with words, so he just came out with it. "What happened? How'd you end up back here? Last I heard, you were in Texas."

Her eyes darted away, as if the question embarrassed her. "Mom and Dad are getting up there. I came back to spend more time with them." She shrugged. "So here I am. On the cutting edge of medical science."

Redd looked her straight in the eyes. "You and I never resolved anything. We just went our separate ways."

Emily shook her head. "Matty, don't. Don't go opening up old wounds. I didn't bring any nylon thread to stitch 'em back up."

Too late.

"I thought about going to Texas to see you a thousand times, especially when I was stationed at Pendleton."

"Maybe you should have."

"I did once. Remember?"

"Yeah. Once. My first semester at TCU, you came down for a New York minute, and then you left."

"You ignored me." His voice rose a little. "What was I supposed to do?"

"I was in the middle of final exams. It was my first semester. You could've picked a better time to decide you needed a booty call."

"Now hold on—"

"You ghosted me, Matty Redd. You checked out of my life without ever telling me why."

"You never asked."

Her scowl revealed the degree to which his retort failed to impress. "Oh yes. I should have come to you on hands and knees, begging you to come back into my life."

"You know what happened to J. B. I had to work the ranch. I didn't have time for anything else and you, well . . ." Redd bit off his last words.

This seemed to mollify her a little. "Actually, I didn't know about you and J. B. and all of that. Not until he told me. He felt horrible about it. To tell you the truth, so did I when he finally told me. When you stopped calling, I thought you had dumped me and found somebody else. It broke my heart."

Redd didn't know what to say to that, so he said the first thing that sounded right. "Yeah. I really screwed it up." He blinked to clear his stinging eyes.

She shrugged. "We were just kids. Hardly anyone marries their high school sweetheart."

It was a true statement, but the way she said it felt too simple for Redd. Yeah, they were young back then, but he'd only truly loved three people in his life, and she was one of them.

"Did you ever? Get married, I mean?"

She shook her head. "Had a couple of chances, though. Doctors who wanted to 'rescue' me from the drudgery of nursing—like I need rescuing. I love what I do. It's important work."

Redd started to nod, but then her words hit like a secondary explosion. *"I love what I do. It's important work."*

He might have said the same thing . . . probably had said it.

And look where it got me. I failed everyone. The team. J. B. Emily . . . I let them all down.

What am I even doing here?

He clapped his hands to his thighs. "Wow. Sorry. I'm going to make you late for work."

She didn't move. "Do you want me to leave?"

"No," he said, maybe a touch too fast.

I want the opposite, he thought. But he didn't know how to say that.

He also didn't know how to tell her that being around her was the best part of being back in Montana.

Emily sighed and reached across the table and touched his hand. "You believe in second chances, Matty?"

He thought immediately of his teammates, blown to bits in Mexico. About the end of his career . . . his honor. About losing J. B. So much had already been lost. No second chances for any of it.

She must have misinterpreted the agony in his eyes as indecision. Before he could even think to take her hand in his, she withdrew it. She looked away, embarrassed. "Sorry; I guess I got my signals crossed."

"Look," he said, his voice cracking. "I don't how to do this, okay?"

"What does *this* mean?"

"Me and you."

"Forgive me for touching you, Matty. I didn't mean—"

"It's not like that."

Emily sat back in her chair. "Okay, what's it like?"

She knew he wasn't the best with words, and yet she always seemed to get him to talk to her anyways. Even when nobody else could.

"It took a long time to get over you, Em. I didn't expect to see you here, and now . . ."

"Well, I'm sorry I came at a bad time." There was an edge of sarcasm in her tone, which she seemed to regret immediately. "I am really sorry, Matty. For everything. For how stuff went down between us. For J. B. All of it. I'm just really sorry."

Redd didn't know what to say, so he just nodded. "I'm sorry too."

"You're right, though. I do need to get going." She stood.

Redd stood as well.

Emily stopped at the front door. "Tuesday at five, here, right?"

"You're coming?"

"I traded shifts so I could make it. I told you I wouldn't miss it for the world."

Redd managed a smile. "Thanks. I appreciate it."

Suddenly her arms were around him, her face pressed against his chest. "Take care of yourself, Matty. You're a good man. It'll all work out. You'll see."

He squeezed her tight. "Thanks for stopping by." He didn't want to let go, but he did.

"Now I'm late. See ya." She bolted for her truck but stopped and looked back just before climbing inside. "Hey, Matty?"

"Yeah?"

"Promise me that before you just take off again, we can sit down and, I don't know, maybe have a cup of coffee somewhere or something?"

"I'm not really a Starbucks kind of guy."

"Well then, you better get yourself a new coffee maker." She smiled, and so did Redd. "Doesn't have to be coffee. I just . . . I'd like to be able to talk to you again. Feels like we have more catching up to do."

Redd nodded. "Promise."

Emily climbed into her truck without saying another word, and Redd watched her rocket away in a cloud of dust.

There was so much more he had wanted to tell her, but if he had, then maybe he would have fallen in love with her all over again. That was the last thing he needed right now. Because loving someone was a weakness that an enemy could exploit.

As Redd watched her truck disappear over the horizon, his thoughts once again turned to Wyatt Gage. Any chance of further reconnecting with Emily would have to come later.

First, he had a score to settle.

FORTY-TWO

After another restless but uneventful night, Redd rose early to let Remington out to graze in the pasture. Then he dressed in jeans and a clean T-shirt and headed into town. His first stop was at the unimaginatively named Coffee Stop, where he bought three extra-large coffees, two of which he poured into J. B.'s old thermos, along with a toasted bagel and a little packet of cream cheese. Not exactly Starbucks—there were no big corporate stores or franchises in Stillwater County—but that was fine with Redd.

His next stop was at the courthouse, where he went directly to the county assessor's office. Redd stood at the front desk waiting for someone to take notice of him. It was hard not to see him, given his size. Finally one of the clerks glanced up from his desk and feigned surprise. Round like a butter bean and bald as a baby, he hurried over to the wide front desk.

"May I help you, sir?"

"I'd like to see some property records."

"Of course. That's what we do here." He tugged at his collar with a fat finger. "Which property did you want to look up?"

Redd returned a patient smile. "All of them."

✴ ✴ ✴

Emily's statement that the Gage family had been buying up property all across the state had been eating at him like an earworm. Anton Gage didn't strike him as the kind of guy who liked to play Monopoly with real money. He was a tech guy, not a real estate guy. So what was the point of buying all that land?

The clerk who had greeted him at the front desk pointed Redd in the general direction of the property records but offered no additional help, explaining that he had work to attend to.

Redd spent the next few hours at a computer terminal in an unused workstation, poring over first the county and then state land ownership records. His presence clearly caused a stir, albeit an understated one. The tax clerks hovered nearby, pretending to be busy when they weren't making runs to the coffee machine or the restroom down the hall. The clerk who greeted Redd made it a point to pass by him directly, casting careful glances over Redd's shoulder, trying to figure out what he was up to.

His eyes glued to the screen, Redd didn't notice a man approach from behind. "Excuse me, sir," he said over Redd's shoulder. "It's Mr. Redd, isn't it?"

Redd looked up to find a tall, slim man with silver hair, attired in a Western-style sport coat and dress boots with pointed toes, polished to a high gloss. "That's right."

"You inherited the Thompson spread?"

Redd nodded. "J. B. was my father."

The man inclined his head. "I'm Randall Shaw, the county assessor. I'm sorry for your loss." His eyes flicked over Redd's shoulder, lighting briefly on the screen, which showed a large plot in the sparsely populated but aptly named Wheatland County. "Something in particular that you're looking for?"

"Just curious."

"Well, if you need assistance, don't hesitate to ask. We're at your service."

"Appreciate it."

Shaw frowned and headed back to his office. Redd turned back to the computer and kept digging. What he discovered was that Wyatt Gage had started buying land in Montana seven years ago, two years before he bought the land for Anton's mountain escape. After that, Wyatt kicked into high gear, focusing on farmland, particularly wheatland in Montana's Golden Triangle.

Farmland?

Neither Wyatt nor Anton Gage was involved in agribusiness. Nor did they seem to be developing the land, turning productive soil into suburban wastelands. Redd was no economist and he certainly wasn't any kind of investor, but he knew how to google stuff.

His suspicions were confirmed by a USDA database. The average value of an acre of farm real estate in the Mountain region was just over twelve hundred dollars. An acre of cropland could be rented out for just under ninety dollars, and pasture rented for just under six dollars an acre.

Spend millions to make hundreds?

It made no sense.

Or did it?

He recalled Hannah telling him how her father was deeply committed to the problem of food security and had formed the Gage Food Trust charity to make that happen. If Gage wanted to feed the world, maybe he needed a lot of farmland to do it. He made a mental note to access the property tax records of other farmland states to see if the Gages were buying in them as well.

So why buy J. B.'s place? It had been a working cattle ranch until J. B. let the operation fall away. It could be so again, if managed correctly, but why would an avowed vegan want to grab up all the rangeland?

He heard approaching footsteps and saw Shaw in the reflection on the screen.

"Mr. Redd?"

Redd sighed and turned around.

"I'm afraid I have some . . . unfortunate news." Shaw slipped his hand into his sport coat, pulled out a printed envelope, and handed it to Redd.

"What's this?" Redd saw the official tax assessor's logo on the return address.

"Your father's ranch is in arrears for a considerable amount of delinquent taxes. A lien was put against it."

Redd slipped a thumbnail under the flap and opened it. "Yeah, I heard."

"And as I'm sure you're well aware, a lien is a legal device that collects taxes upon the sale of the property. Since you've indicated that you don't plan to sell, I'm afraid we have no choice but to levy the property."

Redd pulled the letter out. His eyes narrowed.

"As that letter informs you, your property is now being put up for auction so that the lien might be satisfied."

"When?"

"A week from tomorrow."

"What? How is that possible? Why wasn't I notified?"

Shaw nodded at the letter. "That is your notification."

"But I've only just arrived in town. I need more time."

"I understand your concern. But the lien and auction are in regard to your father's delinquency over the last few years. It must seem sudden to you, but it's not to us."

Redd sensed the whole office was listening in now even if they weren't looking at them.

"I can't afford to pay this bill."

"Then the auction of your property must move forward."

Redd looked at the letter again. *This is BS.*

"I'm sorry to be the bearer of bad news. I hope you realize this isn't personal—"

Redd stood. "It's nothing but personal. And I'm willing to bet that Wyatt Gage had something to do with this, didn't he?"

Shaw glanced around the room, his eyes searching for physical if not moral support. None came. He swallowed hard. "As a matter of fact, yes, Mr. Gage has expressed interest in your situation. But I assure you, there is nothing illegal about this course of action. In fact, I probably should have acted on this earlier, but with your father's illness and all, I just thought—"

Redd crushed the letter in his fist and tossed it to the floor. So much for Wyatt Gage respecting his own father's wishes. "I guess I'm done here."

FORTY-THREE

Redd stomped down the long, creaking hallway of the courthouse, nearly bowling over someone coming out of the county clerk's office. It turned out to be Duke Blanton in his daily uniform of jeans, custom, high-gloss cowboy boots, and a buffalo plaid shirt. His shining silver crew cut was hidden beneath a gray felt Stetson.

"Whoa, son? Where's the fire?" Blanton's weathered face cracked a wide, welcoming laugh, throwing crow's-feet around his bright eyes.

Redd was still full of rage, but his lawyer's smiling face brought his temperature down a few degrees. "Sorry, Mr. Blanton."

"It's Duke, Matt." Blanton squinted. "I'm no doctor, but judging by that look on your face, you must have just swallowed a big ol' cat turd."

"Something like that."

Blanton's calloused hand grabbed Redd by the bicep and led him toward the exit.

"You come with me, young man. Dr. Blanton knows where we can find the cure."

✖ ✖ ✖

Redd and Blanton sat at the end of the bar at Spady's. Redd had half expected the staff to show him the door, but evidently Jarrod had not put his name on the Wall of Shame.

Not yet, anyway.

It was too early for happy hour, and the clientele consisted of a dozen or so men in ranch attire—the fact that they were drinking and not working suggested they were currently unemployed. Lynyrd Skynyrd's "On the Hunt" rocked the jukebox. Blanton insisted on a whiskey shot to toast J. B. and Redd reluctantly agreed.

"To your old man. He was one of the good guys."

"To J. B."

They tossed back their whiskeys and Blanton ordered a round of Bozone beers. "All right, Matt. Why don't you tell me what put your knickers in such a twist?"

As Redd told him, Blanton nodded in comprehension. "Sounds like someone wants to play hardball."

"Yeah" was all Redd could say.

"Well, there are a few legal measures we could take to slow this down, maybe give you an opportunity to raise enough cash to settle the debt. Is that something you could do?"

Aside from prostituting himself to Hannah Gage . . . or perhaps making another appeal to Anton Gage to get Wyatt to call off his dogs, he saw only one solution. "I could try to sell my truck. It's in good shape. I'm sure I could get thirty for it."

Blanton rolled his pint glass between his palms. "Maybe down in Bozeman. But then again, maybe not. Not many folks can make a cash offer like that these days."

"It's all I've got," Redd replied helplessly.

"I'll look into it for you," Blanton said. "But I would be remiss if I didn't offer you some good advice."

Redd had a feeling he wasn't going to like Blanton's advice. He wasn't wrong.

"That property is like a millstone hung around your neck. It dragged J. B. down, and it will drag you down too. Sure, you might be able to save it in the short term, but then what? You gonna stay here and run it all by your lonesome?"

"I did it before."

"You might have done the chores, but Jim Bob was still around to take care of the business side of things. You didn't see that at the time, but his military pension was what kept the ranch from going bust. You do this, and you'll be working without a net. On the other hand, you sell now, before the auction, and you'll walk away with enough cash to live well, at least for a while."

"I won't sell to Wyatt Gage."

"Then sell to someone else. I know a few folks who'd—"

"Who'd give me fair market value and then turn around and sell to Gage." Redd's volume had increased to the point where the bartender—not Jarrod, but a slightly dowdy fortysomething female—gave him a sharp look.

Blanton spread his hands in a gesture of surrender. "Just showing you all the options on the table. I respect what you're trying to do."

He drained the last of his beer and stood, pulled out his wallet, and threw bills onto the bar, then clapped Redd's broad shoulder. "Hold the good thought, Matt. Maybe things will work out for you after all."

Redd nodded. "Thanks for the drinks, Duke. And the advice."

He didn't follow Blanton's exit, which was probably why he didn't see the pair that entered just as the lawyer was leaving. It was the sound of footsteps, growing louder and then stopping right behind him, that finally prompted Redd to swivel his barstool around.

"Hello, Matt," Wyatt Gage said. Roman Shevchenko stood right behind his employer.

Redd wasn't quite able to maintain his flat expression, especially when he saw the hatred smoldering in the Ukrainian's eyes.

"I hear you and my father had a little talk the other day," Wyatt said.

"Nice guy," Redd said. "Good manners. Guess that's not a hereditary trait."

"Yeah, Dad's a peach." Wyatt cocked his head to the side. "What is it you think he told you about your property?"

"He said you had overreached by trying to pressure me to sell. Said you should leave it alone."

Wyatt came alongside him and leaned on the bar. "Well, you know how fathers can be. They don't always get their stories straight."

"Are you calling your father a liar? Or an idiot?" Redd sensed more than saw nearby patrons suddenly paying attention, quiet and alert, like gazelles on the veldt watching two lions circling each other.

"Oh, Matty, Matty, Matty. I know you think my father is on your side, but I can assure you, he's not. He's not on anyone's side but his own. Oh, he said nice things to make you feel better, but that's just to protect his public image. If he really wanted to help you, he'd have paid off your father's debts and given you a stake to make a go of things. Instead, he made some BS promise about buying your stock sometime down the road. Like he'd ever do that. And you fell for it like the white trash sucker you are.

"Now? I get to be the bad guy, snatching up your land for a song at auction. And he gets it in the end anyway. He wins. You lose. And I win, because I'm the one who gets to bury the knife in your back."

"Screw you."

Wyatt just laughed. "You're as stupid as your old man and just as stubborn."

"I'll take that as a compliment."

Wyatt's smile faded. He moved closer to Redd, who finally turned on the stool to face him. "Listen carefully because I'm only going to say this once. I heard you've been snooping around in my family's business affairs. I don't know what your problem is, but I'm telling you right now, you're going to knock that off. Understood?"

"And if I don't?"

Wyatt's grin returned as he stood. "Next time, I won't ask politely."

"That's your idea of polite?"

Behind him, Shevchenko chuckled.

Redd turned away and leaned back, his elbows on the bar. "Just tell me one thing. Why is it you want my daddy's property so bad?"

"Badly," Shevchenko said.

"What?" Redd said.

"*Bad* is an adjective. But it is modifying the verb *want*, so the word you should use is *badly* because it is an adverb. How are you so ignorant about your own language?"

Wyatt chuckled. "Told you he was smarter than you."

"You're right, Sasquatch. My bad. Tell me, Mr. Gage, why do you want my dad's property so *badly*?"

Wyatt blew air through his teeth as he glanced up at the coffered ceiling, thinking. "That's an interesting question. I suppose I could say something clever like 'The heart has its reasons of which reason knows nothing,' but I've had it with that philosophical crap. Or I could point to Darwinian selection and tell you that the strong always absorbs the weak, the superior consumes the inferior, and so on. But that's a tiresome tautology, isn't it?

"The actual reason why I want your property is just because it's next to mine, which means they are already joined in a sense, so in my mind, that makes it my property. And the fact you won't sell it to me no matter how much money I offer makes me want it even more."

"You're not used to people telling you no, are you?"

"Come to think of it, I can't remember the last time someone did—and got away with it."

Redd's heart raced. "Maybe today's the day that all turns around for you."

Wyatt smiled. "I doubt it. See you at the auction—if you're still around." He turned and headed toward his reserved booth in the back of the restaurant.

Shevchenko stayed put.

Redd nodded at Wyatt's back. "Your owner is leaving. Better catch up or he won't leave you treats in your cage tonight."

Shevchenko stepped closer, staring down at him, his dark eyes radiating hate.

Redd couldn't remember being around a guy this big in person. The Ukrainian was a great wall of muscle, bone, and mean. Redd remembered what had happened the last time they'd squared off. He'd won that encounter, but just barely.

"I think it is time you left Montana," Shevchenko said. "There is nothing here for you. Certainly not that delicious little nurse friend of yours. But where will you go? You have nothing and no one." His wide mouth grinned. "Of course, you could go back to the Marines . . . unless . . . you can't go back."

Redd's jaw clenched.

Is he guessing? Or does he know?

"Yes, that's right. Just sit there and take it, like your old man. He was pathetic and weak too. Maybe all of you Marines are cowards. It made me laugh to see him hobble around like an old woman—"

Redd launched from his stool, his big fist smashing into Shevchenko's smirking face like a Hellfire missile.

Shevchenko's head jerked back with the blow.

Barely.

Redd had put men down with hits like that. Knocked them out cold. But Shevchenko wasn't an ordinary man.

The Ukrainian laughed through his split upper lip. Blood gushed over his mouth and down his chin in a fearsome mask, staining his big teeth like a bear's fangs after a kill. Then he backhanded Redd with a fist the size of a Christmas ham. Stars flared in Redd's watering eyes as he staggered back into the bar. Shevchenko leaned back and launched a killing roundhouse punch with his knuckled fist right at Redd's temple.

You're getting beat up, he told himself. *Shake it off.*

Training and instinct kicked in. Redd ducked at the last second. He felt the air breezing against his hair as the massive arm swooped over his head.

Redd lunged forward, driving his shoulder into the Ukrainian's chest the way he had once pushed blocking sleds around the football field.

Shevchenko did not have the leverage to resist, and so they both careened into a table. Someone screamed as chairs scraped and toppled and plates crashed to the floor.

Shevchenko's elbow speared into Redd's spine, turning his legs to rubber but not before he staggered back. Redd rabbit-punched the bigger man's ironhard gut—a futile effort. Shevchenko shoved Redd away hard and threw another punch that glanced off the top of Redd's head. The impact knocked him to the floor but missed the stitched scalp wound by a couple inches. Redd rolled to the side, one arm raised to block the kick he knew was coming. He deflected the blow but at the cost of searing pain that ran the length of his arm.

Before Shevchenko could recock, Redd grabbed a chair and used it to get back to his feet. In the same motion, he lofted the chair above his head like an ax and swung it down hard at the Ukrainian's laughing war face.

Sensing the attack, Shevchenko charged forward, ducking below Redd's swing with the chair, blunting its strike against his back. The rushing Ukrainian's massive bulk hit Redd like a freight train, lifting him off his feet and knocking the wind out of him.

Gasping for breath, he felt Shevchenko's arms wrap around his waist like steel bands, lifting him up and driving him down onto a table, smashing plates and glasses as he hit. Somehow Redd managed to grab Shevchenko's neck at the last minute and pull him down with him.

The two of them crashed to the ground, tossed to the side by the angle of the broken table. Redd rolled with the momentum and fell on top of the fallen monster. He raised a fist to smash Shevchenko in the mouth, but the much larger man stiff-armed Redd—the length of his reach was so great that Redd's falling fist barely struck him.

Delivering a blow to the side of Shevchenko's arm, Redd cleared the way and leaned in. He torqued his body, leveraging every ounce of strength he could muster as he fired off one punch after another. More blood began to trickle out from the corner of Shevchenko's mouth.

After whaling on Shevchenko's face, Redd pulled back and went for the knockout blow, but just as he swung a vicious right hand, the Ukrainian relaxed and rolled his hips back.

Shevchenko turned his head, letting Redd's fist connect just above his right jaw. No sooner had the blow landed than Shevchenko shot his legs out, wrapping them around Redd's neck and shoulders. At the same time, he bear-hugged Redd's arm and squeezed—securing the tightest triangle choke that Redd had ever felt.

Uh-oh.

As Shevchenko's thighs cut into Redd's flesh, putting pressure on his carotid artery, the blood slowed to his brain. Redd knew he had three to five seconds to act, tops. Otherwise, he'd be put to sleep—and the fight would be over.

Grabbing the collar of Shevchenko's shirt, Redd grunted and leaned back. He tried to lift his head. Even a millimeter of movement would buy him more time, but Shevchenko's legs were like a pair of vise grips.

Getting his legs beneath him, Redd yanked with all his might, pulling up on Shevchenko. Normally, with his own considerable size, such a move was no problem for Redd. But the only way to break Shevchenko's hold was to pick him completely off the ground and slam him back down.

His muscles screaming, Redd clawed harder at Shevchenko's collar. He found his grip and hoisted the big man into the air just as his vision went fuzzy. Had he been able to see, he would have noticed Shevchenko's eyes getting bigger the farther he got from the ground.

Letting Newton's law do the bulk of the work, Redd put whatever strength he had left into the return trip—slamming Shevchenko down, driving him into the floor with enough force to make the ground shake slightly beneath them.

Rolling to the side, Redd sucked in some much-needed oxygen. His vison came back, and he watched as Shevchenko shook off the body slam and made his way to his feet.

Hurrying to match the monster's pace, Redd climbed off the ground and charged Shevchenko, spearing him in the rib cage. Both men locked onto each other and, as they fought to gain the upper hand, rolled across the room.

Redd had a decision to make. Clearly Shevchenko was comfortable on his back. He'd already let Redd into his guard once, and that triangle choke nearly put an end to him. Still, from a tactical standpoint, Redd knew his best bet was to mount the Ukrainian and secure the dominant grappling position. He'd done enough judo over the years to feel comfortable on his back, but when fighting three hundred-plus pounds of pissed-off muscle, he figured the safest bet was to keep it beneath him.

Besides, if Redd could get to Shevchenko's right arm, he could put him in an Americana lock hard enough to just maybe end the Ukrainian's punching days for good—and leave the goon seeing more than just stars.

"Redd!"

The shout rebounded off his conscious awareness like a pebble off an alligator's back—not quite enough to distract him, but enough to break his concentration.

"Redd! Stand down!"

It was Shane Hepworth, and from the corner of his eye, Redd saw that the deputy was in uniform, with his pistol drawn and aimed at Redd.

"Stand down, or I will put you down," Hepworth shouted.

Redd stared dully at the barrel of the gun and then, with an effort, mastered his rage. For a second time, someone with a firearm had deprived him of a victory . . . of revenge. Only this time, the gun wasn't loaded with rock salt.

He rolled off Shevchenko, then shoved off, putting some distance between himself and his beaten foe. Hepworth's weapon remained trained on him.

"Go to your knees," Hepworth said, his voice taut as a garotte. "Interlace your fingers behind your head."

Redd did but moved slowly as the pain of old injuries and new seized his nervous system. "Okay. Put the gun away, Shane. I'll go along peacefully."

Hepworth did not lower the pistol but kept it aimed at Redd as he stepped behind him and then deftly slapped a handcuff around Redd's right wrist. Before Redd could protest again, Hepworth twisted both arms down, shackled his left wrist, and then shoved Redd forward onto his face.

"Matthew Redd, you have the right to remain silent. Anything you say can and will—"

"I know my rights, Shane. For crying out loud, it was a bar fight. Let me up, and I'll walk out of here."

"Only place you're going is a cell," Hepworth said. "Matthew Redd, you're under arrest for suspicion of murder."

FORTY-FOUR

Anton Gage sat in the back of his Rivian pickup. His security supervisor was up front with the driver. They were driving past a vast ocean of wheat he owned on either side of the narrow two-lane north of Three Forks, Montana.

Gage's eyes were fixed on dozens of quadcopter drones flying in precise automated patterns just a few inches above the long rows of golden wheat fields ripening with grain. Armed with a variety of sensors and cameras, the drones provided live, high-throughput data for plant growth, stress indicators, insect infestation, and disease symptoms. The diagnostic technology, which was akin to facial recognition for plants, was applicable to all of the cereal crops the Gage Food Trust was developing around the world. The drone analysis helped the trust determine which varieties they would ultimately move forward with next year when the global mass planting program would begin. The exhaustive development process required his researchers to plant multiple fields with genetically engineered drought- and insect-resistant varieties of ultrahigh-protein cereals.

Gage was particularly proud of this drone technology; one of his original firms had pioneered it. It made him feel even closer to the project, the first step in a vision that had been the primary focus of all his endeavors over the last decade. The rest of the Twelve had their own parts to play. But this was his alone.

Though he held no religious beliefs whatsoever, his mission gave him a deep spiritual satisfaction, like some ancient Hebrew prophet invested by the power of Yahweh, bringing truth and judgment to a wicked generation.

He was one step closer to saving the planet.

✖ ✖ ✖

Gage entered the main lab of the Gage Food Trust Research Facility and greeted the beefy security man behind the desk with a nonchalant smile.

"Good to see you, Bob. How are the kids?"

"Jenny's the starting pitcher for her team this Saturday, and Billy's off at space camp. Thank you for asking. Is everything well with you, sir?"

"Couldn't be better."

Gage placed his hand on the biometric reader before being allowed to pass through the metal detector. Clearing both, he boarded a small electric cart.

"Where to, Mr. Gage?" the cart driver said.

"Lab number one."

"Right away." The cart driver called ahead, his famous passenger the picture of serenity.

Gage was anything but serene. He could hardly contain his excitement. He was on his way to a sacred place, built by his own hands, to meet his own high priest, called and consecrated by him these last several years.

It was time to meet with Willow.

✖ ✖ ✖

Dr. Rafael Caldera, aka Willow, stood beneath the wide-screen display, studying several dozen images from the Mexico clinic. He focused on the photo of one newborn child. A boy.

The infant's cloudy blind eyes were almost lost in the misshapen mouth that extended from what should have been the lower jaw all the way to the eye sockets.

He hadn't survived more than a few minutes.

None of them had.

His shoulder-length silver ponytail matched the color of his neatly trimmed beard. Since he wasn't in a clean room, he felt at ease in sandals, jeans, and his favorite blue-and-scarlet FC Barcelona soccer jersey.

"Rafe, it's good to see you," Gage said as he entered the room.

Dr. Caldera turned around. "It's been too long, old friend."

The two men embraced, clapping each other on the back. It had been a long time since they'd seen each other or communicated in any way. Gage conducted all of his important business only in person. As a technology pioneer, he did not trust any form of electronic communication.

Gage and Caldera had first met a decade prior. Gage had been the first and only investor in Caldera's revolutionary "prime editing" gene technology. While the gene editing tool CRISPR was a giant leap forward in gene alteration, its essential process was inelegant and sometimes imprecise. CRISPR did a "cut-and-paste" of strands of genetic material the way a kidnapper used magazine letters to create a ransom note.

But Caldera's quantum-leaping approach was akin to the world's greatest word processor hunting down exact genetic letters, replacing and reorganizing them at will to create the perfect full-length, laser-printed, error-free manuscript.

Error-free, so long as the writer knew how to spell. The Mexico clinic mutations were a last, hard spelling lesson. A typo on the last line of the last chapter of Caldera's perfect novel. After careful analysis, Caldera had spell-checked the sequence error. Problem solved.

Gage nodded at the horror show on the screen behind them. "Why torture yourself?"

"Not torture, just a reminder. In my line of work, I seldom get to see things on the macro scale. In genetics, I play with the bricks but I never get to see the house. It's good to know this will never happen again."

"Your family is well?"

"Yes, all good. And yours?"

"Thriving. I apologize for the dramatics down in Mexico. It was unpleasant but necessary."

Caldera had been less than thrilled at being used as bait to draw out Vasquez, the leak they hadn't been able to identify, but the ruse had the added benefit of destroying the American assault team and humiliating the FBI.

The FBI had been hunting Caldera—or rather his alter ego Willow—for some time. He was rumored to be the money and point man for several science-based WMD programs involving at least five different terror organizations. In this they were half-right.

Dr. Caldera was responsible for developing a variety of weapons programs and distributing monies funded by mysterious donors through various shell corporations. But since the FBI didn't have Caldera's actual identity, they couldn't know he was one of the world's premier geneticists and that the Gage project was his most important mission.

Caldera pointed to the conference table, where coffee and bottled water waited on a tray. "Something to drink?" Caldera poured himself a glass of purified water.

Gage pulled up a chair. "Later, perhaps. You have news for me?"

"Yes. Excellent news. My team isolated the genetic sequence that caused the birth defects. It is now eliminated entirely from GFT-17."

"That means we can move forward?" Gage asked with a hopeful smile.

"Yes, we can, at least on our end." He checked his digital watch. "By this time tomorrow, I should have enough for initial deployment."

"For all three locations?"

The Gage Food Trust Research Facility in Montana was one of three such facilities where different grains were being modified for widespread cultivation. While the Montana facility focused on wheat, the lab in Louisiana specialized in rice, and the facility outside Córdoba, Argentina, some seven hundred kilometers northwest of Buenos Aires, specialized in maize. Together, wheat, rice, and corn made up over 50 percent of the world's entire caloric intake. One or more of them were consumed all over the globe, particularly by the poor who could ill afford expensive animal proteins.

"I'll deliver the GFT-17 to them on Friday, on the return leg of the trip from Argentina."

Gage thought of his last meeting with the Twelve. They had emphasized the immutability of the timeline. Gage had guaranteed delivery on his self-imposed date. They, in turn, made costly commitments and deployed irreplaceable assets to ensure its success. It was a tremendous vote of confidence in Gage, the newest and youngest member of the Twelve.

He smiled and gripped Caldera's shoulder. "Remember this day, Rafe! This is the day we put an end to hunger and human suffering forever!"

Caldera nodded.

After one last look at the photos from the clinic, Gage flicked a switch, turning the screen off, then walked out.

FORTY-FIVE

"This is ridiculous," Redd said from the back of the sheriff's department SUV, his hands still cuffed behind him. "I didn't kill anyone."

Deputy Hepworth's eyes flicked up to meet his gaze in the rearview mirror. "For your own sake, it's probably better if we have this conversation with your legal counsel present."

"I don't need a freaking lawyer, Shane." Even as he said the words, Redd felt a sense of déjà vu. The last time he had refused counsel, it had cost him his career in the Marines. Had that been the wrong call? He didn't think so. He probably deserved a lot worse. But this time? This time he had a clear memory on his side. "I didn't kill anyone."

"That'll be for a jury to decide. I just follow the evidence."

"What evidence? Who did I supposedly kill?"

Hepworth spat a laugh. "Here's a bit of free advice. Cop to manslaughter. Tell Judge Reynolds you were just trying to get your stuff back and things got out of hand. You'll probably get off with a slap on the wrist . . . two to five years at the most."

"Get my stuff back? What are you talking about?"

"I'll probably take some heat for showing you their camp," Hepworth went on. "But don't even think about trying to drag me down with you."

"What, those tweakers? They're dead?"

"Shot with your Ruger. Imagine that. Practically blew their heads right off. Dug the rounds out of the shallow grave where you buried them."

"My Ruger was stolen, Shane. You know that."

Hepworth shrugged. "So you said. But we found it at your place."

"My place?"

"We had a search warrant, if that's what you're thinking."

Redd's mind reeled from this revelation. "Shane, I'm being set up."

Another shrug. "Tell it to the judge, man. I tried to help you out. Told you I'd handle things, but you just had to go about doing it your way."

Suddenly it all made sense. "You did this. You're working for Gage. What did he promise you? Blackwood's job? Did you kill them yourself, or did Gage have his gorilla do it?"

"Now see, that's the kind of talk that's going to get you put away for a long, long time."

Redd threw his head back in disgust. He saw it all clearly now. The break-in at the ranch, the attack, the theft of his gun . . . and a couple of unsuspecting dirtbags sacrificed to make the frame-up complete. "I guess this really shouldn't come as much of a surprise. You were willing to kill J. B. to get his land. What's a couple of tweakers that no one will even miss?"

"Nobody murdered Jim Bob," Hepworth said defensively.

Redd raised an eyebrow at the tacit admission that the second half of his accusation was true. But then Hepworth really didn't care, because it was Redd's word against his, and the deputy had a badge to hide behind.

✖   ✖   ✖

Redd's dinner was a sack lunch from, of all places, Spady's. A pulled pork sandwich, coleslaw in a cup, a dill pickle in wax paper, and a bag of Lay's classic potato chips.

"What? No beer?" Redd asked as he unpacked the paper bag.

"Tap water or burnt coffee," replied his jailer, an older deputy whose nameplate read *McKibben*. "Your choice."

"Can't go wrong with water."

McKibben left, then returned a moment later with a swallow's worth of tepid tap water.

"You guys aren't going to like my Yelp review," Redd muttered as he took the cup.

He'd seen neither hide nor hair of Shane Hepworth since he'd been delivered to the lockup. There had been no interview nor any formal presentation of charges, and he had not been allowed his obligatory phone call. Not that there was anyone to call.

As Redd ate, he mulled over Hepworth's admission.

"Nobody murdered Jim Bob."

He had sounded almost offended at the idea, as if he actually believed it was true. That meant Hepworth wasn't read in on the plan to kill J. B. He'd been duped along with everyone else. But if his story about finding J. B. on the ground next to Remington was true, what had happened to J. B.'s phone?

If he could find that phone, maybe he'd be able to find the proof that Wyatt Gage had murdered J. B.

It wasn't much, but it was something to occupy his mind while cooped up in this tiny cell.

And maybe for the next twenty years of his life, behind bars in Montana State Prison.

I gotta get out of here, Redd told himself. But he had no idea how to make that happen.

FORTY-SIX

All the lights were blasting through the floor-to-ceiling glass of Wyatt's place at Dancing Elk not far from his father's mountain mansion. Wyatt's home looked like a lighthouse overlooking a sea of green forest now black in the moonlight.

Hannah skidded her G-Rex to a halt in front of her brother's place and stormed up the stairs. She was hit by a wall of thundering rap music that thumped against her flesh as she dashed for the main living area on the top floor. She swore as she climbed the floating staircase two steps at a time, worried how the vile sound would affect her horses, to say nothing of the wildlife in the surrounding woods.

She mounted the top landing, which brought her to the expansive, wide-open living area. There were semi-naked couples tangled up on the massive leather sectional, doing their thing next to other people in various stages of dress and drug-altered consciousness, fixated on the swirling images thrown against the screen by the massive overhead digital projector.

She refused to look at the trophy heads of African and North American big game staring down at her like a hanging jury, each slaughtered by Wyatt's own hand—or more accurately, his high-powered rifles and long-range glass.

A hand reached out to grab her as she passed one of the couches, but she swatted it away without breaking stride. She made a beeline for the outdoor porch and the massive hot tub steaming the cool night sky like a Yellowstone hot pot.

Wyatt lay in the tub, a massive gold chain draped around his neck and a buxom young Chinese woman draped over his lap. He cooed in her ear and she giggled as Hannah approached.

"What the hell, Wyatt."

Wyatt rolled his head toward his half sister. He blinked a few times, either to clear away the steam or the chemical fog in his brain. His glistening eyes finally widened with recognition.

"Why, hello to you too, Sister. Come on in. There's plenty of room."

The woman in his lap giggled again.

Hannah fixed the woman with a cold stare. *"Zǒu kāi jìnǔ."*

The girl bolted upright in the bubbling water, terrified, looking to Wyatt for instruction. He frowned and shooed her away with a flick of his hand. She scurried out of the tub, pulling a towel around herself before disappearing into the house.

"Well, that was rude," Wyatt said, his head still lolling back. "What's your problem, anyway?"

He didn't wait for an answer but rose out of the water. He padded over to a glass table, picked up a pair of dark dress pants, then quickly slipped them on.

Hannah followed him. On the glass table she saw a flickering candle illuminating a small mirror with snow-white powder already arranged in neat little rows. He fell into one of the chairs.

Hannah squared off across the table from him. "You know exactly what my problem is. You're a fool, Wyatt."

"And you're a buzzkill. Come on. Do a couple of lines with me, like in the old days, and I'm sure you'll realize that whatever's bothering you just isn't that important."

Wyatt bent over and sniffed a line through a glass tube. He sat up, his eyes closed, his mouth open in ecstasy. "Oh, gosh!" He shook himself all over like a dog, laughing and smiling, quite pleased with himself.

Hannah swept a hand across the table, scattering the cocaine and inadvertently splashing hot wax onto her half brother's pants.

He jumped out of the chair. "What are you doing?"

"What did *you* do, Wyatt?"

"What are you talking abou—?"

"Two of the Buffalo Warriors were shot dead in the woods. Matthew Redd is in jail for their murder, but we both know he didn't do it. Did you kill them?"

He glared at her. "How dare you—"

"Shut up and answer my question."

"Of course I didn't kill them."

"Did Roman?"

"Hannah—"

"He did. He murdered those boys so you could get back at Redd. Do you realize the damage this could do to us?"

Wyatt rolled his eyes. "You worry too much, Sis."

She shook her head. "Matt isn't going to just roll over and take this. He'll say you did this to set him up, and people will believe him. We don't need that kind of attention, Wyatt. Father doesn't need that kind of attention."

"That's rich. This isn't about the reputation of Saint Anton the Divine, our holy father. It's about you wanting to sleep with Redd because he's the only dude in five counties who hasn't tried." Wyatt made a dismissive gesture and then began carefully peeling wax off the thigh of his trousers.

"You have no idea what you're talking about."

"Oh, I don't, do I? We inherited the same disease, the Gages' original sin. We want what we can't have—and so we take it anyway." He looked away from her again, his gaze falling upon the long buffet table laid out on the far side of the deck. Their father's personal chef, Erica, stood behind it along with a couple of young, voluptuous servers who were also on the menu. "Man, I'm starving."

As he started for the table, Hannah chased after him. "Wyatt. I'm talking to you."

"I know, and it's such a drag." He pointed at mounds of fried chicken and fresh grilled tri-tips. The servers obliged and giggled as Wyatt made faces at them.

"We need to talk." Hannah grabbed Wyatt's arm, nearly spilling his plate. "In private."

"Fine." He grabbed a flute of champagne. "Let's go to my office."

✖ ✖ ✖

Hannah waited until her brother was seated comfortably behind his desk to deliver her ultimatum. "You need to fix this, Wyatt."

Using thumb and forefinger, he plucked a piece of tri-tip off his plate and popped it in his mouth. "And how, pray tell, should I do that?"

"I assume that Shane Hepworth is doing all this on your orders. Tell him to cut Redd loose."

"Why don't you tell him?" Wyatt replied with a mischievous grin. "As I recall, he used to dance to your little tune pretty well when you gave him what he wanted. Oh, but wait. You'd rather be with Redd. Shane's not going to like that very much."

"You need to cut Redd loose. And then you need to back off trying to take his land."

Wyatt pressed his hands against his bare chest in a *who me?* gesture. "It's not my fault he can't pay his taxes."

"*I'll* pay his taxes."

"Why? So he'll stay here? So he can make a go of it on that filthy little ranch of his and fall in love with you and the two of you live happily ever after?" Wyatt laughed. "Don't make me puke."

"You still don't get it, do you? This isn't about me and it's not about you. It's about our father. You can't hurt his reputation. His work is too important."

"Trust me, I know his work is too important. It's been more important than anything else in his life—or yours or mine. Both of our mothers can testify to that."

Hannah scowled. "Matthew Redd is innocent. Eventually the DA is going to realize it and he'll be released anyway. And then he's going to come for you."

"Ooh! I'm so scared!"

"You don't want to mess around with Redd. He's not some half-witted cowpoke. Do you have any idea who the Marine Raiders are? I looked them up. They're the best of the best, and Redd was one of them."

"I'm not worried about Matthew Redd." He picked another morsel from his plate, chewed thoughtfully, then leaned over his desk and keyed the intercom button on the phone console. "Roman, come in here, please."

Almost before the words were uttered, the interior door opened and Shevchenko strode through. Hannah could see the fresh bruises and abrasions from his latest tussle with Redd.

Wyatt looked up at his bodyguard. "Roman, Hannah here is worried that Matthew Redd might try to hurt me. What do you think of that?"

"I think I would like to see him try."

Wyatt laughed. "See?"

Hannah glowered at him. "You haven't heard a word I've said, have you? Father was right about you."

"Of course he's right about me. He's right about everything. He's a genius, just like you, and that's why you're his perfect little angel and I'm just a long-forgotten rug burn."

"I'm not going to let you ruin everything. Not over this."

"And what is that supposed to mean?"

Hannah allowed her lips to curl into a smile. "Enjoy your dinner, Brother dear."

She turned to leave and found Shevchenko staring at her with dead shark eyes.

She held his gaze.

Almost imperceptibly, he nodded.

FORTY-SEVEN

Rachel Culp was supposed to be testifying before a closed-door subcommittee later that afternoon. Preparing for it should have been foremost in her thoughts, but at the moment, all she could think about was why Gavin Kline wasn't picking up his cell phone.

He'd disappeared since the Dudek killing. At first she had assumed that he was merely busy carrying out his new assignment to dig into Dudek's personal life and find the next link in the chain to Willow. But it had been twenty-four hours without a check-in, and she was getting a little concerned.

She picked up her phone and dialed his office.

"FBI special annex. Amy speaking. May I help you?"

"This is Executive Assistant Director Culp calling for Agent Kline."

"Hello, Ms. Culp. I'm sorry, but Agent Kline isn't in."

"I know. I've been trying to reach him. He isn't answering his cell."

"He's out of the office. Taking a few personal days."

Personal days? Culp's blood pressure skyrocketed. *In the middle of this nightmare?* With an effort, she kept the fury out of her voice. "Do you know where he went?"

"Let me check."

Culp heard keys clacking on the other end of the line.

"Yes, ma'am. He's heading to Wellington, Montana."

Culp felt another spike in her BP. "Did you say Montana?"

"Yes, ma'am."

"Did he give a reason? I mean, other than personal days?"

"No, ma'am."

"Well, if he contacts you, please let him know I'm looking for him."

"I will, ma'am."

She ended the call and began drumming her fingers on the desk, thinking. *What are you up to, Gavin?*

She'd built a reputation as a door kicker, charging in first, guns up. The insecure men who were threatened by her called her a reckless cowboy. They were half-right. What they didn't understand was that she wasn't reckless. Ever. She always did her research. If she was going in, she needed to know who and what she was going up against.

She never trusted luck.

But the other thing she had going for her was her intuition. She might kick in a door because it was the only logical tactical decision, but her limbic system or lizard brain or whatever it was helped her sense as much as see the danger crouching in every corner.

Just like she was sensing now.

She doubted very much that Kline was actually taking personal leave. He had found something, some clue everyone else had missed, and it had pointed him to Montana.

She rang her assistant and told him to hold her calls for the rest of the morning, then opened her computer and pulled up everything she could find related to Willow.

The answer was just out of reach. She could feel it. It was buried somewhere in this virtual stack of case files.

Rachel Culp could read twelve hundred words per minute with near-perfect retention. It was how she had sailed through university while hardly studying and finished top of her class at Quantico.

It didn't take her long to get through most of the Willow case file. The name she was looking for was that idiot Marine who had gone UA before the disastrous raid.

Redd, Matthew J. She found it and scrolled through his DD214 and the rest of his service records.

Birthplace: Detroit, Michigan.

She kept scanning. Redd's last home address before enlisting in the Marines?

Wellington, Montana.

That was one heck of a coincidence.

Rachel Culp didn't like coincidences.

She closed the file and picked up her phone to call Stephanie Treadway. The call went to voice mail. Culp frowned. Technically Treadway answered to Kline, and so only indirectly to her, but there was no reason why Treadway shouldn't have been available to take her call.

Unless . . .

She allowed the thought to germinate, take root, and bloom and then reached a decision.

Kline, you bastard.

FORTY-EIGHT

MONTANA

The jangling of keys in the cell door lock woke Redd up from another night of fitful sleep. Judging by the dim light in the small glass window high above his cot, it was early morning.

The door swung open. Sheriff Blackwood, disheveled and unshaven, stood in the doorway.

"Visitors." He stepped out of the cell and plodded back to the front office.

Redd sat up and rubbed his eyes as Reverend Lawrence stepped into the cell wearing a brown Carhartt barn coat and faded jeans. His cloud of thick, white hair was wet from a shower, but his fingernails were still caked with grease.

Redd frowned. "What are you doing here?"

Emily followed in right behind her father. She wore nurse's scrubs beneath a coat.

Redd stood when she entered. "Oh, hey." He looked around apologetically, then pointed at the empty cot. "You want to sit?"

"I'm okay," Emily said. Her eyes seemed to take in the massive bruise on his face and the smaller ones on his hands and arms. "How are you?"

Redd shrugged. "Okay." He nodded at the rest of the cell. "Seen better, seen worse."

"How are the stitches?"

"I checked them last night. All good. You do good work." Redd smiled.

Emily didn't. "You need to see a doctor."

"Why? I've got you to look out for me."

"Honey, will you go bring the truck around?" Lawrence said. "I'd like a word with Matthew."

"Sure thing." She cast a pitying look at Redd, then headed out to get the truck.

When she was gone, Lawrence stepped right up to Redd, though he had to raise his head to look into Redd's eyes. "To answer your question, Matthew, we came down here to bail you out."

"Why would you do that?"

"I grant you that a cage is the best place for a wild animal, but I'm not having Jim Bob Thompson's no-account son sitting in the hoosegow while I'm preaching his memorial service today."

Redd shut his eyes, ashamed. He'd totally forgotten about it. A curse escaped his lips.

"Watch your mouth."

Guilt opened Redd's eyes. "You're right. Sorry."

"I'm a Christian man, Matthew, but I wasn't always. I sowed a few wild oats in my youth and I'm not proud of it. But I learned a thing or two. I've known men like you. You were a bad seed when you showed up at J. B.'s ranch, you were a bad seed as a teenager, and you're a bad seed now."

Redd stiffened. Lawrence was probably right but it still hurt.

"But you're not a murderer," Lawrence went on. "Turns out, that gun of yours that was used in the killing was wiped clean of prints. Which really doesn't make a lot of sense when you think about it. Why would you wipe the prints off a gun you claimed had been stolen and then leave it in your house for someone to find? Now, the district attorney still thinks you're probably guilty, but Duke Blanton convinced him that he'd never be able to make the case stick because your prints weren't on that gun. You're being released, pending further investigation, but Duke seems to think this will be the end of it."

Even though he knew he was innocent of the charges, Redd felt a wave of relief. "Why did Blanton get involved?"

"Took it upon hisself when he heard they'd arrested you. Criminal law isn't his forte, but he knows enough to get by."

"I'll be sure to thank him."

Lawrence nodded. "Let's get out of here."

FORTY-NINE

Redd stood in front of the bathroom mirror and examined the purpling bruises on his torso. His ribs were sore to the touch, but his breathing wasn't impaired and they didn't seem to be broken. The rest of him looked pretty banged up too. He spent the next thirty minutes letting the steaming hot water wash away the jail cell stink and massage the aches and pains while he waited for the extra-strength Tylenol caps to start working.

As usually happened when he showered, his thoughts gained focus and clarity. He returned to the idea that J. B.'s missing phone seemed to be the most promising clue to unlock the mystery of his death. The memorial service was still about eight hours away, and that was plenty of time to do a little figurative digging.

After toweling off and getting dressed, Redd sat down at J. B.'s desk and pulled a small ringed binder out of a drawer. J. B. had been keeping his passwords in it for as long as Redd could remember. When he opened the book, he saw the entry for J. B.'s AOL account and then later Netscape—whatever that was—along with several others. He ran his finger down the list looking for J. B.'s Gmail account. Though J. B. rarely used email, he had created the account so that, when people pestered him for his email address, he had something to tell them other than "Don't have one."

If J. B. had location services enabled on his phone and *if* J. B. used Google Maps, there was a chance Redd could track it.

A couple of really big *if*s.

Redd flipped through a few more pages until he found J. B.'s Google account information. The password was *MATTY**REDD*.

Redd sighed. Using such familiar things was bad OPSEC as far as digital security was concerned, but it meant a lot to him to see the password on the page in J. B.'s own hand.

Redd opened Google on his own iPhone, logged out, and then logged back in with J. B.'s particulars. As he was typing, Redd prayed that J. B. had enabled Location Services on his iPhone. The default setting would be to enable it, and it would have required J. B. to hunt it down and disable it, which was certainly in the realm of possibility. The old man wasn't exactly computer savvy, but on the other hand, he wasn't an idiot. Redd had long since disabled that feature on any phone in his possession, and his heart sank when he remembered advising J. B. to do the same.

Redd breathed a sigh of relief when the Google Maps Timeline appeared on the screen, showing the locations of where J. B.'s phone had been.

The most important location was the last, because that would be the day he called asking for help.

Only it wasn't. The last location had pinged the day after J. B.'s body had been found.

Redd zoomed in on the location, then zoomed back out again to find a reference point.

I've got you now.

FIFTY

Redd made a hard right turn onto the access road and pointed the nose of the Raptor straight at the gate of Dancing Elk Ranch. The tires threw dirt and rock as the big truck fishtailed, seeking traction. He had no way to get through that wrought iron gate and no gun to shoot the guards who would keep him from pulling it. He didn't care.

He mashed the throttle to the floorboard.

The Raptor was a weapon too.

This wasn't how he'd been trained to do things. SOP was to gather intel, assess objectives, determine necessary resources, set timetables, formulate plans, and execute the mission tactically.

But all of that was flying out the window.

All he could think of was killing Wyatt Gage with his bare hands.

But as he drew close, he saw that the gate was open and, to all appearances, unguarded.

He didn't believe in luck, but he wasn't going to look a gift horse in the mouth either. The truck boomed through the open gate and stormed up the dirt track leading over the hill to the residential area. He was just rounding a corner when he came almost nose-to-nose with an ambulance heading the opposite direction. He pulled his foot off the gas and stomped his brakes, steering for the roadside to avoid a collision. The ambulance braked for just a second, then continued down the road. Redd watched it go for a moment, then looked back to the house, where he saw two county sheriff's vehicles, along with many of the familiar vehicles used by Gage's security men. Redd pulled up alongside them.

A group of Gage security men stood on the porch, staring Redd down as he jumped from the truck. He took the steps two at a time, but two of the security guards closed ranks to block his way.

"Sorry, sir, only family—"

Redd stiff-armed both of them like a couple of turnstiles and blew past them, heading inside.

The two security men chased after Redd.

One of them caught up as Redd's boot hit the stairs leading up to the commotion. He grabbed Redd by the shoulder.

"You're trespassing—"

Redd turned and clocked the man on the jaw, dropping him. Lights out.

The other guard reached for his pistol, but Redd's big hand covered his as it reached the holster. The guard threw his free hand in a weak punch at Redd's head but Redd ducked it, then headbutted him. The man fell backward, blood gushing from his broken nose, and his gun in Redd's hand.

Redd pointed at him. "Don't move."

He hit the mag release and dumped the mag, then cleared the bullet in the chamber in a single fluid motion before tossing the gun to the floor.

Redd turned around and bounded up the stairs, two at a time. He glanced up at the landing and his eyes locked on Hepworth's pistol, pointed at his face.

Redd froze. He slowly raised his hands in a show of surrender.

"Well, this is getting to be a bad habit," the deputy said. The pistol didn't waver. "Wanna tell me what you're doing here?"

"Where is Wyatt?"

"You just missed him. He's taking a ride down to Pitt-Bateman."

The news took the wind out of Redd's sails. "Dead? How?"

Hepworth glanced down the stairs at the guard writhing on the ground, his cupped hands over his face oozing blood. He holstered his weapon. "What's got you so fired up?"

"I've got . . . or I guess *had* business with Wyatt."

"That a fact?"

"I suppose you're going to accuse me of killing him?"

Hepworth gave a mirthless chuckle. "Come on. Let me show you where we found him."

Hepworth beckoned him to continue up the stairs and led him into the main living area. The great room looked like the aftermath of a police raid, strewn with lost clothes, empty liquor bottles, stuffed ashtrays, and discarded drug paraphernalia. The air reeked of burnt weed and sex.

Hepworth pointed down at a white leather couch, which was stained with dried vomit. "Right there is where they found Wyatt. OD'd. Of course, we'll have to wait for the tox screen and the autopsy to confirm. But I've seen enough of them. He checked himself out on one massive bender."

Redd didn't know what to think. He'd wanted to kill Wyatt, but he also wanted resolution. Now his questions would go forever unanswered.

"Where's my brother?"

The familiar voice, half-frightened, half-enraged, rose up the stairs from behind them, and a moment later, Hannah appeared on the landing.

Hepworth pulled off his Stetson. "Sorry to tell you this, Ms. Gage, but we found your brother dead this morning. Right here."

Hannah's eyes widened and teared up. She seemed on the verge of a complete breakdown but she fought for control. Her face finally softened, and she wiped her nose with her hand. "How?"

"Overdose, looks like."

"Where have they taken him?"

"He'll be taken to the funeral home. That's where they'll perform the autopsy."

Hannah looked around the room. "It had to happen eventually. He failed rehab twice. He promised our father that he had it licked, but I knew better."

"I'm sorry for your loss, Ms. Gage," Hepworth said.

"Are you? Really?"

"Of course."

"My brother was a jerk."

"Your brother was my friend."

"Your friend was a jerk and a—" She broke down into sobs. Hepworth immediately took her in his embrace and held her.

Redd watched them for a moment, unsure of what to do.

J. B.'s iPhone had sent its last ping from somewhere within a hundred meters of the house. It wasn't the kind of evidence that would hold up in court, but it was all the proof Redd needed that Wyatt Gage had murdered J. B.

But Wyatt was dead. It wasn't exactly justice, but it would have to do. Now all that was left was to say goodbye to J. B.

He nodded at Hepworth, who was still holding Hannah, then turned on his heel and headed for the stairs.

✖   ✖   ✖

After Redd was gone, Hannah pulled herself back together, wiping away the tears with a sleeve.

"Do you want me to call your father and tell him the news?" Shane asked.

"No, I'll do it. It's better if it comes from me." She smiled, wiping away more tears. "Thanks."

"Of course. If there's anything I can do, you let me know, okay?"

She nodded.

His voice lowered. "Anything."

✖   ✖   ✖

Hepworth checked with the two guards Redd took out, asking if they wanted to file assault charges against him. He hoped they would. Matthew

Redd was a mad dog that needed to be locked up . . . or put down. But the guards demurred, evidently embarrassed that the big former Marine had bested them so easily.

He cast one last glance up at Hannah, her back to him, a cell phone pressed to her ear.

Oh, how he wanted that woman.

✖   ✖   ✖

Hannah told her father exactly what happened to Wyatt.

He thanked her for the detailed explanation and for the call, then apologized for ending it so quickly. He had important work to attend to.

Besides, Wyatt's death was not unexpected. Not even a little.

FIFTY-ONE

Redd stood on the porch with Reverend and Mrs. Lawrence. His black, long-sleeved Carhartt shirt still had creases in it. He had bought it that afternoon, along with a new pair of Laredo ropers. The ripstop shirt with white snap buttons was the only thing he could find at Hohman's that was black and respectful and fit his broad shoulders. He would have preferred to be in his Marine dress uniform. He hoped J. B. would understand why he wasn't.

A dozen trucks and cars were parked around the yard. Most belonged to the select group Lawrence had invited, who were presently in the yard at the back of J. B.'s house, where Emily was playing hostess, waiting for the service to begin. The latest to arrive, however, had been a delivery. The driver unloaded a bale of green alfalfa from the bed of the pickup truck and carried it over to Remington, who was saddled and tied to the fence post. The horse's nostrils flared as he sniffed the sweet aroma of alfalfa coming his way.

A woman, who had arrived in the same truck, mounted the steps with a huge bouquet of bright flowers.

"Mr. Redd? These are for you," the woman said as she reached the porch. She handed him the giant glass vase. "Our sincerest condolences."

"They're beautiful," Mrs. Lawrence said.

"Who are these from?" Redd asked.

"The card is attached." The florist smiled sadly. "So sorry for your loss. Jim Bob was one of the good guys."

"Thank you, ma'am," Redd said with a nod. He set the flowers down on a small patio table and pulled the card.

"What does it say, dear?" Mrs. Lawrence asked.

"'Remembering our friend Jim Bob Thompson. Our deepest condolences. From your friends, the Gages.'" It was written in a feminine hand. Either the florist's or Hannah's, Redd assumed.

"How very sweet of them. Especially considering . . ." Her voice trailed off. News of Wyatt's death had swept across the county like wildfire.

"Such a waste of God's most precious gift," Lawrence said gravely.

"Yeah. A real waste," Redd said, meaning something altogether different.

The reverend shot him a scathing look.

Redd ignored it. "When can we get this show on the road?"

Reverend Lawrence nodded toward a cloud of dust coming up the road. "Any minute now."

Redd watched the blue SUV race up to the yard and swing into an empty spot between two pickups.

The driver pulled his suit coat off the front seat and pulled it on as he marched toward the porch, obviously in a hurry.

"Why is *he* here?" Redd asked.

"Because I invited him," Lawrence said.

"And why did you do that?"

Lawrence pointed at the man mounting the stairs. He whispered harshly, "Because he's your father. And Jim Bob's friend."

Redd shook his head. As far as he was concerned, his father was dead. The man approaching him might have impregnated his mother twenty-seven years ago, but that was all. And while that man had stayed in touch and, in his own pathetic way, made sure that all the needs of his offspring were taken care of, it wasn't nearly enough for Redd to even consider calling Gavin Kline his father.

✖ ✖ ✖

"Sorry I'm late," Kline said, gripping Lawrence's hand. "My flight was delayed."

"Just glad you made it," Lawrence said.

Mrs. Lawrence gave Kline a big hug around the neck. "It's been too long, Gavin. So good to see you."

"You always make me feel so welcome," Kline said.

"That's because you are, dear."

Kline turned to Redd. "Matt."

"Gavin."

They held each other's gaze for a long while, each man sizing up the other one. Like two bulls squaring off. That was as close as they could get to a display of affection.

"We should get started," Lawrence said, ushering both men toward the front door.

"Yeah, let's do that," Redd said.

✖ ✖ ✖

The deck on the back of the cabin was as big as a dance floor and looked out over the swift-moving fingerling creek that spilled down from the mountain. The water was greener than usual but sparkling white where it broke over the shallow rocks. A light breeze flooded the blue sky with bright, fleecy clouds, but the temperature held steady in the high sixties. A perfect Montana evening.

Just beyond the deck was a stone firepit full of ashes with split-log benches circling it, cut and fashioned by J. B. A big iron grate lay over the pit for cooking, but right now there wasn't a fire or anyone else sitting around it.

Everybody in attendance was on the porch and facing J. B. himself, or more accurately, a small table with an eight-by-ten framed photo of him as a much younger man, in Marine dress blues and a white peaked hat, and the black plastic box Redd had taken from the Pitt-Bateman funeral home.

Reverend Lawrence had opened with a prayer, then nodded to Redd, who was standing next to him, signaling that it was his turn to speak.

Redd stood to one side of the table and faced the group. Several familiar faces looked back at him, including Mr. Hohman from the feedstore; his lawyer, Duke Blanton; and even the mortician, Mr. Pitt. But it was Emily's that he kept coming back to. Her smile urged him on.

"J. B. was a man of few words. So am I. If he were here, he'd say you all shouldn't have made such a fuss, but he'd be glad you're here and he'd thank you for coming. So do I."

Redd pointed at the reverend's wife standing next to him on the other side of the memorial. "I know he'd thank Mrs. Lawrence for preparing us some fine food that we'll all be enjoying in just a little bit, and he'd thank Reverend Lawrence for saying a few words over him." Redd's smile widened. "The key word being *few*."

Most of the folks chuckled at the joke, including Mrs. Lawrence.

The reverend wasn't amused.

"If J. B. were here, he'd tell you he lived a good life, served his country in his beloved corps, and lived out the last of his days on the land he cherished."

Redd gazed up into the trees, letting the waning sunshine warm his face, as he gathered his thoughts. "And as for me? What would I say about Jim Bob Thompson?" He glanced back over at the photo and the ash box. "I'd say he was the best man I ever knew." He didn't intend it as a slight against Gavin Kline, but as soon as he said it aloud, he knew and did not regret it.

"He loved this land and he loved me." Redd nearly choked on the last few words. "And that's all I've got to say."

He turned away and stepped through the back door into the house.

Lawrence's compact but powerful voice trailed after him. "Thank you, Matthew. The book of Ecclesiastes tells us that it is better to go to the house of mourning than to go to the house of feasting: for death is the end of all of us . . ."

❌ ❌ ❌

Redd made his way through the house, stopping to retrieve an old Folgers coffee can from the room that had once been his own bedroom, and then headed out the door and over to Remington.

"It's just the three of us now," Redd said as he mounted the big horse and coaxed him toward the mountain path.

Remington didn't need much encouragement to make the climb. The tall trees quickly shaded them from the fading sun. The higher they climbed, the cooler it got and the freer Redd felt. At a muddy fork in the trail, Redd nudged Remington to the right. The left fork led away to the fence line, which separated J. B.'s spread from the Gage holdings. The right continued up toward the summit of the low, pine-topped mountain, where stood an old log cabin J. B. had used as a base camp during hunting season. Redd had climbed the hill on horseback and on foot a thousand times in his childhood. He and Emily had gone up to the cabin together more than once. Those memories arose unbidden to accompany him along the way.

Remington's sure footing and steady gait lulled Redd into a sense of deep, abiding calm. The smell of the pines and saddle leather, the infinite hues of green, and the cool air cradled him, shielding him from a thousand worries and a million regrets. Even holding J. B.'s remains in the coffee can brought a comforting closure to the whole ordeal of losing him.

Redd smiled, thinking about the laugh J. B. would have at seeing his friends talking to the plastic box full of firepit ashes, thinking it was him, while he and Redd snuck away into the mountains.

And something else happened to Redd as he and Remington and J. B. made the climb. His own words came back to him, probably at J. B.'s prompting, Redd thought.

"He loved this land and he loved me."

Redd knew right then that he was going to stay. Somehow he would find a way because he loved this land, too.

✖   ✖   ✖

At the summit, Redd was greeted by a glorious Western sky, brazen and blue. A great herd of shadowing clouds grazed overhead, all at once swollen white and iron gray and burned to brass by the golden sunlight shimmering on their edges. A carpet of green-black pine fell away below, giving way to grass-covered hills rolling like an emerald sea toward the distant snowcapped mountains. A slim asphalt ribbon meandered in the valley between them all.

Remington nickered into the slight breeze that cooled Redd's skin.

Redd opened the coffee can, said an awkward prayer, and let J. B. take to the wind.

"I know how much you loved this land, Dad," Redd said as J. B. ran through his fingers. "It's your legacy. Always will be."

A chill wind raised the hairs on the back of Redd's neck. He swore he heard J. B.'s voice.

No, Son. It's yours.

FIFTY-TWO

Most of the mourners had left by the time Redd got back to J. B.'s house.

My house.

He pulled Remington's saddle and put him up in his stall after giving him a long drink of water in the trough. By the time he was ready to go inside, Emily and Mrs. Lawrence were finishing the dishes.

"We made you up a plate and put it in the icebox," the reverend's wife said. "Are you okay?"

"I'm doing fine, ma'am. Thank you for everything."

"It's our pleasure." She nodded at Emily. "Isn't it?"

"Of course," Emily said.

Redd saw Gavin and Reverend Lawrence putting up the last of the chairs. "Let me go out back and help," he said.

"No need, they're already done." Emily wiped her hands with a towel.

"I'm glad you're here," Redd said. "For J. B., I mean."

Her head cocked to the side. "Jim Bob isn't the only reason I'm here, Matty."

Redd's mouth was suddenly very dry.

"I've been thinking about our conversation the other day," she said, holding his gaze. "Replaying it my head. I feel like I didn't express myself very well."

"We haven't exactly been talking to each other for the last eight years," he said. "I guess we're out of practice."

"That must be it. So we've got some catching up to do. Unless . . ."

"Unless?"

"Unless you're leaving again."

"I'm not." The words were out of his mouth before he had time to think about it, but he did not regret them. The clarity of purpose he'd felt up on the mountain continued to burn within him. "I'm staying. Somehow I'm going to find a way to keep this place."

She nodded, then let her eyes drop. "It's gonna take some time."

He smiled. "I've got nothing but time, Em."

It was true. Wyatt Gage was dead. He couldn't bring back J. B. any more than he could go back in time and save his teammates . . . or join them. But he could honor J. B.'s memory by making the ranch thrive again.

Was there a place for Emily in that plan?

Before he could say more on the subject, Gavin Kline strode into the kitchen. "Well, I guess I'm outta here."

Mrs. Lawrence dried her hands on her towel and rushed over to give him a hug.

"Matty," Emily whispered, "you need to ask Gavin to stay with you while he's here."

"Me? Why?"

Emily smiled, her sweet eyes turning sweeter. "Because that's what Jim Bob would want you to do."

Redd hated the idea of asking Kline anything, especially something that might mistakenly give the impression that he was looking to build a bridge between them, but he knew she was right. It was what J. B. would have wanted.

✖   ✖   ✖

Burning logs crackled in the firepit warming the chill night air. Redd and Kline sat across from each other looking over the flames, drinking twelve-year-old Cardhu, a single malt Scotch whisky Kline brought with him from Dallas.

"So tell me something, Matt. Why did I have to hear about J. B.'s death from Reverend Lawrence? Why not you?"

"Because I knew you were too busy buying or selling oil . . . or whatever it is you do."

"For J. B. I would make time." He must have realized the foolishness of the statement, because he threw his hands up. "I know, I know. I've got time for an old friend, but not for my own flesh and blood. I'm a jerk—I get it."

Redd raised his glass to signal full agreement.

"J. B. and I went through hell together in the corps. He was like a big brother to me, saved me on more than one occasion. I'm sorry for your loss, Matt. I really am. But this is my loss too. So cut me a little slack, will ya?"

"I can do that." Redd held out his glass. "At least for one night."

"More than I probably deserve." Kline tapped Redd's glass with his. They tossed back their whiskeys. "So Emily said you left the corps. What's next for you?"

For a second, Redd thought Kline was going to ask him why he left the service. He was surprised to find that he *wanted* to tell Kline everything. Confess. Get it off his chest. Dead Marines burned alive, and probably his fault. Discharged without honor. J. B. dead, maybe murdered, and he wasn't there to help him.

He needed absolution. He needed forgiveness. He needed something he knew Kline couldn't give him.

But Kline hadn't asked why. Only *what's next?*

"I don't know what's next. I really don't." He decided to not reveal his decision to keep the ranch. "Maybe you can get me a job as a petroleum executive."

It was only half a joke.

"You'd hate it. Really boring work." Kline leaned in close and jabbed Redd's chest with his finger. "And you listen up. Leaving the service isn't the end of the world. You have your health; you have your youth." He waved a hand at the property. "You have all of this. And best of all, you have Emily."

"Emily? Are you drunk?"

"Well, probably. But I'm not blind. Don't you see the way she looks at you?"

Redd waved a dismissive hand. Kline was the last person he wanted dating advice from.

"Life's full of second chances, Matt."

"Funny. She said the same thing."

"It's true."

"Tell that to the dead."

"You're not dead." Kline let out a long, slow breath. "All right, I gotta piss."

"Me too." Redd followed Kline over to the tree line. They drenched a couple of pines, both grunting with pleasure and relief.

Bonding.

✗   ✗   ✗

They swapped J. B. stories for half the bottle, then grabbed leftovers from the fridge, wolfed them down, and headed back out to the firepit to finish the bottle and tell more stories about the man they both loved and lost.

What they came to understand was that in a way J. B. had fathered them both, which made them, in a weird way, brothers. Their shared Marine experiences made them brothers in another way, too.

What the two of them forgot was a lesson J. B. taught them both years ago. Hard liquor was best left half in the bottle. Their moods darkened as their minds clouded and their inhibitions faded. Even in their stupor, they both realized that their shared grief was bringing them together, but their shared history still separated them.

"I wish you'da been here for me when I needed you," Redd finally blurted out.

"That's why I gave you to J. B. I would've been a terrible dad anyway."

"That woulda been better than nothing, which is what I got."

"Bull. You got J. B. Look at you. You turned out pretty good as far as I can see."

"You can't see anything."

"Touché."

"There's something you should know," Redd said. "J. B. called me the day he died, left a voice mail. I didn't get the message right away. By the time I did, he was already gone. I actually didn't find out he was dead until I got up here last week."

"What did he say?"

Redd took out his phone, scrolled to the message. Although he had heard it in his head over and over again, he had not actually played it since learning of J. B.'s death. Now he could hear the pain in the old man's voice:

"Matty . . . I heard . . . Trouble's come knocking . . . Might need your help."

Redd put the phone away. "You know J. B. He wouldn't ask you to spit on him even if his hair was on fire."

"What are you saying?"

"I think he was murdered."

Kline sat up. *"Murdered?"*

"Officially J. B. died from a broken neck after being thrown from his horse."

"It happens, Matty."

Redd shook his head. "J. B. was sick. Cancer. Did you know that?"

Kline's shocked expression was answer enough.

"Emily says there's no way he could have been riding Remington in his condition. And there was no reason for him to be riding. He sold off all his stock."

Kline crossed his arms over his chest. "I'll admit that does sound suspicious. Let's say you're right. Who would have wanted to hurt him?"

"I think Wyatt Gage was behind it."

"Is he related to Anton Gage? That billionaire environmentalist?"

"His son. He wanted the ranch. J. B. wouldn't sell. So he arranged a little accident for J. B."

"Did you take this to the sheriff?"

"I don't trust the sheriff. Honestly, I'm not sure who to trust in this town. That's why I'm telling you."

Kline shifted. "Me?"

"You were J. B.'s friend. Someone needs to know the truth, even if it doesn't matter anymore. Wyatt Gage is dead. Died this morning. OD'd on drugs at his place."

Kline nodded slowly. "So that's the end of that. Hard to get answers from a dead man."

Redd shrugged. "Maybe. I'm not entirely sure that I've read the situation correctly."

"How so?"

"I know Wyatt wanted J. B.'s property—"

"You mean *your* property."

Redd nodded, coming to grips with it. "Yeah. You're right. My property. But I'm not so sure I know *why*."

"You think there are mineral rights here or something else involved?"

"That's possible. Wyatt told me to my face that he wanted it just because he wanted it. He was an entitled little jerk. But I also know that Wyatt was buying the land on his father's orders. And they were buying land all over the state. Makes me think maybe there's more to it.

"What I can't shake, though, is J. B. asking for help. You knew him. He never asked for nothing. And he wasn't afraid of anything. I can't imagine he was afraid of Wyatt Gage."

"I never knew him to back down from a fight."

"Maybe J. B.'s 'trouble' was that he needed help figuring out some*thing* and then dealing with it. He was bothered or maybe threatened by some*thing*, not some*one*."

"Like what?"

Redd spread his hands. "That's what I'm trying to work out."

Kline stood. "My head is in the rinse cycle right now. I say we tackle it tomorrow. Together. That work for you?"

Redd stood. "Sounds like a plan."

Kline stuck out his hand, and Redd took it. Then both men headed for bed.

Tomorrow, Redd promised himself as he fell asleep.

Tomorrow . . .

FIFTY-THREE

Kline arose before sunrise and stole from the house to go for a run. The crisp air and overall stillness were a welcome relief from the noise and pollution of DC. He understood now why Jim Bob had, in the end, chosen this over transitioning from the corps to a career in intelligence or law enforcement.

He headed up the trail, intending to go all the way to the old hunting cabin at the top of the mountain, but soon realized that his lake circuits in the nation's capital had not prepared him for running up actual mountains more than four thousand feet above sea level. It didn't help that he and Redd had probably had a few too many the night before. After only going about a quarter of a mile, his head was pounding and he felt like his lungs were going to burst, so he turned back, walking back down instead of running.

As he descended, he mulled over the conversation from the night before. He didn't want to believe that Jim Bob had been the victim of foul play, and yet he couldn't dismiss his son's instincts. The fact that the

Gage family was involved added a wrinkle to the problem. The Gages weren't simply wealthy. They were in the top tier of wealth, and that kind of money bought unparalleled influence. He wondered if Matty truly understood that the uberwealthy occupied a different world than everyone else—a world where laws and morality had little meaning.

If Wyatt Gage was responsible for Jim Bob's death, then his overdose was a rare sort of justice.

Still, Kline thought, maybe there was more to it than simple greed and entitlement. He decided to take a deeper look into the activities and the many enterprises of the Gage family, especially in Montana.

That was how he dealt with grief and loss. He'd been a terrible friend to Jim Bob and a terrible father to Matty—no, even that was too generous—but at least he could do something with his position.

He was still debating whether the time had come to tell Matt the truth about what he did. If he was ever going to have any kind of relationship with his son, he would have to begin with that. If anyone could understand why he had chosen to put his career in national service ahead of family, Matty could. Without even knowing it, he'd followed in his old man's footsteps, leaving the ranch behind to join the Marines. The only difference between them was that Matty hadn't slipped up and fathered a child during a drunken one-night stand.

Kline supposed things might have been different if Linda Redd had told him that they had a son together, let him be a part of Redd's early life. Maybe he could have found a way to split the difference. But by the time he'd found out, it was already too late. The best he could do was give the kid to Jim Bob.

On balance, that had worked out pretty well.

Now that they were both grown men, maybe the things they had in common could bring them together. Kline was playing a dangerous game and he could use more help—the kind of help only a former Marine Raider could give. Helping Redd learn the truth about Jim Bob's death might be just the opportunity he needed to reveal the truth about his career in the FBI.

On the other hand, the kid was smart enough that he might be able to put two and two together, and if that happened . . .

His son—yes, his *son*—was a warrior and loyal. Father or not, if Matty ever found out what he had done, he'd kill him.

✖ ✖ ✖

Redd was in the kitchen frying up a can of Spam when Kline returned. As soon as he came inside, Redd poured a cup from his brand-new Mr. Coffee and slid it across the counter to Kline.

"Thanks," Kline said, savoring the brew. "How'd you sleep?"

"Like the dead for an hour or two, thanks to the Scotch. After that . . ." He shook his head. "Brain wouldn't shut off. You?"

"Same." The toaster—another acquisition from the day before—popped. Redd dropped a thick slice of Texas toast on each of two plates. He then tonged thick slices of crispy Spam from the frying pan onto the plates and brought the repast over to the dining table.

Kline forked a slice of Spam onto the bread. "I haven't had this in years."

"J. B.'s favorite." Redd smashed his slice of toast around several pieces of Spam, forming a crude sandwich.

"Reverend Lawrence told me last night that J. B. got religion toward the end," Kline said.

Redd shrugged. "He told me the same. Wish I'd had the chance to talk to him about it myself."

"Well, you know how he was. Even if he found Jesus, he wasn't the sort to go around talking about it. And you know, facing what he was facing . . . it's not that surprising that he'd be thinking about God, especially if he thought he was about to meet Him."

Redd took a sip of his coffee. He'd come to a similar conclusion, unsatisfying though it was. "Why'd you bring it up?"

"Last night when I couldn't sleep, I saw that big Bible next to his bed. I actually read some of it. Haven't done that in a long while."

"So now it's your turn to find Jesus?"

Kline gave a rueful grin. "That Bible had a bunch of handwritten notes in the margins, all of them in Jim Bob's hand. Interesting notes, too. He was serious about it."

"And your point is?"

"It got me to thinking. That Bible was important to him. Maybe there's some insights to be had there."

"Sort of like talking to his ghost?"

"Sort of." Kline stood and padded down the hall to J. B.'s bedroom, returning a moment later with the Bible in hand. He offered it to Redd.

"Now?"

"Why not?"

Redd shrugged and took the Bible. He remembered looking at the endleaf, seeing his own name added to the family roll. Until now, he had not considered how the book might serve any purpose besides family heirloom.

He opened it, thumbing through the pages chosen at random. He quickly saw what Kline had been talking about. The edges of the thin white pages were filled with notes written in fine pencil. Observations and ruminations, questions that even Lawrence probably would not have been able to answer to J. B.'s satisfaction.

"Wonder how long it took him to go through this," Redd murmured.

There was a ribbon marker running down the center of the book. Redd was no Bible student, but he knew that the Psalms were in the middle. He flipped to the marked page and saw that it was Psalm 23—a favorite of warriors in the special operations community.

"Yea, though I walk through the valley of the shadow of death, I will fear no evil."

J. B. had walked alone into that valley. Redd wondered what the old man had to say about it.

But as he spread the pages open, he realized there was a small piece of folded paper tucked securely into the crease. He teased it out and saw a name printed in shaky letters across the front.

Matty.

"What's that?" Kline asked, leaning over him.

"Not sure." Redd unfolded the paper and saw more of J. B.'s spidery writing. He read it silently.

Matty. Tried to call but couldn't get through. If you're reading this . . . Well, never mind. I've got to get it down anyway. Overheard a couple talking tonight. They were acting squirrelly. The woman said they shouldn't be talking about it in public and said something about security protocols. That's what got my attention. The man switched to what I thought at first was Russian. Couldn't make sense of much, but I did catch one phrase. I'll write it the way I heard it.

Redd sounded the words out to the best of his ability. *"Hotovyy koly verba pryyde."*

Kline stiffened. "What's that?"

Redd waved the note. "J. B. overheard a couple of people talking in Russian. He did a tour at the embassy in Moscow, didn't he?"

Kline didn't answer.

Redd went on. "Whatever he heard spooked him enough to call." He looked back to the last few words J. B. had written, which consisted of his best attempt to translate the phrase.

Hotovyy=ready, finished
koly=when
verba=9K333 VERBA MANPADS???
pryyde=will come

Redd swore under his breath. "I think J. B. might have stumbled onto a plot to smuggle in Verba MANPADS."

"MANPADS?" Kline breathed out the word.

"Man-portable air defense system. The Verba is a Russian-made shoulder-launched SAM, capable of knocking down aircraft up to four miles away. It's basically the Russian answer to the Stinger. I've trained with them. They're idiotproof. Fire and forget. Imagine what some of these local militia types might do if they got their hands on something like that. If these smugglers suspected that he understood what they were talking about, they might have come after him."

He sat back and clapped his hand to his head. "I don't believe this. Maybe I got it all wrong. What if Wyatt Gage didn't kill J. B., but these Russians did?"

"It's not Russian," Kline said.

Redd raised an eyebrow in surprise. "How can you tell?"

"I do a lot of business overseas, kid." He took the note from Redd's hand and pointed to the translation. "See this word? J. B. heard the Russian word *verba* but it's a cognate in another Slavic language, Ukrainian."

"Ukrainian?" Now Redd's wheels were turning. "Like that dude Shevchenko."

"Same word, same sound, same meaning. *Verba* translates exactly the same way."

"So what are you saying? Russian or Ukrainian, makes no difference. They realized J. B. overheard and they killed him. MANPADS are serious—"

"This isn't about MANPADS."

Redd eyed Kline suspiciously. "Why do you say that?"

"In both languages, *verba* translates to *Willow*."

Redd flinched, poleaxed at the sound of the word. "Willow? Are you sure?"

"Yeah, I'm sure. This isn't about man-portable air defense. This is about a man. A very dangerous man."

Redd blinked furiously, trying to process. "How in the hell do you know that?"

Kline sighed heavily. "I'm not a petroleum executive, Matt. I'm FBI. Intelligence directorate. Have been since before you were born."

Redd could only stare at him, stunned. Finally he found the words. "I don't believe you."

"I'm serious, Matt. Swear on my life."

"Did J. B. know?"

"Yeah, he did."

"Why didn't he tell me? Why didn't *you* tell me? I deserved to know the truth."

"I'm not just a field investigator. I deal with some dangerous people. The only way to protect the people I care about is to keep them as far away as I can. That's why I sent you to live with Jim Bob."

"I don't believe it," Redd said again as he twisted away, repelled by the mere sight of Gavin Kline. He ran a hand through his hair, pacing the floor. "You think that somehow makes up for it? For not being a father?"

"Of course not. But I have a job to do, Matt. A dangerous job. Maybe that makes me an awful parent, but at least I kept you safe."

Redd's shoulders slumped. He realized he wasn't as shocked at Kline's lie as he was at J. B.'s omission.

"I saw your reaction when I said the name Willow." Kline took a sip of coffee from his mug. "What do *you* know about him?"

Redd shrugged. "Only what they briefed us on. My last mission was a snatch and grab down in Mexico to get him. We didn't have any intel on him other than his pseudonym and his location and that he was a high-priority target." Redd's eyes narrowed as comprehension dawned. "An *FBI* target." He could feel his pulse throbbing in his temples. "What do *you* know about Willow?"

"I developed the intel."

Redd was suddenly blind with rage. He lunged at Kline, grabbing him by the shirtfront, and drove him backward, slamming him against the table. Kline's mug flew from his hand, splattering hot coffee everywhere across the room. The mug shattered against the wall.

"You got my men killed!" Redd shouted, his face mere inches from Kline's.

Kline didn't blink. "Not me. Willow got them killed. Or whoever was protecting him. And there's a chance that whoever killed your team killed J. B."

Redd's raging eyes searched Kline's for any sign of deceit. Somewhere deep beneath his rage, he knew the truth of it. He relaxed his grip. Let go. Backed away.

Redd's voice softened like a scolded child's. "Then you know what happened to me."

"I was briefed. Said a Marine went UA before the mission launched. No name was given. I knew you were in a Raider team, but I had no idea it was you or that it was your unit that went in. I only provided the intel. I don't do ops."

Redd's mood darkened as he made an emotional retreat.

"Look, Matt. What happened out there wasn't your fault. You weren't even there—"

"But I probably blew the mission by spilling my guts to . . ." He shook his head. "Just before the mission, I stopped to help this woman change a flat. She dosed me, probably got me to talk. That's what got them all killed. My fault. If I ever find her—"

"Forget about her, Matt. The op was already compromised. How do you think they knew to grab someone from your team? All they got from you was confirmation. And a scapegoat. So ditch the pity party and man up. We don't have time for your emotional stuff right now."

The insult dope-slapped Redd, surprising him.

Kline took a step closer and dropped a hand on the bigger man's shoulder. "You want to get justice for your team? For J. B.?"

Redd nodded.

"Then let's chase down what we can from this note and find the men who did this. After that, we'll sort out *our* crap. Got it?"

Redd nodded again. "Got it."

"All right, start with what's happened since you've been here."

Redd went back into the kitchen, refilled his mug, and then got a new one for Kline. As he did, he began recounting everything that had transpired since his return to Wellington, omitting nothing. Kline asked for clarification once or twice and headed him off when he started to editorialize or draw conclusions, especially where Wyatt Gage and Roman Shevchenko were concerned.

"Just the facts, ma'am," Kline said with a grin.

When Redd was done, Kline rolled his mug between his palms for a moment. "All right, it sounds like the sheriff or his deputy . . . or maybe both of 'em were working with Wyatt to set you up for that murder, but that doesn't necessarily mean they're involved with Willow. It sounds like the deputy honestly believes J. B.'s death was an accident. The question is, do we trust him enough to show him the note?"

Redd thought about it. "No."

"Then it's you and me."

"What about the bureau? Can't you rope them in on this?"

Kline scratched his unshaven chin, as if giving the suggestion serious consideration. "A very small circle of people at the bureau are in the loop on Willow. That makes it complicated. The leak that got your team killed might have come from inside my department. Bottom line, I don't know who I can trust right now about any of this. Except you."

Redd nodded. "Then it's like you said. Just you and me. What's our first move?"

"Let's start with the obvious. Gage's bodyguard—"

"Shevchenko," Redd confirmed.

"Him. The Ukrainian connection could be a coincidence, but it's a place to start. Tell me about him."

"A real bruiser. But he's smarter than he looks. My guess is former service, maybe even Spetsnaz."

"A lot of those ex–spec ops guys from the old Eastern Bloc ended up working for mobsters."

"Is that who you think is bankrolling Willow? The Bratva?"

Kline shook his head. "Hard to say. The trick here is to see if there's a line from Wyatt Gage to Willow that goes through the bodyguard." He paused to take a sip of coffee. "I know his boss, Wyatt, is dead, but you thought Wyatt was connected to J. B.'s death. Was that just a hunch or did you have any actual proof?"

"I know that Gage wanted the ranch bad." He chuckled, then corrected himself. "Badly. But really, the only piece of hard evidence was J. B.'s phone. It went missing after he died. Shane Hepworth said he never saw it, and it wasn't with his personal effects. The last signal it gave off was at Wyatt's place. That's why I ran up there yesterday morning to confront him. And that's when I found out the idiot OD'd."

Kline stared up at the ceiling. "J. B.'s phone dying at Wyatt's place doesn't prove Wyatt did anything. Anybody who had access to his place could have brought the phone there." His gaze came back to Redd. "How did you figure that out?"

"A Google Map history. J. B. never turned off the self-reporting feature."

"Do you still have that history handy?"

"I took a screenshot." Redd picked up his phone and brought up the saved image.

"You said he called you for help the day he was killed. What day was that?"

"They found him on Saturday but he sent the message Friday night."

"What time did he call you?"

Redd didn't have to consult his call history. "8:31 p.m. local time."

"So J. B. called you when he got worried at half past eight." Kline picked up J. B.'s note and glanced at it. "He wrote this down after he tried to call you. Let's assume that was more or less right after he overheard this conversation about Willow."

"We need to figure out where he was when he heard it and who those Ukrainians are."

"Exactly. We find them, we find J. B.'s killers—and maybe even the bastards who killed your team."

Redd went back to the Google Maps Timeline and zoomed in on the location of J. B.'s phone at 8:31. Then he looked up at Kline and said just one word.

"Spady's."

FIFTY-FOUR

Spady's was just opening for business when Redd pulled the Raptor into the nearly empty parking lot. As he and Kline headed into the empty dining room, the bartender looked up, then stiffened as he recognized Redd.

Redd flashed his best disarming grin. "Hey, Jarrod. How's business? I heard there might be a change in management coming."

Jarrod shifted uncomfortably. "Look, Mr. Redd, I don't—"

Kline stepped forward and stuck out his hand in a friendly if assertive gesture. "Jarrod, is it? I'm Gavin. Jim Bob Thompson was an old friend of mine. I'm in town for his service."

Jarrod looked uncertainly at Kline's hand, then took it. "My condolences. We all loved Jim Bob here."

"You know, Matt here figured that J. B. was in here the night before he passed. Were you working that night? Would have been a Friday? 'Bout two weeks ago?"

"I always work Friday, so . . . yeah, I guess I do recollect that."

"We're just trying to put a couple of puzzle pieces together. I know it's been a little while, but do you remember a couple of out-of-towners in here?"

Jarrod shrugged. "Lots of people were here. I mean, most days this place is full up."

"But these two people were speaking a foreign language. It would have sounded like Russian. That sound familiar?"

Jarrod tugged at his lower lip, thinking. "Yeah, come to think of it. There were two people like that. A man and a woman. Sat right where you're standing."

"You get their names?"

"No. Didn't ask."

"Any chance they paid with a credit card and we can see the transaction?"

Jarrod's eyebrows came together in a frown. "Are you with the police? If you are, you might need a warrant for something like that. I'm not sure."

On the drive over, Kline had explained to Redd that he would not identify himself as FBI unless the situation warranted. "Just a friend of J. B.'s. Trying to figure out what happened to him at the end."

Jarrod thought about this for several seconds, then shrugged again. "Well, as I think on it, I do remember they paid in cash. I only remember because they paid with a couple of crisp hundred-dollar bills. Looked so new, it seemed like they was hot off the press. I even joked with them about that, which is why I remember."

Redd thought this story sounded a little contrived—an embellishment intended to supply authenticity to a false narrative.

"Can you remember what they looked like?" Kline pressed.

"Vaguely. They both had brown hair or maybe black. They were kinda ordinary-looking. Nothing unusual. Nice clothes but nothing fancy. Both wore glasses. Not working-class people. More like office people."

"Fat? Tall? Old?"

Jarrod's eyes darted back and forth as he searched his memory again. "Like I said. Ordinary. He was five-foot-eight or ten. She was a couple of inches shorter. Maybe in their late twenties or thirties. I think they were married."

"Why do you say that?"

"They acted like it. Even got into an argument, I think."

Kline nodded. "Did you get a look at their vehicle?"

"Why would I? It was kinda busy when they left. Listen, what's this all about?"

"J. B. might have had words with these folks," Redd volunteered. "In the lot after they left. If so, they might have been the last people to see him alive."

"Heard he fell off a horse," Jarrod said.

"Could be."

Jarrod's posture changed, telegraphing that he was done answering questions. "Well, I'm sorry. I don't know anything about that. I've got to get back to work. Sorry I can't be more help. I liked ol' Jim Bob."

Redd was about to lean on the bartender a little harder, but Kline headed him off. "Thanks for your time, Jarrod. We'll see ourselves out."

"Now what?" Redd muttered as they headed outside.

"Patience, grasshopper. Watch and learn." Kline took out his phone and a little white case that held wireless AirPods.

"Finally calling the Feebs?" Redd asked.

"Not exactly."

Kline dropped the white buds into his ears, shutting out Redd's ability to follow both sides of the conversation, but it wasn't hard to fill in the gaps.

"Need you to run something for me. I want you to search the list of H-1B visa workers from Ukraine or Ukrainian nationals. One male, one female, both dark hair and eyes. Probably married. Age range twenty-five to forty working in a technical field . . . Yesterday, if not sooner."

Then his expression darkened. "You're kidding me." He was quiet for several seconds, and Redd couldn't tell if he was listening or thinking. Finally he said, "That doesn't mean he's not our guy . . ." He nodded. "Yeah. Do that. But first see what you can dig up on those Ukrainians . . . You know it."

He ended the call.

"What was all that about?" Redd asked once they were ensconced in the Raptor.

"Another case I'm working on," Kline said, waving away the question.

Redd didn't press him. "So you think you can find them through their work visas?"

"It's a long shot. There are nearly six hundred thousand H-1B visa holders in the US right now. The number of Ukrainians is bound to be a lot smaller, but it's still probably close to a thousand. And of course, there's no guarantee that this couple is here on a specialty work visa."

"So if this doesn't work, where does that leave us?"

"The bartender said they were out-of-towners. They probably didn't drive all the way out to Wellington just for dinner. We can check the Diamond T, see if they stayed there. Check Airbnb listings . . . if there are any out here. Maybe ask around a few other places."

"We keep asking questions, and someone's bound to take notice," Redd pointed out.

"It's a chance we'll have to take. But look on the bright side. If Willow comes after us, at least we'll know we're on the right track." His phone chimed with a notification. He glanced at it, then broke into a grin. "Jackpot. Viktor and Anastasia Petryk. Both employed at . . . wait for it . . . Gage Food Trust Research Facility, outside Voight, Montana. I've got work and home addresses, along with photos for ID."

"Outstanding." Redd pounded a triumphant fist on the steering wheel. "Gage and Willow. Son of a gun."

Kline punched the address into Redd's GPS, and the route map appeared on the screen. Voight was an unincorporated community in Wheatland County, a ninety-minute drive from Wellington.

Redd turned the key and the truck roared to life.

✖ ✖ ✖

Jarrod watched the Raptor rocket out of the parking lot. When the truck was no longer in view, he took out his phone and dictated a quick text message.

"They just left."

FIFTY-FIVE

Redd kept to the speed limit after spotting a state trooper's vehicle shooting radar on the other side of the highway, about ten miles east of Bozeman. The unchanging landscape outside—endless fields of wheat under the broad blue sky—left him plenty of time to begin processing everything he had learned since daybreak.

"So FBI, eh?" Redd asked.

Kline continued staring straight ahead. "Yeah."

"Anything else you haven't told me?"

"Lot of things, actually."

"Like what?"

"Everything." Kline shot him a look. "Look, just because I let you in on a couple things doesn't change who I am. I deal in sensitive, classified information. I can't share that with you, Matt. It would be illegal."

The rebuke stung. As a Raider, Redd's security clearance would have cleared him to discuss those secrets. One more reminder of what he'd lost. "We might be heading into a crap storm," he said. "I need to know if you've got my back."

"To say I've let you down before is the understatement of a lifetime. I get that."

"Agreed."

"Well, I'm doing what I can to make up for it. Trust me. I've got your back."

Exactly what Redd hoped he'd say. All his life.

It was also what a practiced liar would say.

Kline added, "If not for your sake, then mine."

Redd looked him hard in the eyes.

He decided it was time to trust the man.

If he was wrong, he'd find out soon enough.

✳   ✳   ✳

Redd pulled the Raptor to a stop in front of the Gage Food Trust Research Facility, about ten miles up the highway from Voight. A barrier arm on either side of the small but fortified security booth prevented vehicles from entering or leaving without permission. Double rows of cyclone fencing topped with razor wire circled the facility like a prison yard. The only thing missing was guard towers with armed guards patrolling them, though Redd caught sight of dozens of security cameras located around the facility.

A female guard approached Redd's window, a *GFTR Security* ball cap on her head and a big, chromed M1911 semiauto in a thigh holster. She smiled behind a pair of dark aviator sunglasses. "Can I help you, sir?"

"We're here to see a couple of old friends of ours, Drs. Viktor and Anastasia Petryk."

"Very good, sir. Your permit?"

"Excuse me?"

"Your friends would have arranged a permit for you to enter the facility."

Redd fumbled around with his shirt pockets. "Must have left it at home."

"Then I'm afraid you can't enter the facility."

"Can we just contact them?"

"Who?"

"The Petryks."

"I'm sorry, sir. I'm not at liberty to confirm or deny that anyone with that name is employed here."

Redd pointed at the big facility. "But you just said they worked here."

"No, I said that if you have friends here, they would have arranged for your permits."

"Can't you look them up on your computer?"

"I'm afraid I don't have access to that information."

"How can I get a permit to get in?"

"Contact your friends and have them make the arrangements through the security office."

Kline pointed at a small building off to the side of the parking lot with a sign that read *Security Office*. "Why can't I just go in there and get one?"

"Because you need a permit to get past this gate and you don't have one."

Another guard, a square-jawed male, approached Kline's window. He knocked on the glass with his knuckle and Kline lowered it.

"There a problem here, gentlemen?"

"No problem." Kline pulled out his FBI service wallet and flashed his credentials. "We're here to see a couple of people that work inside your facility. Just wanted to ask a few questions."

The guard examined the credentials. "Well, Special Agent Kline, thank you for your service to our great nation. You can certainly enter our facility and question any employee you care to so long as you have a visitation permit issued by the security office or a properly authorized search warrant."

"We can do this the hard way or the easy way," Kline said. "The hard way is that I go get that warrant and then I ask a whole lot more questions of a whole lot more people. Or we can do it the easy way and you just let us in out of professional courtesy."

The male guard smiled. "Guess it'll be the hard way."

Redd pointed at the razor wire. "What exactly are you people hiding in there?"

The guard's smile vanished. "This is a world-class research facility, not a petting zoo. Dr. Anton Gage is trying to feed the world. What have you done to feed a hungry child today, sir?"

"Thanks," Kline said as he rolled the window back up. He turned to Redd. "We're wasting time here. Let's go."

✖ ✖ ✖

Ten minutes later, Redd pulled off I-90 and onto the frontage road heading into Voight.

The quaint town of fewer than two thousand souls wasn't much larger than a postage stamp, but it was clean and the residential streets were tree-lined. Redd couldn't recall having ever been here, but it didn't look all that different from Wellington, except maybe smaller.

He steered the Raptor onto a quiet street off the main drag, slowing to the posted speed limit of twenty miles per hour. Kline pointed up ahead. "Up there on the left."

"Got it." A late-model blue Toyota 4Runner was parked in the driveway, its rear hatch open. A thirtysomething brunette roughly matching Anastasia's DMV photo shut the hatch and headed back inside.

"I think we're in luck."

"Do we just drive up and knock on the door?" Redd asked. "The two of us might scare them off. They might even be armed."

"You have a better idea?" Kline asked.

"Are you packing?"

"Wasn't out here on official business. I left my sidearm at home. I don't suppose you're armed?"

Redd shook his head. The Ruger was, as far as he knew, still evidence in the death of the two Buffalo Warriors, and given his shaky status with the sheriff's department, he'd decided it best to leave the pistol he'd taken from the Infidels biker behind.

"Then we take our chances."

"I have another idea." Redd drove past the house, made a left, and drove back to Main Street.

"Where are you headed?"

"I don't know about you, but I'm starved."

×   ×   ×

Twenty minutes later, Redd walked up to the porch of the Petryk house with a smile on his face and a massive pizza box perched on one hand. The Raptor was parked half a block away, just out of the direct line of sight from the porch.

Redd tapped on the doorframe, and a moment later, a woman he recognized as Anastasia Petryk appeared, looking flustered. Judging by her dusty and wrinkled work clothes and the stacks of moving boxes behind her in the living room, she'd been busy packing. She looked at Redd from behind the closed screen door. "Yes?"

"Big Sky Supreme with double cheese, for Viktor."

"Are you sure?" she asked with a lilting Ukrainian accent.

Redd checked the address numbers screwed into her doorframe, then tapped a receipt atop the box. "It's the address I was given." He frowned. "Don't tell me this is another one of those prank orders. That comes out of my check."

She scrunched up her face, frustrated, and turned her head. "Viktor! Did you order—?"

It was the opening Redd had been waiting for. He tossed the pizza box and yanked the screen door open with such force that it ripped the flimsy screw holding the security latch out of the old doorframe.

Before Anastasia could react, Redd had his big hand wrapped around the lower half of her face. He pushed her inside and moved her toward a couch as Kline slipped in behind him and pulled the main door shut.

Heavy footfalls thudded on the wooden staircase leading up from the basement, accompanied by muttered curses in Ukrainian. Then Viktor Petryk turned the corner into the living room. "What is it—?" He froze when he saw the two men, one of them holding his wife. "What do you want?"

"Information," Kline said. He threw a thumb at Redd. "You can volunteer it, or my goon here can beat it out of you."

Petryk swallowed nervously. "What do you want to know?"

✖ ✖ ✖

Kline found a roll of packing tape in the living room. Working together, he and Redd had the couple bound back-to-back in dining room chairs in less than a minute.

"Goon?" Redd muttered. "That's the best you could come up with?"

Kline shrugged. "It did the trick."

Redd just rolled his eyes.

Kline pulled up another chair, positioned it in front of Viktor, and dropped into it. "Look, you two don't have much time here, so I'll make it easy. When does Willow arrive?"

"Willow?" Viktor answered, just a little too quickly. "Who is Willow?"

"*Verba!*" Kline shouted. "Don't play stupid."

"I don't—"

Redd slapped the scientist across the jaw. It was barely more than a tap, but Petryk's head snapped to the side as if it had been a haymaker. A giant red welt rose on the side of his face.

Anastasia screamed. "Leave him alone, you animal!"

Redd glanced over at Kline. "Is that better or worse than *goon*?"

Kline ignored the aside. "Tell me about Willow, or your wife gets it next."

Redd barely managed to hide a frown. He knew . . . or rather, he hoped Kline was bluffing.

"*Never hit a woman, Matty,*" J. B. had always told him. "*No matter how she riles you.*"

Viktor looked truly terrified, but not because of Kline's threat. "We were warned to never speak of him or his project outside of the lab."

"Or else?"

"You have no idea."

"You are afraid?" Kline asked.

Viktor nodded.

Redd raised his hand as if preparing to strike. Anastasia cursed and spat.

Kline lifted Viktor's chin with his hand. "Right now you should be more afraid of my friend here."

Viktor swallowed. "What do you want to know?"

"Tell me about Willow."

"Willow? You are referring to Dr. Caldera, yes?"

Kline ran with it, raising the threat in his voice. "Is Caldera already there, at the facility?"

Viktor frowned, even more confused. "He was. I think he left just before we did."

"Where did he go?"

"I don't know."

Redd cracked his hand across Viktor's jaw again, this time with a little more force.

"He doesn't know anything!" Anastasia screamed.

"Don't mess around, Viktor," Kline rumbled. "My friend isn't a patient man."

"I swear I don't know. He has been here for a week . . . ten days, maybe . . . But the work is done."

"What work?" Redd asked.

Anastasia looked up at him, eyes wide with terror. "I don't know! He was the project lead. He worked in the finishing lab. We worked in a lower division."

"Explain," Kline said.

"We are divided into departments, each working on separate components—like an assembly line for cars. Do you understand?"

"Why?"

"Secrecy. No one is supposed to understand the entire project. Dr. Caldera and Dr. Gage are very protective of their intellectual property. The finishing lab is where the final product was being assembled."

"Go on."

"I don't know specifics, but generally we have been developing a strain of genetically modified wheat. High protein, high nutrient, insect- and drought-resistant. Our part was to develop a trigger response to rust."

"Rust?"

Anastasia found her voice. "*Puccinia.* A fast-spreading fungal infection. We were trying to design a genetic defense against the infection. Like an immune response."

Viktor now chorused in. "Dr. Gage wants to feed the world through the distribution of this new strain of wheat, subsidized in price by his foundation."

Kline and Redd exchanged a worried look. Was this really all about a humanitarian food project?

But no. Intellectual property or not, Gage and Caldera were killers. The Raider team. J. B. Whatever he was up to here, it couldn't be good.

"Where is Caldera going now?"

"Who are you?" Viktor asked, evidently mistaking the slightly more cordial exchange of information as an opportunity for renewed defiance.

"It doesn't matter who we are," Redd said, his voice like gravel in a rock crusher. "You two were talking about Willow at Spady's Saloon. An old man overheard it. And you know he overheard it because you called your security people."

Viktor swallowed hard, and Redd knew he had at last discovered the truth.

"Let me tell you how this works," Kline said, taking over. "That old man is dead—killed by Gage's security team because you opened your big mouths. If they killed him because they were afraid of what he might know, what do you think they're going to do to you now that the project is finished?"

"Then why aren't we already dead?" Anastasia asked.

"I guess the work you were doing was too important. But now that the project is completed?" Kline shrugged. "You're loose ends. Your only chance here is to tell us everything you know. Not just the dumbed-down version, but hard data about your research. In return, protective custody for now. Maybe a deal that keeps you out of prison."

The two scientists exchanged whispers in Ukrainian. Redd could tell by the look in Kline's eyes that he understood every word of it.

"Okay, okay," Viktor said to Kline. "Caldera is taking the product to another facility."

"Where?"

"I don't know."

Redd raised the back of his hand.

"I don't know! I swear!"

Kline raised a hand to forestall Redd. "How many facilities are there?"

"In the world? I'm not sure. Five? Perhaps more. It was never discussed openly."

"Where are they?"

"We don't know," Anastasia said. "The entire organization is compartmentalized."

"In the US? Overseas?"

"Yes, no. Maybe both. We don't know," Anastasia said.

"Okay, fine. You don't know where he's going. When is he leaving?"

"I think . . . *now*," Viktor said.

As the last syllable exited his mouth, the right side of Viktor's head exploded outward, splattering blood and tissue on the yellowing wallpaper behind him. His head rocked to the side, and then he went limp, with only a web of packing tape to keep him upright in his chair.

Anastasia opened her mouth to scream. Kline launched from his chair, intending to knock her down and save her, but he was a fraction of a second too late. A second bullet grazed the top of his shoulder on its way into her face. The contents of Anastasia Petryk's cranium joined with her husband's on the wall as the chair crashed over sideways, with Kline on top of them both.

Redd hit the deck as a dozen more rounds smashed through the windows and into the kitchen wall. Even before the fusillade ended, he was scrabbling across the floor toward the front door, hoping to at least fix the shooter's location. He realized, too late, that the shooting had stopped and that caution was no longer required, but nevertheless edged his way through the door. He was just in time to see the back end of a big SUV disappearing down the street. Despite the distance, he recognized it immediately—a black Range Rover that he'd last seen occupying two "reserved" parking spaces outside Spady's.

Shevchenko.

FIFTY-SIX

Kline found a kitchen towel to use as a compression bandage for the wound in his shoulder. It was only a graze, but it stung worse than he expected. Beneath the towel, his shirt was already dark and damp with blood oozing from the graze.

Redd rushed back inside a moment later. "It was Shevchenko. Let's go! We can catch him!"

"Forget him," Kline said. "Caldera is the primary target. We'll deal with the Ukrainian later."

Redd looked down at the lifeless bodies of the Petryks. "If you don't, I will." He paused a beat, then added, "Where do you think he's going next? Back to Mexico?"

Kline motioned for the door, indicating that they could talk about it on the way. As they hiked back to the Raptor, he said, "I think his work in Mexico is done. We never caught wind of anything connecting Willow to Anton Gage."

Redd used his remote to unlock the truck, then got in and fired it up. "Well, if he's leaving the country, he sure ain't driving there. If I put the pedal to the metal, I bet we can make it to Bozeman airport in about an hour and quarter."

Beside him, Kline buckled up. "Well, I suppose it won't do any good to tell you not to get us killed on the drive. Don't forget about that speed trap we passed on the way in."

"Just wave your magic FBI shield at them as we go by." Redd threw the truck into gear and left rubber on the road.

Kline slipped in his AirPods and made a call.

"Where are you?" Stephanie Treadway asked. "Culp is nosing around. She knows you're in Montana."

"Forget her. I need you to look up the passenger manifests for every flight leaving out of Bozeman International, starting now until the rest of the evening or even tomorrow."

"On it."

Redd navigated through Voight, and now that he was back on the highway heading back toward Bozeman, he delivered on his promise to redline the engine. The Raptor's twin turbo 450 horsepower engine roared beneath the hood as the speedometer arm swept past eighty-two miles per hour, matching the digital readout. Kline unselfconsciously gripped the overhead handhold.

Outside the town limits, the vestiges of civilization surrounding Voight had given way to endless fields of gold under the incredible vastness of the Big Sky. Fortunately, there was hardly any traffic to contend with. The noise of the Raptor's big BFGoodrich all-terrain tires eating up the pavement was almost deafening. Without the AirPods, Kline would have been unable to hear anything at all.

Treadway came back a moment later. "Okay, who am I looking for?"

"A man named Caldera. He's a geneticist."

There was another brief pause. "No one with that name booked on any of the flights departing out of BZN. Is it possible he's using an alias?"

"Anything is possible. I guess we'll have to use a brute force attack." He glanced over at Redd, who was listening intently, and explained himself even though he knew Treadway understood. "Run down every passenger. Check them against ID records."

"On it. Oh, I found something else."

"What?"

"A private charter. It's heading to Denver. Your guy's name isn't on the manifest, but that doesn't necessarily mean anything."

"Who's the private charter?"

"Some outfit called the Gage Charitable Trust. They're a fixed-base operator at Bozeman as well. And get this. It's an electric airplane."

"Bingo." He looked at Redd. "Gage has a private flight leaving out of Bozeman. When's it leaving?"

"Scheduled time of departure is 3 p.m."

Kline glanced at the clock in the corner of the GPS screen. It was showing military time—1424.

"We're not gonna make it."

Redd shot him a dark look, then pressed the accelerator even harder. Kline admired him for trying, but there was no way they could travel eighty-plus miles in thirty-five minutes.

Murphy's Law strikes again.

"I can call the guys at the Bozeman field office," Treadway was saying. "Or get the FAA to ground the plane."

Kline considered it but knew that any action against Caldera or Gage would tip their hand. Without knowing who the leak was, doing so might not only let Willow slip through their fingers again but be potentially fatal. "No. But see if you can find some excuse to delay takeoff. Half an hour should do."

"Like what?"

"How should I know? Get creative. You're good at that." He hung up and turned to Redd. "We need to haul."

Redd just grinned, but as he turned his eyes back to the road, his expression creased into a sudden frown. "What the hell?"

Kline looked and saw it too. Barely visible in the distance, maybe half a mile down the road, a large black shape at the road's edge stood in stark contrast to the golden fields.

"It's him," Redd growled. "Shevchenko."

"What's he doing—?"

A noise like a gunshot inside the cab cut him off. A moment later, the world turned upside down.

FIFTY-SEVEN

Shevchenko watched as the Raptor's front left tire came apart. Chunks of flying steel-belted rubber flew out behind it amid a cloud of black smoke. The Raptor immediately began to swerve as the driver—*Redd,* Shevchenko thought with a smirk of satisfaction—fought a losing battle to maintain control. At such high speeds, he might as well have tried to ride a tornado.

An instant later, the half-ton truck lost contact with the pavement and began tumbling end over end, carried by the momentum of its weight and speed, flinging off pieces of itself as it went. Its trajectory took it off the road, barely two hundred yards from where Shevchenko stood. It smashed through a barbed wire fence and into a muddy pasture. Clods of dirt and vegetation flew up into the air like confetti. The truck finally came to a crunching halt a hundred muddy yards from the pavement, belly-up and dead like smoking roadkill.

Shevchenko put away his phone, which he had just used to detonate the small IED he had affixed to the inside of the Raptor's front wheel, but remained where he was a moment longer, watching for any signs of life.

A quick glance up the road showed no traffic coming in either direction. He alone had borne witness to Redd's end. Satisfied that Redd was incapacitated, if not already dead, he got into the Range Rover and started it up.

He carved a tight U-turn and then rolled down the highway to the place where Redd had blown through the fence. He eased the Range Rover off road and crept forward until he was alongside the broken remains of the Raptor. He scanned the area again, expecting a passerby to come running up to help, but no one came.

Shevchenko had chosen the perfect killing ground. The surrounding acreage was owned by the Gage Food Trust, so there would be no farmers about. In fact, the wreck might not be discovered for days. Provided, of course, that both men in the truck were unable to get a phone call out.

He left the SUV running as he got out and made his way over to the wreck. He'd used a scoped Winchester .30-30 to take down the Petryks, but if it proved necessary to finish off Redd or the FBI agent with a bullet, he would use the Glock 40 Gen 4 10mm with a Trijicon RMR red dot sight holstered on his hip. Despite America's many faults, the fact that a man could open carry his weapon in a state like Montana and not even earn a second look from passersby made it seem almost civilized.

Almost.

Shevchenko approached the passenger window. He knelt down at a discreet distance and peered in. The older man hung upside down, his body suspended by his seat belt. Blood dripped from a gash in his forehead and streamed down his unconscious face. A small puddle of blood and pieces of glass pooled on the roof below his head. He appeared dead. If he wasn't already, he would probably bleed out before long.

Good.

He moved a little closer until he could see Redd, likewise hanging upside down in the driver's seat. It was hard to tell whether he was alive from that vantage point, so Shevchenko stood and walked over to the opposite side, knelt down again, and peered through the empty window frame.

Redd appeared to be unconscious, though not as bloody as the other man. It was hard to believe that both men weren't shredded like red beets in a blender after the horrific crash. No matter.

He edged closer, then reached in to feel Redd's pulse.

✖   ✖   ✖

Redd was groggy from the crash but fought off the stars he was seeing just in time to note Shevchenko's silhouette moving down toward them. He waited, watching as the man circled the truck, first looking at Kline before making his way to the driver's side.

When he did, Redd was ready to strike.

The Ukrainian let out a howl as Redd slashed his arm to the bone with J. B.'s razor-sharp Case folding knife. Shevchenko scrambled back in a panic, his left hand trying to stanch the eruption of blood from his other arm.

Redd quickly slashed the thin blade across the shoulder strap and curled himself into a ball as he dropped eighteen inches onto the inverted truck's headliner. He ignored the multiple pinpricks of pain as his body ground into broken glass and thrust himself through the window opening, diving after Shevchenko.

Shevchenko glanced up in time to see Redd roll out of the cab, his back covered in pellets of broken glass. Still clutching his bleeding right forearm, the Ukrainian braced himself to meet Redd's charge. They collided like a pair of bighorn sheep jousting for control of a mountaintop, muscle and bone slamming together with a resounding thud. Redd bounced back but managed to stay on his feet.

"I'm going to kill you!" Shevchenko growled.

"I'm right here," Redd yelled as he held his arms out wide, taunting the giant Ukrainian.

It was a mistake. Despite his size, Shevchenko moved like lightning, and hampered by his own injuries, Redd was a heartbeat too slow. Shevchenko came in fast, planting one foot and whipping the other around in a kick that drove into Redd's midsection, punching him back into the side of the Raptor. The knife fell from Redd's nerveless fingers as he doubled over.

Shevchenko marched forward. "This will be much more satisfying than killing that old man," he sneered, then drew back to launch another kick.

The declaration opened an untapped reservoir of rage in Redd. He heaved himself off the truck and threw his arms around Shevchenko's planted leg. The kick mostly missed, grazing against Redd's shoulder. With the Ukrainian now off-balance, Redd leveraged all of his weight against Shevchenko's planted leg, upending the larger man and dropping him into the grass.

Redd bounded to his feet to throw himself onto the fallen giant, but Shevchenko launched his other boot and knocked Redd sideways. His gun arm disabled, the Ukrainian reached across his body with his good arm for his Glock and wrapped his hand around the pistol butt. But his Safariland holster, a favorite of military and law enforcement units around the world, had a locking system that could only release the gun when the shooter gripped the pistol and engaged the release button with his thumb. With the wrong hand gripping the pistol in the wrong direction, Shevchenko couldn't unholster the Glock.

In the seconds it took him to realize this, Redd fell on him. He wrapped his hands around the Ukrainian's neck, choking the life out of him.

"Matt, don't! We need him alive!" Kline called from inside the cab as he worked his safety belt.

Redd heard Kline through the fog of his murderous rage. Kline was right. Shevchenko was a living weapon. Redd had suspected all along that the Ukrainian had been J. B.'s executioner, but he had been wrong about the identity of the man who wielded that weapon—not Wyatt but Anton Gage.

The moment of uncertainty gave Shevchenko the respite he needed. His reddening face broke into a grin. His reach was longer than Redd's by four inches, and Redd's marginally loosened grip allowed Shevchenko to reach up with his good arm and grab Redd by the face. His thick fingers caught Redd's skull just below the eye sockets.

Redd shouted, letting go of his choke hold and grabbing Shevchenko's good arm with his left hand to break the agonizing grip on his face. Shevchenko's iron hand squeezed even harder.

Focused on Redd's face, Shevchenko didn't see Redd's right hand close on the fallen Case folder, but he sure felt it when the blade sliced open his wrist, cutting through the cables in his hands down to the bone, flaying muscle and skin.

Shevchenko yanked his bleeding hand away, screaming, as he scrambled to his feet.

Without any hesitation, Redd plunged the high carbon steel blade into Shevchenko's eye. Before Shevchenko could tear himself away, Redd let go of the knife body, then hammered the heel of his hand into the exposed end, driving the knife and half of the hilt deep into Shevchenko's brain.

Even that was not enough to slay the monster. Shevchenko just stood there, a bemused look on his skillet face, blood streaming like tears from his ruined eye. His arms hung at his sides, gushing with each beat of his heart.

Why won't this guy just die?

Redd drove his right fist into Shevchenko's face, staggering him back another step. He followed with a left, then another right, landing one sledgehammer blow after another, until the giant finally went down.

Exhausted, Redd looked down at Shevchenko's lifeless body.

I got him, J. B. I got him.

FIFTY-EIGHT

Redd stared down at his vanquished foe, breathing heavily until the last of his rage boiled away. He spat on the Ukrainian, then knelt to pull J. B.'s old pocketknife from the dead man's eye socket. He wiped it clean on Shevchenko's shirtfront, folded it, and returned it to his pocket.

A hand clapped on his shoulder. It was Kline. He'd regained consciousness and managed to extract himself from the truck, but he didn't look good at all. His face was ashen, with scores of minor lacerations weeping blood. When he spoke, he seemed to have trouble getting the words out. "We need to get going."

"He destroyed my truck."

Kline gestured to the idling Range Rover. "We'll take that. He doesn't need it. We have to catch Caldera."

Redd nodded, but before rising, he reached down and pulled Shevchenko's Glock 40 pistol from its holster. He press-checked it to confirm there was a round in the chamber, then shoved it into his waistband.

Kline started for Shevchenko's SUV but stumbled and knelt to the ground, breathing sharply.

"You're hurt."

"Just gotta . . . catch my breath. Something punched me in the chest."

"I think it was the dashboard." Redd helped him get back up and walked him to the passenger side of the Range Rover. He searched the vehicle in vain for something to stanch the bleeding from Kline's shoulder wound and was finally forced to return to the sad wreck of the Raptor to retrieve the towel Kline had taken from the Petryks' house. When he returned, he found Kline talking wearily into his phone. He ended the call and then turned to Redd.

"We may have caught a break," he said. The utterance seemed to tax him. He drew several short breaths before continuing. "The Gage plane requested a one-hour delay."

Redd grasped the significance of this. "They're waiting for Shevchenko."

Kline nodded. "Could be. But if they try calling him and he doesn't answer, they won't wait one minute longer."

Redd circled the vehicle and got in behind the wheel. "Then we'd better move."

✖ ✖ ✖

The Eviation Alice all-electric airplane sat idle on the Bozeman airport tarmac outside of its hangar, its tail and wingtip motors still as there was no need to start the electric motors until just before takeoff. With its long wings, vee tail, and bulbous aerodynamic shape, the Alice looked like a prop plane designed for *The Jetsons*. Eviation was an Israeli company but had received an early investment from Anton Gage, which was why he now possessed the first and only production model in the US. The high-efficiency 920kW battery put the lightweight composite aircraft in easy range of the Denver airport, where Rafael Caldera would board one of Gage's *other* planes—a Gulfstream V that would take him on to Argentina.

"You said one hour," Caldera said, clutching an aluminum case in his hands. "It's time to go."

"Not yet," the pilot said. "We're waiting for Shevchenko."

"Leave him. My mission is more important."

"He's your security. We wait."

"The timeline—"

"There's plenty of time."

"I demand that you leave *now*."

"You don't get to make demands of me, Doctor," the pilot said, glowering. "Still, it's not like Shevchenko to be late for anything. I'll try calling him again. If we can't reach him, we'll call the tower and request clearance to depart."

✖ ✖ ✖

"We're not gonna make it," Redd said, narrowly swerving around a giant John Deere tractor rumbling down the middle of the road. The hour delay Gage's pilot had requested was nearly up, and Redd and Kline were still ten minutes out.

"Gotta try."

"Can't you get your contact to delay them? Call in a bomb threat or—"

Redd swerved hard and Kline grimaced as he grabbed the overhead bar with both hands.

A rusted-out Subaru Outback pulled off a dirt track and onto the county road just up ahead. Redd honked and flashed lights as he rocketed past the slow-moving wagon still blissfully unaware of its near-death experience.

"I'm not calling in a bomb threat." Kline took several shallow breaths, his face twisted in pain.

"What's wrong with you?"

Kline ignored the question. "That puts my hide in a sling for a federal crime, and they likely won't do anything about it for a while anyway, if at all, if they don't deem it credible. Willow will be long gone. Our only hope is to get there and stop him."

Kline leaned back, his mouth half-open, his face slicked with sweat.

"You're hurt."

"Banged up. No big deal."

But Redd had more than a little combat medical training. "You've got a pneumothorax. Your chest cavity is filling up with air, and it's preventing your lungs from inflating."

"I'll live," Kline wheezed. "Willow—"

"Forget Willow. We need to get you to a hospital."

"I'm not asking you; I'm telling you. Just get us to the airport. Now!"

✖   ✖   ✖

Bozeman Yellowstone International Airport was one of the best small airports Redd had visited. Its one runway capable of handling large commercial aircraft, designated "12/30," made it "international" because it linked to larger, genuinely international airports like Dallas and Denver. Like Montana, BZN was wide-open, unpretentious, and friendly.

After nearly breaking the sound barrier and somehow managing to avoid any law enforcement, Redd sped through the roundabout on screeching tires onto Airway Boulevard and then turned onto the access road, heading straight for the Gage Jet Center, the FBO located right across from the runway.

Redd pointed at the only airplane on the tarmac, an all-white vee tail, carbon fiber aircraft standing on the far end of the long "30" runway to his far right, its three propellers whirring as it waited for takeoff. With a slightly flattened teardrop profile and oversize nacelles, the plane looked more like a stylized art deco image from an old world's fair poster than a functional aircraft.

"It's gotta be that thing."

Even as he said it, the plane began rolling.

"We're too late." Kline grimaced.

"Screw that." Redd punched the gas.

The big Range Rover plowed through the cyclone gate without slowing. Redd made a hard left on the service tarmac and aimed the SUV at the big grassy divide between the service tarmac and the main runway.

"What do you think you're doing?" Kline shouted.

"Gonna block the runway. Keep it from taking off."

✖ ✖ ✖

"What is going on?" Caldera asked, his face nearly pressed against the oval window where he sat. He watched a black SUV bouncing across the grass at a high rate of speed.

On a headset waiting for tower instructions, the pilot couldn't hear him. When there was no response to his panicked question, Caldera unbuckled his seat belt and bolted through the open cockpit door just a few feet away. He shook the pilot's shoulder and pointed out the wide, sloping windscreen to the left.

"¡*Mira!* Look!"

✖ ✖ ✖

Redd swore as the strange airplane shot forward.

"Matt . . ."

Redd stomped the gas, his boot hitting the floorboard. The Range Rover bucked and swerved in the soft turf but rocketed ahead.

The plane increased speed.

So did Redd.

He calculated the difference between the speed of the plane and the Range Rover. He was losing ground. "Come on!" he growled.

Only one thing he could do. He yanked the wheel.

"Matt . . ." Kline's voice was barely louder than a whisper.

The Range Rover swerved, accelerating, closing the gap.

"*Matt.*" Somehow Kline managed to increase his volume.

The white plane loomed large in the windshield.

"*Matt!*"

The plane accelerated. The front wheel began to lift. But Redd got there first.

Like a sledgehammer hitting an empty beer can, the Range Rover slammed into the plane's fuselage with enough force to send it cartwheeling across the tarmac, snapping the landing gear and driving one of its twenty-six-foot-long wings into asphalt, breaking it. The plane folded in the middle like a bent elbow.

Redd braked an instant after the collision, avoiding the spinning airplane. Equipped with a steel bumper cage, the SUV had weathered the impact well, sustaining only cosmetic damage. Once clear, Redd threw the gear lever into park and jumped out of the truck. Off in the distance, he could hear the wail of approaching sirens. Fire engines probably, but maybe law enforcement as well.

Redd charged over to the cabin door and busted it open. He bent down low to get inside. The interior was already clouded with acrid black smoke. Through it, Redd glimpsed a struggling form in the cockpit—the pilot trying to escape the burning wreckage.

Then he saw another figure, spread-eagle on the cabin floor, head canted at a crazy angle from the crash. The man hadn't been belted in when the collision had occurred, and the impact had hurled him against a bulkhead.

It had to be Caldera.

Willow.

Redd knelt over him, checking for a pulse.

"Dead," he announced. "Broke his neck."

"That carrier," Kline said, leaning against the doorframe. He was pointing at an aluminum case, about the size of J. B.'s old tackle box, resting on the deck a few steps behind the dead scientist.

As Redd started toward it, the pilot succeeded in unbuckling and hit the deck with a grunt. Redd reflexively turned toward the commotion and saw the bloodied pilot rising to her feet.

Hannah Gage.

Redd's jaw dropped. *You've got to be kidding me.*

Despite the fact that blood was streaming from a gash in her forehead, she bared her teeth in a fierce smile. "Come to see me off, Matty?"

Redd reached for the Glock in his waistband, but Hannah was faster. She raised her right hand, which held a small but nevertheless deadly Sig P238, aimed it at Redd's heart, and pulled the trigger.

FIFTY-NINE

The bullet creased the air mere inches from Redd's left ear. In the instant that Hannah had pulled the trigger, Kline had stepped in and clocked her in the face, spoiling her aim, though not by much. She dropped like a stone.

Redd let out a breath he hadn't realized he'd been holding and retrieved the aluminum case. He thrust it into Kline's hands, then went back for Hannah.

"Leave her; let's go," Kline said, coughing. "We have what we came for."

"No way." Redd snatched Hannah up in his arms just as a fire truck screeched to a stop. Two men in full turnout gear leaped out and charged over to them.

"How bad is she hurt?" asked one of the firefighters.

Redd pushed past him. "Just fainted."

The second man grabbed Redd's arm. "Where do you think you're going with her?"

Kline flashed his FBI credentials. "Gentlemen, this is a national security emergency. I'll take it from here. But whatever you do, save that plane!"

The two firefighters exchanged an uncertain look, then returned to their truck to begin carrying out Kline's command.

Redd tossed Hannah in the back seat of the Range Rover and crawled behind the wheel as Kline slammed his door shut, wheezing, "Go! Go! Go!"

Redd punched the gas and pointed the Range Rover back the way they'd come. The SUV bounced off the tarmac and across the grassy margin as two more emergency vehicles braked to a halt near the experimental airplane, which was now fully engulfed in flames and black, oily smoke.

The burning aircraft was enough distraction for them to get away.

"Now what?" Redd asked as he threaded the vehicle through the gate he'd blown through earlier.

"We've kicked a hornet's nest," Kline said. "We've got to go to ground. And we need backup. Any chance we can call local law enforcement?"

Redd shook his head. Sheriff Blackwood was in Gage's pocket, and Shane Hepworth was so infatuated with Hannah that he couldn't be counted on to act rationally.

"Care to explain why you brought her along?" Kline asked, jerking a thumb at the motionless figure in the back seat. "I mean she's not bad-looking, but . . ."

"That's Hannah Gage."

Kline's eyes widened. "Welp, I don't know if that's the stupidest thing you've done today or the smartest."

Redd shrugged. "I can't believe you hit a woman."

"Yeah, well, I abandoned my kid too," Kline sighed. "I've done all kinds of terrible stuff in my lifetime. Besides, she tried to kill you." He looked back at Hannah, then to Redd. "We've got Willow's project. We don't need her."

"She's part of it somehow. I need to know what part. We're still only on the bottom rung of this thing. And she has to pay."

Kline did not respond immediately but stared forward. They were heading down a two-lane that cut through a mostly empty landscape. "Where are we going?"

"I know a place where we'll be safe." Redd punched the gas. "Hang on."

✖ ✖ ✖

With the help of the onboard GPS, Redd navigated through a series of unused service and farm roads, making a wide, sweeping circle away from heavily trafficked roads, well away from the places where state police vehicles might be on the lookout for them. What the GPS couldn't show him were the fire watch and ranch roads that ran through a couple of the big ranches in the area and would lead them back in the direction of Wellington, but Redd didn't need help with that. He knew those like the back of his hand.

Kline had not said much, but his breathing had grown increasingly labored.

"You all right?" Redd asked. Stupid question. Obviously he wasn't.

"How much longer?"

"Maybe half an hour. We're taking the scenic route for a reason."

Kline grunted, then looked down at the case that had been in his lap since they'd left the airport. "What do you think's in here?"

"Probably nothing we should be messing with. If Caldera really is . . . *was* . . . Willow, then it's probably some kind of bioweapon. Or maybe it's booby-trapped to destroy the contents if you force it open. Don't you have people at the FBI who can take care of it?"

"One problem with that. I don't know who I can trust at the bureau."

Redd glanced in his rearview mirror and saw Hannah stirring. He nodded to Kline. "I'll bet she can tell us what's in there."

Kline turned in his chair to look back at her. "Hannah Gage?"

Her face was streaked with crusted blood, but her eyes were clear and angry. "Who are you?"

"Special Agent Gavin Kline, FBI. And you're under arrest."

"For what?"

"I can think of half a dozen charges. For starters, transporting weapons of mass destruction, terrorism, murder. Should I go on?"

She tossed her head back. "I haven't done any of that."

Kline held up the case. "We know what's in here, and we know Caldera, aka Willow, is behind it all. But he's dead and you're not, so you're the one going to jail for a very, very long time."

Hannah didn't bother hiding her grin. "You don't know what's in there. You're just guessing. There's no way you opened it."

"How do you know that?"

"Because we'd all be dead if you had."

Redd sensed she was bluffing but decided to let Kline handle the interrogation. Despite his weakened condition, he seemed to be holding his own.

"I don't need to open it to know what's in it."

She leaned forward. "You two idiots have no idea who or what you're dealing with, do you?"

"Enlighten us."

Her eyes found Redd's in the mirror. "Is he a friend of yours, Matty?"

"Not exactly."

Kline darkened. "You don't get to call him Matty."

Hannah's eyes lingered on Redd. "How interesting. Agent Kline, is it? Maybe you should call your superiors before you screw things up even further."

"Why would I do that?"

"Because your boss, or maybe your boss's boss, will tell you to leave this alone. You're in way over your head."

"We'll see about that," Kline said.

Hannah continued to stare at Redd, then abruptly declared, "I want a deal. Immunity in exchange for information."

Kline laughed at the abruptness of her reversal. "So much for being in over our head."

"Why are you suddenly cooperating?" Redd asked.

"Because now they'll probably just kill me anyway. They'll find out what you've just done, if they haven't already, and they'll come for you. I don't want to die. And on the off chance we all survive until tomorrow, I don't want to go to jail."

"I don't have the authority to make that deal," Kline said. "But if you give me something now, I'll start making calls."

"What do you want to know?"

"Well, let's start with who you think will want to kill you. I thought your father was the one running all of this."

She shook her head. "He's only a small cog in a much larger machine."

"What kind of machine?"

Her eyes lit up. "A time machine. A way to roll back the Earth's clock and save the planet."

"You're not making any sense."

"Our planet is dying. There are too many people fighting over too few resources. The only way we're going to make it through this century is to dramatically reduce the population. There's a small but very powerful group of men who are dedicated to making that happen."

"Sounds like the plot of a James Bond movie," Redd remarked.

"It's true." She pointed to the case in Kline's lap. "And that's the key to it."

"Go on."

"Are you familiar with the Georgia Guidestones?"

Redd glanced over at Kline, who just shrugged.

Hannah went on. "They're a monument erected in Elbert County, Georgia, in 1980. Inscribed upon them are the ten guidelines—the principles that will usher in a golden age of humanity, if only we have the courage to follow them."

"Sounds like some kind of cult," Redd muttered. "Who built this monument anyway?"

"The group I told you about. Informally, they are called the Twelve because there are only ever twelve leaders. My father is one of them. I don't know the identity of any others. But I can assure you they're not a cult. The guidelines are based in reason and logic, not superstition or magical thinking. They call for us to put aside our differences, unite in a common language. Avoid petty laws. Balance personal rights with social duties. Seek harmony with the infinite. Leave room for nature."

"Sounds like paradise," Kline said. "What do the guidelines say about developing weapons of mass destruction?"

"The first guideline holds that the world's population should not exceed half a billion people."

It took a moment for the significance of this to dawn on Redd. "You're not serious. You want to exterminate seven billion people?"

Hannah did the head flip again. "Of course not. We're not monsters. The key to reducing population isn't to kill, but rather to reduce the number of live births."

Kline looked down at the case. "So this is some kind of sterilization agent?"

"Broadly speaking. Dr. Caldera's early experiments did not prevent women from conceiving children but instead produced horrifying birth defects. That would have accomplished the same goal, but my father is not in the business of killing babies. Rather, we want to spare the unborn the horrors of living on a planet with too few resources."

"How does it work?"

Hannah pursed her lips together as if trying to decide how much to reveal.

"It's something to do with your GMO grains, isn't it," Redd prompted. Then, remembering what Viktor Petryk had told him, he guessed, "Something to do with leaf rust."

Hannah gave him a sly smile. "I knew you were more than just a pretty face. The Gage Food Trust is dedicated to developing fast-growing strains of wheat, maize, and rice to feed the hungry in developing nations. Our grains are already feeding millions. Hundreds of millions. One of the traits we've engineered into the grains is a resistance to the *Puccinia* fungus—commonly called 'rust.' The plants are impervious to ordinary rust, but Dr. Caldera engineered the plants to be vulnerable to a specially engineered strain of *Puccinia*. Caldera's strain of rust fungus is unique in that it does not harm the plant but instead causes it to manufacture a hormone that reacts with cholesterol, which is naturally biosynthesized in the human body, to create increased levels of estrogen in anyone who consumed the grains as part of their regular diet. The result would be a significant decline in fertility rates in developing countries."

"So this—" Kline held up the case again—"is the GMO fungus? How much more is there?"

"That's everything Dr. Caldera cultivated, but it's enough. Once released, it will propagate exponentially in our engineered crops."

"What will it do to regular grain crops?"

Hannah shrugged as if the question did not concern her.

"Let me get this straight," Redd said. "The wheat and the rust work together to produce the hormone, and then a natural process in the body reacts with the hormone."

Hannah nodded. "This way, no one will suspect what's causing the reduction in birth rates."

"I don't buy it," Kline said. "Cutting birth rates in the world's poorest nations won't get you down to half a billion. Not in a hundred years."

Hannah shrugged again. "The Twelve have other initiatives, but I'm afraid I don't know anything about them."

Other initiatives? Redd thought. *So much for not being monsters.*

"Twelve people are going to do all this?"

"The Twelve are the leaders, coordinating their efforts through a network of operatives who have infiltrated the world's most powerful governments."

"You're talking about the deep state," Kline said.

"That's one name for it. My father refers to them as 'the Five Hundred.'"

"And that's why you told me to call my boss. You've got someone in the FBI. Who?"

Redd felt his pulse quicken. Kline had hinted at a leak in his office, a leak that might have been responsible for compromising the Raider team ahead of the mission to take down Willow.

"Does the name Dudek ring any bells?" Kline pressed. "Kevin Dudek?"

Hannah folded her arms across her chest. "I think I've said enough. I won't say another word unless I get total immunity from any and all crimes. No matter how this plays out, I get my life back."

"Who's this Dudek?" Redd asked, speaking low so that Kline knew the question was for him. "Is he the guy that got my team killed?"

"He worked out of my office. He was one of a handful of people who knew that we were closing in on Willow. Routine surveillance turned up the fact that he had a burner phone and was arranging clandestine meetings."

"That's not exactly an airtight case. For all you know, the guy could have just been having an affair."

"He *was* having an affair. I just found out about it earlier today. But the thing is, somebody stabbed him to death a couple nights ago. It's possible that the affair was what compromised him, and whoever was running him decided he was a weak link." Kline leaned back in his seat as if the effort of explaining this had taken a huge toll.

Redd made a decision. "Let's get where we're going. We can figure out our next move once we get there."

SIXTY

Anton Gage politely declined the offer of a flute of champagne, just as he had an earlier presentation of canapés. Despite the fact that the room was packed with people and buzzing with conversation, the refusal did not go unnoticed.

"If champagne is not to your liking," said the host of the affair, one Senator Winston Lamott, "I do have a bottle of single malt hidden in the bookshelf."

Gage smiled. "Thank you, Senator, but I like to keep a clear head when swimming in shark-infested waters."

A tentative smile lifted the corners of the senator's mouth. He was a fleshy man who exuded the kind of down-on-the-farm bonhomie that was the province of used car salesmen, televangelists, and career politicians. Gage, who was a dedicated student of human nature, did not understand why that patently fake geniality was so attractive to American voters of a certain class, but he knew that it could be reliably exploited, which was why he made such generous donations to the senator's reelection campaign.

"Shark-infested?" Lamott clucked. "I do believe you are paying me a compliment, Anton. But fear not, I know better than to bite the hand that feeds. That's why I'm so concerned when I see you standing here with empty hands."

Gage clapped a hand to the other man's bicep. "There's nothing amiss with your hospitality, Winston. I'm just not at my festive best." He lowered his voice and stepped closer. "I've managed to keep this out of the news, but I lost my son, Wyatt, yesterday."

While this was a factual statement, it was not the reason for Anton Gage's pensiveness. He had wasted no tears on his wayward offspring. In truth, it had not been difficult at all to approve Hannah's suggestion to remove Wyatt from the board. The boy was beyond rehabilitation, beyond redemption, and his excesses threatened everything Gage had worked so hard to accomplish.

With the finish line at last in sight, there were so many things that could go wrong.

"He struggled with addiction," Anton went on, embellishing, though he wasn't really sure why. "I hope he's found peace at last."

"My word," the senator breathed with practiced sympathy. "What a terrible thing. You have my condolences."

"Thank you, Winston. I'd be obliged if you'd keep that information to yourself. At least until . . ." He trailed off as he saw Darla, his personal assistant, searching the room with his phone in her hand.

Gage felt a wave of apprehension. He never carried communication devices into meetings of any sort, believing that real-world interactions took precedence. Darla knew this only too well, so for her to intrude could only mean something bad had happened.

No, no, no. Not after all we've gone through.

The Twelve would not be happy.

"Would you excuse me, Senator?" He did not wait for a reply but strode over to intercept Darla. She met his gaze with a look of abject terror.

"I'm so sorry, sir—" she began, but he waved her off.

"You're just following my orders," he assured her. "I never kill the messenger."

He took the phone. A glance at the screen showed a call on hold from the Montana facility.

"You might want to take this in private," she said gravely.

He nodded and followed her to the exit, taking the call off hold as soon as he was away from the bustle of the cocktail party. "I'm here. Go ahead."

"It's Bob Simpson from the security office, Mr. Gage. There's been an incident at the airport."

Gage listened without interrupting as Simpson relayed the news of the plane crash and the discovery of Dr. Caldera's body. He wanted to ask about the GFT-17 and whether it had been recovered, but Simpson wasn't fully briefed on the details of the operation. Instead, when Simpson's tale ended, he asked, "What about Hannah? And Roman?"

"Initial reports on the scene are that Hannah was removed from the crash by an FBI agent and another unidentified man. There wasn't anyone else on the plane."

"FBI?" Gage's voice rose an octave.

"That's what we were told."

Gage brought his tone back to its customary measured cadence and tone. "Thank you for contacting me, Bob. I'll follow up." Then he added, "Just to be on the safe side, put the facility on standby for sterilization protocol."

"Sir?"

"You heard me, Bob." He ended the call, then immediately opened a GPS application on the phone. He typed in a ten-digit identification code and watched as the map refreshed with the exact location of the corresponding tracking chip.

It was still transmitting.

The location dot was moving slowly, cross-country or possibly on an unmarked road, about forty miles north of Bozeman.

Gage nodded to himself, then called Simpson again with further instructions. Once that task was completed, he felt a degree of calm returning. The crisis was not yet past, but because of his decisive action, it just might be possible to keep the situation from devolving into a full-blown nightmare.

There was just one more detail to take care of. He put in a call to his contact in the FBI Intelligence Division.

She picked up on the first ring.

"What is going on in Montana?" he snapped.

"I'm just getting the brief now," she replied. Her tone suggested that she was just as alarmed as he was. "I'm not sure how Kline was tipped to this, but he's way off the reservation."

"He has my daughter."

"I'm aware of that. I'm on my way to the Bozeman field office. As soon as he calls in, I'll instruct him to bring her in. We can handle this discreetly."

"It's too late for discreet!" Gage's voice had risen again, and he was grateful that Darla had urged him to seek privacy. "I'm sending in a retrieval team. They'll take care of it."

"You know where she is?"

Gage chose his words carefully. "Hannah is carrying a tracker chip."

"Give me the frequency. I'll get her back. There's no need to go kinetic with this."

"The decision has already been made. I just need you to provide political cover for the operations."

"Wait—"

Gage ended the call, handed the phone back to his assistant, and then leaned heavily against the wall.

The plan had already taken his son, and now, barring a miracle, it would take his daughter as well. Memories of Hannah flooded his mind, but just as fast as they arrived, he pushed them from his memory. There would be a time to grieve—and Gage knew it would be a painful experience—but first he had a mission to accomplish.

God supposedly sacrificed His Son to save mankind from their sins. I've given two children—what does that make me?

The thought brought him a measure of comfort, but if the retrieval team failed to recover the GFT-17, his sacrifice would be for nothing.

SIXTY-ONE

MONTANA

The sun was lowering in the west when the Range Rover finally arrived at the old hunting cabin near the summit. It was actually only about a twenty-minute drive from the ranch house, but on the off chance that the house and main entrance were already under surveillance, Redd had elected to make a covert approach on a rutted, seldom-used, old jeep trail that ran down the back side of the mountain and connected to Dry Creek Road.

The cabin, nestled amid lodgepole pine and western larch, had been one of Redd's favorite places growing up. It was a single-room affair, no plumbing or electricity. The rough-hewn boards were iron black with age. There was a small woodstove for heat and a Coleman LED lantern that J. B. kept in the place. Luckily, the batteries still worked. J. B. had also added a rain catchment system, using a fifty-gallon PVC barrel to store the water that ran through the tin roof gutters and a purification hand pump to clean it for drinking, and had always kept a small supply of canned food in the root cellar under the cabin floor.

"Well, it's not the Ritz," Redd told the others as they entered, "but it will do for now."

"Quaint," Hannah said with a sneer.

"Make yourself comfortable," Redd said, pointing at one of the two racks of plywood bunk beds. There weren't any linens or creature comforts on them. They were meant for sleeping bags.

"I was hoping our first time sleeping together would be a little less rustic."

He ignored the innuendo. "There's an outhouse out back. Make sure you check for spiders before you go."

"You're such a romantic."

Redd settled Kline in on the lower bunk. The latter was still conscious, but his breathing was shallow and rapid. His face was pale and soaked in sweat, and his skin had taken on a bluish cast. Redd was certain now of his earlier diagnosis. Pneumothorax.

"Your friend's in trouble," Hannah said from behind him. "He needs a doctor."

She was right, and they both knew it. But if they tried to go to a hospital, Gage's people . . . or the Twelve . . . or whomever . . . would find them.

"We can't take him to the hospital," Redd stated flatly. "But maybe we can bring the hospital to him."

✖ ✖ ✖

Emily Lawrence normally didn't hear her cell phone buzzing when she was busy at work, but it was a slow night and so quiet that the vibration almost startled her. She pulled it out and saw a number she didn't recognize but decided to answer anyway.

"Hello?"

"Em, it's me."

She frowned, confused. "Matty?"

Now he calls?

"Em, listen. Gavin's injured. We were in a car wreck earlier, and he's having a hard time breathing. I think he has a pneumo—"

She forgot about her pique. "Call an ambulance."

"I can't."

"Then bring him here."

"Can't do that either. Look, it's complicated, but we really need you to make a house call. Life or death."

"Why can't you bring him in?"

Emily heard a familiar voice in the background.

"What's wrong, Matt? Your old flame too busy for you?"

Emily's face went hot. "Why is Hannah Gage with you?"

"Gavin arrested her."

"Arrested? Gavin can't arrest people. He's not a cop."

"Em, I can't explain over the phone. But we can't leave and I'm worried that Gavin won't make it without medical attention."

She wanted to tell him to . . . to stop playing cowboy and grow up. But she could hear the sincerity in his voice. "Where are you?"

"Remember where we used to go when we didn't want anyone to find us?"

Emily flushed again, but this time it wasn't with anger. "You couldn't have picked somewhere more convenient? Like maybe the moon?"

"We're trying to stay off the grid."

"Well, you're in the right place for that." She grabbed her backpack from the nurses' station and started filling it with supplies. "I'll head out now, but it'll take me at least an hour to get there. Do what you can to keep him stable."

"Thanks, Em. You're a lifesaver."

"Are you in danger?"

"Nothing I can't handle."

She heard Hannah in the background. *"Oh yeah. Big, strong Matty can handle anything."*

"I'm on my way." Emily killed the call, hefted the pack onto her shoulder, and headed for the exit. She pushed through the door and was about to tell the receptionist that she was stepping out for a while, but before she could, she slammed right into Shane Hepworth.

Emily startled. "What are you doing here?"

"It's nice to see you too." He grinned. "Slow night. Thought I'd come have a cup of coffee with the hardest-working people in Stillwater County."

This wasn't unusual for Hepworth. He had a habit of dropping by the health center to flirt with Emily and the other female staff. The deputy's persistence was alternately charming and annoying, but he seemed to know where the line was and never crossed it.

"I think there's a fresh pot at the nurses' station," she said and pushed past him, heading for the door.

She was halfway across the parking lot when she heard his boots pounding to catch up. "Hey, slow down. Where's the fire?"

She glanced back, saw the determined look in his eyes, and knew that she wouldn't be able to fob him off with a flimsy excuse. "I'm going to see Matty, if you must know."

Hepworth raised an eyebrow. "Is that a fact? You and he . . ." He waggled his hand in a gesture that was probably meant to be suggestive but instead seemed juvenile.

"Not that it's any of your business, but no. A friend of his was injured in a car accident. He asked me to make a house call." She turned and continued toward her truck.

Hepworth cut around and interposed himself between her and the door. "What friend?"

She frowned. "Technically, I don't have to tell you that, Shane. HIPAA regulations require me to protect patient privacy."

"Bull crap. You said there was a car accident. That makes it my business. And I don't need to tell you that Matt's been stirring the pot since he's been back in town." He pointed to his patrol vehicle. "I'll drive."

She saw no alternative. Besides, if Matty was in trouble, then maybe he would need the kind of help only Hepworth could provide.

"Fine. Let's go."

✖ ✖ ✖

In his darkened office, Sheriff Stuart Blackwood sat with his friend Jim Beam. The bottle was unopened, but Blackwood would not have given odds to the likelihood of it staying that way much longer.

It had been a good run—almost a full year. The meetings helped, and most nights he didn't even feel like he was white-knuckling his sobriety, but the demons were always there, waiting for a moment of weakness.

Or distraction.

Unlike some of his fellow officers, he wasn't cynical about the job. He didn't even think of himself as corrupt. He just did what he had to do to get through the day, even if it meant bending rules that nobody really cared about anyway. The bottle inured him to the resulting self-loathing, just as it had helped quiet the screams of the Iraqi soldiers he'd buried alive in their trenches during the push to break through the Saddam Line back in '91.

It was only when he hit rock bottom that he understood just how long he'd been in the downward spiral. He had lost everything—his family, his self-respect—everything but the job, and even that was a lie; the only reason he still wore a badge was because the Gages had practically handed it to him. They had offered him a chance to reinvent himself. A chance to leave the wreckage of his life behind and lose himself in the openness of Big Sky Country. He would get a steady paycheck and, more importantly, respectability in the community. All he would have to do is look the other way.

But then Wyatt Gage went and killed himself on drugs in my county, and who do you think's gonna take the heat for that?

He knew he should call his sponsor. Or Dr. Emily over at the health center . . . She'd talked him down more than once. But he couldn't find it in him to care.

Oblivion was so much easier.

He reached for the bottle . . .

And knocked it over when someone knocked loudly at his door.

"Crap," he muttered, catching the bottle before it could crash to the floor. He hurriedly stashed it in a lower drawer, then took a moment to compose himself before calling out, "Come in."

The door opened and an athletic-looking young woman with short, dark hair stepped through. She faltered a step upon entering, as if his despair was tangible in the air, but then composed herself and continued forward. When she reached the desk, she produced a shield wallet and flashed her creds.

"Special Agent Treadway," she announced. "Are you the sheriff round these parts?"

"Is that supposed to be funny?" he growled, trying to hide his displeasure at this unexpected visit. The appearance of a federal agent on his doorstep seemed to confirm his worst fears.

She ignored the question. "Sheriff, I'm in a bit of a hurry here, so I'll come right to the point. I need to speak with a member of your community, one Matthew Redd. Can you direct me to his residence?"

SIXTY-TWO

Alpha Team was in position.

The GPS signal put out by the aluminum case pointed them here like a targeting laser.

They had parked a mile below and out of sight, staying off the road but moving parallel to it, working their way up by foot, silent as shadows. It was slow going, but worth it to maintain the element of surprise.

In the branches high above, the wind moaned, a cold lament, blowing snow fine as ash.

The team leader, designated Alpha 6, gradually became aware of light flickering through the woods off to their left. He keyed his lip mic. "Alpha element, hold position."

He switched off his night vision goggles, then raised his rifle, which was equipped with a Trijicon ACOG TA110 3.5x35 scope, and scanned the woods until he spotted the source of the illumination—a 4x4 truck bucking over the rutted road like a gut-shot feral hog.

A voice crackled in his ear. "Alpha 6, this is Alpha 5. I've got eyes on

the occupants of that vehicle. One driver, male; one passenger, female."
He went on to supply a few more details, none of which changed a thing.

Their orders were clear: No loose ends. No survivors. What did a couple more guests to the party matter?

The truck passed them, the glow from the headlights diminishing with the distance. Alpha 6 switched on his night vision device again and keyed his mic. "Alpha element, we're clear. Charlie Mike."

Charlie Mike—continue mission.

They resumed their advance, crawling over broken granite and fallen tree trunks, finally taking cover in the thick stand of lodgepole pine surrounding the cabin. The headlights of the recently arrived truck and the light shining out through the cabin's open door was enough to render their night vision devices useless, so Alpha 6 gave the order to switch them off. Out here, away from city lights, the moon and stars were plenty bright enough, especially once their eyes adjusted. They would do this the old-fashioned way.

Alpha 6 peered through the ACOG again, settling the glowing, horseshoe-shaped reticle on the open door and the backlit figures standing there. The female proceeded inside, but the man remained in the doorway, all but eclipsing Alpha 6's view of the cabin's occupants. Every now and then, the man would move just enough to give Alpha 6 a glimpse of the primary target standing just inside, but a clean shot eluded him. Then, after a brief exchange, the man stepped inside and the door closed, plunging the world once more into darkness.

Without lowering his weapon, Alpha 6 keyed his mic. "Alpha 5, establish security on the road. Everyone else, move up and stack on the door."

The team crept forward, smooth and silent as ghosts, while Alpha 6 provided overwatch, keeping the reticle of his ACOG trained on the sturdy wooden door. The combat optical device was designed to be aimed with both eyes open and through his nondominant eye, Alpha 6 could see his men advancing toward the cabin, weaving around the two vehicles outside. When they reached the building, they would coalesce into a line, and once he gave the signal to execute, they would breach the door and sweep into the small enclosure, killing everyone in a matter of seconds. They had performed variations on this tactical insertion thousands of times in rehearsal and hundreds of times in combat. This time would be no different.

✖ ✖ ✖

Redd watched the bouncing headlights of a four-wheel drive vehicle climbing the steep road. It had to be Emily, but he nevertheless snugged the butt of the rifle into the pit of his shoulder and tracked the vehicle's final approach. He'd found the rifle—a Winchester .30-30 that was a favorite of hunters—in the back the Range Rover, along with a partial box of ammo. That and the Glock he'd taken off Shevchenko comprised his arsenal of defense. If Gage or the Twelve or whoever figured out where they were and arrived in force, he would make a stand.

Despite the primeval darkness of the surrounding forest, Redd could still make out the vehicle. The pale three-quarter moon behind the high clouds diffused light bright enough to reveal a sheriff's department SUV. It came to a stop and two figures got out—Emily and Shane Hepworth. The deputy produced a big Maglite and used it to illuminate the way to the cabin entrance.

"Shouldn't have brought him, Em," Redd muttered.

He rose from his prone firing position near the cabin door, rested the barrel of the rifle against his shoulder, and went out to meet them. "Thanks for coming."

Emily, with a large backpack slung over her shoulder, pushed past him and headed directly into the cabin. Hepworth moved to follow her.

"Why are you here?" Redd said, blocking his entrance.

Hepworth bowed up. "Doing my job, Matt. Emily said there was a car accident, but nobody reported it." He shone the light in Redd's face. "You look pretty busted up, but then as I recall, you've picked your share of fights since coming back here."

"The accident didn't happen in Stillwater County," Redd countered. "So it's not your problem. Which means you're trespassing here, Deputy. So get that light out of my face, and get off my ranch."

Before Hepworth could reply, however, a voice from the cabin called out, "Shane? Is that you?"

Then Hannah appeared framed in the cabin doorway. Hepworth did not look particularly surprised to see her. "Hannah? You okay?"

"I'm so glad you're here, Shane. Matthew has been holding me captive up here."

Hepworth's forehead creased as if he couldn't tell if she was serious, but his hand dropped to the butt of his holstered sidearm. He turned to Redd. "Matt, I'd feel a whole lot better if you'd put that rifle down."

Redd frowned. He didn't trust Hepworth, especially not where Hannah Gage was concerned, and he was pretty sure that Hepworth had been behind the attempt to frame him for murder, but he didn't think the deputy was involved in Anton Gage's schemes. He brought the Winchester off his shoulder and held it by the barrel so that his hand was far from the trigger. "Come inside. I'll explain everything."

Emily had immediately gone to Kline's side to begin assessing him. Redd placed the Winchester in a corner, well away from everyone in the room. He made sure not to show Hepworth his back or the big Glock tucked in his waistband.

Hepworth stared at Kline for a moment, then turned back to Redd. "Start talking."

"They kidnapped me, Shane," Hannah said quickly, before Redd could speak. "Brought me up here at gunpoint. You should arrest them!"

This prompted the deputy to slip the strap of his sidearm.

"She's lying," Kline wheezed. "I'm a federal officer. Hannah Gage is in my custody."

Hepworth was momentarily paralyzed with confusion.

"You've got a pneumothorax," Emily said, seemingly oblivious to the conversation. She took a pair of trauma shears from her pack and neatly cut away Kline's shirt, exposing his rib cage, blue and purple with bruising.

"Now hold on a minute," Hepworth said. "Somebody explain to me just what's going on here."

"Hannah Gage is a terrorist," Redd answered. "She and her father are up to some pretty heinous stuff. They killed J. B. when he got too close to it. We caught her at the airport trying to smuggle out a biological weapon." He indicated the aluminum case on the floor beside Kline.

"She agreed to cooperate in exchange for a deal," Redd went on, "but evidently she's having second thoughts." He glared at Hannah for a moment. "I think you can kiss immunity goodbye."

"Don't tell me you believe this conspiracy nonsense," Hannah interjected. "This is a kidnapping, plain and simple."

Hepworth's hand did not leave his weapon. "So first it was Wyatt that murdered Jim Bob. And now it's Hannah. You'd better get your story straight."

Redd jerked a thumb at Kline. "He'll explain everything as soon as he can talk again. Gavin, show him your creds."

Kline grunted loudly as Emily cut an incision in his chest.

"Sorry, no time for local anesthetics," Emily said.

Redd started in Kline's direction, but Hepworth drew his weapon, a Smith & Wesson M&P semiauto 9mm, and pointed it at Redd's face. "Back up."

"Both of you, shut up!" Emily shouted over her shoulder. She pulled a clear plastic pulmonary tube out of its sanitary sleeve, then opened the incision with a pair of forceps and inserted one end of the tube into it. Air immediately flowed out of the tube with a loud hiss. Condensation beaded inside the tube. Kline let out an audible sigh. Emily was already stitching up the wound to hold the vent tube in place.

Redd could see Hepworth's gun hand trembling with indecision. That made him even more dangerous. "Shane, listen to me. Gavin is an FBI agent. I can prove it if you'll just put that gun down."

"I don't know who to believe," Hepworth said slowly. "But I think it might be best if I take Hannah out of here."

"I can't let you do that," Redd said.

Hepworth's finger curled around the trigger. "Try and stop me."

"Matt . . . let them go," Kline rasped.

Redd glanced over at him, then raised his hands halfway to signal his assent.

Hepworth nodded at Hannah. "Come with me."

"I may have underestimated you, Deputy." She leaned in, kissed him on the cheek, then moved around behind him so that he was between her and Redd.

"Don't try anything stupid, Matt," Hepworth said. "I can tell your friend there needs a real hospital. So here's what we're gonna do. I'm gonna take Hannah out in my rig. The rest of you can follow me. Once we get back to town, we'll figure out who's telling the truth."

Hannah opened the door and a cool breeze filled the cabin.

✖   ✖   ✖

Alpha 6 squinted as light from the cabin door filled the scope. The rest of the team ducked down or simply froze in place.

"Hold position," he whispered into his mic. A silhouette appeared in the doorway, then another—two people exiting. Alpha 6 couldn't tell if either one was the primary target, but it didn't matter. He placed the reticle onto the larger of the two and whispered, "On my signal, execute."

That signal took the form of a single trigger squeeze.

A cloud of red mist floated across the open doorway—confirmation that his round had found its target.

SIXTY-THREE

Redd hit the deck reflexively, then rolled away from the open door. He felt Shane Hepworth's hot blood all over his face. "Em! You okay?"

"What's going on?" Emily was stretched over Kline's body, protecting him.

"Someone's sent a kill team." Redd figured they had about sixty seconds before things got real ugly.

Maybe less.

He knew the drill. Knew exactly what the operators outside would do next. He used to lead a kill team himself.

It would be cover and move. Demo the doors with charges, spray the room with automatic gunfire, or just toss in a grenade and shred everyone.

No survivors.

That's how he'd do it.

"We're sitting ducks in here," Kline managed to say.

"I ain't sitting." Redd grabbed the Winchester from the corner and raced back over to the bunk. "I've got to get out there," he said, then passed Shevchenko's pistol over to Kline. The Glock held fifteen rounds plus one of hard-hitting 10mm. When the attackers eventually made it through the door, Kline would need every bullet to make his last stand.

Kline reached for it but Emily snatched it out of Redd's hand. "Give me that. He can't even sit up."

"You know how to handle one of these?"

She dropped the Glock's mag and checked it, saw that it was full up. Reinserted it. Press-checked it. Two seconds.

"I guess you do."

She smiled. "Get out there, Matty. I've got us covered in here."

Redd nodded. "If someone comes through that door, it probably won't be me. Don't you hesitate."

Emily touched his arm. "You better come through that door, Matty Redd. Just let me know it's you first."

"I will." He smiled to cover his lie.

✖ ✖ ✖

"Go! Go! Go!" Alpha 6 shouted and then began firing into the glowing rectangle, controlled pairs at one- to two-second intervals, providing covering fire so that the rest of his team could advance.

In the brief space between reports, he heard a voice in his earpiece. "Six, this is Five. I've got another vehicle approaching. Looks like a sheriff's rig."

What? These people were supposed to be in hiding, not organizing a parade. Alpha 6 squeezed off another shot before sending his reply. "Five, engage and destroy."

"Acknowledged."

A moment later, a report echoed through the woods, indicating that Alpha 5 had taken care of that latest wrinkle in the plan.

But in that instant, a shadow passed across the backlit cabin door. A hulking shape, almost certainly the primary target, had erupted out of the structure as if shot from a cannon. Despite his size, he moved fast, hunched over to stay below the angle of Alpha 6's fire. Before the latter could adjust his aim, the figure was gone, disappearing behind one of the parked vehicles.

Alpha 6 glimpsed one of his men creeping along the opposite side of the same vehicle. "Alpha 2, hostile on your ten—"

Suddenly Alpha 2 wasn't there anymore. Alpha 6 registered a blur of motion as the assaulter was yanked off his feet and dragged around the front end of the pickup. He shifted his aimpoint to the spot and squeezed off two shots. He wasn't worried about hitting his own man—Alpha 2 was almost certainly dead already.

But then, as if to give the lie to this assumption, a figure in the familiar camouflage dress and tactical gear staggered into view. It was Alpha 2, still on his feet . . .

Except instead of brandishing his carbine, the assaulter had both hands raised to his neck. He took a backward step, then dropped to his knees. The impact jostled his hands just enough to allow an arterial spurt—black in the silver moonlight—to slip through his clutching fingers.

Alpha 6 swore under his breath, then resumed scanning for a target. He spied Alpha 3 and 4 moving toward the cabin from the far-right side, their weapons at the high ready and trained on the cabin door, evidently unaware of the threat lurking behind the truck.

"Alpha team, contact left!"

Even as the words went out over the net, the report of a large rifle split the night, and the round from the unseen discharge split the head of Alpha 4.

Two more shots followed in quick succession, but neither found Alpha 3, who had already gone prone, low crawling for the relative safety of the trees.

A flurry of shots erupted from the left side of the cabin—Alpha 1, trying to engage the hostile. Answering reports accompanied the return fire, and then the muzzle flashes from Alpha 1's position ceased altogether.

"Alpha 1, report in."

No reply.

"One, do you copy?" Still nothing. Alpha 6 muttered a curse, then keyed his mic again. "All Alpha elements, report in."

Silence on the comms.

"Alpha 5, do you copy?"

Alpha 6 swore again. His team was down. He was the last man standing. Somehow, despite tactical superiority, the primary target had wiped them out.

But breaking contact wasn't an option. It was still possible for him to win.

He fired off several more shots into the area where he thought the primary target was hiding and then broke from cover, sprinting across open ground toward the second vehicle. He threw himself down behind it and pulled a frag grenade from a pouch on his plate carrier. His deft fingers stripped away the metal retaining band and plucked out the safety pin. He let the spoon fly and started counting . . .

One . . . two . . . On three, he rose up and hurled the baseball-size explosive device at the illuminated rectangle that was the open doorway into the cabin, thirty yards away. He dropped back down just as quickly but continued the count in his head. Somewhere between five and six, there was a simultaneous flash and boom as the grenade's explosive payload detonated, filling the tiny enclosure with a storm of molten metal. The blast alone would have been enough to kill anyone inside, but the shrapnel guaranteed that they would not merely be dead, but completely shredded.

Now we're even.

Alpha 6 waited another second to see how the remaining hostile—the primary target hunched down behind the other vehicle—would respond, and then he was up and moving again, sprinting for the cabin.

The log structure had weathered the detonation surprisingly well, which only confirmed his belief that it would be an eminently defensible position from which to deal with the primary target. The only sign of what had happened was the cloud of dust and smoke billowing out from the doorway.

The interior was pitch-black, the source of artificial light evidently destroyed by the blast, so he switched on his night vision goggles again and went in, his rifle at the high ready on the off chance that, by some unbelievable fluke, one of the targets inside had survived.

But there was no one, alive or dead, in the cabin.

There was debris everywhere but no bodies. No pieces of bodies. Nothing.

He sensed movement behind him and whirled to face the approaching figure. He was a fraction of a second too slow.

In the monochrome display of his night vision goggles, he beheld a monster of a man, his ghost-green face welded to one of the carbines his team had been armed with.

The barrel spat a tongue of incandescent flame.

The first round caught Alpha 6 in the groin, shattering his mind with searing pain. The shooter allowed the muzzle to rise to do the rest. As Alpha 6 staggered back under the assault, rounds stitched his body from crotch to sternum.

At such close range, his Kevlar plate carrier might as well have been made of tissue paper. The high-velocity rifle rounds perforated armor as easily as they did flesh, driving Alpha 6 backward until he hit the wall opposite the door. He tottered there for a moment after the incoming fire ceased, and then, like a marionette with its strings cut, collapsed to the rough-hewn boards in a bloody heap.

Perversely, his night vision goggles continued to illuminate the interior of the cabin, and while they could not penetrate the darkness that was closing in on him, they did permit him to gaze up into the face of his executioner—a face he had only seen in a still photo in a target file. The big man still had the stock of his captured carbine glued to his shoulder, and as he approached, Alpha 6 found himself staring into the muzzle bore.

What are you waiting for? Do it!

The words never reached his throat.

But then, as the world closed in around him, the dying man glimpsed another figure standing in the doorway, one arm extended, holding a pistol.

It was not one of his men, Alpha 6 knew. The silhouette was decidedly feminine, as was the voice that spoke the last words he would ever hear.

"You're a hard man to kill, Matty Redd."

SIXTY-FOUR

Despite the ringing in his ears, the voice was clear as day. Redd felt adrenaline dump into his bloodstream.

How?

"Any last words?"

Hannah. I forgot about Hannah.

"I wish I would have killed you when I had the chance."

He spun on his heel, bringing the carbine up even though he knew there was no possible way he would be able to get the shot off in time.

He saw her, an indistinct figure in the doorway, limned in moonlight, with Hepworth's service weapon aimed at his own heart.

A shot thundered in the darkness, but it didn't come from the weapon Redd was looking at. Hannah's head snapped backward, her body pitching through the open door.

Redd let out his breath as light filled the cabin behind him. He turned and saw Emily, or at least her head and shoulders, protruding from a rectangular hole in the floor—the opening to the old root cellar. Backlit by the blazing LED lantern, she looked like an angel. She offered a quick smile. "I told you I had it covered."

Redd lowered the rifle, sighing with relief, then reached down and helped her up. Her hands were shaking, and Redd instinctively pulled her to his chest before wrapping his free arm around her. "It's just the adrenaline, Em. It'll pass soon, promise."

She nodded.

"How's Gavin?"

Kline's head popped up out of the root cellar, the aluminum case still clutched in his hands. "Can't hear a lick, but otherwise feeling 100 percent better."

"Well, get a move on," Redd urged. "We can't stay here."

Working together, Emily and Redd helped Kline up from the root cellar, though his condition appeared greatly improved following the aspiration procedure. Emily continued to hold his arm, but Redd guessed this was more because she wanted to keep him from overexerting himself. Kline stopped as they stepped over Hannah's body.

"What a shame," he muttered.

"She was about to kill Matty," Emily said, a little defensively.

"And I don't think she had any intention of testifying against her father," Redd added. "I think she was just stalling, waiting for her daddy to send in the cavalry to rescue her."

"This look like a rescue to you?" Kline countered. He held up the aluminum case. "They were after this. Probably got a tracker inside."

"So they'll come after us no matter where we go."

Kline shrugged. "It may take a while for them to regroup. Hate to say it, but our best option right now may be to go somewhere very public."

"Is the hospital in Bozeman public enough?" Emily asked. "Because that's where you should be."

Kline grunted his assent.

Redd shrugged. "Do you think she was telling the truth?"

Kline nodded. "If she was going to lie, she would have come up with a story that wasn't so crazy. In any event, without her testimony, it's going to be tough to pin this to Anton Gage."

Redd pointed to the case. "We've got that."

"I don't know if it will be enough. We need to get back out to the Gage Food Trust facility. This time with a warrant."

Redd headed over to inspect the vehicles. The Range Rover was riddled with holes from stray rounds, and two of the windows on the driver's side had been shot out, but the tires were all still inflated, and when Redd tried the starter, the engine turned over without complaint. He let it idle and was circling around to help Kline get in when he heard someone call for help.

Redd was instantly on guard, bringing the carbine up and scanning the surrounding area until he saw two figures illuminated in the SUV's headlights. It was Sheriff Blackwood and a dark-haired woman in civilian attire. Blackwood was clutching his left shoulder, and Redd could see blood on his hands. Emily immediately went to assist him.

"Em, wait. Don't—"

She disregarded Redd's exhortation, crossing the distance between them to begin assessing the sheriff's injuries. Though Redd remained wary, he shifted the carbine to port arms and went to join her.

"Looks like it passed clean through," she said and dug into her pack for the appropriate first aid supplies. "We'll get a bandage on it to stop the bleeding."

"What are you doing here?" Redd asked.

"Someone shot up my rig," Blackwood said through clenched teeth. "Then he made the mistake of coming in close to finish us off." He tilted his head in the direction of his companion. "Fortunately, Special Agent Treadway here still had two functional arms."

"That's not what I asked. Why are you out here in the first place?"

"She told me you might be in a spot of trouble. Didn't see anyone at the house, so I thought we'd try up here."

Behind them, Kline called out, "Stevie? Late to the party as always."

The woman managed a wry smile. "You didn't tell me to expect a hot reception."

Something about the woman's voice was familiar to Redd, prompting him to give her a second look. She was very attractive, and Redd was sure that he had seen her somewhere before but could not recall having met a dark-haired, female FBI agent . . . or any FBI agents, aside from Kline. Then he saw how the headlights glinted in her dark-green eyes.

Sammy?

Without even thinking, he brought the gun up, putting the front sight center mass and his finger on the trigger. She reacted just as quickly, reaching for the pistol in her shoulder rig.

Redd's finger tightened, taking out the slack in the trigger. He almost took the shot and would have if the woman had moved her hand one more inch. Instead, she froze and then, with painstaking slowness, began moving her hand away from the weapon.

Even then, it was tempting. But he needed answers, and for that, she needed to keep breathing.

At least a little while longer.

Suddenly Kline was standing in front of him, shielding the woman with his body.

"Matt, stop! She's with me!"

Redd shook his head. "She's your leak. She drugged me. She got my team killed."

Kline spread his arms out in a protective gesture. "No, Matt. You got this all wrong. Put the gun down and let me explain."

Through his black rage, pinpoints of comprehension appeared like fireflies. *"She's with me . . . Let me explain . . ."*

And suddenly it all made sense.

Redd elevated the barrel of the carbine until the muzzle was between Kline's eyes.

SIXTY-FIVE

"You're the leak?" Redd asked.

"What? No!"

Redd was dimly aware of Emily, who had stepped away from the stunned Sheriff Blackwood to stand at his side. "Matty, whatever's going on, we can talk it out." She spoke in a calm, soothing voice, but she had the Glock in her hand, pointed at Kline. Even though she didn't know what was going on, she had his back. "Now what's going on?"

"He knew I was on the team that was going after Willow." Redd knew that he was practically screaming. He didn't care. "He had her grab me, drug me. And then leaked the plan to Willow. My entire team got fragged because of them!"

"Matt, that's not how it happened," Kline said. "Whatever you may think about me, I would never betray my country or another Marine. Now if you'll just put that weapon on 'safe,' I'll explain."

"You have about two seconds before I squeeze this trigger, Gavin. Say what you gotta say, but do it quick."

Kline nodded slowly. "I hear you. You do what you have to do, Matty. But leave Agent Treadway out of this, okay? She was following my orders."

"Isn't that what they said at Nuremberg?" Emily remarked.

Blackwood shook his head, then took a cautious step toward Redd and Emily, keeping his gaze fixed on Kline. "I'm not sure what's going on here, but so far I ain't heard a reason why this boy shouldn't blow your fool head off."

Kline did not look away from Redd. "Stevie, I'm ordering you to stand down. Assume the position and allow the sheriff to disarm you."

Behind him and out of Redd's view, the woman he knew as Sammy hissed, "Are you serious? I'm not giving up my weapon."

"You're going to do as I say," Kline asserted. "And if Matthew here decides he doesn't like what I have to say, you're going to testify that he was acting in self-defense. Now do it." He let his voice rise a little at the end, leaving no doubt regarding his sincerity.

With an angry grunt, Special Agent Treadway dropped to her knees. Blackwood moved in, quickly removed her gun from its holster, tossed it aside, and then slapped his handcuffs on her wrists using only one arm. "I do apologize for this," he murmured. "Especially after you saved my life back there. Something tells me putting these bracelets on you just might give me a chance to return the favor."

Treadway remained silent but offered no resistance as Blackwood raised her to her feet and escorted her away from Redd's line of fire.

"Happy?" Redd snarled. "Now start talking."

Kline nodded slowly. "I did know that your team was assigned to the Willow mission. I advised against it, but my boss, EAD Culp, overruled me. I knew there was a very good possibility that the mission was already compromised, and I . . ." He faltered, choked up, then tried again. "I couldn't bear the thought of losing you, Matt."

"That's bull. If you knew, if you even suspected that the mission was compromised, you could have told someone. You didn't, and those men died. And if you think I'm going to somehow forgive you for that or *thank* you for pulling me out—"

"I couldn't stop the mission! I didn't have enough proof, and I didn't know who to trust. I couldn't let you die down there. I don't expect forgiveness or your thanks. I did what I had to do, and I'd do it again."

"You could have told *me*. You could have trusted me. We could have figured this out together."

Kline winced as if only now realizing that was exactly what he should have done. He lowered his head. "I'm sorry, Matty. Sorry I did this to you. Sorry I wasn't a better father to you."

Redd ground his teeth together, wanting nothing more in the world than to pull the trigger. But that wouldn't bring his teammates back. It wouldn't even make him feel better. He moved his finger off the trigger, thumbed the selector to "safe," and lowered the carbine.

"Get off my ranch. I don't ever want to see you again."

Kline nodded. "I understand you feel that way. But, Matt, this isn't over. Gage is still out there, and we need to stop him."

"Leave before I change my mind, Gavin."

"Matt, who do you think killed your team? Anton Gage and the people working for him. If you want to hold someone responsible, help me bring him down."

"You're the FBI. You don't need me."

"There's still a leak in my division. I don't know who to trust with this, and we're running out of time."

Kline's plea penetrated Redd's fury. The threat was still extant. Anton Gage, the man ultimately responsible for killing both J. B. and the Raiders team, was still at large, and the only way to take him down was to find proof of his scheme.

"Fine." Redd lowered the carbine. "I'll take care of it."

He stepped forward and tore the case from Kline's hands, then turned on his heel and circled around to the driver's side of the Range Rover. It wasn't until he put the SUV in gear that anyone realized what he was doing.

"Matt, don't go there alone. Gage will have people waiting for you. You'll get yourself killed!" Kline shouted. "You can't take on a small army all by yourself. Let me help you."

Emily appeared at the passenger window. She worked the door handle, but Redd had already locked her out. She pounded on the glass. "Matty. Stop it. Let me in!" Tears were rolling down her face.

He lifted his foot off the brake and the Range Rover began to move.

"Matthew Redd, don't you leave me again. Not like this!"

Before she could think about trying to block his exit with her own body, Redd punched the accelerator, leaving her and everyone else behind.

SIXTY-SIX

Although it was nearly midnight, it looked like dawn in the sky to the northeast. When Redd was sure that he was not hallucinating, he pulled the truck over and got out, climbing into the bed for a better look.

Before leaving the ranch, he had stopped to exchange the shot-up Range Rover for J. B.'s F-250, which he thought would appear less conspicuous rolling down the highway in the middle of the night. He also took a moment to empty the gun safe, grab a few tools from the barn, and change into a set of desert pattern cammies. Even though he was planning to go full cowboy on Gage's research facility, he was going to do it the Marine way.

Although standing in the bed of the truck only raised his profile by a few feet, it was enough to confirm his initial observation. And one whiff of the burnt toast odor in the air told him what he was actually seeing.

Fire, Redd thought as he surveyed the burning landscape. *Fields of fire.*

It wasn't unusual for farmers and ranchers to use prescribed burns in the spring, but those were usually done earlier, when the ground was still wet. This was something else. Something big. Redd had a pretty good idea what it was.

Gage was burning the evidence.

Redd could think of only one reason for him to do this. Gage was covering his tracks.

Because his plan to effectively sterilize the world relied upon the combination of two genetically modified organisms, the destruction of one of those—the wheat plants—would prevent the authorities from replicating Gage's experiments in a lab and proving what he had intended. Torching a million-plus acres seemed like overkill, but for an ego the size of Anton Gage's, it was a small price to pay.

With the fields already engulfed in flames, continuing on seemed like an exercise in futility, but Redd was not about to give up. Maybe he would find something incriminating in Gage's lab . . . or maybe even *someone*.

Even if he didn't, he still had something that Anton Gage wanted.

He got back in the truck and kept driving.

As he drew closer to Voight, he saw the damage wrought by the fires. To either side of the highway lay a vast emptiness of scorched black earth, above which glowing embers swirled. Farther out, the flames advanced like a wave curling toward a beach, while above the landscape, streams of fire poured down from agricultural drones that had exchanged fertilizer dispensers for drip torches.

The air was thick with smoke, and even with the truck's vents turned off, the miasma soon permeated the interior of the cab. Redd tied a damp bandanna around his nose and mouth, which helped some, but there was nothing he could do to alleviate the sting in his eyes.

He approached the gates to the Gage Food Trust facility fully intending to batter them down with the truck amid a hailstorm of gunfire, but as he drew near, it became apparent that the security forces had either withdrawn or abandoned their post. Rather than risk unnecessary damage to the truck, he slammed on the brakes, screeching to a halt mere inches from the gates.

The bolt cutter Redd had appropriated from the biker made quick work of the chain holding the gates shut, after which he drove through, following the sign to the security office, where he parked and got out. He swapped the bolt cutter for the Fiskars splitting maul he'd unintentionally brought along from California and took down the reinforced metal door of the security office as easily as he had the wooden door of the shoot house at Camp Pendleton. As soon as the breach was effected, he switched to his shotgun and headed inside but found the office empty.

A quick search yielded nothing of interest, save for a map of the facility, which Redd committed to memory. The campus consisted of only a few buildings, most of which were dedicated to specific agricultural functions like irrigation and fertilization. Redd was interested only in the one marked *Laboratory*.

He exited the security office and returned to the truck just long enough to load up on weapons—in addition to the shotgun and the M4 carbine, which he'd kept from the battle at the hunting cabin, he had the biker's semiauto in his waistband and J. B.'s old lever action Henry .45-70. He was a firm believer in the philosophy that too much was always better than not enough, especially when it came to firepower.

With the long rifle, shotgun, and maul slung across his back, he made his way around the security office, leading with the M4—the weapon he was most comfortable with, owing to eight years as a Marine rifleman. He paused at the corner and surveyed the campus. All the buildings were single-story, tilt-up concrete structures with few windows, designed with functionality in mind, not aesthetics. Each low-profile roof was lined with solar panels, but aside from that, the research facility might have been any industrial park in North America. Redd picked out the lab building, marking its location, then began scanning along the route he would need to take to get there. He saw no sign of human activity but knew better than to assume that the facility was completely abandoned.

He moved in quick bounds toward his destination, ducking behind whatever cover he could find when he could find it and zigzagging randomly when he could not. His excessive caution saved his life.

When he was just fifty yards from the door, a bullet split the air where he would have been if not for a random turn a millisecond beforehand. The report echoed between the buildings, but Redd had already fixed the location of the shooter as well as the type of weapon. The shots had come from the roof of the lab building. The weapon was a .22 or 5.56mm rifle, something in the AR-15 family just like the M4 he was carrying. While still on the move, he aimed the carbine in the general direction of the shooter and returned fire. Redd didn't hold out much hope of hitting his target. All he was trying to do was keep the other man's head down until he could reach the front door. The shooter managed to get off two more shots, neither of which came anywhere close, and then Redd reached the entrance to the lab, where the shooter couldn't get a clean shot at him without leaning out over the edge.

The fact that the laboratory building was defended—when even the front gate was not—was an encouraging sign. It meant there was something there that Gage still wanted to protect or, more likely, something that had not yet been destroyed.

Redd unslung the maul and bashed in the door with a single two-handed blow. He was careful to stand to one side of the door, and once more his caution was rewarded. Shots rang out from inside—not the distinctive crack of high-velocity rifle rounds, but the blunter pop of at least two .45 caliber semiautos. Redd switched to the shotgun, extended it around the blind corner, and fired off both barrels, then immediately tossed the weapon aside and went in, leading with the M4.

Redd instantly identified two targets, both wearing the uniform of Gage's security service. One of them, a man, was hunched over, his torso spotted with blood from where at least a few of the buckshot pellets had scored a hit. The other guard was a woman—the same one who had challenged Redd and Kline during their failed attempt to infiltrate the complex earlier in the day. She had her pistol up and was trying to aim it at Redd, but he was faster, taking her out with a controlled pair, then switching to the wounded man and loosing two more rounds.

Both guards went down, mortally wounded by the center mass shots.

Redd swept the entry lobby quickly, looking for more targets, and seeing none, continued through. As he passed the fallen guards, he fired twice more—a pair of head shots—just to be sure.

There was another door at the back of the lobby, leading deeper inside. Although it was equipped with an electronic security lock, it did not look as sturdy as the outer door. Redd decided not to bother switching weapons again and instead opened it with a well-placed kick.

As the door flew open, the guard standing at the far end of the hall fired off a hasty shot from his .45. The round punched into the moving door, which still partly hid Redd from view. Before he could adjust his aim and fire again, Redd stitched him with a controlled pair and then continued down the hallway, his carbine at the high ready.

When he reached the T-junction where the fallen guard lay, he took a knee and quickly switched out the magazine. By his count, there should have been at least eight more rounds in the mag, and possibly as many as ten, but if he turned the corner and found himself facing half a dozen of Gage's men, he did not want to have to pause in the middle of it all to reload.

He shoved the partial mag into his cargo pocket, slapped in a full one, and pied the corner to the left, staying low. When he was fairly certain that there was no one waiting in that direction, he backed off and repeated the process on the opposite corner. As he did, he glimpsed movement at the far end of the corridor behind him, leading back to the lobby. He immediately rolled forward, risking the blind corner, as a burst of automatic rifle fire sizzled past and slammed into the wall.

Redd took a second to clear the transverse hallway where he now found himself, then pivoted back to the intersecting corridor. He surmised that the shooter from the roof had taken the fast way down, dropping over the side of the building to come in from behind—a good sign if true, because it meant that Gage's security team was spread thin.

He took a couple deep, calming breaths and then commenced pieing the corner, his finger ready on the trigger. A moment later, he glimpsed the muzzle of the other man's weapon as he inched forward. Redd let him come a little closer, then swung around the corner and drilled the shooter between the eyes.

After helping himself to the magazine in the fallen guard's AR-15, Redd resumed clearing the lab building. He met no further resistance but nevertheless treated each closed door as hiding a potential ambush. Instead, he found only room after room emptied of anything that might provide context to the research being done at the facility. As he neared the end of the corridor, however, he heard a loud grinding sound coming from behind the door at the end.

Redd went through the doorway with the same determination as he had the others, and as the door flew off its hinges, he quickly acquired the two targets within—one, a guard with his .45 drawn and already swinging in his direction, and a second guard, hunched over a table in the middle of the room. Redd dropped the armed man with two quick shots, then swung the barrel toward the remaining man, who had jerked away from the table in sudden alarm and was reaching for his holstered sidearm.

Driven by a sudden impulse, Redd shifted his aim a degree or two and fired a single shot that caught the man in the right bicep. The guard staggered back, clutching his useless arm, but as Redd closed in on him, he made a cross-body grab for the .45 on his hip.

"Don't do it," Redd warned, his finger poised on the trigger.

For a moment, it looked as if the man would ignore the good advice, but then he relented and moved his left hand back up to the oozing wound on his right arm. Redd now saw the man's face clearly and recognized him from the earlier encounter at the front gate. This was the guard who had been unimpressed by Kline's display of federal authority.

"You wanted the hard way," Redd reminded him. "Now, let me ask again. What are you people hiding in here?"

"Screw you."

Redd shrugged and took aim at the bridge of the man's nose.

"Wait!"

Redd waited.

"Mr. Gage told me to destroy all the data. That's all I know."

A quick glance at the table showed what looked like the remains of a dozen smashed computers. At the far end of the table, where the guard had been standing a moment before, there was a trash can topped with a heavy-duty paper shredder. Redd had interrupted the man in the process of destroying hard drives from the laboratory computers, and by the look of it, he was almost finished. "Why?"

The guard shook his head. "I'm just security."

"Then I guess you're just wasting my time."

As Redd squared his shoulders, preparing to take the shot, the guard turtled, closing his eyes tight. As frustrated as he was to discover that he'd arrived at the facility too late, the pathetic display brought Redd up short. He had no trouble killing an armed enemy, but this man had already surrendered and posed no further threat. Besides, with most of the evidence already destroyed, the case against Anton Gage might depend upon the testimony of his underlings, even if they only knew a very small part of the plan.

Redd reversed his grip and butt-stroked the guard, laying him out on the lab floor. He then knelt and, after removing the man's weapon, holster and all, used strips of his uniform shirt to bind the arm wound. No sense in letting him bleed out.

He was just about to bind the guard's hands together with a computer power cord when he heard a buzzing sound from the man's pocket. He was getting a phone call.

Redd dug out the device—an iPhone 8—and smiled as he read the name on the caller ID display.

He pressed the guard's thumb against the home button to unlock it, then accepted the call. "Hello, Anton."

SIXTY-SEVEN

There was a long moment of silence on the line, and then Anton Gage spoke. "Matthew. Well, this is unfortunate."

"You don't sound very surprised," Redd remarked.

"I'm not. When my retrieval team failed to call in, I guessed that you had somehow neutralized them. After that, it wasn't hard to figure out where you were going."

"And of course you were tracking the chip with Willow's bioweapon."

"It's not a weapon," Gage said, his tone sharpening. "It's a solution. It's a cure to the cancer that is ravaging our biosphere."

"Hannah told me all about your insane plan. She's dead, by the way."

Gage did not sound particularly surprised by this news either. "Did you kill her?"

"Didn't get the chance," Redd answered honestly.

Gage, evidently misinterpreting his truthful reply, said, "Sacrifices sometimes must be made to accomplish great things."

"You're not going to accomplish anything," Redd challenged. "You've failed. And now you're going down."

"This is a setback, Matthew. Nothing more. You won't be able to prove anything."

"I don't need to prove anything. I'm not going to arrest you, Anton. I'm going to kill you. It doesn't matter where you go. I will find you, and when you least expect it, I'll put a bullet in your brain. No sirens. No flashing lights. I'm just going to end you."

There was a long silence on the line. Finally Gage said, "You won't get the chance" and then ended the call.

Redd stared at the phone for a few seconds, then dropped it next to its owner. Gage's ominous parting shot was clear enough. Another hit team was on the way, and as long as Redd held on to Caldera's case, they would know exactly where to find him.

The solution to that problem was obvious. Get rid of the case.

Except doing so would mean surrendering the last shred of evidence of Gage's collusion with Willow, and despite his promise to the man, Redd did care about preserving proof of Gage's misdeeds. It was not enough to simply kill Gage. The billionaire needed to be utterly destroyed—exposed as the monster he was.

No, he needed to hang on to the case, even if it brought the wolves to his doorstep.

Fine, he thought. *Bring 'em on.*

✖ ✖ ✖

Despite the calm assurance he had projected when speaking to Redd, Anton Gage was barely holding it together. He could not believe how quickly things had fallen apart, how his supreme accomplishment had been undone by the actions of a single man.

And then there was the loss of his children.

His mind flashed to Hannah and then to Wyatt. It took everything he had to steel his emotions. Once more he reminded himself that there would be a time to grieve, but right now he had to see his mission through. Otherwise, his children, Hannah especially, would have died in vain. And Gage wouldn't let that happen.

In truth, he did not think he would survive this either. The Twelve were exceedingly intolerant of failure. At a minimum, he would lose his seat at the table, and that was if—only if—he managed to completely erase anything that might connect him to Willow or the plan to effectively sterilize a significant portion of the world's population. Even then, they would probably not accept his mea culpa. He knew too many of their secrets to simply go into exile.

No, it was no longer a matter of survival. All he had left was revenge.

He checked the screen showing the location of the tracker in Caldera's sealed container. It had not moved from its last location—the laboratory at the GFTRC. The concrete walls and solar panels effectively blocked the signal from communicating with the satellite, so until Redd carried it outside once more, it would not refresh. He did not think Redd would leave the case behind, and that could only mean that he had chosen to remain in the lab, perhaps searching for some piece of damning evidence that had escaped the purge.

That was fine with Gage. His men would have the home field advantage.

While he could not simply wave his hand and conjure up another hit squad, he was not without resources. Dancing Elk Ranch employed a small army of security guards, all of them former military with combat experience and all of them intensely loyal to the family. He called his chief of security and told them what he needed.

The chief's response, while affirmative, was not quite as robust as Gage had hoped for, so he added, "You should know Matthew Redd murdered my daughter."

There was an audible gasp. "Hannah's dead?"

"Murdered. And I suspect Redd may also have killed Wyatt, staging it to look like an overdose. He hates my family because he thought we were going to take his land."

"He won't live to see the sunrise," the security chief promised.

"I shall be eternally grateful to you," Gage said. "Before you head out, however, there's one more detail I need to take care of. I'll call you in a few minutes with further instructions."

He ended the call and then dialed another number.

SIXTY-EIGHT

They came in a convoy of Jeeps and trucks. The men had not exchanged their ranch attire for more utilitarian tactical apparel, which gave them the look of a posse of gunslingers rolling into town to challenge the lone marshal at high noon.

In fact, this was not far from the truth. The only differences were that Redd was no marshal, and it was not yet dawn.

There were a dozen of them in all, and one other who was not part of their clique but had, at Mr. Gage's direction, assumed command of the enterprise. That one did not look like a gunslinger and remained behind the wheel of a blacked-out SUV when the others deployed.

The men disgorged from their vehicles and immediately took cover behind them, expecting Redd to make the first move. After a few uneventful minutes had passed, they began advancing in leaps and bounds, cover and move, cover and move. When they reached the front entrance, they split into two elements, with one group holding fast at the main entrance and the other skirting around to cover the rear. Once the second team radioed that they were in position, the first team went in. There was no need for a dynamic entry. The door was already off its hinges.

Just as the last man was heading inside, the first shot rang out.

✖ ✖ ✖

The bullet crossed two hundred yards of empty space faster than the sound of the shot, giving Redd time to work the lever, acquire a second target, and fire before most of the men lined up against the wall at the rear of the laboratory building knew they were under attack. The man who had formerly been lined up in the Henry's sights died without ever realizing it. Redd's second shot took out the man standing next to the first, despite his best attempt to drop and cover.

The earth was hot beneath Redd, the memory of fire lingering in the baked soil hours after this section of the field had been cleared. Everything he'd ever been taught about sniper tactics told him it was a bad idea, but Redd risked taking a third shot. He missed, but the near miss at least gave the surviving men something to think about as Redd sprang to his feet and began running across the scorched emptiness. Hot cinders fell from his clothes as he sprinted away.

Another three hundred yards out, the flames continued to devour Anton Gage's genetically modified wheat plants. Though it was difficult to see from ground level, the fires were being started in systematic fashion by computer-controlled drones traveling back and forth to create a grid pattern of multiple backfires, such that if an unexpected gust of wind fanned the flames, causing them to burn faster and hotter, it would not be long before they encountered a fire line—a section that had already been burned to deprive the moving fire of fuel. From what Redd had seen on the drive in, the same thing was happening all over Gage's land.

Redd had chosen the fields, rather than the hardened structures of Gage's compound, to make his stand. While the buildings provided better cover, they would also have allowed Gage's cowboys to keep him bottled up until reinforcements arrived. No, if he was to survive, he would need the freedom that open ground afforded.

The map of the facility had revealed a series of access roads radiating out from the campus and into the vast fields, and it was to the nearest of these that Redd now sprinted. The road was a gravel path barely wide enough to accommodate a lone vehicle, and as Redd pivoted onto it, he glanced back and saw three vehicles charging toward him.

"Knew that was too good to last," he muttered, kicking into high gear as he hauled off toward the flames.

Distant reports chased after him, but he neither looked back nor made evasive maneuvers. He was well beyond the effective range of their pistols, and while it wasn't inconceivable that a .45 ACP or 9mm round might still find him, it would require extraordinarily good luck for the shooter and extraordinarily bad luck for him. In any case, zigging and zagging would not improve his odds of survival nearly as much as moving quickly in a straight line.

The fields were burning unevenly, with the fire on the right side of the access road closer than on the left, though not by much. As he approached the advancing line of flames, the ambient temperature quickly went from merely uncomfortable to almost intolerable. He'd been close to explosions many times in his career as a Marine, had experienced the blast of heat that pushed out from the center of the detonation riding the overpressure wave, but that was always a fleeting experience, gone almost as soon as it was felt. This was a sustained inferno, and it only got hotter as his proximity increased.

And then he was through, emerging into the smoke-filled crimson hellscape.

Redd turned to the right, running at an angle into the waist-high vegetation in the as-yet unburned field, but after a few steps, he skidded to a stop, turned, and threw himself flat, facing the road. Even though the flames had not reached these plants, the stalks were already wilting as the heat sucked the moisture and the life right out of them. They cracked and broke apart beneath him like dry autumn leaves. The heat remained oppressive. The run had not been particularly taxing, but Redd's heart felt as if it was going to burst in his chest. Nevertheless, he drew in a deep breath of superheated air and held it as he lined up the Henry's sights on the lead vehicle charging down the access road, less than a hundred yards away on the other side of the flames. He had only a second to judge its velocity and adjust to lead the target; then he let his breath out and squeezed the trigger. The Henry barked in his grip.

He didn't linger to assess the results. Whether or not he'd killed the driver, the other vehicles would quickly adjust to the new circumstances and continue the pursuit. He regretted a little having taken the third shot earlier, but there was nothing he could do about that now. The Henry's magazine tube held only four rounds, and while he had a pocket full of cartridges for the weapon, his instincts told him that, one way or another, the battle would be over before he found a spare thirty seconds to reload. He left the Henry on the ground, sprang to his feet, and headed deeper into the parched field.

Fifty yards farther out, the air temperature was a little more tolerable, and Redd flopped down again, rolling sideways twice before coming back up with the M4 in ready position. At almost the same instant, the first vehicle appeared as if from out of the flames.

It was a Jeep Wrangler, emblazoned with the logo of Dancing Elk Ranch, and there was another right behind it, followed by a bright-red Ram Warlock 4x4. The tops of the two Jeeps had been removed, and a pair of cowboys stood in the rear of each, with one hand gripping the roll bar and the other holding a pistol. There were also two men in the bed of the Ram, though they were hunkered down to avoid presenting an easy target. Once past the wall of flame, the pickup slowed to a crawl, while the Jeeps rolled past the spot where Redd lay. It was evident that they had only a general idea of his location. That was about to change.

Redd took aim at the men in the back of the middle vehicle, switched the selector to burst, and let lead fly. All of the men standing in the Jeeps went down, but the two he had targeted did not get back up.

He fired another burst, then rolled right, bounded to his feet again and ran, this time heading back in the direction of the flames.

I'm up, he sees me, I'm down.

Before he finished the timing chant, the air behind him roared with multiple pistol reports. None of the rounds found his flesh, but the hot air around him crackled with the disturbance of their passage. He went down, rolled in the scorched grass, and came back up in a kneeling stance, ready to fire.

Seventy-five yards away, the three vehicles were turning in unison, pulling off the road and heading across the field like a picket line. Redd quickly aimed . . . fired . . . shifted . . . fired, shifted . . . fired.

Three bursts, each one perforating the grille of a pursuing vehicle. Mini geysers sprayed out as the shattered radiators disgorged superheated, pressurized steam. Redd couldn't tell if the shots had incapacitated the vehicles because he was already up and moving, but the eruptions served to partially screen him from view. More shots were fired, but none even came close.

He dropped, rolled, and came up scanning for a target, but this time his choices were not so clear-cut. The three vehicles had all stopped, and he did not immediately see any of the gunmen. He swept the muzzle of the M4 back and forth, waiting for one of Gage's men to break cover and fire at him. They obliged him, but every time one of them leaned out to pop off a shot, they would retreat before he could get a bead on them. He withheld fire at first, considering his options but then realized that he could not survive a prolonged standoff out in the field any better than he could have withstood a siege in the laboratory. The enemy had time and numbers on their side, and the only hope he had of surviving, of winning, was to execute bold and decisive action.

Enough running, he thought, coiling his body like a spring in preparation to launch.

Before he could, however, a loud whining sound from behind him caught his attention. He risked a quick glance back.

For a moment, he couldn't quite make sense of what he was seeing, and in the time it took for him to process, the noise increased and the hovering ribbon of fire got closer. Overcoming his momentary paralysis, Redd threw himself to the right, rolling over and over as the aerial drone sailed past, trailing a line of burning diesel-gasoline mixture that set the wheat plants blazing in its wake.

Pushed by the hot wind created by the neighboring blaze, the flames spread quickly and seemed to seek Redd out as if driven by some malign supernatural intelligence. Momentarily forgetting the half-dozen-plus gunmen, he got up and sprinted away from the advancing conflagration.

Fortunately for Redd, the enemy was similarly occupied by the arrival of the drone. Its preprogrammed flight took it directly over the Ram, and as it passed, it left a stripe of burning fuel right down the middle of the vehicle. The four men who had hidden behind the truck broke cover and fled. Three of them darted across the open ground toward the stalled Jeeps where more of their comrades waited. The fourth, caught on the wrong side of the drone's drip torch, disappeared behind a wall of flame.

Redd had only gone about twenty yards when the men hiding behind the Jeeps started taking shots at him. When he heard the reports, he quickly went to a prone position, then rolled over and came up shooting. He could see muzzle flashes but the men were staying mostly behind cover at the corners of the vehicles. The three men fleeing the destruction of the pickup, however, were in the open, so Redd adjusted his aim and fired off the rest of the magazine in a series of bursts. One of the men went down and didn't get up again.

Redd switched out the magazine, rolled right, and then bounded up for a three-second rush toward the Jeep that was furthest out. At almost the same instant that he dropped prone amid the wheat stalks, the men behind that vehicle began shooting. The incoming rounds snapped through the now-brittle stalks and threw up clods of earth that showered down on Redd's position. Although they could not see him amid the broken wheat, they clearly had a pretty good idea where he was. After a few seconds, however, the shooting stopped.

Ignoring the threat, Redd low crawled forward, moving slowly to avoid disturbing the stalks and further drawing attention to his position. When he'd gone about ten yards, he cautiously shifted into a crouch and raised his head up until he could just see through the crisscrossing stalks.

The Jeep was only about twenty yards away, a dark shape against the red-orange glow that suffused the smoke-thick air. There was no sign of movement, but Redd knew the men were there, waiting for him to reveal himself. He dropped down again and continued low crawling forward, dragging his body along the ground inch by inch.

After moving another five yards, he heard a rustling sound and froze in place. At least one of the men had ventured out into the field to look for him, and as he lay there, he could hear the men exchanging shouts, coordinating their efforts to close in on his location. He risked another look, rising up slowly as if doing a cobra stretch, and glimpsed an upright figure moving alongside him less than eighteen inches away.

Redd went flat again and then laid the M4 aside, switching to a pistol. From here on out, the battle would be strictly up close and personal.

Just the way I like it.

He rolled onto his back, aiming the pistol at the nearly invisible figure moving past, but held his fire. The gunman hadn't seen him, and he wasn't going to give himself away with a shot unless he had no other alternative.

An urgent shout came from the direction of the Jeep, and then Redd's stalker abruptly wheeled around and ran back the way he'd come.

As much as Redd welcomed the unexpected reprieve, it was an ominous development. He rolled back onto his belly, pushed up again, and immediately saw what had prompted the man's retreat.

The drone that had passed through a few minutes earlier was coming around for a return pass, laying down a stream of liquid fire some fifty yards beyond where Redd now lay. To his left, the fire it had started earlier was steadily advancing. Once the drone completed its pass, Redd would be caught between opposing fires. The surviving gunmen had already figured this out and were running full tilt to reach the other side of the fire line before it was too late.

Redd was tempted to follow their example but knew he'd never make it in time, and even if he did, Gage's kill team would be waiting for him. Instead, he shoved the pistol back into his waistband, snatched up the M4 again, took aim at the approaching drone, and started firing on burst.

Bright-yellow flames roared from the carbine's muzzle, but the rounds seemed to have no effect. Redd tracked the drone's advance, swiveling his body as he tried to lead it, squeezing the trigger repeatedly, maintaining constant fire.

His efforts did not go unnoticed by Gage's men. A couple of them wheeled around and began firing at him. Redd ignored the incoming rounds and maintained his focus on the drone. Just as it was about to pass by, one of his shots pierced the fuel reservoir for the drip torch. The drone erupted in a flash and fell to the ground in a shower of flaming debris, which ignited a scattering of small fires between Redd and Gage's men. The latter kept firing at him through the flames, so Redd adjusted his aim and did the same.

One of the men spun like a top as a burst from Redd's M4 ripped through him. Redd shifted to another target, but when he squeezed the trigger, the carbine spat a single round and then went silent. Redd threw the useless weapon down and whipped the pistol from his waistband as he charged headlong toward the flames.

Unlike the backfires set by the drip torch, the little hot spots caused by the drone's destruction were scattered like islands of flame in the sea of wheat. Though they would eventually spread out and join, there was presently a path through for anyone bold or foolish enough to take it. Redd fit at least one of those descriptions.

The inferno felt hot enough to singe his hair and beard, and he was a little worried that the loose rounds in his pocket might cook off, but he kept moving, weaving and dancing around the fire islands. A line from the old Rodney Atkins song, which itself might've been borrowed from Churchill, played in his head like a soundtrack of insanity.

"If you're going through hell, keep on going."

Gage's men either did not see what he was doing or simply refused to believe it. They had backed away from the fires and begun moving around them, perhaps expecting Redd to come around from the other direction, which gave him a chance to take up a solid fighting stance as he emerged, gripping his pistol with both hands as he took aim at the nearest enemy.

Two shots from the M1911 took the man down. Redd saw Gage's men pivoting toward him and lunged forward into a somersault as they began firing. He came up in a crouch and fired again, winging one of the four remaining men, and then felt the bolt on his weapon lock back. Empty.

He pitched forward into another combat roll, even as two more shots were fired, and then, fully expecting to get mowed down at any second, launched himself at the man he had just wounded.

By some miracle, Gage's men did not shoot him, and Redd was able to reach his intended target. He tackled the gunman, pounding him senseless with a single blow, and then reached for the Glock the man had just dropped.

So much for miracles, he thought as he realized that the pistol's slide was locked back. Empty.

He was a sitting duck now, and yet the three remaining gunmen still held back from taking the shot. It took him a few seconds to realize that their weapons were also empty.

Redd almost laughed aloud.

The men stared at Redd for a moment, then looked at each other, exchanged nods, and started moving toward him, fists balled and ready for some old-fashioned brawling.

Three of them and only one of him. Evidently they liked those odds.

So did Redd.

SIXTY-NINE

The fight was over almost before it began. Two of Gage's cowboys tried to flank him, while the third drew a bowie knife from a belt sheath and came straight on. Redd let them all get within a couple steps before making his move. He feinted toward the knife wielder, then backstepped into the man on his left, seized him by one outstretched arm, and whipped him around with such force that the grasped arm was dislocated from the shoulder joint. The man's howl of agony was cut short as Redd slammed him into the man with the knife. Their skulls came together with a crack almost as loud as a gunshot. As both men went down in a heap, Redd charged the remaining man, who, evidently stunned by what had just happened, failed to so much as raise his fists in his own defense.

Redd left them all where they had fallen and headed back to the road at a jog.

He had to brave the flames twice on his trek back to the research facility. As he emerged into the zone of scorched earth, he could see dawn lightening the sky to the east. The long night was nearly at an end, but his fight with Anton Gage was only beginning.

He bypassed the laboratory and was just about to head over to the lot where he'd left J. B.'s old truck when a voice called out from behind.

"Stop right there, Mr. Redd!"

Redd's heart stuttered, but he complied, slowly raising his arms. The voice was husky but definitely belonged to a female. After a moment, he started to turn to look at her, prompting the woman to sound another warning. "Stop. I mean it. I'll shoot."

He froze in place but had already turned far enough to see the woman who stood about twenty yards away, near the front entrance to the laboratory.

"I'd say the fact that I'm not dead already means you want something from me," Redd said. "Let me guess. You're after Willow's bioweapon."

"Where is it?"

Redd allowed himself a small smile of satisfaction. If she didn't already have it, then it meant his countermeasures to block the GPS tracker had worked. "Somewhere safe. I wrapped it in a foil space blanket and hid it somewhere you'll never find it."

He made another quarter turn to face her. Tall and lean, with a blonde bob looking almost white in the strange twilight, she didn't look like one of Gage's security team. She wore a smart black business suit. He could also see the Glock 19 in her right hand, pointed at him. She did not repeat her order to stop but gave the gun a meaningful shake.

"I texted the location to Special Agent Gavin Kline," Redd went on. "He's an FBI agent. So even if you kill me, Gage is still going down."

Her full lips curled into a decidedly unattractive sneer. "Kline." She spat the name like a curse. "What is your connection to him anyway?"

"Long story. What's yours?"

She cocked her head to the side as if trying to decide how much to reveal. "Well, not that it matters much. I'm his boss. So you see, no matter what kind of side deal you've made with him, it won't matter."

Redd nodded slowly in understanding and felt the embers of rage growing hot in his gut. "You must be EAD Culp. Kline told me he thought there was a leak in his office."

Her sneer almost became a smile. "Oh, but you see, Gavin *is* the leak. Or at least, that's what the evidence will show. And he won't be in much of a position to defend himself."

Redd felt his heart rate quicken, exactly as it had when he'd braved the fields of fire, but this time, the heat that caused his blood pressure to soar came from within. "You told Willow that Gavin was closing in on him." Despite his rising fury, Redd's tone was cold as a steel razor. "You warned him that the Marine Raiders were on their way."

He took a step toward her. Her eyes flashed with comprehension and something else.

Fear.

"My father raised me to never strike a woman," he said in that same steely tone. "But you're something else."

She stiffened and brandished the Glock again. "Don't," she warned, but her hand was trembling. She took two quick steps back, maintaining standoff distance. "I mean it. I don't need you alive. I'll kill you and then I'll kill Kline, and it won't matter if that case is never found."

Redd barely heard her through the rush of blood in his ears. She might have been speaking a foreign language for all he cared to listen. He was only vaguely aware of the pistol she was pointing at him, of the damage it might do to him. The only part of his brain that remained coldly rational was occupied with calculating how many steps it would take to reach her and how much force it would take to break her neck.

If he moved fast enough, she would be dead before she could even pull the trigger.

Just as he was about to make his move, however, he saw her eyes dart to the side, looking past him to . . . what?

It didn't matter. She had let her guard down, and he was not going to let the chance slip by.

He pivoted away from the muzzle of the Glock, and before she could shift it back to him, he was on her. He seized the wrist of her gun hand, forcing it skyward, and then stepped around behind her, wrapping his left arm around her neck.

And that was when he saw what had distracted her.

A black SUV was rolling into the parking lot, moving fast on what seemed like a collision course with the two of them.

Prioritizing this new threat, Redd deftly slid his right hand up and stripped the Glock out of Culp's grip, and then, still holding her as a human shield, took aim at the windshield, right where the driver's head would be.

The SUV skidded to a stop twenty yards out, and the doors flew open. A pair of empty hands reached out, and then he heard a familiar voice cry out, "Matty! Don't! It's me."

Redd almost dropped the Glock in his haste to move it away. "Em? What are you doing here?"

Emily slid out from behind the wheel. Kline got out on the opposite side, while Sheriff Blackwood and Special Agent Treadway emerged from the rear. Emily crossed the remaining distance without a trace of fear, and Kline followed, albeit a little more hesitantly.

"Matty," Emily said, speaking in a low, soothing voice. "It's over. Let Gavin take it from here."

Redd blinked at her. "She killed my team, Em."

Emily nodded. "I know she did. And she did it on Anton Gage's orders. She can help bring him down."

"Listen to her, Matt," Kline intoned. "Culp isn't going to take the fall for Gage. She'll roll on him to save her own skin."

"You don't have anything on me," Culp croaked, her voice muffled by Redd's arm.

"We've got plenty, Rachel. But you know what? I'm fine with letting Matt take your head off. Either way, you're a traitor and the world is going to know it."

"You wouldn't."

Kline shrugged, then deliberately turned his back. Redd's biceps flexed almost involuntarily, choking off any further protest. Culp began pounding furiously against his arm.

"Matty!" Emily pleaded. "Don't. This isn't you."

Redd tightened his grip. "You don't even know me anymore, Em."

Her eyes narrowed. "I might be the only person still alive who really *does* know you. Now stop it."

The declaration broke through his rage. He let go of Culp, who collapsed on the ground, gasping and choking. Kline moved quickly to subdue her, though the fight had already gone out of the woman.

Without another word, Redd turned on his heel and began walking toward J. B.'s truck. He didn't know where he would go but knew that he had to keep moving.

"Matty, wait." Emily caught up to him and put a hand on his arm.

It took every ounce of self-control he possessed not to tear free of her grasp.

"It's over. Let's just go home."

"Home?" The word felt strange in his mouth—like some new obscenity he did not fully understand. "What's that?"

She gazed up into his eyes. "Jim Bob's ranch. *Your* ranch. You can rest now, Matty. You won."

Redd didn't feel like he won anything. But for the first time in days, he wasn't thinking about everything that he lost, either. Maybe it was that he'd finally gotten justice for J. B. or that Gage's psychotic plan had been stopped. Either way, he was ready to take off—and this time he had no intention of leaving Emily behind.

Taking her hand, he chinned toward J. B.'s truck and said, "Let's get out of here."

"Matt, wait." This time the call came from Kline. He had stepped away from Culp, who now was restrained with Treadway's handcuffs, and was hurrying to catch up to Redd and Emily. "Matt, you have no idea how big a deal this is. This is a major win, and it's all because of you."

Redd glared back at him. "This doesn't change anything between us, Gavin. I don't ever want to see you again."

"I get that—I really do. But Gage is still out there. And the rest of the Twelve. We need to find him."

Redd shook his head. "Not my problem anymore. I've got a ranch to save."

He felt Emily's hand slide into his. She gave him a reassuring squeeze. "*We* have a ranch to save."

Epilogue

A heavy night snow fell on the house, lit up like a flickering beacon by the roaring fireplace inside.

Emily lay on the couch with her head on Redd's lap, mesmerized by the dancing flames as music played softly in the background. They were both stuffed after a dinner of steak, fried potatoes, and rocky road ice cream, the three things Emily had discovered she most craved. They'd also just finished another episode of *The Big Bang Theory*, Emily's favorite television show.

Redd was new to "bingeing" and streaming in general, but the comedy had grown on him. He didn't know every line the way she did, but he chuckled here and there. Mostly he enjoyed seeing her happy. She had an amazing smile, but her laugh was even better.

It had been a hard six months getting the ranch into shape and starting to pay off J. B.'s debts little by little, but they could not have been happier.

Emily continued working at the health center while Redd ran the ranch, leasing out his property and tending the cattle of other ranchers. Barring any major disasters, come springtime, they'd have enough to pick up some stock of their own.

The two of them talked more than most young newlyweds and made love more often than they thought possible given their mutual fatigue after the long work hours. It was as if they were both desperately trying to make up for the years they'd lost to their mutual stubbornness and pride. Emily's pregnancy hadn't slowed them down much at all.

Reverend Lawrence had agreed to give Redd his daughter's hand. Though initially concerned that Redd might disappear and once again leave Emily with a broken heart, he was thrilled to hear that Matthew intended to stay, fix up the ranch, settle J. B.'s debts, and marry his daughter. The two had even recently began attending Sunday services together. Finally Redd was becoming the man his little girl deserved, and at the wedding, Lawrence declared that his daughter had finally made an honest man of Redd. When Redd and Emily told her parents that they would soon be grandparents, the old man had jumped out of his chair, laughing hysterically as he danced an old Irish jig for joy. Any outsider watching would have thought he was drunk.

With autumn deepening into winter, they spent a lot more time in front of a crackling fire, reveling in the heat that kept the frozen silence outside at bay.

Running his hand through her soft hair, Redd looked down at his wife and smiled.

"What are you thinking right now?" she asked.

Redd noticed that she asked that question a lot and figured it had something to do with his poor communication skills. She was a talker, he wasn't. But he was working on it.

"Nothing really."

"C'mon, Matty. Tell me. You've got a funny look on your face."

"Well," he said, looking for the right words. "You were right. This is home now."

Emily smiled back at him. "See, Montana isn't so bad after all."

She had a point, but that wasn't what Redd had meant. "I guess, but I was thinking more about, you know, this." He waved his free hand around in a circular motion.

Emily's face scrunched up and Redd knew she was confused, frustrated that she still couldn't always understand him. He didn't hold it against her, though. He didn't even always know what he was trying to say. It frustrated him too.

"You mean the ranch?"

"The ranch is great," he said with a nod. "Lot of work, but I see why J. B. always loved this land so much."

Emily tilted her head to the side, still trying to read him.

Redd sighed. Then he finally found the words.

"You're my home, Em. *You.* Not this place, not the ranch. Just being with you. That's where I belong."

Emily's cheeks flushed, and she reached up and wrapped her arms around his neck, pulling him into her as Thomas Rhett's voice echoed through the small speaker behind them.

And I know that I can't ever tell you enough
That all I need in this life is your crazy love . . .
Oh, if all I got is your hand in my hand
Baby, I could die a happy man

✖   ✖   ✖

They were nearly asleep when the sound of a motor and crunching tires startled them out of their stupor.

Redd leaped to his feet and fetched the Winchester off the mantel as Emily sat up.

"Who do you think it is?"

"No clue."

Redd didn't bother pulling on his barn coat as the engine outside shut off. He yanked the front door open.

A man stood in the dark, the orange glow of firelight through the windows playing shadows on his face.

"What are you doing here?" Redd asked.

"I have something I want to talk to you about," Gavin Kline said, jets of vapor pouring out of his mouth with every word. Thick flakes of snow began accumulating in his hair and on his shoulders. He held up his hands, palms toward Redd, in mock surrender.

"I've got nothing to say to you except *leave*."

Emily came up beside Redd and wrapped her arms around him. She squinted. "Gavin? Is that you?"

"Hi, Emily. Sorry I missed the wedding."

"It's not your fault," she said. Despite Kline's unforgivable act of betrayal, Emily had lobbied to extend an invitation to him, but Redd had vetoed the idea in the strongest possible terms.

"Thanks for sending me the pictures," Kline went on. "You were beautiful."

"Thank you."

"And congratulations on the baby. Even from here, you look radiant."

"Well, thanks for stopping by," Redd said. "There's a storm coming." He gestured toward Kline's 4x4. "Get back in your truck, drive to the airport, and get out of here while you still can."

"Matt, just give me a minute. It's important."

Emily tugged on Redd's arm. She whispered in his ear, loud enough for Kline to hear, "Come on, Matty. At least hear him out."

Redd sighed, then folded his thick arms over his chest. "What?"

"I have something for you. I know it won't make up for anything, but—"

"Whatever it is, I don't want it."

"You'll want this." Kline dipped a hand beneath his coat and brought out a manila envelope. He opened it and teased out a printed form that Redd had no difficulty recognizing, even with the low light and the distance separating them.

It was form DD214, the standard Department of Defense document that recorded every single change in the career of an individual service member. Kline pulled another piece of paper from the envelope and laid it over the first. Though this one was less familiar to Redd, he could make out the seal of the Marine Corps on the creamy parchment and the elegant calligraphy across the top reading *Honorable Discharge.*

Redd was speechless.

Kline came forward and held out the documents. When Redd did not move to take them, Emily did. "Gavin, this is amazing. Thank you."

"No thanks are necessary." Kline held Redd's gaze. "I can't ever make up for what I did, but at least this gives you back something that was stolen from you. All mention of your OTH and the circumstances leading up to it have been expunged from your record. You're righteous again."

Redd nodded slowly. He still saw his teammates' faces in his dreams, haunting him when he tried to sleep. He had not forgotten the promise he'd made to Anton Gage.

"It doesn't matter where you go. I will find you."

And yet that promise seemed a little less important with each passing day. Saving the ranch and making up for lost time with Emily had not exactly healed his emotional wounds, but it had covered them over with scar tissue.

Now, in giving him back at least a measure of the dignity he'd lost, Kline had just ripped those wounds open again.

Righteous again, he thought. *But it doesn't bring the team back. Nothing can do that.*

"There is one other thing," Kline went on. "A lot has happened since you stopped Gage from releasing Willow's bioweapon. I've been appointed to head the Intelligence Directorate . . . Culp's old job. And our number one mission is exposing and taking down this so-called Twelve that Hannah talked about, starting with Anton Gage."

"You know where he is?" Emily asked.

Kline shook his head. "Not yet, but he can't hide forever. His assets have been frozen and there are only a handful of places where he can hide. As soon as he comes up for air, no matter where in the world he is, we'll be ready. I'm forming a fly team, answerable only to the FBI director and the president, and finding Gage is our first priority."

Redd blinked, then raised his eyes to meet Kline's imploring stare. "Congratulations on the promotion, Gavin. You deserve it after all the time you've put in and the sacrifices you've made." He rolled his shoulders. "You should probably get a move on." He turned to head back into the house.

"I can pick anyone I want for my team, Matt, and I want you."

Redd stopped but did not turn. He shook his head. "I've got a ranch to run."

"Did you not hear me? We're going after Anton Gage. The man who is actually responsible for killing Jim Bob and your team. Don't you want to be a part of that?"

Now Redd did turn, stepped off the porch, and stalked over until he was nose-to-nose with the other man. "You pulled me off that Mexico mission without asking me. Worse, you let my teammates die. I can't forgive you for that, let alone trust you."

"I'm sorry for what happened, but I'll never apologize for protecting you. It's what a father is supposed to do, no matter what. That might even be the first real fatherly thing I've ever done. You wait until that kid of yours is born, you'll see."

"You killed those men, Gavin. Twist it however you want, but you've got their blood on your hands."

Kline shook his head. "I didn't kill them. Anton Gage did that, and I'm going to make him pay. Him and everyone else that was part of this. The only question is, do you want a piece of that action? Are you in, or are you out?"

Redd turned back to Emily, who was shivering in the cold and snow. Then he shook his head. "I told you. I've got things to do. A ranch to run. A family to take care of. That's what's important to me."

"We're still getting up and running," Kline went on. "Once the unit is up to speed, you'd be on call and only on standby until we're needed. You'll have plenty of time to work the ranch and raise your kid. I promise."

"I'm not like you, Gavin," Redd growled, stabbing a finger in Kline's chest. "I'm not going to abandon my wife and child to chase bad guys. I've lived it, and I'd never put my own kid through that. That's what set you and J. B. apart. He understood that. There are always going to be bad guys, but you only get one chance at family."

Emily stepped off the porch and took Redd by the elbow. "Matty, hold on. Just think about—"

"I won't do that to either of you," Redd said, cutting her off. His eyes dropped to her growing belly.

Emily squeezed his arm. "When I was up at the cabin with Gavin, surrounded by danger, I was scared. The only thing that made me feel like it might be okay was knowing that you were out there. That you were coming back. That you were going to save us."

She reached up and touched the side of his face. "There's a lot of people out there who need you, Matty Redd, and they don't even know it yet. You're a good man, you do what's right—" she rubbed her free hand over her swollen belly—"and we'll be right here waiting for you when you get back."

Redd held her gaze for a long time. Finally he let a smile touch the corners of his mouth. "I love you, Em."

Her smile could have melted winter itself. "I love you too."

Redd turned back to Kline, his face once again hardening. "I will never forgive you. Not for any of it. And I will never be like you."

Kline let his shoulders sag in defeat. "You know, you like to point out what a terrible father I was to you. But at least I did one thing right when I gave you over to Jim Bob." He turned and headed for his SUV. "I won't keep begging, Matt. Last chance. Are you in, or are you out?"

Redd folded his arms across his chest, then looked to Emily one more time. She nodded, signaling her approval.

"If you find Anton Gage, give me a call and I'll go play Whac-A-Mole the second he pops his head up. Until then, I'll be right here."

"Deal," Kline said as he opened the door and climbed inside his SUV. "I'll be in touch."

"See you around, Gavin."

Acknowledgments

First and foremost, I would like to thank my Lord and Savior, Jesus Christ. Without Him, none of this would have been possible.

Writing a book is *not* a one-man show, and there have been more people than I could ever thank who've contributed in various ways, all helping me along this incredible journey. For starters, **Joshua Hood, Mike Maden**, and **Sean Ellis**. Each of you played critical roles in helping me shape *Fields of Fire* into the book that it is today. Gentlemen, thank you for all you've done for me and Matty Redd. More importantly, thank you each for your friendship.

To that end, I would wholeheartedly like to thank the late, great **Vince Flynn**. While I've enjoyed many authors and their works over the years, it is because of Vince—and his character Mitch Rapp—that I fell in love with the genre to begin with. Though I never got to meet him, Vince's life has greatly impacted my own, in ways I never could have imagined when I fell headfirst into his fictional universe all those years ago.

To my parents, **James and Rhonda Steck**, I love you both more than words. Thank you, from the bottom of my heart, for everything. For all the sacrifices. The sage advice. And for always believing in me. To

Joslyn, my sister, thank you too for all your support both growing up and in my adult life. To my **grandparents**, thank you for your contributions to my life.

Unfortunately for my parents, I required more help growing up than most. They say it takes a village to raise a child, but for me, it was more like a small country. **Steve and Janeen Docsa**, you're the closest thing I have to another set of parents. You've done more for me than I could ever thank or repay you for, and I am eternally grateful to have you in my life. Same goes for **Pete and Vickie Asaro**, **Chuck and Sandy Green**, **Rick and Jannie Smith**, and **Christine Jarzeboski**. To all of you, from the bottom of my heart, thank you.

To my July buddies, **Scott Docsa** (and his lovely wife, **Kelci**) and **Lindsay Scheffers** (plus her husband, **Nate**), I love you both like siblings. Thank you both for so many wonderful memories.

To **Mikey and Emily Derhammer**. You guys have become family, and I will always be thankful that you love our children the way you do. Thank you for the many laughs, which were so needed over the last eighteen months, and for all you've done for Melissa, me, and our kids. We love you guys.

Kyle Mills, who I'm honored to call a friend, has done an amazing job keeping Mitch Rapp alive and well. Kyle (and **Kim**, who is the real brains behind the operation), thank you for all that you've done for me. And on behalf of Rapp fans everywhere, thank you for carrying on Vince's legacy. There is nobody else who could do Mitch justice. We sure are lucky to have you.

To the ageless wonder, **David Brown** (aka @AtriaMysteryBus), who is not *my* publicist, but still the gold standard in the business. Without you, whether it be your influence or support, there would have been no "Rappologist" and no Real Book Spy. Thank you for all that you do for everyone in the thriller community.

To **Kimberly Howe**, who is not only my dear friend but also my partner in crime for ThrillerTalk, I appreciate your friendship, support, and advice far more than you know. You do an amazing job with ITW and ThrillerFest, and I cannot wait to see your next book on store shelves.

To **C. J. Box**, **Brad Thor**, **Jack Carr**, **Mark Greaney**, **Brad Taylor** (and of course **Elaine**, the DCOE), **Brad Meltzer**, **Daniel Silva** (as well as **Jamie Gangel**), **Gayle Lynds**, **Don Winslow**, **Ted Bell**, **Ben Coes**, **Matthew Betley**, **Lisa Scottoline**, and **Joel C. Rosenberg**: thank you. Each of you, aside from becoming friends, has inspired me to write. Whether it was a pep talk along the way, offering advice on the side, helping me with story issues, or simply motivating me by delivering yet another up-all-night reading experience, you've all played a major role in my life—even if you didn't know it—and I am forever thankful.

Growing up, there were three teachers who had a profound impact on me. **Nancy Looper**, my freshman English teacher, you are a true gem, and the Parchment community is so lucky to have you. **Kate Kwasny**, may she rest in peace, was the sole reason I even graduated high school. She never gave up on me and always implored her students to "make good decisions!" at the end of each class. I miss you so much. Then, of course, **Mrs. Shay Vanderstelt-Wentz**. You are so special to me, and I thank you for loving, caring, and supporting me way back when. It was in your class that Matty Redd was first born, during a writing assignment that ultimately resulted in me receiving a weeklong suspension. I was mad at the time, but hey, it all worked out and then some. Thank you for everything.

Terry O'Hara. Brother, I would give anything for you to be here right now. A retired NYPD sergeant, Terry passed away from 9/11 esophageal cancer in 2017 (which he contracted working as a first responder at Ground Zero), leaving behind a wife and two beautiful children. **Denise**, you are doing an amazing job raising those wonderful kiddos of yours, and I know Terry is looking down, smiling, cheering you on.

Blair and Travis Hegner. Friday movie nights are the best. You guys are terrific parents and wonderful people. Thank you for always being there and for bingeing on pizza and laughing with us. My work is fiction, but you two have a *real* story to tell, and one day I hope I'm able to pick up *your* book and dive on in. So go write it!

To **Marlene Steck**. I could write a whole book about how much you mean to me and how thankful I am for everything you've ever done for me over the course of my life. You're more than just an aunt to me, and I hope you know that. From daily phone calls of encouragement, sharing your advice, and when all else fails, praying for me. I cannot imagine my life without you and love you so much more than you will ever know. I sure wish Grandma was here to see this. Not only was **Lorraine Steck** the best grandma a kid could have, but she, better than anyone I've ever known, exemplified what it means to be a God-fearing individual and to have a servant's heart.

To my agent, **John Talbot**. What a journey! John, it is because of you that my dreams have finally come true and this book was published. Thank you for never giving up on me and for all the advice, support, and encouragement along the way.

To everyone at Tyndale, thank you so much for taking a chance on me and Matty Redd. I am so honored to be a Tyndale author and cannot tell you what a wonderful experience it has been working with you all. **Karen Watson**, you're the best, and your support and belief in this series means more to me than you'll ever know. **Jan Stob, Stephanie Broene, Andrea Martin, Wendie Connors, Amanda Woods, Dean Renninger, Elizabeth Jackson**, and everyone else who's worked on *Fields of Fire*, you guys are the best of the best, and I am so fortunate for each of your involvement in this project. I'd also like to single out my brilliant editor, **Sarah Rische**. Sarah, I could not have a better partner in bringing both Matty Redd and this story to life than you. Throughout this process, you have made *Fields of Fire* a much better book, and I've learned so much from you. I truly hope this is the first of many projects we're able to work on together.

To my beautiful wife, **Melissa Steck**. I love you more than life and have enjoyed every second of this crazy adventure with you. You are my soul mate. My best friend. My *everything*. While it is my name on the cover of this book, this story is just as much yours as it is mine. I might have locked myself away to write it, but you held down the fort, got kids to and from appointments, made sure dinner was on the table and that everyone was cared for. You sacrificed to make my dream a reality, and I know that. The kids and I are so lucky to have you, babe. Thank you.

And finally to my readers. Both those who've followed me as a Book Spy and now as an author, thank you. The support I've received over the last few years has been incredible. I've bonded with many of you over a love of thrillers, and at the end of the day, I set out to deliver one that I hope you've enjoyed. Matty Redd is on a journey, and I have so much more planned for him. Just wait until the next book. If you thought he was up against it in this one, I promise . . . you haven't seen anything yet!

About the Author

RYAN STECK is an editor, an author, and the founder and editor in chief of The Real Book Spy. Ryan has been named an "Online Influencer" by Amazon and is a regular columnist at CrimeReads. TheRealBookSpy.com has been endorsed by #1 *New York Times* bestselling authors Mark Greaney, C. J. Box, Kyle Mills, Daniel Silva, Brad Thor, and many others. A resident of Michigan, along with his wife and their six kids, Steck cheers on his beloved Detroit Tigers and Lions during the rare moments when he's not reading or talking about books on social media. He can be reached via email at ryan@therealbookspy.com.

KEEP UP-TO-DATE ON NEWS FROM RYAN STECK AT

therealbookspy.com

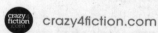
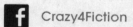
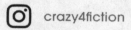
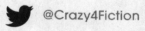

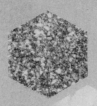